The Swiss Family Robinson

JOHANN DAVID WYSS

CLASSICS

Reprint 2024

FiNGERPRINT! CLASSICS
An imprint of Prakash Books India Pvt. Ltd

113/A, Darya Ganj,
New Delhi-110 002
Email: info@prakashbooks.com/sales@prakashbooks.com

Fingerprint Publishing
@FingerprintP
@fingerprintpublishingbooks
www.fingerprintpublishing.com

ISBN: 978 93 8917 839 5

Born in Bern, Switzerland, on May 28, 1743, Johann David Wyss was a Swiss pastor. Little is known about the early years of his life. It is believed that Wyss was inspired by Daniel Defoe's *Robinson Crusoe.* He authored *The Swiss Family Robinson* for which he is best remembered.

A tale of a family shipwrecked on a deserted tropical island, it follows their exploration and survival in the face of adversities. Edited by his son Johann Rudolf Wyss, *The Swiss Family Robinson* was first published in German in 1812. It was translated into English in 1814. Ever since, this children's classic has remained one of the best-loved adventure stories of all time.

Contents

CHAPTER

I

Storm-tossed—Wrecked—Deserted—Supper—We make swimming-belts for the children—An anxious night—The gale moderates—We examine our cargo—Jack introduces two new acquaintances—How shall we get on shore?—Jack's plan—We adopt it—The use of a lever—Our tug-boat completed—Another night on the wreck—We collect the cargo—And embark—Jack's friends will not be left behind—Steer for the shore—Once more on land—We erect a tent—Glue soup—Jack makes the acquaintance of a lobster—Ernest shirks the water—Oysters and salt—How shall we eat our soup?—Ernest solves the difficulty—Fritz returns—The sucking pig—How to open an oyster and how to eat it—The dogs devour the agouti—Fritz's anger—Our first night in the new country.

For many days we had been tempest-tossed. Six times had the darkness closed over a wild and terrific scene, and returning light as often brought but renewed distress, for the raging storm increased in fury until on the seventh day all hope was lost.

We were driven completely out of our course; no conjecture could be formed as to our whereabouts. The crew had lost heart, and were utterly exhausted by incessant labor.

The riven masts had gone by the board, leaks had been sprung in every direction, and the water, which rushed in, gained upon us rapidly.

Instead of reckless oaths, the seamen now uttered frantic cries to God for mercy, mingled with strange and often ludicrous vows, to be performed should deliverance be granted.

Every man on board alternately commended his soul to his Creator, and strove to bethink himself of some means of saving his life.

My heart sank as I looked round upon my family in the midst of these horrors. Our four young sons were overpowered by terror. "Dear children," said I, "if the Lord will, he can save us even from this fearful peril; if not, let us calmly yield our lives into his hand, and think of the joy and blessedness of finding ourselves forever and ever united in that happy home above."

At these words my weeping wife looked bravely up, and, as the boys clustered round her, she began to cheer and encourage them with calm and loving words. I rejoiced to see her fortitude, though my heart was ready to break as I gazed on my dear ones.

We knelt down together, one after another praying with deep earnestness and emotion. Fritz, in particular, besought help and deliverance for his dear parents and brothers, as though quite forgetting himself.

Our hearts were soothed by the never-failing comfort of child-like, confiding prayer, and the horror of our situation seemed less overwhelming. "Ah," thought I, "the Lord will hear our prayer! He will help us."

Amid the roar of the thundering waves I suddenly heard the cry of "Land, land!" while at the same instant the ship struck with a frightful shock, which threw every one to the deck, and seemed to threaten her immediate destruction.

Dreadful sounds betokened the breaking up of the ship, and the roaring waters poured in on all sides:

Then the voice of the captain was heard above the tumult shouting, "Lower away the boats! We are lost!"

"Lost!" I exclaimed, and the word went like a dagger to my heart; but seeing my children's terror renewed, I composed myself, calling out cheerfully, "Take courage, my boys! We are all above water yet. There is the land not far off; let us do our best to reach it. You know God helps those that help themselves!" With that, I left them and went on deck. What was my horror when through the foam and spray I beheld the only remaining boat leave the ship, the last of the seamen spring into her and push off, regardless of my cries and entreaties that we might be allowed to share their slender chance of preserving their lives. My voice was drowned in the howling of the blast; and even had the crew wished it, the return of the boat was impossible.

Casting my eyes despairingly around, I became gradually aware that our position was by no means hopeless, inasmuch as the stern of the ship containing our cabin was jammed between two high rocks, and was partly raised from among the breakers which dashed the forepart to pieces. As the clouds of mist and rain drove past, I could make out, through rents in the vaporous curtain, a line of rocky coast, and rugged as it was, my heart bounded toward it as a sign of help in the hour of need. Yet the sense of our lonely and forsaken condition weighed heavily upon me as I returned to my family, constraining myself to say with a smile, "Courage, dear ones! Although our good ship will never sail more, she is so placed that our cabin will remain above water, and tomorrow, if the wind and waves abate, I see no reason why we should not be able to get ashore."

These few words had an immediate effect on the spirits of my children, who at once regarded our problematical chance of escaping as a happy certainty, and began to enjoy the relief from the violent pitching and rolling of the vessel.

My wife, however, perceived my distress and anxiety, in spite of my forced composure, and I made her comprehend our real situation, greatly fearing the effect of the intelligence on her nerves. Not for a moment did her courage and trust in Providence forsake her, and on seeing this, my fortitude revived.

"We must find some food, and take a good supper," said she, "it will never do to grow faint by fasting too long. We shall require our utmost strength tomorrow."

Night drew on apace, the storm was as fierce as ever, and at intervals we were startled by crashes announcing further damage to our unfortunate ship.

"God will help us soon now, won't he, father?" said my youngest child.

"You silly little thing," said Fritz, my eldest son, sharply, "don't you know that we must not settle what God is to do for us? We must have patience and wait his time."

"Very well said, had it been said kindly, Fritz, my boy. You too often speak harshly to your brothers, although you may not mean to do so."

A good meal being now ready, my youngsters ate heartily, and retiring to rest were speedily fast asleep. Fritz, who was of an age to be aware of the real danger we were in, kept watch with us. After a long silence, "Father," said he, "don't you think we might contrive swimming belts for mother and the boys? With those we might all escape to land, for you and I can swim."

"Your idea is so good," answered I, "that I shall arrange something at once, in case of an accident during the night."

We immediately searched about for what would answer the purpose, and fortunately got hold of a number of empty flasks and tin canisters, which we connected two and two together so as to form floats sufficiently buoyant to support a person in the water, and my wife and young sons each willingly put one on. I then provided myself with matches, knives, cord, and other portable articles, trusting that, should the vessel go to pieces before daylight, we might gain the shore not wholly destitute.

Fritz, as well as his brothers, now slept soundly. Throughout the night my wife and I maintained our prayerful watch, dreading at every fresh sound some fatal change in the position of the wreck.

At length the faint dawn of day appeared, the long, weary night was over, and with thankful hearts we perceived that the gale had began to moderate; blue sky was seen above us, and the lovely hues of sunrise adorned the eastern horizon.

I aroused the boys, and we assembled on the remaining

portion of the deck, when they, to their surprise, discovered that no one else was on board.

"Hallo, papa! What has become of everybody? Are the sailors gone? Have they taken away the boats? Oh, papa! Why did they leave us behind? What can we do by ourselves?"

"My good children," I replied, "we must not despair, although we seem deserted. See how those on whose skill and good faith we depended have left us cruelly to our fate in the hour of danger. God will never do so. He has not forsaken us, and we will trust him still. Only let us bestir ourselves, and each cheerily do his best. Who has anything to propose?"

"The sea will soon be calm enough for swimming," said Fritz.

"And that would be all very fine for you," exclaimed Ernest, "but think of mother and the rest of us! Why not build a raft and all get on shore together?"

"We should find it difficult, I think, to make a raft that would carry us safe to shore. However, we must contrive something, and first let each try to procure what will be of most use to us."

Away we all went to see what was to be found, I myself proceeding to examine, as of great consequence, the supplies of provisions and fresh water within our reach.

My wife took her youngest son, Franz, to help her to feed the unfortunate animals on board, who were in a pitiful plight, having been neglected for several days.

Fritz hastened to the arm chest, Ernest to look for tools: and Jack went toward the captain's cabin, the door of which he no sooner opened than out sprang two splendid large dogs, who testified their extreme delight and gratitude by such tremendous bounds that they knocked their little deliverer completely head over heels, frightening him nearly out of his wits. Jack did not long yield either to fear or anger; he presently recovered himself; the dogs seemed to ask pardon by vehemently licking his face and hands, and so, seizing the larger by the ears, he jumped on his back, and, to my great amusement, coolly rode to meet me as I came up the hatchway.

When we reassembled in the cabin, we all displayed our treasures.

Fritz brought a couple of guns, shot belt, powder flasks, and plenty of bullets.

Ernest produced a cap full of nails, an ax, and a hammer, while pincers, chisels, and augers stuck out of all his pockets.

Little Franz carried a box, and eagerly began to show us the "nice sharp little hooks" it contained. "Well done, Franz!" cried I; "these fish hooks, which you, the youngest, have found, may contribute more than anything else in the ship to save our lives by procuring food for us. Fritz and Ernest, you have chosen well."

"Will you praise me too?" said my dear wife. "I have nothing to show, but I can give you good news. Some useful animals are still alive; a cow, a donkey, two goats, six sheep, a ram, and a fine sow. I was but just in time to save their lives by taking food to them."

"All these things are excellent indeed," said I; "but my friend Jack here has presented me with a couple of huge, hungry, useless dogs, who will eat more than any of us."

"Oh, papa! They will be of use! Why, they will help us to hunt when we get on shore!"

"No doubt they will, if ever we do get on shore, Jack; but I must say I don't know how it is to be done."

"Can't we each get into a big tub, and float there?" returned he. "I have often sailed splendidly like that, round the pond at home."

"My child, you have hit on a capital idea," cried I. "Now, Ernest, let me have your tools, hammers, nails, saws, augers, and ax; and then make haste to collect any tubs you can find!"

We very soon found four large casks, made of sound wood, and strongly bound with iron hoops; they were floating with many other things in the water in the hold, but we managed to fish them out, and drag them to a suitable place for launching them. They were exactly what I wanted, and I succeeded in sawing them across the middle. Hard work it was, and we were glad enough to stop and refresh ourselves with wine and biscuits.

My eight tubs now stood ranged in a row near the water's

edge, and I looked at them with great satisfaction; to my surprise, my wife did not seem to share my pleasure!

"I shall never," said she, "muster courage to get into one of these!"

"Do not be too sure of that, dear wife; when you see my contrivance completed, you will perhaps prefer it to this immovable wreck."

I next procured a long, thin plank, on which my tubs could be fixed, and the two ends of this I bent upward so as to form a keel. Other two planks were nailed along the sides of the tubs; they also being flexible, were brought to a point at each end, and all firmly secured and nailed together. I felt satisfied that in smooth water this craft would be perfectly trustworthy. But when we thought all was ready for the launch, we found, to our dismay, that the grand contrivance was so heavy and clumsy, that even our united efforts could not move it an inch.

"I must have a lever," cried I. "Run and fetch the capstan bar!"

Fritz quickly brought one, and, having formed rollers by cutting up a long spar, I raised the fore part of my boat with the bar, and my sons placed a roller under it.

"How is it, father," inquired Ernest, "that with that thing you alone can do more than all of us together?"

I explained, as well as I could in a hurry, the principle of the lever; and promised to have a long talk on the subject of Mechanics, should we have a future opportunity.

I now made fast a long rope to the stern of our boat, attaching the other end to a beam; then placing a second and third roller under it, we once more began to push, this time with success, and soon our gallant craft was safely launched: so swiftly indeed did she glide into the water that, but for the rope, she would have passed beyond our reach. The boys wished to jump in directly; but, alas, she leaned so much on one side that they could not venture to do so.

Some heavy things being thrown in, however, the boat righted itself by degrees, and the boys were so delighted that they struggled which should first leap in to have the fun of sitting down in the tubs. But it was plain to me at once that something more was required to make her perfectly safe, so I contrived outriggers to preserve the balance, by nailing long poles across at the stem and stern, and fixing at the end of each empty brandy casks. Then the boat appearing steady, I got in; and turning it toward the most open side of the wreck, I cut and cleared away obstructions, so as to leave a free passage for our departure, and the boys brought oars to be ready for the voyage. This important undertaking we were forced to postpone until the next day, as it was by this time far too late to attempt it. It was not pleasant to have to spend another night in so precarious a situation; but yielding to necessity, we sat down to enjoy a comfortable supper, for during our exciting and incessant work all day we had taken nothing but an occasional biscuit and a little wine.

We prepared for rest in a much happier frame of mind than on the preceding day, but I did not forget the possibility of a renewed storm, and therefore made every one put on the belts as before.

I persuaded my wife (not without considerable difficulty), to put on a sailor's dress, assuring her she would find it much more comfortable and convenient for all she would have to go through. She at last consented to do this, and left us for a short time, reappearing with much embarrassment and many blushes, in a most becoming suit, which she had found in a midshipman's chest. We all admired her costume, and any awkwardness she felt soon began to pass off; then retiring to our berths, peaceful sleep prepared us all for the exertions of the coming day.

We rose up betimes, for sleep weighs lightly on the hopeful, as well as on the anxious. After kneeling together in prayer, "Now, my beloved ones," said I, "with God's help we are about to effect our escape. Let the poor animals we must leave behind be well fed, and put plenty of fodder within their reach: in a few days we may be able to return, and save them likewise. After that, collect everything you can think of which may be of use to us."

The boys joyfully obeyed me, and I selected from the large quantity of stores they got together, canvas to make a tent, a chest of carpenter's tools, guns, pistols, powder, shot, and bullets, rods and fishing tackle, an iron pot, a case of portable soup, and another of biscuit. These useful articles, of course, took the place of the ballast I had hastily thrown in the day before.

With a hearty prayer for God's blessing, we now began to take our seats, each in his tub. Just then we heard the cocks begin to crow, as though to reproach us for deserting them. "Why should not the fowls go with us!" exclaimed I. "If we find no food for *them*, they can be food for *us*!" Ten hens and a couple of cocks were accordingly placed in one of the tubs, and secured with some wire-netting over them.

The ducks and geese were set at liberty, and took to the water at once, while the pigeons, rejoicing to find themselves on the wing, swiftly made for the shore. My wife, who managed all this for me, kept us waiting for her some little time, and came at last with a bag as big as a pillow in her arms. "This is *my* contribution," said she, throwing the bag to little Franz, to be, as I thought, a cushion for him to sit upon.

All being ready, we cast off, and moved away from the wreck. My good, brave wife sat in the first compartment of the boat; next her was Franz, a pretty little boy, nearly eight years old. Then came Fritz, a handsome, spirited young fellow of fifteen; the two center tubs contained the valuable cargo; then came our bold, thoughtless Jack; next him Ernest, my second son, intelligent, well-formed, and rather indolent. I myself, the anxious, loving father, stood in the stern, endeavoring to guide the raft with its precious burden to a safe landing-place.

The elder boys took the oars; every one wore a float belt, and had something useful close to him in case of being thrown into the water.

The tide was flowing, which was a great help to the young oarsmen. We emerged from the wreck and glided into the open sea. All eyes were strained to get a full view of the land, and the boys pulled with a will; but for some time we made no progress, as the boat kept turning round and round, until I hit upon the right way to steer it, after which we merrily made for the shore.

We had left two dogs, Turk and Juno, on the wreck, as being both large mastiffs we did not care to have their additional weight on board our craft; but when they saw us apparently deserting them, they set up a piteous howl, and sprang into the sea. I was sorry to see this, for the distance to the land was so great that I scarcely expected them to be able to accomplish it. They followed us, however, and occasionally resting their fore-paws on the outriggers, kept up with us well. Jack was inclined to deny them this, their only chance of safety. "Stop," said I, "that would be unkind as well as foolish; remember, the merciful man regardeth the life of his beast."

Our passage, though tedious, was safe; but the nearer we approached the shore the less inviting it appeared; the barren rocks seemed to threaten us with misery and want.

Many casks, boxes, and bales of goods floated on the water around us. Fritz and I managed to secure a couple of hogsheads, so as to tow them alongside. With the prospect of famine before us, it was desirable to lay hold of anything likely to contain provisions.

By and by we began to perceive that, between and beyond the cliffs, green grass and trees were discernible. Fritz could distinguish many tall palms, and Ernest hoped they would prove to be coconut trees, and enjoyed the thoughts of drinking the refreshing milk.

"I am very sorry I never thought of bringing away the captain's telescope," said I.

"Oh, look here, father!" cried Jack, drawing a little spyglass joyfully out of his pocket.

By means of this glass, I made out that at some distance to the left the coast was much more inviting; a strong current however, carried us directly toward the frowning rocks, but I presently observed an opening, where a stream flowed into the sea, and saw that our geese and ducks were swimming toward this place. I steered after them into the creek, and we found ourselves in a small bay or inlet where the water was perfectly smooth and of moderate depth. The ground sloped gently upward from the low banks to the cliffs, which here retired inland, leaving a small plain, on which it was easy for us to land. Every one sprang gladly out of the boat but little Franz, who, lying packed in his tub like a potted shrimp, had to be lifted out by his mother.

The dogs had scrambled on shore before us; they received us with loud barking and the wildest demonstrations of delight. The geese and ducks kept up an incessant din, added to which was the screaming and croaking of flamingoes and penguins, whose dominion we were invading. The noise was deafening, but far from unwelcome to me, as I thought of the good dinners the birds might furnish.

As soon as we could gather our children around us on dry land, we knelt to offer thanks and praise for our merciful escape, and with full hearts we commended ourselves to God's good keeping for the time to come.

All hands then briskly fell to the work of unloading, and oh, how rich we felt ourselves as we did so! The poultry we left at liberty to forage for themselves, and set about finding a suitable place to erect a tent in which to pass the night. This we speedily did; thrusting a long spar into a hole in the rock, and supporting the other end by a pole firmly planted in the ground, we formed a framework over which we stretched the sailcloth we had brought; besides fastening this down with pegs, we placed our heavy chest and boxes on the border of the canvas, and arranged hooks so as to be able to close up the entrance during the night.

When this was accomplished, the boys ran to collect moss and grass, to spread in the tent for our beds, while I arranged a fireplace with some large flat stones, near the brook which flowed close by. Dry twigs and seaweed were soon in a blaze on the hearth; I filled the iron pot with water, and giving my wife several cakes of the portable soup, she established herself as our cook, with little Franz to help her.

He, thinking his mother was melting some glue for carpentering, was eager to know "what papa was going to make next?"

"This is to be soup for your dinner, my child. Do you think these cakes look like glue?"

"Yes, indeed I do!" replied Franz, "and I should not much like to taste glue soup! Don't you want some beef or mutton, mamma?"

"Where can I get it, dear!" said she, "we are a long way from a butcher's shop! But these cakes are made of the juice of good meat, boiled till it becomes a strong, stiff jelly—people take them when they go to sea, because on a long voyage they can only have salt meat, which will not make nice soup."

Fritz, meanwhile, leaving a loaded gun with me, took another himself, and went along the rough coast to see what lay beyond the stream; this fatiguing sort of walk not suiting Ernest's fancy, he sauntered down to the beach, and Jack scrambled among the rocks, searching for shellfish.

I was anxious to land the two casks which were floating alongside our boat, but on attempting to do so, I found that I could not get them up the bank on which we had landed, and was therefore obliged to look for a more convenient spot. As I did so, I was startled by hearing Jack shouting for help, as though in great danger. He was at some distance, and I hurried toward him with a hatchet in my hand. The little fellow stood screaming in a deep pool, and as I approached, I saw that a huge lobster had caught his leg in its powerful claw. Poor Jack was in a terrible fright; kick as he would, his enemy still clung on. I waded into the water, and seizing the lobster firmly by the back, managed to make it loosen its hold, and we brought it safe to land. Jack, having speedily recovered his spirits, and anxious to take such a prize to his mother, caught the lobster in both hands, but instantly received such a severe blow from its tail that he flung it down, and passionately hit the creature with a large stone. This display of temper vexed me. "You are acting in a very childish way, my son," said I; "never strike an enemy in a revengeful spirit." Once more lifting the lobster, Jack ran triumphantly toward the tent.

"Mother, mother! A lobster, Ernest! Look here, Franz! Mind,

he'll bite you! Where's Fritz?" All came crowding round Jack and his prize, wondering at its unusual size, and Ernest wanted his mother to make lobster soup directly, by adding it to what she was now boiling.

She, however, begged to decline making any such experiment, and said she preferred cooking one dish at a time. Having remarked that the scene of Jack's adventure afforded a convenient place for getting my casks on shore, I returned thither and succeeded in drawing them up on the beach, where I set them on end, and for the present left them.

On my return I resumed the subject of Jack's lobster, and told him he should have the offending claw all to himself, when it was ready to be eaten, congratulating him on being the first to discover anything useful.

"As to that," said Ernest, "I found something very good to eat, as well as Jack, only I could not get at them without wetting my feet."

"Pooh!" cried Jack, "I know what he saw—nothing but some nasty mussels; I saw them too. Who wants to eat trash like that! Lobster for me!"

"I believe them to be oysters, not mussels," returned Ernest calmly.

"Be good enough, my philosophical young friend, to fetch a few specimens of these oysters in time for our next meal," said I; "we must all exert ourselves, Ernest, for the common good, and pray never let me hear you object to wetting your feet. See how quickly the sun has dried Jack and me."

"I can bring some salt at the same time," said Ernest, "I remarked a good deal lying in the crevices of the rocks; it tasted very pure and good, and I concluded it was produced by the evaporation of sea water in the sun."

"Extremely probable, learned sir," cried I; "but if you had brought a bagful of this good salt instead of merely speculating so profoundly on the subject, it would have been more to the purpose. Run and fetch some directly."

It proved to be salt sure enough, although so impure that it seemed useless, till my wife dissolved and strained it, when it became fit to put in the soup.

"Why not use the sea water itself?" asked Jack.

"Because," said Ernest, "it is not only salt, but bitter too. Just try it."

"Now," said my wife, tasting the soup with the stick with which she had been stirring it, "dinner is ready, but where can Fritz be?" she continued, a little anxiously.

"How are we to eat our soup when he does come?" I asked; "we have neither plates nor spoons, and we can scarcely lift the boiling pot to our mouths. We are in as uncomfortable a position as was the fox to whom the stork served up a dinner in a jug with a long neck."

"Oh, for a few coconut shells!" sighed Ernest.

"Oh, for half a dozen plates and as many silver spoons!" rejoined I, smiling.

"Really though, oyster-shells would do," said he, after a moment's thought.

"True, that is an idea worth having! Off with you, my boys; get the oysters and clean out a few shells. What though our spoons have no handles, and we do burn our fingers a little in baling the soup out."

Jack was away and up to his knees in the water, in a moment, detaching the oysters. Ernest followed more leisurely, and still unwilling to wet his feet, stood by the margin of the pool and gathered in his handkerchief the oysters his brother threw him; as he thus stood he picked up and pocketed a large mussel shell for his own use. As they returned with a good supply we heard a shout from Fritz in the distance; we returned it joyfully, and he presently appeared before us, his hands behind his back, and a look of disappointment upon his countenance.

"Unsuccessful!" said he.

"Really!" I replied; "never mind, my boy, better luck next time."

"Oh, Fritz!" exclaimed his brothers, who had looked behind

him, "a sucking-pig, a little sucking-pig. Where did you get it? How did you shoot it? Do let us see it!"

Fritz then with sparkling eyes exhibited his prize.

"I am glad to see the results of your prowess, my boy," said I; "but I cannot approve of deceit, even as a joke; stick to the truth in jest and earnest."

Fritz then told us how he had been to the other side of the stream. "So different from this," he said; "it is really a beautiful country, and the shore, which runs down to the sea in a gentle slope, is covered with all sorts of useful things from the wreck. Do let us go and collect them. And, father, why should we not return to the wreck and bring off some of the animals? Just think of what value the cow would be to us, and what a pity it would be to lose her! Let us get her on shore, and we will move over the stream, where she will have good pasturage, and we shall be in the shade instead of on this desert, and father, I do wish—"

"Stop, stop, my boy!" cried I. "All will be done in good time. Tomorrow and the day after will bring work of their own. And tell me, did you see no traces of our shipmates?"

"Not a sign of them, either on land or sea, living or dead," he replied.

"But the sucking-pig," said Jack, "where did you get it?"

"It was one of several," said Fritz, "which I found on the shore; most curious animals they are; they hopped rather than walked, and every now and then would squat down on their legs and rub their snouts with their fore-paws. Had not I been afraid of losing them all, I would have tried to catch one alive, they seemed so tame."

Meanwhile Ernest had been carefully examining the animal in question.

"This is no pig," he said; "and except for its bristly skin, does not look like one. See, its teeth are not like those of a pig, but rather those of a squirrel. In fact," he continued, looking at Fritz, "your sucking-pig is an agouti."

"Dear me," said Fritz; "listen to the great professor lecturing! He is going to prove that a pig is not a pig!"

"You need not be so quick to laugh at your brother," said I, in my turn; "he is quite right. I, too, know the agouti by descriptions and pictures, and there is little doubt that this is a specimen. The little animal is a native of North America, where it makes its nest under the roots of trees, and lives upon fruit. But, Ernest, the agouti not only looks something like a pig, but most decidedly grunts like a porker."

While we were thus talking, Jack had been vainly endeavoring to open an oyster with his large knife. "Here is a simpler way," said I, placing an oyster on the fire; it immediately opened. "Now," I continued, "who will try this delicacy?" All at first hesitated to partake of them, so unattractive did they appear. Jack, however, tightly closing his eyes and making a face as though about to take medicine, gulped one down. We followed his example, one after the other, each doing so rather to provide himself with a spoon than with any hope of cultivating a taste for oysters.

Our spoons were now ready, and gathering round the pot we dipped them in, not, however, without sundry scalded fingers. Ernest then drew from his pocket the large shell he had procured for his own use, and scooping up a good quantity of soup he put it down to cool, smiling at his own foresight.

"Prudence should be exercised for others," I remarked; "your cool soup will do capitally for the dogs, my boy; take it to them, and then come and eat like the rest of us."

Ernest winced at this, but silently taking up his shell he placed it on the ground before the hungry dogs, who lapped up its contents in a moment; he then returned, and we all went merrily on with our dinner. While we were thus busily employed, we suddenly discovered that our dogs, not satisfied with their mouthful of soup, had espied the agouti, and were rapidly devouring it. Fritz, seizing his gun, flew to rescue it from their hungry jaws, and before I could prevent him, struck one of them with such force that his gun was bent. The poor beasts ran off howling, followed by a shower of stones from Fritz, who shouted and yelled at them so fiercely that his mother was actually terrified. I followed him, and as soon as he would listen to me, represented to him how despicable, as well as wicked, was such an outbreak, of temper: "for," said I, "you have hurt, if not actually wounded, the dogs; you have distressed and terrified your mother, and spoiled your gun."

Though Fritz's passion was easily aroused, it never lasted long, and speedily recovering himself, immediately he entreated his mother's pardon, and expressed his sorrow for his fault.

By this time the sun was sinking beneath the horizon, and the poultry, which had been straying to some little distance, gathered round us, and began to pick up the crumbs of biscuit which had fallen during our repast. My wife hereupon drew from her mysterious bag some handfuls of oats, peas, and other grain, and with them began to feed the poultry. She at the same time showed me several other seeds of various vegetables. "That was indeed thoughtful," said I; "but pray be careful of what will be of such value to us; we can bring plenty of damaged biscuits from the wreck, which, though of no use as food for us, will suit the fowls very well indeed."

The pigeons now flew up to crevices in the rocks, the fowls perched themselves on our tent pole, and the ducks and geese waddled off, cackling and quacking, to the marshy margin of the river. We, too, were ready for repose, and having loaded our guns, and offered up our prayers to God, thanking Him for His many mercies to us, we commended ourselves to His protecting care, and as the last ray of light departed, closed our tent and lay down to rest.

The children remarked the suddenness of nightfall, for indeed there had been little or no twilight. This convinced me that we must be not far from the equator, for twilight results from the refraction of the sun's rays: the more obliquely these rays fall, the farther does the partial light extend; while the more perpendicularly they strike the earth, the longer do they continue their undiminished force, until, when the sun sinks, they totally disappear, thus producing sudden darkness.

CHAPTER II

A morning consultation—Breakfast—Away on an expedition—Over the stream and through the grass—An unexpected reinforcement—Search in vain for our comrades—Rest by a stream—Fritz finds a "round bird's nest"—Natural history of a coconut—Calabash trees—The use of gourds—How to make a bottle—A lovely but lonely scene—Sugarcanes—Monkeys of use—Coconut milk turned to champagne—Turk kills an unfortunate mother monkey—Carry the orphan home—Display our treasures—A sumptuous supper—Ernest's penguin—Champagne turned to vinegar—A fight with jackals—A curious sentinel—A visit to the wreck—We rig our craft—Stow a cargo—Sleep on board—Floats for our herd—We embark—Encounter a shark—Land—Relate our adventures.

We should have been badly off without the shelter of our tent, for the night proved as cold as the day had been hot, but we managed to sleep comfortably, every one being thoroughly fatigued by the labors of the day. The voice of our vigilant cock, which, as he loudly saluted the rising moon, was the last sound I heard at night, roused me at daybreak, and I then awoke my wife, that in the quiet interval while yet our children slept, we might take counsel together on our situation and prospects. It was plain to both of us that, in the first place, we should ascertain if possible the fate of our late companions, and then examine into the nature and resources of the country on which we were stranded.

We therefore came to the resolution that, as soon as we had breakfasted, Fritz and I should start on an expedition with these objects in view, while my wife remained near our landing-place with the three younger boys.

"Rouse up, rouse up, my boys," cried I, awakening the children cheerfully. "Come and help your mother to get breakfast ready."

"As to that," said she smiling, "we can but set on the pot, and boil some more soup!"

"Why, you forget Jack's fine lobster!" replied I. "What has become of it, Jack?"

"It has been safe in this hole in the rock all night, father. You see, I thought, as the dogs seem to like good things, they might take a fancy to that, as well as to the agouti."

"A very sensible precaution," remarked I. "I believe even my heedless Jack will learn wisdom in time. It is well the lobster is so large, for we shall want to take part with us on our excursion today."

At the mention of an excursion, the four children were wild with delight, and capering around me, clapped their hands for joy.

"Steady there, steady!" said I, "you cannot expect all to go. Such an expedition as this would be too dangerous and fatiguing for you younger ones. Fritz and I will go alone this time, with one of the dogs, leaving the other to defend you."

We then armed ourselves, each taking a gun and a game bag; Fritz in addition sticking a pair of pistols in his belt, and I a small hatchet in mine; breakfast being over, we stowed away the remainder of the lobster and some biscuits, with a flask of water, and were ready for a start.

"Stop!" I exclaimed, "we have still left something very important undone."

"Surely not," said Fritz.

"Yes," said I, "we have not yet joined in morning prayer. We are only too ready, amid the cares and pleasures of this life, to forget the God to whom we owe all things." Then having commended ourselves to his protecting care, I took leave of my wife and children, and bidding them not wander far from the boat and tent, we parted not without some anxiety on either side, for we knew not what might assail us in this unknown region.

We now found that the banks of the stream were on both sides so rocky that we could get down to the stream by only one narrow passage, and there was no corresponding path on the other side. I was glad to see this, however, for I now knew that my wife and children were on a comparatively inaccessible spot, the other side of the tent being protected by steep and precipitous cliffs. Fritz and I pursued our way up the stream until we reached a point where the waters fell from a considerable height in a cascade, and where several large rocks lay half covered by the water; by means of these we succeeded in crossing the stream in safety. We thus had the sea on our left, and a long line of rocky heights, here and there adorned with clumps of trees, stretching away inland to the right. We had forced our way scarcely fifty yards through the long rank grass, which was here partly withered by the sun and much tangled, when we heard behind us a rustling, and on looking round saw the grass waving to and fro, as if some animal were passing through it. Fritz instantly turned and brought his gun to his shoulder, ready to fire the moment the beast should appear. I was much pleased with my son's coolness and presence of mind, for it showed me that I might thoroughly rely upon him on any future occasion when real danger might occur; this time, however, no savage beast rushed out, but our trusty dog Turk, whom in our anxiety at parting we had forgotten, and who had been sent after us, doubtless, by my thoughtful wife.

From this little incident, however, we saw how dangerous was our position, and how difficult escape would be should any fierce beast steal upon us unawares: we therefore hastened to make our way to the open seashore. Here the scene which presented itself was indeed delightful. A background of hills, the green waving grass, the pleasant groups of trees stretching here and there to the very water's edge, formed a lovely prospect. On the smooth sand we searched carefully for any trace of our hapless companions, but not the mark of a footstep could we find.

"Shall I fire a shot or two?" said Fritz; "that would bring our companions, if they are within hearing."

"It would indeed," I said, "or any savages that may be here. No, no; let us search diligently, but as quietly as possible."

"But why, father, should we trouble ourselves about them at all? They left us to shift for ourselves, and I for one don't care to set eyes on them again."

"You are wrong, my boy," said I. "In the first place, we should not return evil for evil; then, again, they might be of great assistance to us in building a house of some sort; and lastly, you must remember that they took nothing with them from the vessel, and may be perishing of hunger."

Thus talking, we pushed on until we came to a pleasant grove which stretched down to the water's edge; here we halted to rest, seating ourselves under a large tree, by a rivulet which murmured and splashed along its pebbly bed into the great ocean before us. A thousand gaily-plumaged birds flew twittering above us, and Fritz and I gazed up at them.

My son suddenly started up.

"A monkey," he exclaimed; "I am nearly sure I saw a monkey."

As he spoke he sprang round to the other side of the tree, and in doing so stumbled over a round substance, which he handed to me, remarking, as he did so, that it was a round bird's nest, of which he had often heard.

"You may have done so," said I, laughing, "but you need not necessarily conclude that every round hairy thing is a bird's nest; this, for instance, is not one, but a coconut."

We split open the nut, but, to our disgust, found the kernel dry and uneatable.

"Hullo," cried Fritz, "I always thought a coconut was full of delicious sweet liquid, like almond milk."

"So it is," I replied, "when young and fresh, but as it ripens the milk becomes congealed, and in course of time is solidified into a kernel. This kernel then dries as you see here, but when the nut falls on favorable soil, the germ within the kernel swells until it bursts through the shell, and, taking root, springs up a new tree."

"I do not understand," said Fritz, "how the little germ manages to get through this great thick shell, which is not like an almond or hazelnut shell, that is divided down the middle already."

"Nature provides for all things," I answered, taking up the pieces. "Look here, do you see these three round holes near the stalk? It is through them that the germ obtains egress. Now let us find a good nut if we can."

As coconuts must be over-ripe before they fall naturally from the tree, it was not without difficulty that we obtained one in which the kernel was not dried up. When we succeeded, however, we were so refreshed by the fruit that we could defer the repast we called our dinner until later in the day, and so spare our stock of provisions.

Continuing our way through a thicket, and which was so densely overgrown with lianas that we had to clear a passage with our hatchets, we again emerged on the seashore beyond, and found an open view, the forest sweeping inland, while on the space before us stood at intervals single trees of remarkable appearance.

These at once attracted Fritz's observant eye, and he pointed, to them, exclaiming,

"Oh, what absurd-looking trees, father! See what strange bumps there are on the trunks."

We approached to examine them, and I recognized them as calabash trees, the fruit of which grows in this curious way on the stems, and is a species of gourd, from the hard rind of which bowls, spoons, and bottles can be made. "The savages," I remarked, "are said to form these things most ingeniously, using them to contain liquids: indeed, they actually cook food in them."

"Oh, but that is impossible," returned Fritz. "I am quite sure this rind would be burnt through directly it was set on the fire."

"I did not say it was set on the fire at all. When the gourd has been divided in two, and the shell or rind emptied of its contents, it was filled with water, into which the fish, or whatever is to be cooked, is put; red hot stones are added until the water boils; the food becomes fit to eat, and the gourd-rind remains uninjured."

"That is a very clever plan: very simple too. I daresay I should have hit on it, if I had tried," said Fritz.

"The friends of Columbus thought it very easy to make an egg stand upon its end when he had shown them how to do it. But now suppose we prepare some of these calabashes, that they may be ready for use when we take them home."

Fritz instantly took up one of the gourds, and tried to split it equally with his knife, but in vain: the blade slipped, and the calabash was cut jaggedly. "What a nuisance!" said Fritz, flinging it down, "the thing is spoiled; and yet it seemed so simple to divide it properly."

"Stay," said I; "you are too impatient, those pieces are not useless. Do you try to fashion from them a spoon or two while I provide a dish."

I then took from my pocket a piece of string, which I tied tightly round a gourd, as near one end of it as I could; then tapping the string with the back of my knife, it penetrated the outer shell. When this was accomplished, I tied the string yet tighter; and drawing the ends with all my might, the gourd fell, divided exactly as I wished.

"That is clever!" cried Fritz. "What in the world put that plan into your head?"

"It is a plan," I replied, "which the negroes adopt, as I have learned from reading books of travel."

"Well, it certainly makes a capital soup-tureen, and a soup-plate too," said Fritz, examining the gourd. "But supposing you had wanted to make a bottle, how would you have set to work?"

"It would be an easier operation than this, if possible. All that is necessary is to cut a round hole at one end, then to scoop out the interior, and to drop in several shot or stones; when these are shaken, any remaining portions of the fruit are detached, and the gourd is thoroughly cleaned, and the bottle completed."

"That would not make a very convenient bottle though, father; it would be more like a barrel."

"True, my boy; if you want a more shapely vessel, you must take it in hand when it is younger. To give it a neck, for instance, you must tie a bandage round the young gourd while it is still on the tree, and then all will swell but that part which you have checked."

As I spoke, I filled the gourds with sand, and left them to dry; marking the spot that we might return for them on our way back.

For three hours or more we pushed forward, keeping a sharp lookout on either side for any trace of our companions, till we reached a bold promontory, stretching some way into the sea, from whose rocky summit I knew that we should obtain a good and comprehensive view of the surrounding country. With little difficulty we reached the top, but the most careful survey of the beautiful landscape failed to show us the slightest sign or trace of human beings. Before us stretched a wide and lovely bay, fringed with yellow sands, either side extending into the distance, and almost lost to view in two shadowy promontories; enclosed by these two arms lay a sheet of rippling water, which reflected in its depths the glorious sun above. The scene inland was no less beautiful; and yet Fritz and I both felt a shade of loneliness stealing over us as we gazed on its utter solitude.

"Cheer up, Fritz, my boy," said I presently. "Remember that we chose a settler's life long ago, before we left our own dear country; we certainly did not expect to be so entirely alone—but what matters a few people, more or less? With God's help, let us endeavor to live here contentedly, thankful that we were not cast upon some bare and inhospitable island. But come, the heat here is getting unbearable; let us find some shady place before we are completely broiled away."

We descended the hill and made for a clump of palm trees, which we saw at a little distance. To reach this, we had to pass through a dense thicket of reeds, no pleasant or easy task; for, besides the difficulty of forcing our way through, I feared at every step that we might tread on some venomous snake. Sending Turk in advance, I cut one of the reeds, thinking it would be a more useful weapon against a reptile than my gun. I had carried it but a little way, when I noticed a thick juice exuding from one end. I tasted it, and to my delight found it sweet and pleasant. I at once knew that I was standing amongst sugarcanes. Wishing Fritz to make the same discovery, I advised him to cut a cane for his defense; he did so, and as he beat the ground before him, the reed split, and his hand was covered with the juice. He carefully touched the cane with the tip of his tongue, then, finding the juice sweet, he did so again with less hesitation; and a moment afterward sprang back to me exclaiming:

"Oh, father, sugarcanes! Sugarcanes! Taste it. Oh, how delicious, how delightful! Do let us take a lot home to mother," he continued, sucking eagerly at the cane.

"Gently there," said I, "take breath a moment, moderation in all things, remember. Cut some to take home if you like, only don't take more than you can conveniently carry."

In spite of my warning, my son cut a dozen or more of the largest canes, and stripping them of their leaves, carried them under his arm. We then pushed through the cane-brake, and reached the clump of palms for which we had been making; as we entered it a troop of monkeys, who had been disporting themselves on the ground, sprang up, chattering and grimacing, and before we could clearly distinguish them were at the very top of the trees.

Fritz was so provoked by their impertinent gestures that he raised his gun and would have shot one of the poor beasts.

"Stay," cried I, "never take the life of any animal needlessly. A live monkey up in that tree is of more use to us than a dozen dead ones at our feet, as I will show you."

Saying this, I gathered a handful of small stones, and threw them up toward the apes. The stones did not go near them, but influenced by their instinctive mania for imitation, they instantly seized all the coconuts within their reach, and sent a perfect hail of them down upon us.

Fritz was delighted with my stratagem, and rushing forward picked up some of the finest of the nuts. We drank the milk they contained, drawing it through the holes, which I pierced, and then, splitting the nuts open with the hatchet, ate the cream which lined their shells. After this delicious meal, we thoroughly despised the lobster we had been carrying, and threw it to Turk, who ate it gratefully; but far from being satisfied, the poor beast began to gnaw the ends of the sugarcanes, and to beg for coconut. I slung a couple of the nuts over my shoulder, fastening them together by their stalks, and Fritz having resumed his burden, we began our homeward march.

I soon discovered that Fritz found the weight of his canes considerably more than he expected: he shifted them from shoulder to shoulder, then for a while carried them under his arm, and finally stopped short with a sigh. "I had no idea," he said, "that a few reeds would be so heavy."

"Never mind, my boy," I said, "patience and courage! Do you not remember the story of Æsop and his breadbasket, how heavy he found it when he started, and how light at the end of his journey? Let us each take a fresh staff, and then fasten the bundle crosswise with your gun."

We did so, and once more stepped forward. Fritz presently noticed that I from time to time sucked the end of my cane.

"Oh, come," said he, "that's a capital plan of yours, father, I'll do that too."

So saying, he began to suck most vigorously, but not a drop of the juice could he extract. "How is this?" he asked. "How do you get the juice out, father?"

"Think a little," I replied, "you are quite as capable as I am of finding out the way, even if you do not know the real reason of your failure."

"Oh, of course," said he, "it is like trying to suck marrow from a marrow-bone, without making a hole at the other end."

"Quite right," I said, "you form a vacuum in your mouth and the end of your tube, and expect the air to force down the liquid from the other end which it cannot possibly enter."

Fritz was speedily perfect in the accomplishment of sucking sugarcane, discovering by experience the necessity for a fresh cut at each joint or knot in the cane, through which the juice would not flow; he talked of the pleasure of initiating his brothers in the art, and of how Ernest would enjoy the coconut milk, with which he had filled his flask.

"My dear boy," said I, "you need not have added that to your load; the chances are it is vinegar by the time we get home. In the heat of the sun, it will ferment soon after being drawn from the nut."

"Vinegar! Oh, that would be a horrid bore! I must look directly, and see how it is getting on," cried Fritz, hastily swinging the flask from his shoulder, and tugging out the cork. With a loud "pop" the contents came forth, foaming like champagne.

"There now!" said I, laughing as he tasted this new luxury, "you will have to exercise moderation again, friend Fritz! I daresay it is delicious, but it will go to your head, if you venture deep into your flask."

"My dear father, you cannot think how good it is! Do take some. Vinegar, indeed! This is like excellent wine."

We were both invigorated by this unexpected draught, and went on so merrily after it, that the distance to the place where we had left our gourd-dishes seemed less than we expected. We found them quite dry, and very light and easy to carry.

Just as we had passed through the grove in which we had breakfasted, Turk suddenly darted away from us and sprang furiously among a troop of monkeys, which were gamboling playfully on the turf at a little distance from the trees. They were taken by surprise completely, and the dog, now really ravenous from hunger, had seized and was fiercely tearing one to pieces before we could approach the spot.

His luckless victim was the mother of a tiny little monkey, which, being on her back when the dog flew at her, hindered her flight. The little creature attempted to hide among the grass, and in trembling fear watched its mother. On perceiving Turk's bloodthirsty design, Fritz had eagerly rushed to the rescue, flinging away all he was carrying, and losing his hat in his haste. All to no purpose as far as the poor mother ape was concerned, and a laughable scene ensued, for no sooner did the young monkey catch sight of him, than at one bound it was on his shoulders, and, holding fast by his thick curly hair, it firmly kept its seat in spite of all he could do to dislodge it. He screamed and plunged about as he endeavored to shake or pull the creature off, but all in vain; it only clung the closer to his neck, making the most absurd grimaces.

I laughed so much at this ridiculous scene, that I could scarcely assist my terrified boy out of his awkward predicament.

At last, by coaxing the monkey, offering it a bit of biscuit; and gradually disentangling its small sinewy paws from the curls it grasped so tightly, I managed to relieve poor Fritz, who then looked with interest at the baby ape, no bigger than a kitten, as it lay in my arms.

"What a jolly little fellow it is!" exclaimed he, "do let me try to rear it, father. I daresay coconut milk would do until we can bring the cow and the goats from the wreck. If he lives he might be useful to us. I believe monkeys instinctively know what fruits are wholesome and what are poisonous."

"Well," said I, "let the little orphan be yours. You bravely and kindly exerted yourself to save the mother's life; now you must train her child carefully, for unless you do so its natural instinct will prove mischievous instead of useful to us."

Turk was meanwhile devouring with great satisfaction the little animal's unfortunate mother. I could not grudge it him, and continued hunger might have made him dangerous to ourselves. We did not think it necessary to wait until he had dined, so we prepared to resume our march.

The tiny ape seated itself in the coolest way imaginable on Fritz's shoulder, I helped to carry his canes, and we were on some distance before Turk overtook us, looking uncommonly well pleased, and licking his chops as though recalling the memory of his feast.

He took no notice of the monkey, but it was very uneasy at sight of him, and scrambled down into Fritz's arms, which was so inconvenient to him that he devised a plan to relieve himself of his burden. Calling Turk, and seriously enjoining obedience, he seated the monkey on his back, securing it there with a cord, and then putting a second string round the dog's neck that he might lead him, he put a loop of the knot into the comical rider's hand, saying gravely: "Having slain the parent, Mr. Turk, you will please to carry the son."

At first this arrangement mightily displeased them both, but by and by they yielded to it quietly; the monkey especially amused by riding along with the air of a person perfectly at his ease.

"We look just like a couple of mountebanks on their way to a fair with animals to exhibit," said I. "What an outcry the children will make when we appear!"

My son inquired to what species of the monkey tribe I thought his *protégé* belonged, which led to a good deal of talk on the subject, and conversation beguiling the way, we found ourselves ere long on the rocky margin of the stream and close to the rest of our party.

Juno was the first to be aware of our approach, and gave notice of it by loud barking, to which Turk replied with such hearty good will, that his little rider, terrified at the noise his steed was making, slipped from under the cord and fled to his refuge on Fritz's shoulder, where he regained his composure and settled himself comfortably.

Turk, who by this time knew where he was, finding himself free dashed forward to rejoin his friends, and announce our coming.

One after another our dear ones came running to the opposite bank, testifying in various ways their delight at our return, and hastening up on their side of the river, as we on ours, to the ford at which we had crossed in the morning. We were quickly on the other side, and, full of joy and affection, our happy party was once more united.

The boys suddenly perceiving the little animal which was clinging close to their brother, in alarm at the tumult of voices, shouted in ecstasy:

"A monkey! A monkey! Oh, how splendid! Where did Fritz find him? What may we give him to eat? Oh, what a bundle of sticks! Look at those curious, great nuts father has got!"

We could neither check this confused torrent of questions, nor get in a word in answer to them.

At length, when the excitement subsided a little, I was able to say a few words with a chance of being listened to. "I am truly thankful to see you all safe and well, and, thank God, our expedition has been very satisfactory, except that we have entirely failed to discover any trace of our shipmates."

"If it be the will of God," said my wife, "to leave us alone on this solitary place, let us be content; and rejoice that we are all together in safety."

"Now we want to hear all your adventures, and let us relieve you of your burdens," added she, taking my game bag.

Jack shouldered my gun, Ernest took the coconuts, and little Franz carried the gourds; Fritz distributed the sugarcanes amongst his brothers, and handing Ernest his gun replaced the monkey on Turk's back. Ernest soon found the burden with which Fritz had laden him too heavy for his taste. His mother perceiving this, offered to relieve him of part of the load. He gave up willingly the coconuts, but no sooner had he done so than his elder brother exclaimed:

"Hullo, Ernest, you surely do not know what you are parting with; did you really intend to hand over those good coconuts without so much as tasting them?"

"What? Ho! Are they really coconuts?" cried Ernest. "Do let me take them again, mother, do let me look at them."

"No, thank you," replied my wife with a smile. "I have no wish to see you again overburdened."

"Oh, but I have only to throw away these sticks, which are of no use, and then I can easily carry them."

"Worse and worse," said Fritz; "I have a particular regard for those heavy, useless sticks. Did you ever hear of sugarcanes?"

The words were scarcely out of his mouth when Ernest began to suck vigorously at the end of the cane, with no better result, however, than Fritz had obtained as we were on the march.

"Here," said Fritz, "let me show you the trick of it," and he speedily set all the youngsters to work extracting the luscious juice.

My wife, as a prudent housekeeper, was no less delighted than the children with this discovery; the sight of the dishes also pleased her greatly, for she longed to see us eat once more like civilized beings. We went into the kitchen and there found preparations for a truly sumptuous meal. Two forked sticks were planted in the ground on either side of the fire; on these rested a rod from which hung several tempting looking fish; opposite them hung a goose from a similar contrivance, slowly roasting while the gravy dropped into a large shell placed beneath it. In the center sat the great pot, from which issued the smell of a most delicious soup. To crown this splendid array, stood an open hogshead full of Dutch cheeses. All this was very pleasant to two hungry travelers, but I was about to beg my wife to spare the poultry until our stock should have increased, when she, perceiving my thought, quickly relieved my anxiety. "This is not one of our geese," she said, "but a wild bird Ernest killed."

"Yes," said Ernest, "it is a penguin, I think; it let me get quite close, so that I knocked it on the head with a stick. Here are its head and feet, which I preserved to show you; the bill is, you see, narrow and curved downward, and the feet are webbed. It had funny little bits of useless wings, and its eyes looked so solemnly and sedately at me that I was almost ashamed to kill it. Do you not think it must have been a penguin?"

"I have little doubt on the matter, my boy," and I was about to make a few remarks on the habits of this bird, when my wife interrupted me and begged us to come to dinner, and continue our natural history conversation at some future time. We then sat down before the appetizing meal prepared for us, our gourds coming for the first time into use, and having done it full justice, produced the coconuts by way of dessert.

"Here is better food for your little friend," said I to Fritz, who had been vainly endeavoring to persuade the monkey to taste dainty morsels of the food we had been eating; "the poor little animal has been accustomed to nothing but its mother's milk; fetch me a saw, one of you."

I then, after extracting the milk of the nuts from their natural holes, carefully cut the shells in half, thus providing several more useful basins. The monkey was perfectly satisfied with the milk, and eagerly sucked the corner of a handkerchief dipped in it. Fritz now suddenly recollected his delicious wine, and producing his flask, begged his mother to taste it. "Try it first yourself," said I; Fritz did so, and I instantly saw by his countenance that the liquor had passed through the first stage of fermentation and had become vinegar.

"Never mind, my boy," said my prudent wife, when she learned the cause of his wry faces, "we have wine already; but no vinegar; I am really pleased at the transformation."

The sun was now rapidly sinking behind the horizon, and the poultry, retiring for the night, warned us that we must follow their example. Having offered up our prayers, we lay down on our beds, the monkey crouched down between Jack and Fritz, and we were all soon fast asleep.

We did not, however, long enjoy this repose; a loud barking from our dogs, who were on guard outside the tent, awakened us, and the fluttering and cackling of our poultry warned us that a foe was approaching. Fritz and I sprang up, and seizing our guns rushed out. There we found a desperate combat going on; our gallant dogs, surrounded by a dozen or more large jackals, were fighting bravely. Four of their opponents lay dead, but the others were in no way deterred by the fate of their comrades. Fritz and I, however, sent bullets through the heads of a couple more, and the rest galloped off. Turk and Juno did not intend that they should escape so cheaply, and pursuing them, they caught, killed, and devoured another of the animals, regardless of their near relationship. Fritz wished to save one of the jackals that he might be able to show it to his brothers in the morning; dragging, therefore, the one that he had shot near the tent, he concealed it, and we once more returned to our beds.

Soundly and peacefully we slept until cock-crow next morning, when my wife and I awoke, and began to discuss the business of the day.

"It seems absolutely necessary, my dear wife," I began "to return at once to the wreck while it is yet calm, that we may save the poor animals left there, and bring on shore many articles of infinite value to us, which, if we do not now recover, we may finally lose entirely. On the other hand, I feel that there is an immense deal to be done on shore, and that I ought not to leave you in such an insecure shelter as this tent."

"Return to the wreck by all means," replied my wife, cheerfully. "Patience, order, and perseverance will help us through all our work, and I agree with you that a visit to the wreck is without doubt our first duty. Come, let us wake the children, and set to work without delay."

They were soon roused, and Fritz, overcoming his drowsiness before the others, ran out for his jackal; it was cold and stiff from the night air, and he placed it on its legs before the tent, in a most life-like attitude, and stood by to watch the effect upon the family. The dogs were the first to perceive their enemy, and growling, seemed inclined to dispose of the animal as they had disposed of its brethren in the night, but Fritz called them off. The noise the dogs made, however, had the effect of bringing out the younger children, and many were the exclamations they made at the sight of the strange animal.

"A yellow dog!" cried Franz.

"A wolf!" exclaimed Jack.

"It is a striped fox," said Ernest.

"Hullo," said Fritz. "The greatest men may make mistakes. Our Professor does not know a jackal when he sees one."

"But really," continued Ernest, examining the animal, "I think it is a fox."

"Very well, very well," retorted Fritz, "no doubt you know better than your father! He thinks it is a jackal."

"Come, boys," said I, "no more of this quarreling; you are none of you very far wrong, for the jackal partakes of the nature of all three, dog, wolf, and fox."

The monkey had come out on Jack's shoulder, but no sooner did it catch sight of the jackal, than it fled precipitately back into the tent, and hid itself in a heap of moss until nothing was visible but the tip of its little nose. Jack soothed and comforted the frightened little animal, and I then summoned them all to prayers, soon after which we began our breakfast. So severely had we dealt with our supper the previous night that we had little to eat but the biscuits, which were so dry and hard, that, hungry as we were, we could not swallow much. Fritz and I took some cheese to help them down, while my wife and younger sons soaked theirs in water. Ernest roamed down to the shore, and looked about for shellfish. Presently he returned with a few whelks. "Ah," said he, "if we had but some butter." "My boy," I replied, "your perpetual if, if, quite annoys me; why do you not sit down and eat cheese like the rest of us." "Not while I can get butter," he said; "see here, father," and he pointed to a large cask, "that barrel contains butter of some sort or another, for it is oozing out at the end."

"Really, Ernest," I said, "we are indebted to you. I will open the cask." So saying, I took a knife and carefully cut a small hole, so that I could extract the butter without exposing the mass of it to the effects of the air and heat. Filling a coconut shell, we once more sat down, and toasting our biscuits before the fire, spread them with the good Dutch butter. We found this vastly better than the dry biscuits, and while we were thus employed I noticed that the two dogs were lying unusually quiet by my side. I at first attributed this drowsiness to their large meal during the night, but I soon discovered that it arose from a different cause; the faithful animals had not escaped unhurt from their late combat, but had received several deep and painful wounds, especially about the neck. The dogs began to lick each other on the places which they could not reach with their own tongues, and my wife carefully dressed the wounds with butter, from which she had extracted the salt by washing.

A sudden thought now struck Ernest, and he wisely remarked, that if we were to make spiked collars for the dogs, they would in future escape such dangerous wounds. "Oh, yes," exclaimed Jack, "and I will make them; may I not, father?"

"Try, by all means, my little fellow," said I, "and persuade your mother to assist you; and now, Fritz," I continued, "we must be starting, for you and I are to make a trip to the wreck." I begged the party who were to remain on shore to keep together as much as possible, and having arranged a set of signals with my wife, that we might exchange communications, asked a blessing on our enterprise. I erected a signal post, and, while Fritz was making preparations for our departure, hoisted a strip of sailcloth as a flag; this flag was to remain hoisted so long as all was well on shore, but should our return be desired, three shots were to be fired and the flag lowered.

All was now ready, and warning my wife that we might find it necessary to remain all night on the vessel, we tenderly bade adieu and embarked. Except our guns and ammunition, we were taking nothing, that we might leave as much space as possible for the stowage of a large cargo. Fritz, however, had resolved to bring his little monkey, that he might obtain milk for it as soon as possible. We had not got far from the shore, when I perceived that a current from the river set in directly for the vessel, and though my nautical knowledge was not great, I succeeded in steering the boat into the favorable stream, which carried us nearly three-fourths of our passage with little or no trouble to ourselves; then, by dint of hard pulling, we accomplished the whole distance, and entering through the breach, gladly made fast our boat and stepped on board. Our first care was to see the animals, who greeted us with joy—lowing, bellowing, and bleating as we approached; not that the poor beasts were hungry, for they were all still well supplied with food, but they were apparently pleased by the mere sight of human beings. Fritz then placed his monkey by one of the goats, and the little animal immediately sucked the milk with evident relish, chattering and grinning all the while; the monkey provided for, we refreshed ourselves with some wine and biscuits. "Now," said I, "we have plenty to do; where shall we begin?"

"Let us fix a mast and sail to our boat," answered Fritz; "for the current which brought us out will not take us back, whereas the fresh breeze we met would help us immensely had we but a sail."

"Capital thought," I replied; "let us set to work at once."

I chose a stout spar to serve as a mast, and having made a hole in a plank nailed across one of the tubs, we, with the help of a rope and a couple of blocks, stepped it and secured it with stays. We then discovered a lug-sail, which had belonged to one of the ships' boats; this we hoisted; and our craft was ready to sail. Fritz begged me to decorate the masthead with a red streamer, to give our vessel a more finished appearance. Smiling at this childish but natural vanity, I complied with his request. I then contrived a rudder, that I might be able to steer the boat; for though I knew that an oar would serve the purpose, it was cumbrous and inconvenient. While I was thus employed, Fritz examined the shore with his glass, and soon announced that the flag was flying and all was well.

So much time had now slipped away that we found we could not return that night, as I had wished. We signaled our intention of remaining on board, and then spent the rest of our time in taking out the stones we had placed in the boat for ballast, and stowed in their place heavy articles of value to us. The ship had sailed for the purpose of supplying a young colony, she had therefore on board every conceivable article we could desire in our present situation; our only difficulty, indeed, was to make a wise selection. A large quantity of powder and shot we first secured, and as Fritz considered that we could not have too many weapons, we added three excellent guns, and a whole armful of swords, daggers, and knives. We remembered that knives and forks were necessary, we therefore laid in a large stock of them, and kitchen utensils of all sorts. Exploring the captain's cabin, we discovered a service of silver plate and a cellaret of good old wine; we then went over the stores, and supplied ourselves with potted meats, portable soups, Westphalian hams, sausages, a bag of maize and wheat, and a quantity of other seeds and vegetables. I then added a barrel of sulphur for matches, and as much cordage as I could find. All this—with nails, tools, and agricultural implements—completed our cargo, and sank our boat so low that I should have been obliged to lighten her had not the sea been calm.

Night drew on, and a large fire, lighted by those on shore, showed us that all was well. We replied by hoisting four ship's lanterns, and two shots announced to us that our signal was perceived; then, with a heartfelt prayer for the safety of our dear ones on shore, we retired to our boat, and Fritz, at all events, was soon sound asleep. For a while I could not sleep; the thought of my wife and children—alone and unprotected, save by the great dogs—disturbed my rest.

The night at length passed away. At daybreak Fritz and I arose and went on deck. I brought the telescope to bear upon the shore, and with pleasure saw the flag still waving in the morning breeze; while I kept the glass directed to the land, I saw the door of the tent open, and my wife appear and look steadfastly toward us.

I at once hoisted a white flag, and in reply the flag on shore was thrice dipped. Oh, what a weight seemed lifted from my heart as I saw the signal!

"Fritz," I said, "I am not now in such haste to get back, and begin to feel compassion for all these poor beasts. I wish we could devise some means for getting them on shore."

"We might make a raft," suggested Fritz, "and take off one or two at a time."

"True," I replied; "it is easy enough to say, 'make a raft,' but to do it is quite another thing."

"Well," said Fritz, "I can think of nothing else, unless indeed we make them such swimming belts as you made for the children."

"Really, my boy, that idea is worth having. I am not joking, indeed," I continued, as I saw him smile; "we may get every one of the animals ashore in that way."

So saying, I caught a fine sheep, and proceeded to put our plan into execution. I first fastened a broad piece of linen round its belly, and to this attached some corks and empty tins; then, with Fritz's help, I flung the animal into the sea—it sank, but a moment afterward rose and floated famously.

"Hurrah!" exclaimed Fritz, "we will treat them all like that." We then rapidly caught the other animals and provided them, one after the other, with a similar contrivance. The cow and ass gave us more trouble than did the others, as for them we required something more buoyant than the mere cork; we at last found some empty casks and fastened two to each animal by thongs passed under its belly. This done, the whole herd were ready to start, and we brought the ass to one of the ports to be the first to be launched. After some maneuvering we got him in a convenient position, and then a sudden heave sent him plunging into the sea. He sank, and then, buoyed up by the casks, emerged head and back from the water. The cow, sheep, and goats followed him one after the other, and then the sow alone remained. She seemed, however, determined not to leave the ship; she kicked, struggled, and squealed so violently, that I really thought we should be obliged to abandon her; at length, after much trouble, we succeeded in sending her out of the port after the others, and when once in the water, such was the old lady's energy that she quickly distanced them, and was the first to reach the shore.

We had fastened to the horns or neck of each animal a cord with a float attached to the end, and now embarking, we gathered up these floats, set sail, and steered for shore, drawing our herd after us.

Delighted with the successful accomplishment of our task, we got out some biscuits and enjoyed a midday meal; then, while Fritz amused himself with his monkey, I took up my glass and tried to make out how our dear ones on shore were employing themselves. As I was thus engaged, a sudden shout from Fritz surprised me. I glanced up; there stood Fritz with his gun to his shoulder, pointing it at a huge shark; the monster was making for one of the finest sheep; he turned on his side to seize his prey; as the white of his belly appeared Fritz fired. The shot took effect, and our enemy disappeared, leaving a trace of blood on the calm water.

"Well done, my boy," I cried, "you will become a crack shot one of these days; but I trust you will not often have such dangerous game to shoot." Fritz's eyes sparkled at his success and my praise, and reloading his gun carefully watched the water. But the shark did not again appear, and, borne onward by the breeze, we quickly neared the shore. Steering the boat to a convenient landing place, I cast off the ropes which secured the animals, and let them get ashore as best they might.

There was no sign of my wife or children when we stepped on land, but a few moments afterward they appeared, and with a shout of joy ran toward us. We were thankful to be once more united, and after asking and replying to a few preliminary questions, proceeded to release our herd from their swimming belts, which, though so useful in the water, were exceedingly inconvenient on shore. My wife was astonished at the apparatus.

"How clever you are!" said she.

"I am not the inventor," I replied; "the honor is due to Fritz. He not only thought of this plan for bringing off the animals, but saved one, at least, of them from a most fearful death." And I then told them how bravely he had encountered the shark.

My wife was delighted with her son's success, but declared that she would dread our trips to the vessel more than ever, knowing that such savage fish inhabited the waters.

Fritz, Ernest, and I began the work of unloading our craft, while Jack, seeing that the poor donkey was still encumbered with his swimming belt, tried to free him from it. But the donkey would not stand quiet, and the child's fingers were not strong enough to loosen the cordage; finally, therefore, he scrambled upon the animal's back, and urging him on with hand and foot, trotted toward us.

"Come, my boy," I said, "no one must be idle here, even for a moment; you will have riding practice enough hereafter; dismount and come and help us."

Jack was soon on his feet. "But I have not been idle all day," he said; "look here!" and he pointed to a belt round his waist. It was a broad belt of yellow hair, in which he had stuck a couple of pistols and a knife. "And see," he added, "what I have made for the dogs. Here, Juno! Turk!" the dogs came bounding up at his call, and I saw that they were each supplied with a collar of the same skin, in which were fastened nails, which bristled round their necks in a most formidable manner.

"Capital, capital! My boy," said I, "but where did you get your materials, and who helped you?"

"Except in cutting the skin," said my wife, "he had no assistance, and as for the materials, Fritz's jackal supplied us with the skin, and the needles and thread came out of my wonderful bag. You little think how many useful things may be had from that same bag; it is woman's duty and nature, you know, to see after trifles."

Fritz evidently did not approve of the use to which his jackal's hide had been devoted, and holding his nose, begged his little brother to keep at a distance. "Really, Jack," he said, "you should have cured the hide before you used it; the smell is disgusting; don't come near me."

"It is not the hide that smells at all," retorted Jack, "it is your nasty jackal itself, that you left in the sun."

"Now, boys," said I, "no quarreling here; do you, Jack, help your brother to drag the carcass to the sea, and if your belt smells after that you must take it off and dry it better."

The jackal was dragged off, and we then finished our work of unloading our boat. When this was accomplished we started for our tent, and finding no preparation for supper, I said, "Fritz, let us have a Westphalian ham."

"Ernest," said my wife, smiling, "let us see if we cannot conjure up some eggs."

Fritz got out a splendid ham and carried it to his mother triumphantly, while Ernest set before me a dozen white balls with parchment-like coverings.

"Turtles' eggs!" said I. "Well done, Ernest! Where did you get them?"

"That," replied my wife, "shall be told in due course when we relate our adventures; now we will see what they will do toward making a supper for you; with these and your ham I do not think we shall starve."

Leaving my wife to prepare supper, we returned to the shore and brought up what of the cargo we had left there; then, having collected our herd of animals, we returned to the tent.

The meal which awaited us was as unlike the first supper we had there enjoyed as possible. My wife had improvised a table of a board laid on two casks; on this was spread a white damask tablecloth, on which were placed knives, forks, spoons, and plates for each person. A tureen of good soup first appeared, followed by a capital omelette, then slices of the ham; and finally some Dutch cheese, butter, and biscuits, with a bottle of the captain's Canary wine, completed the repast.

While we thus regaled ourselves, I related to my wife our adventures, and then begged she would remember her promise and tell me all that had happened in my absence.

CHAPTER
III

The mother relates her adventures—Proposes that we should build a nest—How Jack treated the jackal skin—How the boys were surprised by a bustard—How they found the mangrove tree—How the dogs caught the crabs—We discuss the possibility of making a house in the tree—To bed once more—We start for the wreck—The shark again—Return to land—Franz's crawfish—Bridge building—We pack up—A family removing in patriarchal style—A prickly enemy—Jack shoots it—We reach our new home—Fritz rids our poultry of an enemy—Little Franz finds the figs—Dinner—We prepare materials for our nest—Flamingoes—Roast and tame—The use of trigonometry—A cord carried over the bough—The rope ladder made—We mount our tree—Sleep under the roots—The building of the nest—Retire to roost for the first time.

"I will spare you a description," said my wife, "of our first day's occupations; truth to tell, I spent the time chiefly in anxious thought and watching your progress and signals. I rose very early this morning, and with the utmost joy perceiving your signal that all was right, hastened to reply to it, and then, while my sons yet slumbered, I sat down and began to consider how our position could be improved. 'For it is perfectly impossible,' said I to myself, 'to live much longer where we are now. The sun beats burningly the lifelong day on this bare, rocky spot, our only shelter is this poor tent, beneath the canvas of which the heat is even more oppressive than on the open shore. Why should not I and my little boys exert ourselves as well as my husband and Fritz? Why should not we too try to accomplish something useful? If we could but exchange this melancholy and unwholesome abode for a pleasant, shady dwelling place, we should all improve in health and spirits. Among those delightful woods and groves where Fritz and his father saw so many charming things, I feel sure there must be some little retreat where we could establish ourselves comfortably; there must be, and I will find it.'

"By this time the boys were up, and I observed Jack very quietly and busily occupied with his knife about the spot where Fritz's jackal lay. Watching his proceedings, I saw that he had cut two long, narrow strips of the animal's skin, which he cleaned and scraped very carefully, and then taking a handful of great nails out of his pocket, he stuck them through the skin, points outward, after which he cut strips of canvas sailcloth, twice as broad as the thongs, doubled them, and laid them on the raw side of the skin, so as to cover the broad, flat nail heads. At this point of the performance, Master Jack came to me with the agreeable request that I would kindly stitch the canvas and (moist) skin together for him. I gave him needles and thread, but could not think of depriving him of the pleasure of doing it himself.

"However, when I saw how good-humoredly he persevered in the work with his awkward, unskilled fingers, I took pity on him, and conquering the disgust I felt, finished lining the skin dog-collars he had so ingeniously contrived. After this, I was called upon to complete in the same way a fine belt of skin he had made for himself. I advised him to think of some means by which the skin might be kept from shrinking.

"Ernest, although rather treating Jack's manufacture with ridicule, proposed a sensible enough plan, which Jack forthwith put into execution. He nailed the skin, stretched flat, on a board, and put it in the sun to dry.

"My scheme of a journey was agreed to joyously by my young companions. Preparations were instantly set on foot; weapons and provisions provided; the two elder boys carrying guns, while they gave me charge of the water flask, and a small hatchet.

"Leaving everything in as good order as we could at the tent, we proceeded toward the stream, accompanied by the dogs. Turk, who had accompanied you on your first expedition, seemed immediately to understand that we wished to pursue the same route, and proudly led the way.

"As I looked at my two young sons, each with his gun, and considered how much the safety of the party depended on these little fellows, I felt grateful to you, dear husband, for having acquainted them in childhood with the use of firearms.

"Filling our water-jar, we crossed the stream, and went on to the height, from whence, as you described, a lovely prospect is obtained, at the sight of which a pleasurable sensation of buoyant hope, to which I had long been a stranger, awoke within my breast.

"A pretty little wood in the distance attracted my notice particularly, and thither we directed our course. But soon finding it impossible to force our way through the tall, strong grass, which grew in dense luxuriance higher than the children's heads, we turned toward the open beach on our left, and following it, we reached a point much nearer the little woods, when, quitting the strand, we made toward it.

"We had not entirely escaped the tall grass, however, and with the utmost fatigue and difficulty, were struggling through the reeds, when suddenly a great rushing noise terrified us all dreadfully. A very large and powerful bird sprang upward on the wing. Both boys attempted to take aim, but the bird was far away before they were ready to fire.

"'Oh, dear, what a pity!' exclaimed Ernest; 'now if I had only had my light gun, and if the bird had not flown quite so fast, I should have brought him down directly!'

"'Oh yes,' said I, 'no doubt you would be a capital sportsman, if only your game would always give you time to make ready comfortably.'

"'But I had no notion that anything was going to fly up just at our feet like that,' cried he.

"'A good shot,' I replied, 'must be prepared for surprises; neither wild birds nor wild beasts will send you notice that they are about to fly or to run.'

"'What sort of bird can it have been?' inquired Jack.

"'Oh, it certainly must have been an eagle,' answered little Franz, 'it was so very big!'

"'Just as if every big bird must be an eagle!' replied Ernest, in a tone of derision.

"'Let's see where he was sitting, at all events!' said I.

"Jack sprang toward the place, and instantly a second bird, rather larger than the first, rushed upward into the air, with a most startling noise.

"The boys stood staring upward, perfectly stupefied, while I laughed heartily, saying, 'Well, you are first-rate sportsmen, to be sure! You certainly will keep my larder famously well supplied!'

"At this, Ernest colored up, and looked inclined to cry, while Jack put on a comical face, pulled off his cap, and with a low bow, called after the fugitive:

"'Adieu for the present, sir! I live in hopes of another meeting!'

"On searching the ground carefully, we discovered a rude sort of nest made untidily of dry grass. It was empty, although we perceived broken eggshells at no great distance, and concluded that the young brood had escaped among the grass, which, in fact, we could see was waving at a little distance, as the little birds ran through it.

"'Now look here, Franz,' said Ernest, presently, 'just consider how this bird could by any possibility have been an eagle. Eagles never build on the ground, neither can their young leave the nest and run as soon as they are out of the egg. That is a peculiarity of the gallinaceous tribe of birds alone, to which then these must belong. The species, I think, is indicated by the white belly and dull red color of the wing coverts which I observed in these specimens, and I believe them to be bustards, especially as I noticed in the largest the fine mustache-like feathers over the beak, peculiar to the great bustard.'

"'My dear boy!' I said, 'your eyes were actively employed, I must confess, if your fingers were unready with the gun. And after all, it is just as well, perhaps, that we have not thrown the bustard's family into mourning.'

"Thus chatting, we at length approached my pretty wood. Numbers of birds fluttered and sang among the high branches, but I did not encourage the boys in their wish to try to shoot any of the happy little creatures. We were lost in admiration of the trees in this grove, and I cannot describe to you how wonderful they are, nor can you form the least idea of their enormous size without seeing them yourself. What we had been calling a wood proved to be a group of about a dozen trees only, and, what was strange, the roots sustained the massive trunks exalted in the air, forming strong arches, and props and stays all around each individual stem, which was firmly rooted in the center.

"I gave Jack some twine, and scrambling up one of the curious open-air roots, he succeeded in measuring round the trunk itself, and made it out to be about eighteen yards. I saw no sort of fruit, but the foliage is thick and abundant, throwing delicious shade on the ground beneath, which is carpeted with soft green herbage, and entirely free from thorns, briars, or bushes of any kind. It is the most charming resting place that ever was seen, and I and the boys enjoyed our midday meal immensely in this glorious palace of the woods, so grateful to our senses after the glare and heat of our journey thither. The dogs joined us after a while. They had lingered behind on the seashore, and I was surprised to see them lie down and go comfortably to sleep without begging for food, as they do usually when we eat.

"The longer we remained in this enchanting place, the more did it charm my fancy; and if we could but manage to live in some sort of dwelling up among the branches of those grand, noble trees,

I should feel perfectly safe and happy. It seemed to me absurd to suppose we should ever find another place half so lovely, so I determined to search no further, but return to the beach and see if anything from the wreck had been cast up by the waves, which we could carry away with us.

"Before starting, Jack persuaded me to sit quietly a little longer, and finish making his belt and the spike-collars for the dogs, for you must know that the child had actually been carrying the board on which these were stretched all this time, so that they should get the full benefit of the sun. As they were now quite dry, I completed them easily, and Jack girded on the belt with great pride, placing his pistols in it, and marching about in the most self-important style, while Ernest fitted the collars on the two dogs.

"On reaching the shore, we found it strewed with many articles, doubtless of value, but all too heavy for us to lift. We rolled some casks, however, beyond high-water mark, and dragged a chest or two also higher on the beach; and, while doing so, observed that our dogs were busy among the rocks. They were carefully watching the crevices and pools, and every now and then would pounce downward and seize something which they swallowed with apparent relish.

"'They are eating crabs,' said Jack. 'No wonder they have not seemed hungry lately.'

"And, sure enough, they were catching the little green crabs with which the water abounded. These, however, did not apparently entirely satisfy them.

"Some time afterward, just as we were about to turn inland toward the ford, we noticed that Juno was scraping in the sand, and turning up some round substances, which she hastily devoured. Ernest went to see what these were, and reported in his calm way that the dog had found turtles' eggs.

"'Oh,' cried I, 'then let us by all means share in the booty!' Mrs. Juno, however, did not at all approve of this, and it was with some difficulty that we drove her aside while we gathered a couple of dozen of eggs, stowing them in our provision bags.

"While thus employed, we caught sight of a sail which appeared to be merrily approaching the shore beyond the cliffs. Ernest declared it must be our raft. Little Franz, always having the fear of savages before his eyes, began to look frightened, and for a moment I myself was doubtful what to think.

"However, we hastened to the stream; and crossing it by the stepping-stones, came in sight of the landing place, where we joyfully met you.

"Now I hope you approve of the proceedings of your exploring party, and that tomorrow you will do me the favor of packing everything up, and taking us away to live among my splendid trees."

"Aye, little wife," said I; "so that is your idea of comfort and security, is it? A tree, I do not know how many feet high, on which we are to perch and roost like the birds? If we had but wings or a balloon, it would, I own, be a capital plan."

"Laugh as much as you like," returned my wife, "my idea is not so absurd as you make it out. We should be safe up there from jackals' visits during the night. And I know I have seen at home, in Switzerland, quite a pretty arbor, with a strong floor, up among the branches of a lime tree, and we went up a staircase to reach it. Why could not we contrive a place like that, where we could sleep safely at night?"

"I will consider the idea seriously, my wife," said I; "perhaps something may come of it, after all! Meantime, as we have finished our supper, and night is coming on, let us commend ourselves to Almighty protection and retire to rest."

Beneath the shelter of our tent, we all slept soundly, like marmots, until break of day; when, my wife and I awaking, we took counsel together as to future proceedings.

Referring to the task she had the previous evening proposed for me, I remarked that to undertake it would involve so many difficulties that it was highly necessary to look closely into the subject.

"In the first place," said I, "I am unwilling hastily to quit a spot to which I am convinced we were providentially led as a landing place. See how secure it is; guarded on all sides by these high cliffs, and accessible only by the narrow passage to the ford, while from this point it is so easy to reach the ship that the whole of the valuable cargo is at our disposal. Suppose we decide to stay patiently here for the present—until, at least, we have brought on shore everything we possibly can?"

"I agree with you to a certain extent, dear husband," replied she; "but you do not know how dreadfully the heat among the rocks tries me. It is almost intolerable to us who remain here all day, while you and Fritz are away out at sea or wandering among the shady woods, where cool fruits refresh, and fair scenes delight you. As to the contents of the ship, an immense deal has been cast ashore, and I would much rather give up all the remainder, and be spared the painful anxiety it gives me when you even talk of venturing again on the faithless deep."

"Well, I must admit that there is much right on your side," I continued; "suppose we were to remove to your chosen abode, and make this rocky fastness our magazine and place of retreat in case of danger. I could easily render it more secure, by blasting portions of the rock with gunpowder. But a bridge must be constructed in the first place, to enable us to cross bag and baggage."

"Oh, I shall be parched to death before we can leave this place if a bridge has to be made," cried my wife impatiently. "Why not just take our things on our backs and wade across as we have done already? The cow and the donkey could carry a great deal."

"That they will have to do, in whatever fashion we make the move," said I; "but bags and baskets we must have, to put things in, and if you will turn your attention to providing those, I will set about the bridge at once. It will be wanted not once but continually; the stream will probably swell and be impassable at times, and even as it is, an accident might happen."

"Well! Well!" Cried my wife, "I submit to your opinion; only pray set about it without delay, for I long to be off. It is an excellent idea to make a strong place among the cliffs here; the gunpowder especially, I shall be delighted to see stored here when we go away, for it is frightfully dangerous to keep so much as we have close to our habitation."

"Gunpowder is indeed the most dangerous and at the same time the most useful thing we have," said I, "and for both these reasons we must be especially careful of it. In time I will hollow out a place in the rock where we can store it safe from either fire or damp."

By this morning's consultation we had settled the weighty question of our change of abode, and also chalked out work for the day.

When the children heard of the proposed move their joy was boundless; they began at once to talk of it as our "journey to the Promised Land," and only regretted that time must be "wasted," as they said, in bridge-building before it could be undertaken.

Every one being impatient for breakfast that work might be begun at once, the cow and goats were milked, and, having enjoyed a comfortable meal of biscuit boiled in milk, I prepared to start for the wreck, in order to obtain planks for the proposed bridge. Ernest, as well as Fritz, accompanied me, and we were soon within the influence of the current, and were carried swiftly out to sea. Fritz was steering, and we had no sooner passed beyond the islet at the entrance of the bay, so as to come in sight of its seaward beach, than we were astonished to see a countless multitude of sea birds, gulls, and others, which rose like a cloud into the air, disturbed by our approach, and deafened us by their wild and screaming cries. Fritz caught up his gun, and would have sent a shot among them had I permitted it. I was curious to find out what could be the attraction for all this swarm of feathered fowl; and, availing myself of a fresh breeze from the sea, I set the sail and directed our course toward the island.

The swelling sail and flying pennant charmed Ernest, while Fritz bent his keen eyes eagerly toward the sandy shore, where the flocks of birds were again settling.

Presently he shouted: "Aha! Now I see what they are after!

They have got a huge monster of a fish there and a proper feast they are making! Let's have a nearer look at it, father!"

We could not take our boat very close in, but we managed to effect a landing at a short distance from the festive scene; and, securing the raft by casting a rope round a large stone, we cautiously drew near the object of interest.

It proved to be a monstrous fish on whose flesh these multitudes of birds were ravenously feeding; and it was extraordinary to watch the ferocity, the envy, the gluttony, and all manner of evil passions, exhibited among the guests at this banquet.

"There was nothing on this sandy beach when we passed yesterday, I am certain, father," said Fritz. "It seems strange to see this creature stranded here."

"Why, Fritz!" cried Ernest, "it must be the shark! Your shark, you know! I believe I can see where you hit him in the head."

"You are right, I do believe, Ernest," said I, "though I think your imagination only can distinguish the gunshot wound among all the pecking and tearing of the voracious birds there. Just look, boys, at those terrific jaws, beneath the strangely projecting snout. See the rows upon rows of murderous teeth, and thank God we were delivered from them! Let us try if we can induce these greedy birds to spare us a bit of the shark's skin; it is extremely rough, and when dry may be used like a file."

Ernest drew the ramrod from his gun, and charged so manfully into the crowd, that striking right and left he speedily killed several, while most of the others took to flight. Fritz detached some broad strips of skin with his knife, and we returned toward the boat.

Perceiving with satisfaction that the shore was strewn with just the sort of boards and planks I wanted, I lost no time in collecting them; and, forming a raft to tow after us, we were in a short time able to direct our course homeward, without visiting the wreck at all. As we sailed along, extremely well pleased with our good fortune, Fritz, by my direction, nailed part of the shark's skin flat on boards to dry in the sun, and the rest on the rounded mast.

"Will that be a good plan, father?" inquired he, "it will be quite bent and crooked when it hardens."

"That is just what I want it to be," said I, "we may happen to find it useful in that form as well as flat. It would be beautiful shagreen if we could smooth and polish it."

"I thought," remarked Ernest, "that shagreen was made from asses' hide."

"And you thought rightly," said I. "The best shagreen is prepared in Turkey, Persia, and Tartary, from the skins of horses and asses. In these skins, the roughness is produced artificially; while the skin is newly flayed and still soft, hard grains of corn are spread on the under surface, and pressed into it as it dries. These grains are afterward removed, and the roughness imparted to the appearance of the skin remains indelibly; shagreen is useful in polishing joiners' work, and it is made in France from the rough skin of a hideous creature called the angel-fish."

"Angel-fish!" exclaimed Fritz; "what a name to give to anything 'hideous,' father!"

"There are bad angels as well as good ones," observed Ernest, in his dry, quiet way; "it is better to leave people to see for themselves which is meant."

By this time we were close in shore; and, lowering the sail, we soon had our craft, with the raft in tow, safely moored to the bank.

No one was in sight, not a sound to be heard, so with united voice we gave a loud cheery halloo, which after a while was answered in shrill tones, and the mother, with her two boys, came running from behind the rocks between us and the stream, each carrying a small bundle in a handkerchief, while little Franz held aloft a landing net.

Our return so soon was quite unexpected, and they anxiously inquired the reason, which we soon explained; and then the mysterious bundles were opened, and a great number of fine crawfish displayed; whose efforts to escape by scuttling away in every direction, directly they were placed in a heap on the ground, caused immense fun and laughter as the boys pursued and brought them back, only to find others scrambling off in a dozen different ways.

"Now, father, have we not done well today!" cried Jack, "did you ever see such splendid crawfish? Oh, there were thousands of them, and I am sure we have got two hundred here at least. Just look at their claws!"

"No doubt you were the discoverer of these fine crabs, eh, Jack?" said I.

"No! Fancy young Franz being the lucky man!" answered he. "He and I went toward the stream while mother was busy, just to look for a good place for the bridge. Franz was picking up pebbles and alabasters, some because they were so pretty, some to strike sparks with in the dark, and some, he insisted, were 'gold.' 'Jack! Jack!' cried he presently, 'come and see the crabs on Fritz's jackal!' You know we threw it away there, and to be sure it was swarming with these creatures. Are you glad we have found them, father? Will they be good to eat?"

"Very excellent, my boy, and we may be thankful that food for our wants is thus provided day by day."

When each party had related the day's adventures, and while the mother was cooking the crawfish, we went to bring our store of planks to land. Even this apparently simple operation required thought, and I had to improvise rope-harness for the cow and the donkey, by which we could make them drag each board separately from the water's edge to the margin of the stream.

Jack showed me where he thought the bridge should be, and I certainly saw no better place, as the banks were at that point tolerably close to one another, steep, and of about equal height.

"How shall we find out if our planks are long enough to reach across?" said I. "A surveyor's table would be useful now."

"What do you say to a ball of string, father?" said Ernest. "Tie one end to a stone, throw it across, then draw it back and measure the line!"

Adopting my son's idea, we speedily ascertained the distance across to be eighteen feet. Then allowing three feet more at each side, I calculated twenty-four feet as the necessary length of the boards.

The question as to how the planks were to be laid across was a difficult one. We resolved to discuss it during dinner, to which we were now summoned. And my wife, as we sat resting, displayed to me her needlework. With hard labor she had made two large canvas bags for the ass to carry. Having no suitable needle, she had been obliged to bore the hole for each stitch with a nail, and gained great praise for her ingenuity and patience. Dinner was quickly dispatched, as we were all eager to continue our engineering work. A scheme had occurred to me for conveying one end of a plank across the water, and I set about it in this way. There fortunately were one or two trees close to the stream on either side. I attached a rope pretty near one end of a beam, and slung it loosely to the tree beside us; then, fastening a long rope to the other end, I crossed with it by means of broken rocks and stones, and having a pulley and block, I soon arranged the rope on a strong limb of the opposite tree, again returning with the end to our own side.

Now putting my idea to the proof, I brought the ass and the cow, and fastening this rope to the harness I had previously contrived for them, I drove them steadily away from the bank. To my great satisfaction, and the surprise and delight of the boys, the end of the plank which had been laid alongside the stream began gently to move, rose higher, turned, and soon projecting over the water, continued to advance, until, having described the segment of a circle, it reached the opposite bank; I stopped my team, the plank rested on the ground, the bridge was made! So at least thought Fritz and Jack, who in a moment were lightly running across the narrow way, shouting joyfully as they sprang to the other side.

Our way was now comparatively easy. A second and third plank were laid beside the first; and when these were carefully secured at each end to the ground and to the trees, we very quickly laid short boards side by side across the beams, the boys nailing them lightly down as I sawed them in lengths; and when this was done, our bridge was pronounced complete. Nothing could exceed the excitement of the children. They danced to and fro on the wonderful structure, singing, shouting, and cutting the wildest capers.

I must confess I heartily sympathized with their triumphant feelings.

Now that the work was done, we began to feel how much we were fatigued, and gladly returned to our tent for refreshment and repose.

Next morning, while we breakfasted, I made a little speech to my sons on the subject of the important move we were about to make, wishing to impress them with a sense of the absolute necessity of great caution.

"Remember," said I, "that, although you all begin to feel very much at your ease here, we are yet complete strangers to a variety of dangers which may surprise us unawares. I charge you, therefore, to maintain good order, and keep together on the march. No darting off into by-ways, Jack. No lingering behind to philosophize, Ernest. And now all hands to work."

The greatest activity instantly prevailed in our camp. Some collected provisions, others packed kitchen utensils, tools, ropes, and hammocks, arranging them as burdens for the cow and ass. My wife pleaded for a seat on the latter for her little Franz, and assuring me likewise that she could not possibly leave the poultry, even for a night, nor exist an hour without her magic bag, I agreed to do my best to please her, without downright cruelty to the animals.

Away ran the children to catch the cocks and hens. Great chasing, fluttering, and cackling ensued; but with no success whatever, until the mother recalled her panting sons; and scattering some handfuls of grain within the open tent, soon decoyed the fowls and pigeons into the enclosure; where, when the curtain was dropped, they were easily caught, tied together, and placed on the cow. This amiable and phlegmatic animal had stood calmly chewing the cud, while package after package was disposed on her broad back, nor did she now object even to this noisy addition to her load. I placed a couple of half-hoops over all; and, spreading sailcloth on them, put the fowls in darkness, and they rapidly became quiet; and the cow, with the appearance of having a small wagon on her back, was ready to start.

Franz was firmly seated on the ass, amidst bags and bundles of all sorts and sizes; they rose about him like cushions and pillows, and his curly head rested on the precious magic bag, which surmounted all the rest.

Having filled the tent with the things we left behind, closing it carefully, and ranging chests and casks around it, we were finally ready to be off, each well equipped and in the highest spirits.

Fritz and his mother led the van.

Franz (the young cavalier) and the sober-minded cow followed them closely.

Jack conducted the goats; one of these had also a rider, for Knips,* the monkey, was seated on his foster-mother, whose patience was sorely tried by his restlessness and playful tricks.

The sheep were under Ernest's care, and I brought up the rear of this patriarchal band, while the dogs kept constantly running backward and forward in the character of aides-de-camp.

"We seem delightfully like those simple and pastoral tribes I have read of," said Ernest, as we proceeded, "whose whole lives are spent in shifting from place to place, without any wish to settle."

"Yes," said I. "Among the Arabs, Tartars, and some other Eastern nations, this mode of life is natural. They for that reason are called Nomads.

"These tribes are amply provided with camels and horses, and effect their journeys more quickly and conveniently than we are likely to do with these deliberate quadrupeds of ours. Whatever you young folks may think, I suspect your mother and I will be quite satisfied with one such undertaking. At least I hope she will be contented with the nest she intends me to build for her up in her wonderful trees."

---

* German, *Knipps*, a mannikin.

With honest pride I introduced my wife to my bridge, and after receiving from her what I considered well-merited praise for my skill in its construction, we passed over it in grand procession, reinforced unexpectedly on the opposite side by the arrival of our cross-grained old sow. The perverse creature had obstinately resisted our attempts to bring her with us, but finding herself deserted, had followed of her own accord, testifying in the most unmistakable manner, by angry grunts and squeals, her entire disapproval of our proceedings.

I soon found we must, as before, turn down to the sea beach, for not only did the rank grass impede our progress, but it also tempted the animals to break away from us, and, but for our watchful dogs, we might have lost several of them.

On the firm open sands we were making good way, when, to my annoyance, both our dogs suddenly left us, and springing into the thick cover to our right, commenced a furious barking, following by howling as if in fear and violent pain.

Not for a moment doubting that some dangerous animal was at hand, I hastened to the spot, remarking as I went the characteristic behavior of my three sons.

Fritz cocked his gun and advanced boldly, but with caution.

Ernest looked disconcerted, and drew back, but got ready to fire.

While Jack hurried after Fritz without so much as unslinging his gun from his shoulders.

Before I could come up with them, I heard Jack shouting excitedly,

"Father! Father! Come quickly! A huge porcupine! A most enormous porcupine!"

Sure enough, the dogs were rushing round and round a porcupine, and having attempted to seize it, were already severely wounded by its quills. Each time they came near, the creature, with a rattling noise, bristled up its spines.

Somewhat to my amusement, while we were looking at the curious defence this creature was making, little Jack stepped close up to it, with a pocket pistol in his hand, and shot it dead, making sure of it by a couple of heavy raps on the head, and then giving way to a burst of boyish exultation, he called upon us to help to convey his prize to his mother. This it was by no means easy to do. Sundry attempts resulted in bloody fingers, till Jack, taking his pocket handkerchief, and fastening one corner round its neck, ran off, dragging it after him to where his mother awaited us.

"Hullo, mother! Here's a jolly beast, isn't it? I shot it, and it's good to eat! Father says so! I only wish you had seen how it terrified the dogs, and heard the rattling and rustling of its spines. Oh, it is a fearful creature!"

Ernest, examining it carefully, pronounced its incisor teeth, its ears and feet, to resemble those of the human race, and pointed out the curious crest of stiff hairs on its head and neck.

"I have read of another species," said he, "called the tuft-tailed porcupine, which must be even more curious looking than this is. It has short, flat quills, and a scaly tail ending in an extraordinary tuft, like a bunch of narrow strips of parchment. It cannot be such a disagreeable enemy to encounter as this fellow."

"Were you not afraid, Jack," asked I, "lest the porcupine should cast some of his quills like darts at you?"

"Of course not," returned he, "I know well enough that is nothing but a fable!"

"A fable!" said I; "why, look at your mother! She is drawing five or six spines out of each of the dogs!"

"Ah, those stuck into them when they so fiercely fell upon it in their attack. Those are the short quills, and seem very slightly fixed in its skin. The long quills bent aside when Juno pressed against them."

"You are perfectly right, my boy," said I; "there is no truth in the old idea of shooting out the spines. But now, shall we leave this prickly booty of yours, or attempt to take it with us?"

"Oh, please father, let us take it! Why, it is good to eat!"

Smiling at the child's eagerness, and willing to please him, I made a somewhat awkward bundle of the porcupine, wrapping it in several folds of cloth, and added it to the donkey's load.

Our party then resumed the march, which, with little interruption, was continued steadily, until we came in sight of our future place of residence.

The wonderful appearance of the enormous trees, and the calm beauty of the spot altogether, fully came up to the enthusiastic description which had been given me. And my wife gladly heard me say that, if an abode could be contrived among the branches, it would be the safest and most charming home in the world.

We hastily unloaded the ass and cow, securing them, as well as the sheep and goats, by tying their forefeet loosely together. The doves and poultry were set at liberty, and we sat down to rest among the soft herbage while we laid our plans for the night.

Fritz soon left us, but presently two shots were fired, and he appeared holding a fine tiger cat by the hind legs, which, with the intensest delight, he exhibited to each in turn.

"Well done, Fritz!" cried I. "Our cocks and hens would have had an unfortunate night of it but for this lucky shot of yours. It is to be hoped he has left no companion near at hand. You must be on the lookout."

"How curious it seems," remarked Ernest, "that God should create hurtful animals like this."

"To our feeble and narrow vision many of the ways of the Infinite and Eternal Mind are incomprehensible," I replied. "What our limited reason cannot grasp, let us be content to acknowledge as the workings of Almighty power and wisdom, and thankfully trust in that 'Rock,' which, were it not higher than we, would afford no sense of security to the immortal soul. That animals should prey upon one another is a means of preserving a due balance in the world of nature, and in many ways these beasts of prey are also useful to man. What beautiful and warm furs are procured by hunters just in those countries where no other covering would defend the inhabitants from the wintery cold!—as, for instance, the skins of bears, wolverines, and arctic foxes, wild cats, and many others."

"The skin of the seal, or sea dog, is also valuable," said Ernest.

"It is," I replied, "and in its own element that creature preys on fish as the dog did on land animals before his race become domesticated by man. But now, Fritz, tell us how you obtained your prize."

"Observing that something moved among the branches," said he, "I went softly around the tree with my gun, and making sure the creature was a wild cat, I fired and brought it down. It was severely wounded, but, rising in a fury, it attempted to climb the tree, when I, luckily having a loaded pistol, gave it a quietus. And do tell me, father, what sort of a cat it is."

"It is a mercy the brute did not fly at your throat instead of attempting to escape," said I. "It belongs to a fierce and bloodthirsty race—that of the ocelots or tiger cats, natives of the tropical parts of America. I should say this was a margay, and it would have proved a cruel foe, not only of our poultry, but also of our sheep and goats. I am well pleased that you have rid us of it."

"May I have the beautiful skin, father? And will you tell me what will be the best use to make of it?"

"I advise you to skin the animal very carefully, and of the handsome black and yellow tail make a hunting-belt for yourself. The paws—let me see—why, I fancy the paws might be made famous cases for knife, fork and spoon, and look well hanging from the belt. The skin of the body you had better preserve until you find some suitable use for it."

"Oh, father, what a splendid plan!" cried Jack; "do tell me some good use for my porcupine."

"I think its feet may make cases also; at least, you may try. The quills, I am sure, may be used for packing needles, and for tipping arrows, and I should try to make defensive armor for the dogs out of the rest. They may fall in with foes more dangerous than any we have yet seen."

"To be sure, father, the very thing!" shouted Jack, in high glee. "I have seen pictures of boar hunts, in which the dogs were protected by a sort of leather coat of mail. That will be grand!"

After giving this advice, I got no peace until I had shown my boys how to act upon it, and in a short time each had his prize fastened up by the hind legs, and carefully slitting the skin, was stripping it from the carcass.

Ernest, meanwhile, was fetching large flat stones in order to form a fireplace, while Franz gathered sticks, as his mother was anxious to prepare some food.

"What sort of a tree do you suppose this to be, father?" inquired Ernest, seeing me examining that under which we were encamping. "Is not the leaf something like the walnut?"

"There is a resemblance, but in my opinion these gigantic trees must be mangroves or wild figs. I have heard their enormous height described, and also the peculiarity of the arching roots supporting the main trunk raised above the soil."

Just then little Franz came up with a large bundle of sticks, and his mouth full of something he was eating with evident satisfaction.

"Oh, mother!" cried he, "this is so good! So delicious!"

"Greedy little boy!" exclaimed she in a fright. "What have you got there? Don't swallow it, whatever you do. Very likely it is poisonous! Spit it all out this minute!" And the anxious mother quickly extracted from the rosy little mouth the remains of a small fig.

"Where did you find this?" said I.

"There are thousands lying among the grass yonder," replied the little boy. "They taste very nice. I thought poison was nasty. Do you think they will hurt me? The pigeons and the hens are gobbling them up with all their might and main, papa!"

"I think you have no cause for alarm, dear wife," I said. "The trees seem to be the fig-bearing mangrove of the Antilles. But remember, Franz, you must never eat anything without first showing it to me, never mind how good it seems. If birds and monkeys eat a fruit or vegetable, it is usually safe to believe it wholesome," added I, turning to the other boys, who, instantly taking the hint, coaxed Franz to give them the figs he still had in his pocket, and ran to offer them to Knips, who was closely watching the skinning of the tiger cat and porcupine, apparently giving his opinion on the subject with much chattering and gesticulation.

"Here, Knips, allow me to present you with a fig!" cried Jack, holding one out to the funny little creature.

Knips took it readily, and after turning it about, and sniffing and smelling it, he popped it into his mouth, with such a droll grimace of delight and satisfaction that the boys all laughed and clapped their hands, crying "Bravo, Knips! You know a good thing when you see it, don't you, old fellow! Hurrah!"

My wife, with her mind set at rest on the question of the figs, now continued her preparations for dinner.

The flesh of the margay was given to the dogs, but part of the porcupine was put on the fire to boil, while we reserved the rest for roasting.

I employed myself in contriving needles for my wife's work, by boring holes at one end of the quills, which I did by means of a red hot nail, and I soon had a nice packet of various sizes, which pleased her immensely. I also laid plans for making proper harness for our beasts of burden, but could not attempt to begin that while so many wants more pressing demanded attention.

We examined the different trees, and chose one which seemed most suited to our purpose. The branches spread at a great height above us, and I made the boys try if it were possible to throw sticks or stones over one of these, my intention being to construct a rope ladder if we could once succeed in getting a string across a strong bough.

Finding we could not succeed in that way, I resolved other schemes in my mind, and meantime went with Jack and Fritz to a small brook close by, where I showed them how to place the skins to steep and soften in the water, with stones placed on them to keep them beneath the surface.

When dinner was over, I prepared our night quarters. I first slung our hammocks from the roots of the tree, which, meeting above us, formed an arched roof, then covering the whole with sailcloth, we made a temporary tent, which would at least keep off the night damps and noxious insects.

Leaving my wife engaged in making a set of harness for the ass and cow, whose strength I intended to employ the following day in drawing the beams up to our tree, I walked down with Fritz and Ernest to the beach to look for wood suitable for building our new abode, and also to discover, if possible, some light rods to form a ladder. For some time we hunted in vain, nothing but rough drift wood was to be seen, utterly unfit for our purpose. Ernest at length pointed out a quantity of bamboos, half buried in the sand. These were exactly what I wanted, and stripping them of their leaves I cut them into lengths of about five feet each; these I bound in bundles to carry to the tree, and then began to look about for some slight reeds to serve as arrows.

I presently saw what I required in a copse at a little distance. We advanced cautiously lest the thicket should contain some wild beast or venomous serpent. Juno rushed ahead; as she did so a flock of flamingoes, which had been quietly feeding, rose in the air. Fritz, instantly firing, brought a couple of the birds to the ground, the rest of the squadron sailing away in perfect order, their plumage continually changing, as they flew, from beautiful rose to pure white, as alternately their snowy wings and rosy breasts were visible. One of those which fell was perfectly dead, but the other appeared only slightly wounded in the wing, for it made off across the swampy ground. I attempted to follow, but soon found that progress was impossible on the marsh; Juno, however, chased the bird and, seizing it, speedily brought it to my feet. Fritz and Ernest were delighted at the sight of our prize.

"What a handsome bird!" exclaimed they. "Is it much hurt? Let us tame it and let it run about with the fowls."

"Its plumage is much more brilliant than that of the dead one," remarked Fritz.

"Yes," said Ernest, "this is a full grown bird, while yours is younger; it is some years before they reach perfection. See what long active legs it has, like those of a stork, while with its great webbed feet it can swim faster than a goose. Earth, air, or water is all the same to the flamingo, it is equally at home in any one of the three."

"Well," said Fritz, "let us take the dead one to mother and get her to introduce it to the other element, and see what it will make of that; if it is young and tender, as you say, it should make a delicious roast."

Fritz and Ernest then carried the birds and bamboos to the trees, while I proceeded to cut my reeds. I chose those which had flowered, knowing that they were harder, and having cut a sufficient quantity of these, I selected one or two of the tallest canes I could find to assist me in measuring the height of the tree. I then bound them together and returned to my family.

"Do you mean to keep this great hungry bird Fritz has brought?" said my wife, "it is another mouth to feed, remember, and provisions are still scarce."

"Luckily," I replied, "the flamingo will not eat grain like our poultry, but will be quite satisfied with insects, fish, and little crabs, which it will pick up for itself. Pray reassure yourself, therefore, and let me see to the poor bird's wound."

So saying, I procured some wine and butter and anointed the wing, which though hurt was not broken. I bound it up, and then took the bird to the stream, where I fastened it by a long cord to a stake and left it to shift for itself. In a few days the wound was healed, and the bird, subdued by kind treatment, became rapidly tame.

While I was thus employed my sons were endeavoring to ascertain the height of the lowest branch of the tree from the ground. They had fastened together the long reeds I had brought, and were trying to measure the distance with them, but in vain; they soon found that were the rods ten times their length they could not touch the branch.

"Hullo, my boys," I said, when I discovered what they were about, "that is not the way to set to work. Geometry will simplify the operation considerably; with its help the altitude of the highest mountains are ascertained. We may, therefore, easily find the height of the branch."

So saying, I measured out a certain distance from the base of the tree and marked the spot, and then by means of a rod whose length I knew, and imaginary lines, I calculated the angle subtended by the trunk of the tree from the ground to the root of the branch. This done, I was able to discover the height required, and, to the astonishment of the younger children, announced that we should henceforth live thirty feet above the ground. This I wanted to know, that I might construct a ladder of the necessary length.

Telling Fritz to collect all our cord, and the others to roll all the twine into a ball, I sat down, and taking the reeds, speedily manufactured half a dozen arrows and feathered them from the dead flamingo. I then took a strong bamboo, bent it, and strung it so as to form a bow. When the boys saw what I had done they were delighted, and begged to have the pleasure of firing the first shot.

"No, no!" said I, "I did not make this for mere pleasure, nor is it even intended as a weapon, the arrows are pointless. Elizabeth," I continued to my wife, "can you supply me with a ball of stout thread from your wonderful bag?"

"Certainly," replied she, "I think a ball of thread was the first thing to enter the bag," and diving her hand deep in, she drew out the very thing I wanted.

"Now, boys," I said, "I am going to fire the first shot," and I fastened one end of the thread to one of my arrows and aimed at a large branch above me. The arrow flew upward and bore the thread over the branch and fell at our feet. Thus was the first step in our undertaking accomplished. Now for the rope ladder!

Fritz had obtained two coils of cord, each about forty feet in length; these we stretched on the ground side by side; then Fritz cut the bamboos into pieces of two feet for the steps of the ladder, and as he handed them to me, I passed them through knots which I had prepared in the ropes, while Jack fixed each end with a nail driven through the wood. When the ladder was finished, I carried over the bough a rope by which it might be hauled up. This done, I fixed the lower end of the ladder firmly to the ground by means of stakes, and was all ready for an ascent. The boys, who had been watching me with intense interest, were each eager to be first.

"Jack shall have the honor," said I, "as he is the lightest; so up with you, my boy, and do not break your neck."

Jack, who was as active as a monkey, sprang up the ladder and quickly gained the top.

"Three cheers for the nest!" he exclaimed, waving his cap. "Hurrah, hurrah, hurrah for our jolly nest! What a grand house we will have up here; come along, Fritz!"

His brother was soon by his side, and with a hammer and nails secured the ladder yet more securely. I followed with an ax, and took a survey of the tree. It was admirably suited to our purpose; the branches were very strong and so closely interwoven that no beams would be required to form a flooring, but when some of the boughs were lopped and cleared away, a few planks would be quite sufficient.

I now called for a pulley, which my wife fastened to the cord hanging beside the ladder. I hauled it up, and finding the boys rather in my way, told them to go down, while I proceeded to fasten the pulley to a stout branch above me, that we might be able to haul up the beams we should require the next day. I then made other preparations, that there might be no delay on the morrow, and a bright moon having arisen, I by its light continued working until I was quite worn out, and then at length descended. I reached the ground, but to my surprise found that the two boys were not there. They had not been seen. A moment afterward, however, all anxiety was dispelled, for among the topmost boughs I heard their young voices raised in the evening hymn. Instead of descending, they had, while I was busy, climbed upward, and had been sitting in silent admiration of the moonlight scene, high above me. They now joined us, and my wife showed me the results of her labor. She had made two complete sets of harness. I congratulated her upon her success, and we then sat down to supper. On a cloth spread out upon the grass were arranged a roast shoulder of porcupine, a delicious bowl of soup made from a piece of the same animal, cheese, butter, and biscuits, forming a most tempting repast. Having done this ample justice, we collected our cattle, and the pigeons and fowls having retired to roost on the neighboring trees, and on the steps of our ladder, we made up a glorious fire to keep off any prowling wild beasts, and ourselves lay down. The children, in spite of the novelty of the hammocks, were quickly asleep. In vain I tried to follow their example; a thousand anxious thoughts presented themselves, and as quickly as I dispelled them others rose in their place. The night wore on, and I was still awake; the fire burned low, and I rose and replenished it with dry fuel. Then again I climbed into my hammock, and toward morning fell asleep.

Early next morning we were astir, and dispersed to our various occupations. My wife milked the goats and cow, while we gave the animals their food, after which we went down to the beach to collect more wood for our building operations. To the larger beams we harnessed the cow and ass, while we ourselves dragged up the remainder. Fritz and I then ascended the tree, and finished the preparations I had begun the night before, all useless boughs we lopped off, leaving a few about six feet from the floor, from which we might sling our hammocks, and others still higher, to support a temporary roof of sailcloth. My wife made fast the planks to a rope passed through the block I had fixed to the boughs above us, and by this means Fritz and I hauled them up. These we arranged side by side on the foundation of boughs, so as to form a smooth solid floor, and round this platform built a bulwark of planks, and then throwing the sailcloth over the higher branches, we drew it down and firmly nailed it. Our house was thus enclosed on three sides, for behind the great trunk protected us, while the front was left open to admit the fresh sea breeze which blew directly in. We then hauled up our hammocks and bedding and slung them from the branches we had left for that purpose. A few hours of daylight still remaining, we cleared the floor of leaves and chips, and then descended to fashion a table and a few benches from the remainder of the wood. After working like slaves all day, Fritz and

I flung ourselves on the grass, while my wife arranged supper on the table we had made.

"Come," said she at length, "come and taste flamingo stew, and tell me how you like it. Ernest assured me that it would be much better stewed than roasted, and I have been following his directions."

Laughing at the idea of Ernest turning scientific cook, we sat down. The fowls gathered round us to pick up the crumbs, and the tame flamingo joined them, while Master Knips skipped about from one to the other, chattering and mimicking our gestures continually. To my wife's joy, the sow appeared shortly after, and was presented with all the milk that remained from the day's stock that she might be persuaded to return every night.

"For," said my wife, "this surplus milk is really of no use to us, as it will be sour before the morning in this hot climate."

"You are quite right," I replied, "but we must contrive to make it of use. The next time Fritz and I return to the wreck we will bring off a churn among the other things we require."

"Must you really go again to that dreadful wreck?" said my wife shuddering. "You have no idea how anxious I am when you are away there."

"Go we must, I am afraid," I replied, "but not for a day or two yet. Come, it is getting late. We and the chickens must go to roost."

We lit our watch-fires, and, leaving the dogs on guard below, ascended the ladder. Fritz, Ernest, and Jack were up in a moment. Their mother followed very cautiously, for though she had originated the idea of building a nest, she yet hesitated to entrust herself at such a terrific height from the ground. When she was safely landed in the house, taking little Franz on my back, I let go the fastenings which secured the lower end of the ladder to the ground, and swinging to and fro, slowly ascended.

Then for the first time we stood all together in our new home. I drew up the ladder, and, with a greater sense of security than I had enjoyed since we landed on the island, offered up our evening prayer, and retired for the night.

CHAPTER IV

A day of rest—A parable for the young people—Quiet recreation—Geographical nomenclature—The margay and porcupine skins made of use—An expedition to Tentholm—Potatoes, potatoes—Tropical vegetation—The use of the karatas—Jack's greediness and its punishment—Ernest discovers cochineal—Arrive at Tentholm—The poultry rebellious—Return to Falconhurst—Ernest roused out early—We collect wood for a sledge—Master Knips turns thief—Franz's plan for the saving of ammunition—Ernest and I take the sledge to Tentholm—Ernest's laziness exemplified—He catches a salmon—We start for home—Kill a kangaroo—And cook it.

Next morning all were early awake, and the children sprang about the tree like young monkeys.

"What shall we begin to do, father?" they cried. "What do you want us to do today?"

"Rest, my boys," I replied, "rest."

"Rest?" repeated they. "Why should we rest?"

"'Six days shalt thou labor and do all that thou hast to do, but on the seventh, thou shalt do no manner of work.' This is the seventh day," I replied, "on it, therefore, let us rest."

"What, is it really Sunday?" asked Jack; "how jolly! Oh, I won't do any work, but I'll take a bow and arrow and shoot, and we'll climb about the tree and have fun all day."

"That is not resting," said I, "that is not the way you are accustomed to spend the Lord's day."

"No! But then we can't go to church here, and there is nothing else to do."

"We can worship here as well as at home," said I.

"But there is no church, no clergyman, and no organ," said Franz.

"The leafy shade of this great tree is far more beautiful than any church," I said; "there will we worship our Creator. Come, boys, down with you: turn our dining hall into a breakfast room."

The children, one by one, slipped down the ladder.

"My dear Elizabeth," said I, "this morning we will devote to the service of the Lord, and by means of a parable, I will endeavor to give the children some serious thoughts; but, without books, or the possibility of any of the usual Sunday occupations, we cannot keep them quiet the whole day; afterward, therefore, I shall allow them to pursue any innocent recreation they choose, and in the cool of the evening we will take a walk."

My wife entirely agreed with my proposal, and having breakfasted, the family assembled round me, as we sat in the pleasant shade on the fresh, soft green grass.

After singing some hymns and offering heartfelt prayers to the Almighty giver of all good, I told the children I would relate to them a parable instead of preaching a sermon.

"Oh, that would be delightful! I like the parables in the Bible better than anything," said Frank. "When can we hear you read out of the Bible again, father?"

"Ah, my little boy, your words reproach me," returned I. "While eagerly striving to procure from the ship what would feed our bodies and provide for *their* comfort, I blush to think that I have neglected the Bread of Life, the word of God. I shall search for a Bible on my next return to the wreck: although our own books were nearly all destroyed, I am pretty sure to find one."

At these words my wife arose, and fetching her magic bag, she drew from it a copy of the Holy Scriptures, which I thankfully received from her hand; and, after reading aloud from its sacred pages, I spoke as follows:

"A Great King, ruling in power and splendor over a vast realm of light and love, possessed within its boundaries a desolate and unfruitful island. This spot he made the object of his special care; and, lavishing on it all the varied resources of his might and goodness, it bloomed in beauty, and became the happy residence of a band of colonists, who were charged not only with the cultivation and improvement of the soil, but each, individually, was bound to cherish in his soul the spirit of love and true allegiance to his Sovereign. While this faithful union was maintained, the colony flourished; and the noblest virtues exalted and rendered happy the existence of every member of the race. That a discontented and rebellious spirit should ever have infected these fortunate subjects of so loving a master, seems incredible, yet so it was; disobedience and pride brought misery and punishment, the fair prospects of the colony were blighted, the labors of the colonists were unblessed, and total separation from the parent kingdom seemed inevitable. A message of pardon—of free forgiveness—was nevertheless accorded to these rebels; and to all who, humbly accepting it, molded their future lives to the will of the Great King (now revealed in a character even more gracious than before), was held out the promise of removal at last from among the ruins caused by the great rebellion, to the glory and undimmed splendor of the realm of Light and Blessedness."

Having interested the children, I then, leaving allegory, pressed simply and earnestly home to each young heart the truths I sought to teach; and, with a short prayer for a blessing on my words, brought the service to a close.

After a thoughtful pause, we separated, and each employed himself as he felt disposed.

I took some arrows and endeavored to point them with porcupine quills.

Franz came to beg me to make a little bow and arrow for him to shoot with, while Fritz asked my advice about the tiger cat skin and the cases he was to contrive from it. Jack assisted with the arrow making, and inserting a sharp spine at one end of each reed made it fast with pack-thread, and began to wish for glue to insure its remaining firm.

"O Jack! Mamma's soup is as sticky as anything!" cried Franz; "shall I run and ask for a cake of it?"

"No, no, little goose! Better look for some real glue in the tool-box."

"There he will find glue, to be sure," said I, "and the soup would scarcely have answered your purpose. But Jack, my boy, I do not like to hear you ridicule your little brother's ideas. Some of the most valuable discoveries have been the result of thoughts which originally appeared no wiser than his."

While thus directing and assisting my sons, we were surprised by hearing a shot just over our heads; at the same moment two small birds fell dead at our feet, and looking up, we beheld Ernest among the branches, as bending his face joyfully toward us, he cried, "Well hit! Well hit! A good shot, wasn't it?"

Then slipping down the ladder, and picking up the birds, he brought them to me. One was a kind of thrush, the other a small dove called the ortolan, and esteemed a very great delicacy on account of its exquisite flavor. As the figs on which these birds came to feed were only just beginning to ripen, it was probable that they would soon flock in numbers to our trees; and by waiting until we could procure them in large quantities, we might provide ourselves with valuable food for the rainy season, by placing them, when half cooked, in cases with melted lard or butter poured over them.

By this time Jack had pointed a good supply of arrows, and industriously practiced archery. I finished the bow and arrows for Franz, and expected to be left in peace; but the young man next demanded a quiver, and I had to invent that also, to complete his equipment. It was easily done by stripping a piece of bark from a small tree, fitting a flat side and a bottom to it, and then a string. Attaching it to his shoulders, the youthful hunter filled it with arrows and went off; looking, as his mother said, like an innocent little Cupid, bent on conquest.

Not long after this, we were summoned to dinner, and all right willingly obeyed the call.

During the meal I interested the boys very much by proposing to decide on suitable names for the different spots we had visited on this coast.

"For," said I, "it will become more and more troublesome to explain what we mean, unless we do so. Beside which, we shall feel much more at home if we can talk as people do in inhabited countries: instead of saying, for instance, 'the little island at the mouth of our bay, where we found the dead shark,' 'the large stream near our tent, across which we made the bridge,' 'that wood where we found coconuts, and caught the monkey,' and so on. Let us begin by naming the bay in which we landed. What shall we call it?"

"Oyster Bay," said Fritz.

"No, no!—Lobster Bay," cried Jack, "in memory of the old fellow who took a fancy to my leg!"

"I think," observed his mother, "that, in token of gratitude for our escape, we should call it Safety Bay."

This name met with general approbation, and was forthwith fixed upon.

Other names were quickly chosen. Our first place of abode we called Tentholm; the islet in the bay, Shark's Island; and the reedy swamp, Flamingo Marsh. It was some time before the serious question of a name for our leafy castle could be decided. But finally it was entitled Falconhurst;* and we then rapidly named the remaining points: Prospect Hill, the eminence we first ascended; Cape Disappointment, from whose rocky heights we had strained our eyes in vain search for our ship's company; and Jackal River, as a name for the large stream at our landing place, concluded our geographical nomenclature.

---

* *Horst*, in German, means "nest" or "eyrie."

In the afternoon the boys went on with their various employments. Fritz finished his cases, and Jack asked my assistance in carrying out his plan of making a cuirass for Turk out of the porcupine skin. After thoroughly cleansing the inside, we cut and fitted it round the body of the patient dog; then when strings were sewn on and it became tolerably dry, he was armed with this ingenious coat of mail, and a most singular figure he cut!

Juno strongly objected to his friendly approaches, and got out of his way as fast as she could; and it was clear that he would easily put to flight the fiercest animal he might encounter, while protected by armor at once defensive and offensive.

I determined to make also a helmet for Jack out of the remainder of the skin, which to his infinite delight I speedily did.

Amid these interesting occupations the evening drew on, and after a pleasant walk among the sweet glades near our abode, we closed our Sabbath day with prayer and a glad hymn of praise, retiring to rest with peaceful hearts.

Next morning, I proposed an expedition to Tentholm, saying I wished to make my way thither by a different route. We left the tree well armed; I and my three elder sons each carrying a gun and game bag, while little Franz was equipped with his bow and quiver full of arrows. A most curious party we formed: Fritz, adorned with his belt of margay skin, and Jack, with his extraordinary head-dress, looked like a couple of young savages. Their mother and I walked together: she, of the whole party, being the only one unarmed, carried a jar in which to get butter from Tentholm; we were preceded by the dogs—Turk armed most effectually with his cuirass of porcupine skin, and Juno keeping at a respectful distance from so formidable a companion. Master Knips fully intended to mount his charger as usual; but when he saw him arrayed apparently in a new skin, he approached him carefully, and touching him with one paw, discovered that such a hide would make anything but an agreeable seat; the grimace he made was most comical, and chattering vociferously he bounded toward Juno, skipped on her back, seated himself, and soon appeared perfectly reconciled to the change of steed. The flamingo saw us starting, and, having been much petted during the last day or two, considered himself entitled to accompany us; for some time he kept beside the children, following first one and then another as they explored the wood on either side; their irregular course, however, at length disgusted him, and, abandoning them, he walked sedately by my side. We strolled on in the cool air, following the course of the stream; the great trees overshadowed us, and the cool, green sward stretched away between them at our feet. The boys roamed ahead of me, intent on exploration. Presently I heard a joyful shout, and saw Ernest running at full speed toward me, followed by his brothers. In his hand he held a plant, and, panting for breath, and with sparkling eyes, he held it up to me.

"Potatoes! Potatoes! Father," he gasped out.

"Yes," said Jack, "acres and acres of potatoes!"

"My dear Ernest," said I, for there was no mistaking the flower and leaf, and the light clear-green bulbous roots, "you have indeed made a discovery; with the potato we shall never starve."

"But come and look at them," said Jack, "come and feast your eyes on thousands of potatoes."

We hurried to the spot: there, spread out before us, was a great tract of ground, covered with the precious plant.

"It would have been rather difficult," remarked Jack, "not to have discovered such a great field."

"Very likely," replied Ernest, smiling; "but I doubt if you would have discovered that it was a potato field."

"Perhaps not," said Jack, "you are quite welcome, at all events, to the honor of the discovery; I'll have the honor of being the first to get a supply of them." So saying, he dug up, with hands and knife, a number of plants, and filled his game bag with the roots. The monkey followed his example, and scratching away with his paws most cleverly, soon had a heap beside him. So delighted were we with the discovery, and so eager were we to possess a large supply of the roots, that we stopped not digging until every bag, pouch, and pocket was filled. Some wished to return at once to Falconhurst, to cook and taste our new acquisition; but this I overruled, and we continued our march, heavily laden, but delighted.

"How," said I, "can we thank the Giver of all these blessings, sufficiently?"

"Oh," said Franz, "we can say, 'We thank thee, O Lord, for all thy goodness and mercy; and bless us for Jesus Christ's sake. Amen.'"

"That would not be sufficient," said Fritz. "Do you think it would be enough, just to say to father and mother: 'Thank you for all you do,' and not to show them we were really thankful, by loving them and doing what we can to please them?"

"You are quite right, Fritz," said I; "Franz did not say all that was necessary, he should have added, 'Give me grace to do Thy will, and to obey Thee in all things.'"

As we thus talked, we reached the head of our streamlet, where it fell from the rocks above in a beautiful, sparkling, splashing cascade. We crossed and entered the tall grass on the other side. We forced our way through with difficulty, so thick and tangled were the reeds. Beyond this, the landscape was most lovely. Rich tropical vegetation flourished on every side: the tall, stately palms, surrounded by luxuriant ferns; brilliant flowers and graceful creepers; the prickly cactus, shooting up amidst them; aloe, jasmine, and sweet-scented vanilla; the Indian pea, and above all the regal pineapple, loaded the breath of the evening breeze with their rich perfume. The boys were delighted with the pineapple, and so eagerly did they fall to, that my wife had to caution them that there were no doctors on our territory, and if they became ill, they would have to cure themselves as best they might.

This advice, however, seemed to have small effect on my sons, and showing Knips what they wanted, they sent him after the ripest and best fruit.

While they were thus employed, I examined the other shrubs and bushes. Among these I presently noticed one which I knew well from description to be the karatas.

"Come here, boys," I said; "here is something of far more value than your pineapples. Do you see that plant with long pointed leaves and beautiful red flower? That is the karatas. The filaments of the leaves make capital thread, while the leaves themselves, bruised, form an invaluable salve. The pith of this wonderful plant may be used either for tinder or bait for fish. Suppose, Ernest, you had been wrecked here, how would you have made a fire without matches, or flint and steel?"

"As the savages do," replied he; "I would rub two pieces of wood together until they kindled."

"Try it," I said; "but, if you please, try it when you have a whole day before you, and no other work to be done, for I am certain it would be night before you accomplish the feat. But see here," and I broke a dry twig from the karatas, and peeling off the bark, laid the pith upon a stone. I struck a couple of pebbles over it, and they emitting a spark, the pith caught fire.

The boys were delighted with the experiment. I then drew some of the threads from the leaves, and presented them to my wife.

"But what," said Fritz, "is the use of all these other prickly plants, except to annoy one? Here, for instance, is a disagreeable little tree."

"That is an Indian fig," said I. "It grows best on dry, rocky ground; for most of its nourishment is derived from the air. Its juice is used, I believe, medicinally, while its fruit is pleasant and wholesome."

Master Jack was off in a moment when he heard of a new delicacy, and attempted to gather some of the fruit, but in vain; the sharp thorns defied his efforts, and with bleeding hands, and rueful countenance, he returned. I removed the thorns from his hands, and making a sharp wooden skewer, I thrust it into a fig, and quickly twisted it from its branch and split it open with a knife, still holding it upon the skewer. The rest followed my example, and we regaled ourselves upon the fruit, which we found excellent. Ernest carefully examined the fig he was eating. "What are these," he exclaimed presently; "little red insects! They cling all over the fruit, and I cannot shake them off. Can they be cochineal?"

He handed me the fig, and I examined it attentively.

"You are quite right, my boy," I said; "there is no doubt this is the real cochineal. However, though it is worth its weight in gold to European traders, it is of little use to us, I am afraid unless any of you care to appear in gay colors. The cochineal you know, forms the most lovely scarlet dye."

"No, thank you," said Jack; "but we will take a lot of it when we go home again. Now let us find something more useful to us." And they thereupon plied me incessantly with questions concerning every plant and shrub we passed.

"Stop, stop," I said at length; "the most learned naturalist would be much puzzled with many of these trees, and I who have never seen any of them before, and know them merely by description, cannot pretend to tell you the names, or explain to you the use of one-quarter of them."

Discussing, however, the properties of such shrubs as I did know, we at length reached Tentholm. Everything was safe, and we set to work to collect what we wanted. I opened the butter cask, from which my wife filled her pot. Fritz saw after the ammunition, and Jack and Ernest ran down to the beach to capture the geese and ducks. This they found no easy matter, for the birds, left so long alone, were shy, and nothing would induce them to come on shore and be caught. Ernest at length hit upon an ingenious plan. He took some pieces of cheese, and tied them to long strings. This bait he threw into the water, and the hungry ducks instantly made a grab at it; then with a little skillful maneuvering he drew them on shore. While Jack and he were thus busily employed catching and tying the rebels together by the feet, we procured a fresh supply of salt, which we packed upon Turk's back, first relieving him of his coat of mail. The birds we fastened to our game bags, and carefully closing the door of our tent, started homeward by the seashore. After a cheerful and pleasant walk, we once more reached our woodland abode. I released the birds and, clipping their wings to prevent their leaving us, established them on the stream. Then, after a delicious supper of potatoes, milk, and butter, we ascended our tree and turned in.

Having remarked a great deal of driftwood on the sands the preceding evening, it occurred to me that it would be well to get some of it, and make a kind of sledge, so that the labor of fetching what we wanted from our stores at Tentholm might not fall so heavily on ourselves.

I awoke early, and roused Ernest as my assistant, wishing to encourage him to overcome his natural fault of indolence. After a little stretching and yawning, he got up cheerfully, pleased with the idea of an expedition while the others still slept, and we made our way to the beach, taking with us the donkey, who drew a large broad bough, which I expected to find useful in bringing back our load.

As we went along, I remarked to Ernest that I supposed he was rather sorry for himself, and grudged leaving his cozy hammock and pleasant dreams at this untimely hour.

"Oh, father, do not laugh at my laziness! Indeed, I mean to cure myself of it. I am very glad to go with you. I intended to shoot some more of the ortolans this morning, but there will be plenty of time afterward. The boys will be shooting at them, I daresay, but I don't expect they will have any great luck."

"Why not, pray?" inquired I.

"I don't believe they will know what shot to use at first, and, besides, they will most likely shoot upward at the birds and be sure to miss them, on account of the great height and thickness of the branches and foliage."

"Well, Ernest, you certainly possess the gifts of prudence and reflection, as well as observation. These are valuable; but sudden action is so often necessary in life, that I advise you to cultivate the power of instantly perceiving and deciding what must be done in cases of emergency. Presence of mind is a precious quality, which, although natural in some characters, may be acquired in a certain degree by all who train themselves to it."

Once on the seashore, our work was quickly accomplished, for, selecting the wood I thought fit for my purpose, we laid it across the broad, leafy branch, and, with some help from us, the donkey dragged a very fair load of it homeward, with the addition of a small chest, which I raised from among the sand, which nearly covered it.

We heard the boys popping away at the birds as we drew near. They hastened to meet us, and inquired where we had been, looking curiously at the chest, which I allowed them to open, while I asked my wife to excuse our "absence without leave," and after submitting to her gentle reprimand, I explained my plan for a sledge, which pleased her greatly, and she already imagined it loaded with her hogshead of butter, and on its way from Tentholm to Falconhurst.

The chest proved to be merely that of a common sailor, containing his clothes, very much wetted by the sea water.

The boys exhibited an array of several dozen birds, and related, during breakfast, the various incidents of failure and success which had attended their guns. Ernest had rightfully guessed the mistakes they would make, but practice was making them perfect, and they seemed disposed to continue their sport, when their mother, assuring them that she could not use more birds than those already killed, asked if I did not think some means of snaring them might be contrived, as much powder and shot would be expended if they fired on at this rate.

Entirely agreeing with this view of the subject, I desired the lads to lay aside their guns for the present, and the younger ones readily applied themselves to making snares of the long threads drawn from the leaves of the karatas, in a simple way I taught them, while Fritz and Ernest gave me substantial assistance in the manufacture of the new sledge.

We were busily at work, when a tremendous disturbance among our fowls led us to suppose that a fox or wild cat had got into their midst.

The cocks crowed defiantly, the hens fluttered and cackled in a state of the wildest excitement. We hastened toward them, but Ernest remarking Master Knips slipping away, as though conscious of some misdemeanor, went to watch him, and presently caught him in the act of eating a new-laid egg, which he had carried off and hidden among the grass and roots. Ernest found several others. These were very welcome to my wife, for hitherto the hens had not presented us with any eggs. Hereafter she determined to imprison the monkey every morning until the eggs had been collected.

Soon after this, as Jack was setting the newly made snares among the branches, he discovered that a pair of our own pigeons were building in the tree. It was very desirable to increase our stock of these pretty birds, and I cautioned the boys against shooting near our tree while they had nests there, and also with regard to the snares, which were meant only to entrap the wild fig-eaters.

Although my sons were interested in setting the snares, they by no means approved of the new order to economize the ammunition. No doubt they had been discussing this hardship, for little Franz came to me with a brilliant proposal of his own.

"Papa," said he, "why should not we begin to plant some powder and shot immediately? It would be so much more useful than bare grain for the fowls."

His brothers burst into a roar of laughter, and I must confess I found it no easy matter to keep my countenance.

"Come, Ernest," said I; "now we have had our amusement, tell the little fellow what gunpowder really is."

"It is not seed at all, Franz," Ernest explained. "Gunpowder is made of charcoal, sulphur, and saltpeter, mixed cleverly together; so you see it cannot be sown like corn, any more than shot can be planted like peas and beans."

My carpentering meantime went on apace. In order to shape my sledge with ends properly turned up in front, I had chosen wood which had been part of the bow of the vessel, and was curved in the necessary way for my purpose. Two pieces, perfectly similar, formed the sides of my sleigh, or sledge, and I simply united these strongly by fixing short bars across them. Then, when the ropes of the donkey's harness were attached to the raised points in front, the equipage was complete and ready for use.

My attention had been for some time wholly engrossed by my work, and I only now observed that the mother and her little boys had been busily plucking above two dozen of the wild birds, and were preparing to roast them, spitted in a row on a long, narrow sword blade, belonging to one of our ship's officers.

It seemed somewhat wasteful to cook so many at once; but my wife explained that she was getting them ready for the butter-cask I was going to fetch for her on the new sledge, as I had advised her to preserve them half-cooked, and packed in butter.

Amused at her promptitude, I could do nothing less than promise to go for her cask directly after dinner. For her part she resolved in our absence to have a grand wash of linen and other clothes, and she advised me to arrange regular baths for all the boys in future.

Early in the afternoon Ernest and I were ready to be off, equipped as usual. Fritz presented us each with a neat case of margay skin to hang at our girdles.

We harnessed both cow and ass to the sledge, and, accompanied by Juno, cheerfully took our departure, choosing the way by the sands, and reaching Tentholm without accident or adventure.

There unharnessing the animals, we began at once to load the sledge, not only with the butter cask, but with a powder chest, a barrel of cheese, and a variety of other articles—ball, shot, tools, and Turk's armor, which had been left behind on our last visit.

Our work had so closely engaged our attention, that when we were ready to leave it and go in search of a good bathing place, we discovered that our two animals had wandered quite out of sight, having crossed the bridge to reach the good pasture beyond the river.

I sent Ernest after them, and went alone to the extremity of the bay. It terminated in bold and precipitous cliffs, which extended into the deep water, and rose abruptly, so as to form an inaccessible wall of rock and crag. Swampy ground, overgrown with large canes, intervened between me and these cliffs. I cut a large bundle of the reeds, and returned to Ernest. It was some time before I found him, comfortably extended full length on the ground near the tent, and sleeping as sound as a top, while the cow and the ass, grazing at will, were again making for the bridge.

"Get up, Ernest, you lazy fellow!" exclaimed I, much annoyed; "why don't you mind your business? Look at the animals! They will be over the river again!"

"No fear of that, father," returned he, with the utmost composure. "I have taken a couple of boards off the bridge. They won't pass the gap."

I could not help laughing at the ingenious device by which the boy had spared himself all trouble; at the same time I observed that it is wrong to waste the precious moments in sleep when duty has to be performed. I then bid him go and collect some salt, which was wanted at home, while I went to bathe.

On coming back, much refreshed, I again missed Ernest, and began to wonder whether he was still gathering salt, or whether he had lain down somewhere to finish his nap, when I heard him loudly calling:

"Father, father, I've caught a fish! An immense fellow he is. I can scarcely hold him, he drags the line so!"

Hastening toward the spot, I saw the boy lying in the grass, on a point of land close to the mouth of the stream, and with all his might keeping hold of a rod. The line was strained to the utmost by the frantic efforts of a very large fish, which was attempting to free itself from the hook.

I quickly took the rod from him, and giving the fish more line, led him by degrees into shallow water. Ernest ran in with his hatchet and killed him.

It proved to be a salmon of full fifteen pounds weight, and I was delighted to think of taking such a valuable prize to the mother.

"This is capital, Ernest!" cried I; "you have cleared yourself for once of the charge of laziness! Let us now carry this splendid salmon to the sledge. I will clean and pack it for the journey, that it may arrive in good condition, while you go and take a bath in the sea."

All this being accomplished, we harnessed our beasts to the well-laden vehicle, and replacing the boards on the bridge, commenced the journey home.

We kept inland this time, and were skirting the borders of a grassy thicket, when Juno suddenly left us, and plunging into the bushes, with fierce barking hunted out, right in front of us, the most singular-looking creature I ever beheld. It was taking wonderful flying leaps, apparently in a sitting posture, and got over the ground at an astonishing rate. I attempted to shoot it as it passed, but missed. Ernest, who was behind me, observed its movements very coolly, and seeing that the dog was puzzled, and that the animal, having paused, was crouching among the grass, went cautiously nearer, fired at the spot he had marked, and shot it dead.

The extraordinary appearance of this creature surprised us very much. It was as large as a sheep, its head was shaped like that of a mouse; its skin also was of a mouse color, it had long ears like a hare, and a tail like a tiger's. The fore-paws resembled those of a squirrel, but they seemed only half-grown, while the hind legs were enormous, and so long that, when upright on them, the animal would look as if mounted on stilts.

For some time we stood silently wondering at the remarkable creature before us. I could not recollect to have seen or heard of any such.

"Well, father," said Ernest at last, "I should say this was about the queerest beast to be met with anywhere. I am glad I knocked it over. How they will all stare when I carry it home!"

"You have had a lucky day altogether, certainly," said I; "but I cannot think what this animal can be. Examine its teeth, and let us see to what class of mammalia it belongs. We may be led to guess at its name in that way."

"I see four sharp incisor teeth, father—two upper, and two under, as a squirrel has."

"Ah! Then he is a rodent. What rodents can you remember, Ernest?"

"I do not know them all, but there are the mouse, the marmot, the squirrel, the hare, the beaver, the jerboa——"

"The jerboa!" I exclaimed, "the jerboa! Now we shall have it. This is really very like a jerboa, only far larger. It must be a kangaroo, one of the class of animals which has a pouch or purse beneath the body, in which its young can take refuge. They were discovered in New Holland, by the great Captain Cook, and I congratulate you on being the first to obtain a specimen in New Switzerland!" I added, laughing, as I extemporized the name.

The kangaroo was added to the already heavy load on our sledge, and we proceeded slowly, arriving late at Falconhurst, but meeting with the usual bright welcome.

Very eager and inquisitive were the glances turned toward the sledge, for the load piled on it surpassed all expectation; we on our part staring in equal surprise at the extraordinary rig of the young folks who came to meet us.

One wore a long night-shirt, which, with a belt, was a convenient length in front, but trailed behind in orthodox ghost fashion.

Another had on a very wide pair of trousers, braced up so short that each little leg looked like the clapper in a bell.

The third, buttoned up in a pea-jacket which came down to his ankles, looked for all the world like a walking portmanteau.

Amid much joking and laughter, the mother explained that she had been washing all day, and while their clothes were drying, the boys amused themselves by dressing up in things they found while rummaging the sailor's chest, and had kept them on, that Ernest and I might see the masquerade. It certainly amused us, but made me regret that so little belonging to ourselves had been saved from the wreck, in consequence of which the children had scarcely a change of linen.

Turning now to our new acquisitions, we excited great interest by exhibiting each in turn; the large salmon, but more especially the kangaroo, surprised and delighted every one.

Fritz alone wore a look expressive of dissatisfaction, and I saw that he was envious of his younger brother's success. Vexed that so noble a prize had fallen to Ernest's gun, instead of his own, he treated it rather slightingly; but I could see that he was struggling against his jealous feelings, and he, after a while, succeeded in recovering his good humor, and joined pleasantly in the conversation.

"What a famous day's sport you have had altogether!" said he, coming close up to me. "It will be my turn to go out with you next, will it not, father? Just about here there is nothing to shoot, and I have found it very dull."

"Still you have been doing your duty, my dear boy; you were entrusted with the care of the family, and a youth of manly character will not depend for happiness on mere excitement."

As the shades of night approached, we made haste to conclude the day's work, by preparing the kangaroo, part for immediate use, and part for salting. The animals were fed, and a plentiful allowance of salt made to them. Our own supper of broiled salmon and potatoes was dispatched with great appetite, and we retired, with thankful hearts, to sound and well-earned repose.

CHAPTER V

Jack and Ernest disappear—Fritz and I start for the wreck—The boys ambuscade—We form a raft—Ransack the vessel—Again embark—A turtle in sight—Fritz harpoons it—The turtle acts as "Steam Tug"—Safe ashore—Return home—Jack's clay field—A fresh discovery—The mother's cellar—A trip to the wreck—The pinnace—Jack's raid on the Lilliputians—A secret revealed—A new method of grinding flour—Wholesome or poisonous?—Bread-making in earnest.

Next morning, while the breakfast was getting ready, I attended to the beautiful skin of the kangaroo, which I was anxious to preserve entire; and afterward, when Fritz had prepared everything in readiness for our trip to the wreck, I called Ernest and Jack in order to give them some parting injunctions. They, however, had disappeared directly after breakfast, and their mother could only guess, that, as we required potatoes, they might have gone to fetch a supply. I desired her to reprove them, on their return, for starting away without leave; but, as it appeared they had taken Turk, I satisfied myself that no harm was likely to befall them, although it was not without reluctance that I left my dear wife alone with little Franz, cheering her with hopes of our speedy return with new treasures from the wreck.

Advancing steadily on our way, we crossed the bridge at Jackal River, when suddenly, to our no small astonishment,

Jack and Ernest burst out of a hiding place where they had lain in wait for us, and were enchanted with the startling effect of their unexpected appearance upon their unsuspecting father and brother. It was evident that they fully believed they might now go with us to the wreck.

To this notion I at once put a decided stop, although I could not find in my heart to scold the two merry rogues for their thoughtless frolic, more especially as I particularly wished to send back a message to my wife. I told them they must hurry home, so as not to leave their mother in suspense, although, as they were already so far, they might collect some salt. And I instructed them to explain that, as my work on board would take up a long time, she must try to bear with our absence for a night. This I had meant to say when we parted, but my courage had failed, knowing how much she would object to such a plan, and I had resolved to return in the evening.

On consideration, however, of the importance of constructing a raft, which was my intention in going, and finishing it without a second trip, I determined to remain on board for the night, as the boys had, unintentionally, given me the chance of sending a message to that effect.

"Goodbye, boys, take care of yourselves! We're off," shouted Fritz, as I joined him in the tub-boat, and we shoved off.

The current carried us briskly out of the bay; we were very soon moored safely alongside the wreck, and scrambling up her shattered sides, stood on what remained of the deck, and began at once to lay our plans.

I wanted to make a raft fit to carry on shore a great variety of articles far too large and heavy for our present boat. A number of empty water casks seemed just what was required for a foundation; we closed them tightly, pushed them overboard, and arranging twelve of them side by side in rows of three, we firmly secured them together by means of spars, and then proceeded to lay a good substantial floor of planks, which was defended by a low bulwark. In this way we soon had a first-rate raft, exactly suited to our purpose.

It would have been impossible to return to land that same evening, for we were thoroughly fatigued by our labors, and had eaten only the light refreshment we had brought in our wallets, scarcely desisting a moment from our work.

Rejoicing that we were not expected home, we now made an excellent supper from the ship's provisions, and then rested for the night on spring mattresses, a perfect luxury to us, after our hard and narrow hammocks.

Next morning we actively set about loading the raft and boat: first carrying off the entire contents of our own cabins; and passing on to the captain's room, we removed the furniture, as well as the doors and window-frames, with their bolts, bars, and locks. We next took the officers' chests, and those belonging to the carpenter and gunsmith; the contents of these latter we had to remove in portions, as their weight was far beyond our strength.

One large chest was filled with an assortment of fancy goods, and reminded us of a jeweler's shop, so glittering was the display of gold and silver watches, snuff-boxes, buckles, studs, chains, rings, and all manner of trinkets; these, and a box of money, drew our attention for a time; but more useful to us at present was a case of common knives and forks, which I was glad to find, as more suited to us than the smart silver ones we had previously taken on shore. To my delight we found, most carefully packed, a number of young fruit trees: and we read on the tickets attached to them the names, so pleasant to European ears, of the apple, pear, chestnut, orange, almond, peach, apricot, plum, cherry, and vine.

The cargo, which had been destined for the supply of a distant colony, proved, in fact, a rich and almost inexhaustible treasure to us. Ironmongery, plumber's tools, lead, paint, grindstones, cart wheels, and all that was necessary for the work of a smith's forge, spades and ploughshares, sacks of maize, peas, oats, and wheat, a hand-mill, and also the parts of a saw-mill so carefully numbered that, were we strong enough, it would be easy to put it up, had been stowed away.

So bewildered were we by the wealth around us that for some time we were at a loss as to what to remove to the raft. It would be impossible to take everything; yet the first storm would complete the destruction of the ship, and we should lose all we left behind. Selecting a number of the most useful articles, however, including of course the grain and the fruit trees, we gradually loaded our raft. Fishing lines, reels, cordage, and a couple of harpoons were put on board, as well as a mariner's compass.

Fritz, recollecting our encounter with the shark, placed the harpoons in readiness; and amused me by seeming to picture himself a whaler, flourishing his harpoon in most approved fashion.

Early in the afternoon, both our crafts were heavily laden, and we were ready to make for the shore. The voyage was begun with considerable anxiety, as, with the raft in tow, there was some danger of an accident.

But the sea being calm and the wind favorable, we found we could spread the sail, and our progress was very satisfactory.

Presently, Fritz asked me for the telescope, as he had observed something curious floating at a distance. Then handing it back, he begged me to examine the object; which I soon discovered to be a turtle asleep on the water, and of course unconscious of our approach.

"Do, father, steer toward it!" exclaimed he.

I accordingly did so, that he might have a nearer look at the creature. Little did I suspect what was to follow. The lad's back was turned to me, and the broad sail was between us, so that I could not perceive his actions; when, all of a sudden, I experienced a shock, and the thrill of line running through a reel. Before I had time to call out, a second shock, and the sensation of the boat being rapidly drawn through the water, alarmed me.

"Fritz, what are you about?" cried I, "you are sending us to the bottom."

"I have him, hurrah! I have him safe!" shouted he, in eager excitement.

To my amazement, I perceived that he really had struck the

tortoise with a harpoon; a rope was attached to it, and the creature was running away with us.

Lowering the sail and seizing my hatchet, I hastened forward, in order to cut the line, and cast adrift at once turtle and harpoon.

"Father! Do wait!" pleaded the boy, "there is no danger just yet? I promise to cut the line myself the instant it is necessary! Let us catch this turtle if we possibly can."

"My dear boy, the turtle will be a very dear bargain, if he upsets all our goods into the sea, even if he does not drown us too. For Heaven's sake be careful! I will wait a few minutes, but the minute there is danger, cut the line."

As the turtle began to make for the open sea, I hoisted the sail again; and, finding the opposition too much for it, the creature again directed its course landward, drawing us rapidly after it. The part of the shore for which the turtle was making was considerably to the left of our usual landing place. The beach there shelved very gradually, and at some distance from land we grounded with a sharp shock, but fortunately without a capsize.

The turtle was evidently greatly exhausted, and no wonder, since it had been acting the part of a steam tug, and had been dragging, at full speed, a couple of heavily laden vessels. Its intention was to escape to land; but I leaped into the water, and wading up to it, dispatched it with my ax. Such was its tenacity of life, however, that it did not cease its struggles, until I had actually severed its head from its body.

As we were by no means far from Falconhurst, Fritz gave notice of our approach by firing off his gun, as well as shouting loudly in his glee; and, while we were yet engaged in securing our boats and getting the turtle on shore, the whole family appeared in the distance, hastening eagerly toward us; and our new prize, together with the well-laden boat and raft, excited the liveliest interest; my wife's chief pleasure, however, consisted in seeing us back, as our night's absence had disturbed her, and she was horrified by the description of our dangerous run in the wake of the fugitive turtle.

Being anxious to remove some of our goods before night, the boys ran off to fetch the sledge; while I, having no anchor, contrived to moor the boats by means of some of the heavy blocks of iron we had brought.

It required our united strength to get the turtle hoisted on to the sledge, its weight being prodigious; we found it, indeed, with the addition of the sapling fruit trees, quite a sufficient load.

We then made the best of our way home, chatting merrily about our various adventures. The first thing to be done on arriving was to obtain some of the turtle's flesh and cook it for supper. To my wife this appeared necessarily a work of time, as well as of difficulty; but I turned the beast on its back, and soon detached a portion of the meat from the breast with a hatchet, by breaking the lower shell: and I then directed that it should be cooked, with a little salt, shell and all.

"But let me first cut away this disgusting green fat," said my wife, with a little shudder. "See how it sticks all over the meat. No one could eat anything so nasty."

"Leave that fat, whatever you do!" exclaimed I. "Why, my dear, that is the very best part, and the delight of the epicure. If there be really too much, cut some off—it can be used as lard, and let the dogs make a supper of the refuse."

"And the handsome shell!" cried Fritz; "I should like to make a water-trough of that, to stand near the brook, and be kept always full of clear water. How useful it would be!"

"That is a capital idea," I replied, "and we may manage it easily, if we can find clay so as to make a firm foundation on which to place it."

"Oh, as to clay," said Jack, "I have a grand lump of clay there under that root."

"Well done, my lad! When did you find it?"

"He found a bed of clay near the river this morning," said his mother, "and came home in such a mess, I had regularly to scrape his clothes and wash him thoroughly!"

"Well, mother, I can only tell you I should never in all my days have found the clay, if I had not slipped and fallen among it."

"That I can well believe," returned his mother; "only, to hear your talk this morning, one would have thought your discovery of clay the result of very arduous search indeed."

"When you have ended the question of the clay and the turtle shell," said Ernest, "I should like to show you some roots I found today; they are getting rather dry now. They look something like radishes, although the plant itself was almost a bush; but I have not ventured to taste them, although our old sow was devouring them at a great rate."

"In that you did wisely, my boy. Swine eat many things injurious to men. Let me see your roots. How did you discover them?"

"I was rambling in the wood this morning, and came upon the sow, very busy grubbing under a small bush, and eating something ravenously; so I drove her away, and found a number of these roots, which I brought for you to see."

"Indeed, Ernest," I exclaimed, after taking the roots in my hand and considering them attentively, "I am inclined to believe that you have really made a brilliant discovery! If this proves to be, as I expect, the manioc root, we might lose every other eatable we possess, and yet not starve. In the West Indies, cakes called cassava bread are made from it; and, already having potatoes, we shall be very independent if we can succeed in preparing flour from these roots. Great care must be taken in the manufacture to express the juice, otherwise the flour may be injurious and even poisonous.

"If we can collect a sufficient quantity, we will attempt bread-making. I think I know how to set about it."

Finding there was still time to make another trip with the sledge, I went off with the elder boys, leaving Franz with his mother; and we all looked forward with satisfaction to the prospect of the princely supper they were to have ready for us, for our day's work had been none of the lightest.

"I have been thinking about my turtle, father," said Fritz, as we went along; "is not the shell very valuable? Surely beautiful combs, boxes, and a number of ornamental things are made of tortoise shell, and if so, it seems a pity to use it for a water trough."

"Your turtle, Fritz, is only fit for eating, its shell is worthless as regards ornament; whereas the species whose shell is prized so much is unfit for food. Tortoise shell is subjected to the action of the heat, the outer layer peels off, leaving a beautifully marked, semi-transparent surface, which is susceptible of a very high polish."

The sledge quickly received its second load from the raft. Chests, four cart-wheels, and the hand-mill were placed on it, with all manner of smaller articles, and we lost no time in returning to Falconhurst.

The mother welcomed us joyfully, for she said we had been regularly overworked during the last two days. "However, now you are come home to rest," said she, "and you little think what refreshment awaits you here in the shade. Come and see my cellar!" and she smilingly exhibited a small cask, half sunk in the ground, and well sheltered with leaves and branches.

"Ah! You wonder where this came from," continued the mother; "well, I found it myself on the sands, today, while you were all absent; and fancying it was wine of some sort, I got it up here on purpose to be ready for you. The boys are most anxious to know what sort of wine it will prove to be."

As the simplest method of ascertaining this, I inserted a straw at the vent-hole, and presently announced, that in all my life I had never enjoyed a more delicious draught of Canary sack. The mother was immediately pleased to find that her exertions in my behalf had not been thrown away, and the boys pressed around me, armed with straws and begging for a taste.

After so strongly expressing my own enjoyment of the wine, it seemed unreasonable to deny them this, and I let them come in turns, but was speedily obliged to call a halt; for the rogues got so eager and excited that I had to reprove them for their greediness, and warn them of the risk they ran of being intoxicated. In fact, I blamed myself for allowing them to have this strong wine as a beverage at all. They were wholly unaccustomed to it, and were, besides, fatigued and very hungry. Supper was more to the purpose; and, as the turtle proved delicious, it was heartily enjoyed, and gave us strength to haul the mattresses we had brought from the ship up into our sleeping rooms, so that very refreshing slumbers closed the day.

Early next morning I got up without rousing any of the others, intending to pay a visit to the beach; for I had my doubts about the safety of my vessels on the open shore. The dogs were delighted when I descended the ladder, and bounded to meet me; the cocks crowed and flapped their wings; two pretty kids gamboled around; all was life and energy; the ass alone seemed disinclined to begin the day, and as I especially required his services, this was unfortunate. I put his morning dreams to flight, however, and harnessed him to the sledge; the cow, as she had not been milked, enjoyed the privilege of further repose, and, with the rest of the family, I left her dozing.

My fears as to the safety of the boats were soon dispelled, for they were all right; and, being in haste to return, the load I collected from their freight was but a light one, and the donkey willingly trotted home with it, he, as well as I, being uncommonly ready for breakfast. Approaching the tree, not a sound was to be heard, not a soul was to be seen, although it was broad day; and great was my good wife's surprise, when, roused by the clatter and hullabaloo I made, she started up, and became aware of the late hour!

"What can have made us oversleep ourselves like this?" she exclaimed. "It must be the fault of those mattresses; they are delightful, but really too lulling; see, the children are sound asleep still."

With much stretching and many yawns, the boys at last came tumbling down from the tree, rubbing their eyes and seeming but half awake; Ernest last, as usual.

"Come, my boys," said I, "this will never do! Your beds were too luxurious last night, I see." In my own opinion, however, I felt there was something else to blame besides the comfortable mattresses, and I made a mental resolve that the captain's fine Canary should be dealt with very sparingly in future. "So now for prayers and breakfast," I continued, "and then off to work. I must have our cargo landed in time to get the boats off with the next tide."

By dint of downright hard work, we accomplished this, and I got on board with Fritz as soon as they were afloat; the rest turned homeward, but Jack lingered behind with such imploring looks, that I could not resist taking him with me.

My intention had been simply to take the vessels round to the harbor in Safety Bay, but the calm sea and fine weather tempted me to make another trip to the wreck. It took up more time than I expected, so that, when on board, we could only make a further examination of the cargo, collect a few portable articles, and then avail ourselves of the sea-breeze which would fail us later in the evening.

To Jack the pleasure of hunting about in the hold was novel and charming, and very soon a tremendous rattling and clattering heralded his approach with a wheelbarrow, in the highest spirits at his good fortune in having found such a capital thing in which to bring home potatoes.

He was followed by Fritz, whose news was still more important. He had found, carefully packed and enclosed within partitions, what appeared to be the separate parts of a pinnace, with rigging and fittings complete, even to a couple of small brass guns. This was a great discovery, and I hastened to see if the lad was right. Indeed he was, but my pleasure was qualified by a sense of the arduous task it would be to put such a craft together so as to be fit for sea. For the present we had barely time to get something to eat and hurry into the boat, where were collected our new acquisitions, namely, a copper boiler, iron plates, tobacco-graters, two grindstones, a small barrel of powder, and another of flints, two wheelbarrows, besides Jack's, which he kept under his own especial care.

As we drew near the shore, we were surprised to see a number of little figures ranged in a row along the water's edge, and apparently gazing fixedly at us. They seemed to wear dark coats and white waistcoats, and stood quite still with their arms dropping by their sides, only every now and then one would extend them gently, as though longing to embrace us.

"Ah! Here at last come the pigmy inhabitants of the country to welcome us!" cried I, laughing.

"Oh, father!" exclaimed Jack, "I hope they are Lilliputians! I once read in a book about them, so there must be such people, you know, only these look rather too large."

"You must be content to give up the Lilliputians and accept penguins, my dear Jack," said I. "We have not before seen them in such numbers, but Ernest knocked one down, if you remember, soon after we landed. They can neither fly nor run."

We were gradually approaching the land as I spoke, and no sooner was the water shallow, than out sprang Jack from his tub, and wading ashore, took the unsuspecting birds by surprise, and with his stick laid half a dozen, right and left, either stunned or dead at his feet. The rest escaped into the water, dived, and disappeared.

As these penguins are disagreeable food, on account of their strong, oily taste, I was sorry Jack had attacked them; but going to examine them when we landed, some of the fallen arose from their swoon, and began solemnly to waddle away, upon which we caught them, and tying their feet together with long grass, laid them on the sand to wait until we were ready to start.

The three wheelbarrows then each received a load, the live penguins, seated gravely, were trundled along by Jack, and away we went at a great rate.

The usual noise of our approach set the dogs barking furiously, but discovering us, they rushed forward with such forcible demonstrations of delight, that poor little Jack, who, as it was, could scarcely manage his barrow, was fairly upset, penguins and all. This was too much for his patience, and it was absurd to see how he started up and cuffed them soundly for their boisterous behavior.

This scene, and the examination of our burdens, caused great merriment: the tobacco-grater and iron plates evidently puzzling everybody.

I sent the boys to catch some of our geese and ducks, and bid them fasten a penguin to each by the leg, thinking that it was worth while to try to tame them.

My wife had exerted herself in our absence to provide a good store of potatoes, and also of manioc root. I admired her industry, and little Franz said, "Ah, father! I wonder what you will say when mother and I give you some Indian corn, and melons, and pumpkins, and cucumbers!"

"Now, you little chatterbox!" cried she, "you have let out my secret! I was to have the pleasure of surprising your father when my plants were growing up."

"Ah, the poor disappointed little mother!" said I. "Never mind! I am charmed to hear about it. Only do tell me where did these seeds come from?"

"Out of my magic bag, of course!" replied she. "And each time I have gone for potatoes, I have sown seeds in the ground which was dug up to get them; and I have planted potatoes also."

"Well done, you wise little woman!" I exclaimed. "Why, you are a model of prudence and industry!"

"But," continued she, "I do not half like the appearance of those tobacco-graters you have brought. Is it possible you are going to make snuff? Do, pray, let us make sure of abundance of food for our mouths, before we think of our noses!"

"Make your mind easy, my wife," said I. "I have not the remotest intention of introducing the dirty, ridiculous habit of snuffing into your family! Please to treat my graters with respect, however, because they are to be the means of providing you with the first fresh bread you have seen this many a long day."

"What possible connection can there be between bread and tobacco-graters? I cannot imagine what you mean, and to talk of bread where there are no ovens is only tantalizing."

"Ah, you must not expect real loaves," said I. "But on these flat iron plates I can bake flat cakes or scones, which will be excellent bread; I mean to try at once what I can do with Ernest's roots. And first of all, I want you to make a nice strong canvas bag."

This the mother willingly undertook to do, but she evidently had not much faith in my powers as a baker, and I saw her set on a good potful of potatoes before beginning to work, as though to make sure of a meal without depending on my bread.

Spreading a piece of sailcloth on the ground, I summoned my boys to set to work. Each took a grater and a supply of well-washed manioc root, and when all were seated round the cloth—"Once, twice, thrice! Off!" cried I, beginning to rub a root as hard as I could against the rough surface of my grater. My example was instantly followed by the whole party, amid bursts of merriment, as each remarked the funny attitude and odd gestures of his neighbors while vehemently rubbing, rasping, grating, and grinding down the roots allotted to him. No one was tempted by the look of the flour to stop and taste it, for in truth it looked much like wet sawdust.

"Cassava bread is highly esteemed in many parts of the New World, and I have heard that some Europeans there prefer it to the wheaten bread of their own country. There are various species of manioc. One sort grows quickly, and its roots ripen in a very short time. Another kind is of somewhat slower growth. The roots of the third kind do not come to maturity for two years. The two first are poisonous, if eaten raw, yet they are preferred to the third, which is harmless, because they are so much more fruitful, and the flour produced is excellent, if the scrapings are carefully pressed."

"What is the good of pressing them, father?" inquired Ernest.

"It is in order to express the sap, which contains poison. The dry pith is wholesome and nourishing. Still, I do not mean to taste my cakes, until I have tried the effect on our fowls and the ape."

By this time our supply of roots being reduced to damp powder, the canvas bag was filled with it, and tying it tightly up, I attempted to squeeze it, but soon found that mechanical aid was necessary in order to express the moisture. My arrangements for this purpose were as follows: A strong, straight beam was made flat on one side, smooth planks were laid across two of the lower roots of our tree; on these we placed the sack, above the sack another plank, and over that the long beam; one end was passed under a root near the sack, the other projected far forward. And to that we attached all the heaviest weights we could think of, such as an anvil, iron bars, and masses of lead. The consequent pressure on the bag was enormous, and the sap flowed from it to the ground.

"Will this stuff keep any time?" inquired my wife, who came to see how we were getting on. "Or must all this great bagful be used at once? In that case we shall have to spend the whole of tomorrow in baking cakes."

"Not at all," I replied; "once dry, the flour in barrels will keep fresh a long time. We shall use a great deal of this, however, as you shall see."

"Do you think we might begin now, father?" said Fritz. "There does not seem the least moisture remaining."

"Certainly," said I. "But I shall only make one cake today for an experiment; we must see how it agrees with Master Knips and the hens before we set up a bakehouse in regular style."

I took out a couple of handfuls of flour for this purpose, and with a stick loosened and stirred the remainder, which I intended should be again pressed. While an iron plate, placed over a good fire, was getting hot, I mixed the meal with water and a little salt, kneaded it well, and forming a thickish cake, laid it on the hot plate, when one side presently becoming a nice yellow-brown color, it was turned and was quickly baked.

It smelt so delicious that the boys quite envied the two hens and the monkey, who were selected as the subjects of this interesting experiment, and they silently watched them gobbling up the bits of cake I gave them, until Fritz turned to me, saying, "Suppose the cake is poisonous, what effect will it have on the creatures? Will they be stupefied, or will they suffer pain?"

"That depends upon the nature of the poison. Some cause

violent pain, as colchicum, hellebore, and aconite. Others produce stupefaction and paralysis, as opium, hemlock, and prussic acid; while others again, as strychnine, are followed by violent convulsions, or, as belladonna, by delirium. The effects of course vary according to the quantity taken, and such remedies should be applied as will best counteract the effect of each poison: emetics in any case, to remove as much as possible of thenoxious substance, combined with oils and mucilaginous drinks to soothe and protect the stomach in case of irritants; stimulants, such as spirits, ammonia, or strong coffee to rouse from the stupor of the narcotics; and sedative drugs, which are perhaps in themselves poisons, to counteract the over stimulation of the nerves caused by the convulsant poisons. But now let us think no more of poisons; here is supper ready and we need not be afraid to eat roast penguin and potatoes."

No sooner said than done; we left the fowls picking up the least crumb they could find of the questionable food, and assembled to enjoy our evening meal. The potatoes were, as usual, excellent, the penguin was really not so bad as I expected, although fishy in taste and very tough.

Next morning every one expressed the tenderest concern as to the health of Knips and the hens; and lively pleasure was in every countenance when Jack, who ran first to make the visit inquiry, brought news of their perfect good health and spirits.

No time was now to be lost, and the bread-baking commenced in earnest. A large fire was kindled, the plates heated, the meal made into cakes, each of the boys busily preparing his own, and watching the baking most eagerly. Mistakes occurred, of course; some of the bread was burnt, some not done enough; but a pile of nice, tempting cakes was at length ready, and with plenty of good milk we breakfasted right royally, and in high spirits at our success.

Soon after, while feeding the poultry with the fragments of the repast, I observed that the captive penguins were quite at ease among them and as tame as the geese and ducks; their bonds were therefore loosed, and they were left as free as the other fowls.

CHAPTER VI

Now for the pinnace—Repeated visits to the wreck—The pinnace built—How shall we cut her out—The difficulty solved—We fit her out—Fire a salute—The mother's surprise—We visit Falconhurst—Attend to our fruit trees—Athletics—The lasso—An excursion—A bustard captured—Ernest discovers a magician—Jack fights him—The Liane Rouge—We turn carvers—Ernest's alarm—The old sow again—We discover a sleeping beauty—Return with it to the camp—Knips pronounces our apples "good"—Return to Falconhurst.

Having now discovered how to provide bread for my family, my thoughts began to revert to the wreck and all the valuables yet contained within it. Above all, I was bent on acquiring possession of the beautiful pinnace, and aware that our united efforts would be required to do the necessary work, I began to coax and persuade the mother to let me go in force with all her boys except Franz.

She very unwillingly gave her consent at last, but not until I had faithfully promised never to pass a night on board. I did so with reluctance, and we parted, neither feeling quite satisfied with the arrangement.

The boys were delighted to go in so large a party, and merrily carried provision bags filled with cassava bread and potatoes.

Reaching Safety Bay without adventure we first paid a visit to the geese and ducks which inhabited the marsh there, and having fed them and seen they were thriving well, we buckled on each his cork belt, stepped into the tub-boat, and, with the raft in tow, steered straight for the wreck.

When we got on board, I desired the boys to collect whatever came first to hand, and load the raft to be ready for our return at night, and then we made a minute inspection of the pinnace.

I came to the conclusion that difficulties, well-nigh insuperable, lay between me and the safe possession of the beautiful little vessel. She lay in a most un-get-at-able position at the further end of the hold, stowed in so confined and narrow a space, that it was impossible to think of fitting the parts together there. At the same time these parts were so heavy, that removing them to a convenient place piece by piece was equally out of the question.

I sent the boys away to amuse themselves by rummaging out anything they liked to carry away, and sat down quietly to consider the matter.

As my eyes became used to the dim light which entered the compartment through a chink or crevice here and there, I perceived how carefully every part of the pinnace was arranged and marked with numbers, so that if only I could bestow sufficient time on the work, and contrive space in which to execute it, I might reasonably hope for success.

"Room! Room to work in, boys! That's what we need in the first place!" I cried, as my sons came to see what plan I had devised, for so great was their reliance on me that they never doubted the pinnace was to be ours.

"Fetch axes, and let us break down the compartment and clear space all round."

To work we all went, yet evening drew near, and but little impression was made on the mass of woodwork around us. We had to acknowledge than an immense amount of labor and perseverance would be required before we could call ourselves the owners of the useful and elegant little craft, which lay within this vast hulk like a fossil shell embedded in a rock.

Preparations for returning to shore were hastily made, and we landed without much relish for the long walk to Falconhurst, when, to our great surprise and pleasure, we found the mother and little Franz at Tentholm awaiting us. She had resolved to take up her quarters there during the time we should be engaged on the wreck. "In that way you will live nearer your work, and I shall not quite lose sight of you!" said she, with a pleasant smile.

"You are a good, sensible, kind wife," I exclaimed, delighted with her plan, "and we shall work with the greater diligence, that you may return as soon as possible to your dear Falconhurst."

"Come and see what we have brought you, mother!" cried Fritz; "a good addition to your stores, is it not?" and he and his brothers exhibited two small casks of butter, three of flour, corn, rice, and many other articles welcome to our careful housewife.

Our days were now spent in hard work on board, first cutting and clearing an open space round the pinnace, and then putting the parts together. We started early and returned at night, bringing each time a valuable freight from the old vessel.

At length, with incredible labor, all was completed. The pinnace stood actually ready to be launched, but imprisoned within massive wooden walls which defied our strength.

It seemed exactly as though the graceful vessel had awakened from sleep, and was longing to spring into the free blue sea, and spread her wings to the breeze. I could not bear to think that our success so far should be followed by failure and disappointment. Yet no possible means of setting her free could I conceive, and I was almost in despair, when an idea occurred to me which, if I could carry it out, would effect her release without further labor or delay.

Without explaining my purpose, I got a large cast-iron mortar, filled it with gunpowder, secured a block of oak to the top, through which I pierced a hole for the insertion of the match, and this great petard I so placed, that when it exploded it should blow out the side of the vessel next from which the pinnace lay. Then securing it with chains, that the recoil might do no damage, I told the boys I was going ashore earlier than usual, and calmly desired them to get into the boat. Then lighting a match I had prepared, and which would burn some time before reaching the powder, I hastened after them with a beating heart, and we made for the land.

We brought the raft close in shore and began to unload it; the other boat I did not haul up, but kept her ready to put off at a moment's notice; my anxiety was unobserved by anyone, as I listened with strained nerves for the expected sound. It came!—a flash! A mighty roar—a grand burst of smoke!

My wife and children, terror-stricken, turned their eyes toward the sea, whence the startling noise came, and then, in fear and wonder, looked to me for some explanation. "Perhaps," said the mother, as I did not speak, "perhaps you have left a light burning near some of the gunpowder, and an explosion has taken place."

"Not at all unlikely," replied I quietly; "we had a fire below when we were caulking the seams of the pinnace. I shall go off at once and see what has happened. Will any one come?"

The boys needed no second invitation, but sprang into the boat, while I lingered to reassure my wife by whispering a few words of explanation, and then joining them, we pulled for the wreck at a more rapid rate than we ever had done before.

No alternation had taken place in the side at which we usually boarded her, and we pulled round to the further side, where a marvelous sight awaited us. A huge rent appeared, the decks and bulwarks were torn open, the water was covered with floating wreckage—all seemed in ruins; and the compartment where the pinnace rested was fully revealed to view. There sat the little beauty, to all appearance uninjured; and the boys, whose attention was taken up with the melancholy scene of ruin and confusion around them, were astonished to hear me shout in enthusiastic delight: "Hurrah! She is ours! The lovely pinnace is won! We shall be able to launch her easily after all. Come, boys, let us see if she has suffered from the explosion which has set her free."

The boys gazed at me for a moment, and then guessing my secret, "You planned it yourself, you clever, cunning father! Oh, that machine we helped to make was on purpose to blow it up!" cried they; and eagerly they followed me into the shattered opening, where, to my intense satisfaction, I found everything as I could wish, and the captive in no way a sufferer from the violent measures I had adopted for her deliverance.

The boys were deeply interested in examining the effects of the explosion, and in the explanation I gave them of the principle and proper way to manage a petard.

It was evident that the launch could now be effected without much trouble; I had been careful to place rollers beneath the keel, so that by means of levers and pulleys we might, with our united strength, move her forward toward the water. A rope was attached by which to regulate the speed of the descent, and then, all hands putting their shoulders to the work, the pinnace began to slide from the stocks, and finally slipped gently and steadily into the water, where she floated as if conscious it was her native element; while we, wild with excitement, cheered and waved enthusiastically. We then only remained long enough to secure our prize carefully at the most sheltered point, and went back to Tentholm, where we accounted for the explosion; saying that having blown away one side of the ship, we should be able to obtain the rest of its contents with a very few more days' work.

These days were devoted to completing the rigging, the mounting of her two little brass guns, and all necessary arrangements about the pinnace. It was wonderful what martial ardor was awakened by the possession of a vessel armed with two real guns. The boys chattered incessantly about savages, fleets of canoes, attack, defense, and final annihilation of the invaders.

I assured them that, brilliant as their victories would doubtless be, we should have good cause to thank God if their fighting powers and new-born valor were never put to the test.

The pinnace was fully equipped and ready to sail, while yet no idea of the surprise we were preparing for her had dawned upon my wife, and I permitted the boys, who had kept the secret so well, to fire a salute when we entered the bay.

Casting off from the ship, and spreading the sail, our voyage began. The pinnace glided swiftly through the water. I stood at the helm, Ernest and Jack manned the guns, and Fritz gave the word of command, "Fire!" Bang! Bang! Rattled out a thrilling report, which echoed and re-echoed among the cliffs, followed by our shouts and hurrahs.

The mother and her little boy rushed hastily forward from near the tent, and we could plainly see their alarm and astonishment; but speedily recognizing us, they waved joyfully, and came quickly to the landing place to meet us.

By skillful management we brought the pinnace near a projection of the bank, and Fritz assisted his mother to come on board, where, breathless with haste and excitement, she exclaimed, "You dear, horrid, wonderful people, shall I scold you or praise you? You have frightened me out of my wits! To see a beautiful little ship come sailing in was startling enough, for I could not conceive who might be on board, but the report of your guns made me tremble with fear—and had I not recognized your voices directly after, I should have run away with Franz—Heaven knows where! But have you really done all this work yourselves?" she continued, when we had been forgiven for terrifying her with our vainglorious salute. "What a charming little yacht! I should not be afraid to sail in this myself."

After the pinnace had been shown off, and received the admiration she deserved, while our industry, skill, and perseverance met with boundless praise: "Now," said my wife, "you must come with me, and see how little Franz and I have improved our time every day of your absence."

We all landed, and with great curiosity followed the mother up the river toward the cascade; where, to our astonishment, we found a garden neatly laid out in beds and walks; and she continued, "We don't frighten people by firing salutes in honor of our performances; although, by and by, I too shall want fire in a peaceable form. Look at my beds of lettuce and cabbages, my rows of beans and peas! Think what delicious dinners I shall be able to cook for you, and give me credit for my diligence."

"My dear wife!" I exclaimed, "this is beautiful! You have done wonders! Did you not find the work too hard?"

"The ground is light and easy to dig hereabouts," she replied. "I have planted potatoes, and cassava roots; there is space for sugarcane, and the young fruit trees, and I shall want you to contrive to irrigate them, by leading water from the cascades in hollow bamboos. Up by the sheltering rocks I mean to have pineapples and melons; they will look splendid when they are spread there. To shelter the beds of European vegetables from the heat of the sun, I have planted seeds of maize round them. The shadow of the tall plants will afford protection from the burning rays. Do you think that is a good plan?"

"I do, indeed; the whole arrangement is capital. Now, as sunset approaches, we must return to the tent for supper and rest, for both of which we are all quite ready."

The time passed in happy talk over our many new interests; every one had the pleasant sensation which attends successful labor, as well as experiencing the joy of affording unexpected pleasure to others; and I especially pointed out to my sons how true, genuine happiness consists in that, rather than in mere self-gratification.

Next morning, my wife said: "If you can exist on shore long enough to visit Falconhurst, dear husband, I should like you to attend to the little fruit trees. I fear they have been too much neglected. I have watered them occasionally, and spread earth over the roots as they lay, but I could not manage to plant them."

"You have done far more than I could have expected, my wife," I replied, "and provided you do not ask me to give up the sea altogether, I most willingly agree to your request, and will go to Falconhurst as soon as the raft is unloaded, and everything safely arranged here."

Life on shore was an agreeable change for us all, and the boys actively went to work, so that the stores were quickly brought up to the tent, piled in order, and carefully covered with sailcloths, fastened down by pegs all round. The pinnace being provided with an anchor, was properly moored, and her elegant appearance quite altered the looks of our harbor, hitherto occupied only by the grotesque tub boat, and flat, uninteresting raft.

Taking an ample supply of everything we should require at Falconhurst, we were soon comfortably reestablished in that charming abode, its peaceful shade seeming more delightful than ever, after the heat and hard work we had lately undergone.

Several Sundays had passed during our stay at Tentholm, and the welcome Day of Rest now returned again, to be observed with heartfelt devotion and grateful praise.

I did not attempt too much in the form of preaching, as I could not have secured the attention of my hearers to any long-winded discourse, but they were interested in the Bible reading and simple instructions I drew from it, and their young voices joined sweetly in favorite hymns, which my wife sang from memory.

In the evening I desired the boys to let me see their dexterity in athletic exercises, such as running, leaping, wrestling, and climbing; telling them they must keep up the practice of these things, so as to grow strong, active men, powerful to repel and cope with danger, as well as agile and swift-footed to escape from it. No man can be really courageous and self-reliant without an inward consciousness of physical power and capability.

"I want to see my sons strong, both morally and physically," said I; "that means, little Franz," as the large blue eyes looked inquiringly up at him, "brave to do what is good and right, and to hate evil, and strong to work, hunt, and provide for themselves and others, and to fight if necessary."

On the following day, the boys seeming disposed to carry out my wishes by muscular exercise of all sorts, I encouraged them by saying I meant to prepare a curious new weapon for them, only they must promise not to neglect the practice of archery; as to their guns, I had no reason to fear they would be laid aside.

Taking a long cord, I attached a leaden bullet to each end and had instantly to answer a storm of questions as to what this could possibly be for.

"This is a miniature lasso," said I; "the Mexicans, Patagonians, and various tribes of South America, make use of this weapon in hunting, with marvelous dexterity, only, having no bullets, they fasten stones to their ropes, which are immensely longer than this. One end is swung round and round the mounted hunter's head, and then cast with skill and precision toward the animal he wishes to strike; immediately drawing it back, he can repeat the blow, and either kill or wound his prey. Frequently, however, the intention is to take the animal, wild horse, or buffalo, or whatever it may be, alive; and in that case, the lasso is thrown, while riding in hot pursuit, in such a way as to make the stone twist many times round the neck, body, or legs of the fugitive, arresting him even in full career."

"Oh, father, what a splendid contrivance! Will you try it now? There is the donkey, father! Do catch the donkey."

Not at all certain of my powers, I declined to practice upon a live subject, but consented to make a trial of skill by aiming at the stump of a tree at no great distance.

My success surpassed my own expectations; the stump was entwined by the cord in such a way as to leave no doubt whatever as to the feasibility of the wonderful performances I described; and I was assailed by petitions from the boys, each anxious to possess a lasso of his own without a moment's delay.

As the manufacture was simple, their wishes were speedily gratified, and lasso practice became the order of the day.

Fritz, who was the most active and adroit, besides having, of course, the greatest muscular strength, soon became skilled in the art.

That night a change came over the weather, and early next morning I perceived that a gale of wind was getting up. From the height of our trees I could see that the surface of the sea was in violent agitation.

It was with no small satisfaction that I thought of our hard-won pinnace, safely moored in the harbor, and recollected that there was nothing to call us to the wreck for the next few days.

My attention was by no means monopolized by my sons and their amusements. The good mother had much to show me demanding my approval, advice, or assistance, as the case might be.

A good supply of wild pigeons and ortolans had been snared, partly cooked, and preserved in lard. Of these she showed me her small cask well filled.

Then the nests of various pairs of tame pigeons were exhibited, but her chief care was the unpromising condition of her dear little fruit trees, for, having been forgotten, they were so dry and withered, that unless planted without further delay, she feared we should lose them.

This needful work we set about, therefore, at once, proposing afterward an excursion to the Calabash Wood, in order to manufacture a large supply of vessels and utensils of all sorts and sizes.

Every one was inclined for this expedition; consequently the planting of the orchard was carried on with surprising vigor, but was not completed until toward evening; and then all sorts of arrangements were made for an early start next day. The mother and Franz were to be of the party, and their equipment took some time, for we meant to make a grand family excursion, attended by our domestic pets and servants!

By sunrise we were all astir, and everything quickly made ready for a start.

The sledge, loaded with ammunition and baskets of provisions, and drawn by the donkey, was to be used for carrying home our gourd manufactures, as well as any other prize we might fall in with.

Turk, as usual, headed the procession, clad in his coat of mail.

Then came the boys with their guns and game bags. Their mother and I followed, and behind trotted Juno, not in very good spirits, poor dog! Because Master Knips, who had no idea of being left alone, must needs ride on her back.

On this occasion I took two guns with me, one loaded with shot for game, another with ball for our defense against beasts of prey.

Flamingo Marsh was quickly crossed, and the magnificent country beyond lay extended in all its beauty and fertility before our eyes. It was new to my wife and two of the boys, and the lovely prospect enchanted them.

Here Fritz and Jack turned aside into the bush, where presently loud barking was followed by the quick report of a gun, and a large bird, which had risen from thicket, fell heavily to the ground before us. Far from resigning itself, however, to death or captivity, it sprung to its feet, and, unable to fly, rushed away with extraordinary speed, hotly pursued by the excited dog, while Fritz ran, panting, in the same direction, and Juno, eager to join the chase, sprang aside so suddenly that her rider was flung unceremoniously on the sand, as she darted to intercept the retreat of the active bird. This she cleverly accomplished, but its defense was maintained so fiercely, as it struck out with its powerful legs and sharp claws, that neither Fritz nor the dogs could master it.

I hastened to their assistance, and found Juno holding on nobly by the wing she had seized, while the bird, which proved to be a magnificent bustard, struggled and fought fiercely. Watching my opportunity, I threw a large handkerchief over it, and with difficulty succeeded in binding its legs and wings. It was borne in triumph to the rest of our party, who meantime had been reclining on the sand.

"What have you got?" "What has Fritz shot?" cried the boys, starting up at our approach. "A bustard! Oh, that is splendid!"

"To be sure, it is the one we missed that day, don't you remember, mother? Ah, ha! Old fellow, you are done for this time!" said Jack.

"I think this is a hen bustard; it is the mother bird," said Ernest.

"Ah, yes, poor thing!" exclaimed my wife, in a tone of concern; "it is most likely the same, and I know she had a brood of young birds, and now they will be left unprotected and miserable. Had we not better let her go?"

"Why, my dear, kind-hearted wife, that was weeks and weeks ago! Those little birds are all strong and big by this time, and I dare say Mrs. Bustard here has forgotten all about them. Besides, she is badly wounded, and we must try to cure the hurt. If we succeed, she will be a valuable addition to our poultry yard; if we cannot, you shall roast her for dinner."

Resuming our march, we next arrived at the Monkey Grove, which was the scene of the tragi-comic adventure by which Fritz became the guardian of the orphan ape.

While he amused us all by a lively and graphic description of the scene, Ernest was standing apart under a splendid coconut palm, gazing in fixed admiration at the grand height of the stem, and its beautiful, graceful crown of leaves. The cluster of nuts beneath these evidently added interest to the spectacle, for, drawing quietly near him, I heard a long-drawn sigh, and the words:

"It's awfully high! I wish one would fall down!"

Scarcely had he uttered these words, than, as if by magic, down plumped a huge nut at his feet.

The boy was quite startled, and sprang aside, looking timidly upward, when, to my surprise, down came another.

"Why, this is just like the fairy tale of the wishing-cap!" cried Ernest. "My wish is granted as soon as formed!"

"I suspect the fairy in this instance is more anxious to pelt us and drive us away than to bestow dainty gifts upon us," said I. "I think there is most likely a cross-eyed old ape sitting up among those shadowy leaves and branches."

We examined the nuts, thinking they were perhaps old ones, and had fallen, in consequence, naturally, but they were not even quite ripe.

Anxious to discover what was in the tree, we all surrounded it, gaping and gazing upward with curious eyes.

"Hullo! I see him!" shouted Fritz presently. "Oh, a hideous creature! What can it be? Flat, round, as big as a plate, and with a pair of horrid claws! Here he comes! He is going to creep down the tree!"

At this, little Franz slipped behind his mother, Ernest took a glance round to mark a place of retreat, Jack raised the butt-end of his gun, and every eye was fixed on the trunk of the tree, down which a large land-crab commenced a leisurely descent. As it approached within reach, Jack hit at it boldly, when it suddenly dropped the remaining distance, and opening its great claws, sidled after him with considerable rapidity, upon which he fairly turned tail and ran. We all burst into a roar of laughter, which soon made him face about, and then, to our infinite amusement, the little fellow prepared for a fresh onset; laying down all he was carrying, pulling off his jacket and spreading it wide out in both hands, he returned to the charge, suddenly threw his garment over the creature, wrapped it well round it, and then pummeled it with all the strength of his fists.

For a few minutes I could do nothing but laugh, but then running to him with my hatchet, I struck several sharp blows on his bundle, which we opened carefully, and found within the land-crab perfectly dead.

"Well, this is an ugly rascal!" cried Jack; "if he hadn't been so hideous, I should not have dealt so severely with him. I wasn't a bit afraid. What is the creature's name?"

"This is a crab, a land-crab," said I, "of which there are many varieties, and this, I think, is called a coconut crab, or at least it deserves the name, for it is evidently very fond of eating these nuts, since it takes the trouble to climb the trees for them; the difficulty of getting at the kernel, too, is considerable. You showed no little presence of mind, Jack, when you thought of catching it in your jacket; in fact, it might have been more than a match for you otherwise, for some are most determined fighters, and are very swift, too. Now let us take it, as well as the nuts, to the sledge, and go on our way."

Progress became difficult, for we were constantly stopped in passing through the wood, by having to cut away the hanging boughs and creeping plants which interlaced them. Ernest was behind, and by-and-by called me back to see what proved to be an important discovery; from the several stalks of one of these creepers flowed clear cold water, and I recognized the "liane rouge," which is known in America, and is so precious to the thirsty hunter or traveler. This is truly one of God's good gifts to man!

The boys were much delighted with this curious plant. "Only fancy, mother," said Ernest, as he showed it to her, "how cheering and refreshing to find this if one were lost and alone in a vast forest, wandering for days and days without being near a natural spring of water."

"But are you certain it is safe to drink this?" asked she.

I assured her it was so, and advised the boys to cut enough to quench the thirst of the whole party, including our animals. This they did, only finding it necessary, as with the sugar canes, to cut air holes above the joints.

After struggling onward for a short time, we emerged from the thickets into open ground, and saw the calabash trees in the distance. As we drew near, their curious appearance and singular fruit caused much surprise and also amusement, for we were speedily established among the trees, where, as I chose and cut down the gourds most likely to be useful, every one engaged merrily in the work of cutting, carving, sawing, and scooping some manner of dish, bowl, cup, jar, or platter, according to his several taste or ability.

We were to dine here, and after a time Fritz and Jack began to prepare a fireplace, their great ambition being to heat the stones red hot, and cook the crab in a hollow gourd. Their mother, therefore, left them to their own devices, and attended to the hungry animals, unharnessing the ass to graze, and giving coconut milk to the poor little monkey, who had been obliged to travel in a covered basket for some time, lest he should be lost in the woods. The wounded bustard had been completely forgotten, and from heat and thirst was suffering greatly until her friendly care revived it, and it was tied to a tree and allowed to move about, its fierce spirit greatly tamed by adversity.

The cooking operations came to a stand soon after the fire was lighted, for it appeared that we had no more water in the jars we had brought, so the boys proposed to go in search of a spring. I agreed to accompany them; Ernest also wished to join us, and as our intention was to examine merely the surrounding wood, I saw no objection to leaving their mother and Franz for a short time.

Very soon after our exploration began, Ernest, who was in front, turned with a face of terror, shouting, "A wild boar! An immense wild boar, father! Do come, quick!" And sure enough, I heard a loud snorting and puffing as some large animal passed hastily through the thick underwood beyond us. "After him lads, after him!" cried I, hurrying forward. "Call the dogs! Stand ready to fire!" And we pressed through the bushes to the spot where Ernest had seen the creature. The ground was grubbed up, and some potatoes lay about, showing that we had disturbed him at his midday meal. Ernest and Jack were more disposed to gather the roots than to follow up the chase. Fritz and I alone went after the dogs, who eagerly pushed on, and by the sounds we heard had evidently attacked the boar at no great distance. Terrific barking, snarling, and grunting guided us to the scene of action, and we beheld our mastiffs one on each side of a large respectable-looking pig, holding on by the great ears, while the animal, on seeing us, appeared rather to beseech our interference than to propose to offer a desperate resistance.

In a moment the truth became apparent! The captive grunter was no fierce native of the forest, but our own runaway sow! Our excitement had been wound to so high a pitch that the discovery was quite a shock, and we felt half angry with the creature who had disappointed us; then the absurdity of the whole thing made us laugh heartily, and calling off the dogs, the old lady was released from her ignominious position. Our laughter resounding through the wood, brought Ernest and Jack from their potatoes, to see what was going on.

“Much use you two would have been suppose we had required help,” cried Fritz, as they recognized their old friend.

“Ah, well, you see,” returned Jack, “Ernest and I had a sort of a kind of presentiment that this was going to be the old sow. And just look at our fine potatoes!”

A good deal of joking on the subject ensued, but was interrupted by Ernest, who drew our attention to fruit resembling apples on the surrounding bushes, and on the grass beneath them.

The sow was making amends for the fright and pain she had endured by munching and crunching this fruit at a great rate. Fritz feared that it might be the poisonous manchineel, against which I once warned them, but on examining it, I was induced to pronounce a more favorable opinion, and we collected a quantity in hopes that, if the monkey approved of it as well as the old sow, we might be able to enjoy a feast ourselves.

All this time not a drop of water had we seen, and our own thirst increasing, we felt eager to procure some before returning to our resting-place.

Jack preceded us, and we made our way toward a high rock, which rose above the thickets, when he suddenly startled us by a loud cry of “A crocodile! Father! Father! A crocodile!”

“Nonsense, boy! A crocodile, of all things, in this dry, parched forest, where we can’t get so much as a mouthful of water!”

On advancing to where Jack stood, I perceived that his mistake was not so very silly after all, for I beheld an iguana, one of the largest of the lizard species, and a truly formidable-looking fellow. I was glad to assure Jack that the strange creature he had found was perfectly harmless, and that its flesh being esteemed a delicacy, it would be a valuable prize to carry back with us.

In another moment Fritz would have fired, but arresting his hand, “Your shot,” I said, “would probably only wound the animal, and being extremely tenacious of life, it would certainly escape; we must gain possession of the sleeping beauty by a gentler method.”

"You are not going to kiss it, are you, father?" asked Jack, with a grin.

I tried to rebuke him for his impertinence, but, failing, I commenced operations. I first attached a cord and running-noose to a stout stick, and holding a light switch in my other hand, I began to approach the creature with soft, slow steps, while the boys looked on with the utmost curiosity.

Presently I began very softly to whistle a sweet, yet very lively air, which I continued more and more distinctly as I drew near the lizard; until, awaking, it seemed to listen with pleasure—raising its head as though better to catch the sounds, or to discover whence they came.

When near enough, I began gently to stroke and tickle him with the wand, continuing to whistle the prettiest tunes I could think of; and the lizard gave signs of pleasurable contentment, stretching his limbs and moving his tail in token of enjoyment.

Suddenly, availing myself of a movement of his head, I cast the noose over it, drew the cord tight, and placing my foot on the body, I was about to kill it by piercing the nostril—almost the only vulnerable part in this singular reptile—when Jack received such a blow from its tail, which was furiously driving in all directions, as sent him rolling over like a ninepin. At the same time he opened his jaws, when the boys took fright at the row of sharp teeth, and thinking that the sooner he was dead the better, were for battering him with sticks; but I assuring them my method would kill him more quickly and without pain, thrust my rod into his nostril, on which the blood flowed and the lizard soon expired.

The boys seemed to think me as wonderful a person as a snake charmer, and the success of my stratagem, as well as of the means by which the lizard was slain, called forth great admiration, since they had never heard of the animal, nor of the method of capturing it so commonly practised in the West Indies.

Now came the question of how we were to carry this unwieldy burden. I had a great dislike to killing any creature and leaving it useless behind me; so, without more ado, I fairly took it on my back, and marched off with it.

As we came toward the Calabash Wood, we could hear the voices of the deserted mother and child calling us in anxious tones; for indeed our protracted absence alarmed them. We shouted joyously in reply, and our appearance, as we issued from the woods, afforded them welcome relief from their fears, although the dreadful creature on my back startled them not a little.

There was so much to tell, so much to be seen, that for a time hunger and thirst were forgotten; and no one thought even of the water we had vainly gone in search of, until Master Knips, having slyly possessed himself of some of our new-found apples, was discovered munching away and enjoying them amazingly—which instantly gave the boys a strong wish to eat some also; and as the bustard likewise pecked at them without hesitation, I felt sure there could be no danger; and on tasting them, I concluded it was the fruit of the guava, a West Indian plant, which we were delighted to have.

Although refreshing, this fruit rather sharpened than appeased our appetites, and we were glad to eat the provisions we had brought from home, without waiting to cook anything, as we had originally intended.

It was, in fact, high time to move homeward, and we thought it best not to encumber ourselves with the sledge and the greater part of its load, but to leave it until the next day. The ass was laden with the iguana and the bustard; and little Franz, tired as he was, looked in vain for a spare seat on its back.

Our road home lay through a majestic forest of oak trees, beneath which lay numberless acorns, some of which we gathered as we went along; and at length, before night closed in, we all reached Falconhurst in safety.

When supper was ready, we were thankful to recruit our exhausted strength by eating heartily of a piece of broiled iguana, with potatoes and roast acorns, which tasted like excellent chestnuts.

CHAPTER VII

Fritz and I return to the Calabash Wood—Fritz shoots a ruffed grouse—We come across waxberry bushes—Sociable grosbeaks—Fritz captures a parrot—A lecture on ants—Caoutchouc trees—The sago-palm and the edible worms—Return with sugarcanes to Falconhurst—Candle-making—How to make butter without a churn—Plant trees and adorn Tentholm—Last visit to the wreck—The first ducklings on the island—Falconhurst again—An excursion—We pitch our tent—Fritz and Jack ascend the coconut trees—Ernest brings us a delicacy—Loss of Grizzle—Jack and I go in pursuit—Giant bamboos—Encounter with buffaloes—The buffalo calf—Find a jackal's lair—Reach our camp—What happened in our absence—Fritz's pet—Sago manufacture—Meet with our sow and her family again—How Ernest tamed the eagle.

The first thing to be done on the following day was to return to the Calabash Wood, to fetch the sledge with the dishes, bowls, and baskets we had made.

Fritz alone accompanied me. I desired the other boys to remain with their mother, intending to explore beyond the chain of rocky hills, and thinking a large party undesirable on the occasion.

Passing through the wood of evergreen oaks, we observed our sow feasting on the acorns, evidently not a whit the worse for the fright we had given her the previous day—in fact, she appeared more friendly disposed toward us than usual, possibly considering us as her deliverers from the jaws of the savage dogs.

Many birds tenanted this grove, and were undisturbed by our movements, until Fritz fired and shot a beautiful blue jay and a couple of parakeets, one a brilliant scarlet, the other green and gold.

Fritz was in the act of reloading his gun, when an unaccountable noise struck our ears, and put us instantly on the alert, because it appeared like the dull thumping sound of a muffled drum, and reminded us of the possible presence of savages.

With the greatest caution we drew near the sound, concealing ourselves among the low bushes and thick grass and creepers, until we reached an open glade; where, standing on an old prostrate log, was a beautiful bird, about the size of a cock, of a rich chestnut brown color, finely mottled with dark brown and gray. On the shoulders were curious tufts of velvety black feathers, glossed with green. He was ruffling his wings, erecting his tail and neck feathers, strutting and wheeling about in a most strange and stately fashion. After maneuvering for some time in this manner, greatly to the edification of a party of birds resembling him, but without any ruff, who, assembled round the stump, were enjoying his performances, he spread out his tail like a fan, stiffened his wings, and began to strike with them in short, rapid beats, faster and faster, until a rumbling sound like very distant thunder was produced, and the whirring wings enveloped him as in a cloud. This was the drumming noise which had alarmed us, increased, as I imagine, by the wing strokes falling at times on the decayed and hollow stump on which the curious pantomime was acted.

I was watching it with the utmost interest, when a shot from behind me was fired, and in a moment the play was at an end; my over-hasty son had changed the pretty comedy into a sad and needless tragedy. The enthusiastic drummer fell dead from his perch, and the crowd of admiring companions fled in dismay.

The cruel interruption of a scene so rare and remarkable annoyed me extremely, and I blamed Fritz for firing without my leave. I felt sure the bird was the ruffed grouse, and a very fine specimen. We placed it on the ass, which was patiently awaiting our return, and went on our way.

The sledge was quite safe where we had left it; it was early in the day, and I resolved to explore, as I had intended, a line of cliff and rocky hills, which, at more or less distance from the seashore, extended the whole length of coast known or visible to us.

I desired to discover an opening, if any existed, by which to penetrate the interior of the country, or to ascertain positively that we were walled in and isolated on this portion of the coast.

Leaving Calabash Wood behind us, we advanced over ground covered with manioc, potatoes, and many plants unknown to us; pleasant streamlets watered the fruitful soil, and the view on all sides was open and agreeable.

Some bushes attracted my notice, loaded with small white berries, of peculiar appearance like wax, and very sticky when plucked. I recognized in this a plant called by botanists *Myrica cerifera*, and with much pleasure explained to Fritz that, by melting and straining these berries, we might easily succeed in making candles, and afford very great satisfaction to the mother, who did not at all approve of having to lay her work aside and retire to rest the moment the sun set. The greenish wax to be obtained would be more brittle than beeswax, but it would burn very fairly, and diffuse an agreeable perfume. Having the ass with us, we lost no time in gathering berries enough to fill one of the large canvas bags he carried, and we then continued our route.

Very soon we met with another natural curiosity, the curious appearance of which surprised us much. This was the abode, under one roof, of a whole colony of birds, about the size of yellow hammers, but of plain brown plumage. The nests were built in a mass round the stem and among the branches of a tree standing alone, and a kind of roof formed of grass, straws, and fibers covered them all, and sheltered the community from rain and the heat of the sun. There were numbers of openings into the irregular sides of the group of dwellings, the nests resembling different apartments in a house common to all; twigs and small branches emerged here and there from the walls, and served as perches for the young birds, and resting-places and posts of observation for all. The general appearance of the establishment reminded us of a huge bath-sponge. The feathered inhabitants swarmed in and out by thousands, and we saw among them many beautiful little parrots, who seemed in many instances to contest possession of the nest with the lawful owners.

Fritz, being an expert climber and exceedingly anxious to examine the nests more closely, ascended the tree, hoping to obtain one or two young birds, if any were hatched. He put his hand into several holes, which were empty; but at last his intended theft and robbery met with repulse and chastisement he little expected; for, reaching far back into the nest, his finger was seized and sharply bitten by a very strong beak, so that with a cry he withdrew his hand, and shook it vigorously to lessen the pain. Recovering from the surprise, he again and more resolutely seized the unkind bird, and, despite its shrieks and screams, drew it from its retreat, crammed it into his pocket, buttoned up his coat, and slid quickly to the ground, pursued by numbers of the captive's relations, who darted from the other holes and flew round the robber, screeching and pecking at him in a rage.

Fritz's prize was not one of the real owners of the nests, which were those of the sociable grosbeak, but a very pretty small green parrot, with which he was greatly pleased, and which he at once determined to tame and teach to speak; for the present it was carefully remanded to prison in his pocket.

This curious colony of birds afforded us matter for conversation as we went on our way; their cheerful, sociable habits, and the instinct which prompted them to unite in labor for the common good, appearing most wonderful to us.

"Examples of the kind, however," said I, "are numerous, in various classes of animals. Beavers, for instance, build and live together in a very remarkable way. Among insects, bees, wasps, and ants are well known as social architects; in like manner, the coral insect works wonders beneath the ocean waves, by force of perseverance and united effort."

"I have often watched ants at work," said Fritz; "it is most amusing to see how they carry on the various works and duties of their commonwealth."

"Have you ever noticed how much trouble they take with the eggs?" inquired I, to see how far he understood the process; "carrying them about in the warmth of the sun until they are hatched?"

"Ah! That is rather the chrysalis of the antworm, or larva which is produced from an egg. I know they are called ants' eggs, but, strictly speaking, that is incorrect."

"You are perfectly right, my boy. Well, if you have taken so much interest in watching the little ants of your native country, how delighted and astonished you would be to see the wonders performed by the vast tribes of large ants in foreign lands.

"Some of these build heaps or nests, four or six feet high and proportionately broad, which are so strong and firm that they defy equally sunshine and rain. They are, within, divided into regular streets, galleries, vaults, and nurseries. So firmly are these mounds built, that with interior alterations, a deserted one might be used for a baking-oven.

"The ant, although respected since the days of King Solomon as a model of industry, is not in itself an attractive insect.

"It exudes a sticky moisture, its smell is unpleasant, and it destroys and devours whatever eatable comes in its way. Although, in our own country it does little harm, the large ants of foreign lands are most destructive and troublesome; it being very difficult to check their depredations. Fortunately they have enemies by whose exertions their numbers are kept down; birds, other insects, and even four-footed beasts prey upon them. Chief among the latter is the ant-bear, or tamanoir, of SouthAmerica, a large creature six or seven feet in length, covered with long coarse hair, drooping like a heavy plume over the hind quarters. The head is wonderfully elongated and very narrow; it is destitute of teeth, and the tongue resembles somewhat a great red earth-worm. It has immensely strong curved claws, with which it tears and breaks down and scratches to pieces the hard walls of the ant-heaps; then, protruding its sticky tongue, it coils and twists it about among the terrified millions disturbed by its attack; they adhere to this horrible invader, and are drawn irresistibly backward into the hungry, toothless jaws awaiting them.

"The little ant-eater is not more than about twenty-one inches in length, has a shorter and more natural looking head, and fine silky fur. It usually lives in trees."

I was pleased to find my memory served me so well on this subject, as it interested my boy amazingly; and occupied us for a considerable time while we traveled onward.

Arriving presently at a grove of tall trees, with very strong, broad thick leaves, we paused to examine them; they bore a round, fig-like fruit, full of little seeds and of a sour, harsh taste.

Fritz saw some gummy resin exuding from cracks in the bark, and it reminded him of the boyish delight afforded by collecting gum from cherry-trees at home, so that he must needs stop to scrape off as much as he could. He rejoined me presently, attempting to soften what he had collected in his hands; but finding it would not work like gum, he was about to fling it away, when he suddenly found that he could stretch it and that it sprang back to its original size.

"Oh, father, only look! This gum is quite elastic! Can it possibly be India rubber?"

"What!" cried I; "let me see it! A valuable discovery that would be, indeed; and I do believe you are perfectly right!"

"Why would it be so very valuable, father?" inquired Fritz. "I have only seen it used for rubbing out pencil marks."

"India rubber," I replied, "or, more properly, caoutchouc, is a milky, resinous juice which flows from certain trees in considerable quantities when the stem is purposely tapped. These trees are indigenous to the South American countries of Brazil, Guiana, and Cayenne. The natives, who first obtained it, used to form bottles by smearing earthen flasks with repeated coatings of the gum when just fresh from the trees, and when hardened and sufficiently thick, they broke the mold, shook out the fragments, and hung the bottles in the smoke, when they became firmer and of a dark color. While moist, the savages were in the habit of drawing rude figures and lines on the resin by way of ornament; these marks you may have observed, for the bottles obtained from the natives by the Spaniards and Portuguese have for years been brought to Europe, and cut into portions to be sold for use in drawing. Caoutchouc can be put to many uses, and I am delighted to have it here, as we shall, I hope, be able to make it into different forms; first and foremost, I shall try to manufacture boots and shoes."

Soon after making this discovery, we reached the coconut wood, and saw the bay extending before us, and the great promontory we called Cape Disappointment, which hitherto had always bounded our excursions.

In passing through the wood, I remarked a smaller sort of palm, which, among its grand companions, I had not previously noticed. One of these had been broken by the wind, and I saw that the pith had a peculiar mealy appearance, and I felt convinced that this was the world-renowned sago-palm.

In the pith I saw some fat worms or maggots, and suddenly recollected that I had heard of them before as feeding on the sago, and that in the West Indies they are eaten as a delicacy.

I felt inclined to try what they tasted like; so at once kindling a fire, and placing some half-dozen, sprinkled with salt, on a little wooden spit, I set them to roast.

Very soon rich fat began to drop from them, and they smelt so temptingly good that all repugnance to the idea of eating worms vanished; and, putting one like a pat of butter on a baked potato, I boldly swallowed it and liked it so much that several others followed in the same way. Fritz also summoned courage to partake of this novel food, which was a savory addition to our dinner of baked potatoes.

Being once more ready to start, we found so dense a thicket in the direct route that we turned aside without attempting to penetrate it, and made our way toward the sugar brake near Cape Disappointment. This we could not pass without cutting a handsome bundle of sugarcanes, and the donkey carried that, in addition to the bag of wax berries.

In time we reached the sledge in Calabash Wood: the ass was unloaded, everything placed on the sledge, and our patient beast began calmly and readily to drag the burden he had hitherto borne on his back.

No further adventure befell us, and we arrived in the evening at Falconhurst, where our welcome was as warm as usual—all we had to tell listened to with the greatest interest, all we had to show most eagerly examined, the pretty green parakeet enchanting the boys most particularly.

An excellent supper was ready for us, and with thankful hearts we enjoyed it together; then, ascending to our tree-castle, and drawing up the ladder after us, we betook ourselves to the repose well earned and greatly needed after this fatiguing day.

The idea of candle-making seemed to have taken the fancy of all the boys; and next morning they woke, one after the other, with the word candle on their lips. When they were thoroughly roused they continued to talk candles; all breakfast-time, candles were the subject of conversation; and after breakfast they would hear of nothing else but setting to work at once and making candles.

"So be it," said I; "let us become chandlers."

I spoke confidently, but to tell the truth, I had in my own mind certain misgivings as to the result of our experiment. In the first place, I knew that we lacked a very important ingredient—animal fat, which is necessary to make candles burn for any length of time with brilliancy. Besides this, I rather doubted how far my memory would recall the various operations necessary in the manufacture. Of all this, however, I said nothing; and the boys, under my direction, were soon at work. We first picked off the berries and threw them into a large shallow iron vessel placed on the fire. The green, sweet-scented wax was rapidly melted, rising to the surface of the juice yielded by the berries. This we skimmed off and placed in a separate pot by the fire, ready for use; repeating the operation several times, until we had collected sufficient liquid wax for our purpose. I then took the wicks my wife had prepared, and dipped them one after the other into the wax, handing them as I did so to Fritz, who hung them up on a bush to dry. The coating they thus obtained was not very thick; but, by repeating the operation several times, they at length assumed very fair proportions, and became real sturdy candles. Our wax being at an end, we hung these in a cool, shady place to harden; and that same night we sat up like civilized beings three whole hours after sunset, and Falconhurst was for the first time brilliantly illuminated.

We were all delighted with the success of our experiment.

"You are indeed clever," said my wife; "I only wish that with your ingenuity you would show me how to make butter. Day after day I have the annoyance of seeing a large supply of good cream go bad under my very eyes, simply because I have no use to which to put it. Invent a plan, please do."

"I think that perhaps I can help you," I replied, after a little consideration; "not that I can claim the honor of the invention of my plan; that is due to the Hottentots. I will see what I can do. Jack, bring me one of our gourd bottles."

I took the gourd, one of those I had previously prepared, with a small hole at one end and well hollowed out and cleaned; this I partially filled with cream and then corked up the hole tightly.

"Here, boys," said I, "you can continue the operation, while I turn carpenter and make a cart to take the place of our sledge."

I gave them their directions, and then set about my own work. They fixed four posts in the ground, and to them fastened a square piece of sailcloth by four cords attached to the corners. In this cradle they placed the gourd of cream, and each taking a side rolled it backward and forward continuously for half an hour.

"Now," I cried, looking up from my work, "open the gourd and take the contents to your mother, with my compliments."

They did so; and my good wife's eyes were delighted with the sight of a large lump of capital fresh butter.

With my son's assistance the cart was in time completed; a clumsy vehicle it was, but strong enough for any purpose to which we might put it, and, as it proved, of immense use to us in collecting the harvest.

We then turned our attention to our fruit-trees, which we had planted in a plot ready for transplanting. The walnut, cherry, and chestnut trees we arranged in parallel rows, so as to form a shady avenue from Falconhurst to Family-bridge; and between them we laid down a tolerable road, that we might have no difficulty in reaching Tentholm, be the weather bad as it might. We planted the vines round the arched roots of our great mangrove, and the rest of the trees in suitable spots; some near Falconhurst, and others away over Jackal River, to adorn Tentholm. Tentholm had been the subject of serious thoughts to me for some time past, and I now turned all my attention thither. It was not my ambition to make it beautiful, but to form of it a safe place of refuge in a case of emergency. My first care, therefore, was to plant a thick, prickly hedge capable of protecting us from any wild animal, and forming a tolerable obstacle to the attack of even savages, should they appear. Not satisfied with this, however, we fortified the bridge, and on a couple of hillocks mounted two guns which we brought from the wreck, and with whose angry mouths we might bark defiance at any enemy, man or beast.

Six weeks slipped away while we were thus busily occupied, six weeks of hard, yet pleasant, labor. We greeted each Sunday and its accompanying rest most gratefully, and on that day always, especially thanked God for our continued health and safety. I soon saw that this hard work was developing in the boys remarkable strength, and this I encouraged by making them practise running, leaping, climbing, and swimming; I also saw, however, that it was having a less satisfactory effect upon their clothes, which, though a short time before remarkably neat, were now, in spite of the busy mother's mending and patching, most untidy and disreputable.

I determined, therefore, to pay another visit to the wreck, to replenish our wardrobe and to see how much longer the vessel was likely to hold together. Three of the boys and I went off in the pinnace. The old ship seemed in much the same condition as when we had left her; a few more planks had gone, but that was all.

"Come, boys," cried I, "not an article of the slightest value must be left on board; rummage her out to the very bottom of her hold."

They took me at my word: sailors' chests, bales of cloth and linen, a couple of small guns, ball and shot, tables, benches, window shutters, bolts and locks, barrels of pitch, all were soon in a heap on the deck. We loaded the pinnace and went on shore. We soon returned with our tub-boat in tow, and after a few more trips nothing was left on board.

"One more trip," said I to my wife, before we started again, "and there will be the end of the brave ship which carried us from Switzerland. I have left two barrels of gunpowder on board and mean to blow her up."

Before we lighted the fuse, I discovered a large copper cauldron which I thought I might save. I made fast to it a couple of empty casks, that when the ship went up it might float. The barrels were placed, the train lighted, and we returned on shore.

The supper was laid outside the tent, at a spot from whence we might obtain a good view of the wreck. Darkness came on. Suddenly a vivid pillar of fire rose from the black waters, a sullen roar boomed across the sea, and we knew that our good old ship was no more.

We had planned the destruction of the vessel; we knew that it was for the best; and yet that night we went to bed with a feeling of sadness in our hearts, as though we had lost a dear old friend.

Next morning all our sadness was dispelled, and it was with pleasure that we saw the shore lined with a rich store of planks and beams, the remnants of the wreck. I soon found, too, the copper cauldron which was successfully floated by the casks; this I got on shore, and hauling it up among the rocks, stored under it the powder casks we had landed the day before. Collecting all these valuables gave us some little trouble, and while we were thus engaged my wife brought us good news. She had discovered that two ducks and a goose had each reared a large family among the reeds by the river; and they presently appeared waddling past us, apparently vastly well-pleased with their performance. We greeted them joyfully.

"Hurrah!" cried Ernest, "we'll be able to afford duck and green peas some day soon, and imagine we're once more civilized mortals."

The sight of these birds reminded me of our family at Falconhurst, and I announced my intention of paying them a visit.

Every one was delighted and every one would come with me. As we approached Falconhurst I noticed that several young trees in our avenue were considerably bent by the wind, and this resolved me to make an expedition next day to cut bamboos for their support. As Fritz was the only one besides myself who had visited Cape Disappointment and the surrounding country, my wife and the younger boys begged hard to be allowed to accompany me. I consented; and next morning we started, bringing with us the cart, drawn by the cow and ass, and laden with everything necessary for an expedition of several days—a tent, provisions, a large supply of ammunitions, and all sorts of implements and utensils; for I intended to make a great collection of fruits and the produce of different trees. It was a lovely morning, and passing gaily through the plantations of potatoes, manioc, and cassavas, we came to the nests of the sociable grosbeak, the sight of which charmed the children immensely.

We reached the wax trees, and there I called a halt, for I wished to gather a sack or two of the berries that we might renew our stock of candles. The berries were soon plucked; and I stored them away among the bushes, marking the spot that we might find them on our return.

"Now for the caoutchouc tree," said I; "now for the waterproof boots and leggings to keep your feet dry, Ernest." To the caoutchouc tree we directed our steps, and were soon busily engaged in stabbing the bark and placing vessels beneath to catch the sap. We again moved forward; and, crossing the palm wood, entered upon a delightful plain bounded on one side by an extensive field of waving sugarcane, on the other by a thicket of bamboos and lovely palms, while in front stretched the shining sea, calm and noiseless.

"How beautiful!" exclaimed Jack, "let us pitch our tent here and stay here always instead of living at Falconhurst. It would be jolly."

"Very likely," replied I, "and so would be the attacks of wild beasts; imagine a great tiger lying in wait in the thicket yonder, and pouncing out on us at night. No, no, thank you, I much prefer our nest in the tree, or our impregnable position at Tentholm. We must make this our headquarters for the present, however; for, though perhaps dangerous, it is the most convenient spot we shall find. Call a halt and pitch the tent."

Our beasts were quickly unyoked, the tent arranged, a large fire lit, supper started, and we dispersed in various directions, some to cut bamboos, and some to collect sugarcane. We then returned; and, as supper was still not ready and the boys were hungry, they decided to obtain some coconuts. This time, however, no assistance was to be had from either monkeys or land-crabs, and they gazed up with longing eyes at the fruit above them.

"We can climb," said Fritz, "up with you, boys."

Jack and he each rushed at one of the smooth, slippery trunks; right vigorously they struggled upward, but to no purpose; before they had accomplished one-quarter of the distance they found themselves slipping rapidly to the ground.

"Here, you young athletes," cried I, "I foresaw this difficulty, and have provided for it." So saying I held up buskins of shark's skin which I had previously prepared, and which I now bound on to their legs. Thus equipped they again attempted the ascent, and with a loop of rope passed round their body and the trunk of the tree, quickly reached the summit. My wife joined me, and together we watched the boys as they ascended tree after tree, throwing down the best fruit from each.

They then returned and jestingly begged Ernest to produce the result of his labor. The professor had been lying on the grass grazing at the palms; but, on this sarcastic remark, he sprang to his feet. "Willingly," he exclaimed, and seizing a pair of buskins, he quickly donned them. "Give me a coconut shell," said he. I gave him one, and he put it in his pocket. He ran to a tree, and, with an agility which surprised us all, quickly reached the top. No sooner had he done so than Fritz and Jack burst into a roar of laughter. He had swarmed a tree which bore no nuts. Ernest apparently heard them; for, as it seemed in a fit of anger, he drew his knife and severed the leafy crest, which fell to the ground. I glanced up at him, surprised at such a display of temper. But a bright smile greeted me, and in a merry tone he shouted:

"Jack, pick that palm-cabbage up and take it to your father; that is only half my contribution, and it is worth all your nuts put together."

He spoke truly; the cabbage palm is rare, and the tuft of leaves at its summit is greatly prized by the South Americans for its great delicacy and highly nutritive qualities.

"Bravo!" I cried, "you have retrieved your character; come down and receive the thanks of the company. What are you waiting up there for?"

"I am coming presently," he replied, "with the second half of my contribution; I hope it will be as fully appreciated as the first."

In a short time he slipped down the tree, and, advancing to his mother, presented her with the nut shell he had taken up with him.

"Here," he said, "is a wine which the greatest connoisseur would prize. Taste it, mother."

The shell was filled with a clear, rosy liquor, bright and sparkling. My wife tasted it. "Excellent, excellent," she exclaimed. "Your very good health, my dear boy!"

We drank the rosy wine in turn, and Ernest received hearty thanks from all.

It was getting late, and while we were enjoying our supper before our tent, our donkey, who had been quietly browsing near us, suddenly set up a loud bray, and, without the least apparent cause, pricked up his ears, threw up his heels, and galloped off into the thicket of bamboos. We followed for a short distance, and I sent the dogs in chase, but they returned without our friend, and, as it was late, we were obliged to abandon the chase.

I was annoyed by this incident, and even alarmed; for not only had we lost the ass, but I knew not what had occasioned his sudden flight. I knew not whether he was aware, by instinct, of the approach of some fierce wild beast. I said nothing of this to my family, but, making up an unusually large fire, I bade them sleep with their arms by their sides, and we all lay down.

A bright morning awoke us early, and I rose and looked out, thinking that perhaps our poor donkey might have been attracted by the light of the fires, and had returned. Alas! Not a sign of him was to be seen. As we could not afford to lose so valuable a beast, I determined to leave no attempt untried to regain him. We hurriedly breakfasted, and, as I required the dogs to assist me in the search, I left my elder sons to protect their mother, and bade Jack get ready for a day's march. This arrangement delighted him, and we quickly set out.

For an hour or more we trudged onward, directed by the print of the ass's hoofs. Sometimes we lost the track for a while, and then again discovered it as we reached softer soil. Finally this guide failed us altogether, for the donkey seemed to have joined in with a herd of some larger animals, with whose hoof-prints his had mingled. I now almost turned back in despair, but Jack urged me to continue the search; "For," said he, "if we once get upon a hill we shall see such a large herd, as this must be, at almost any distance. Do let us go on, father."

I consented, and we again pushed forward, through bushes, and over torrents, sometimes cutting our way with an ax, and sometimes plunging knee-deep through a swamp. We at length reached the border of a wide plain, and on it, in the distance, I could see a herd of animals browsing on the rich grass. It struck me that it might be the very herd to which our good donkey had joined himself; and, wishing to ascertain whether this was so, I resolved to make a detour through a bamboo marsh, and get as near as possible to the animals without disturbing them. The bamboos were huge, many of them over thirty feet in height; and, as we made our way through them, I remembered an account of the giant cane of South America, which is greatly prized by the Indians on account of its extreme usefulness; the reeds themselves make masts for their canoes, while each joint will form a cask or box. I was delighted, for I had little doubt that the bamboos we were among were of the same species. I explained this to Jack, and as we discussed the possibility of cutting one down and carrying a portion of it home, we reached the border of the marsh, and emerged upon the plain. There we suddenly found ourselves face to face with the herd which we sought—a herd of buffaloes. They looked up and stared at us inquisitively, but without moving. Jack would have fired, but I checked him. "Back to the thicket," I said, "and keep back the dogs!"

We began to retreat, but before we were again under cover the dogs joined us; and, in spite of our shouts and efforts to restrain them, they dashed forward and seized a buffalo calf. This was a signal to the whole herd to attack us. They bellowed loudly, pawed the ground, and tore it up with their horns, and then dashed madly toward us. We had not time to step behind a rock before the leader was upon us. So close was he that my gun was useless. I drew a pistol and fired. He fell dead at my feet. His fall checked the advance of the rest. They halted, snuffed the air, turned tail, and galloped off across the plain. They were gone, but the dogs still held gallantly to the calf. They dragged and tussled with him, but with their utmost efforts they could not bring him to the ground. How to assist them without shooting the poor beast I knew not; and this I was unwilling to do, for I hoped that, if we could but capture him alive, we might in time manage to tame him, and use him as a beast of burden. Jack's clever little head, however, suddenly devised a plan for their aid, and with his usual promptitude, he at once put it into execution. He unwound the lasso, which was coiled round his body, and, as the young bull flung up his heels, he cast, it and caught him by his hind legs. The noose drew tight, and in a twinkling the beast was upon the ground. We fastened the other end of the cord round a stout bamboo, called off the dogs, and the animal was at our mercy.

"Now we have got him," said Jack, as he looked at the poor beast, lying panting on the ground, "what are we to do with him?"

"I will show you," said I; "help me to fasten his forelegs together, and you shall see the next operation."

The bull, thus secured, could not move; and while Jack held his head I drew my knife and pierced the cartilage of his nose, and when the blood flowed less freely, passed a stout cord through the hole. I felt some repugnance at thus paining the animal, but it was a case of necessity, and I could not hesitate. We united the ends of the cord, freed the animal, set him upon his legs, and, subdued and overawed, he followed us without resistance. I now turned my attention to the dead buffalo, but as I could not then skin it, I contented myself with cutting off the most delicate parts, its tongue, and a couple of steaks, and, packing them in salt in my wallet, abandoned the rest to the dogs. They fell upon it greedily, and we retired under the shade to enjoy a meal after our hard work. The dogs, however, were not to have undisputed possession of the carcass; vultures, crows, and other birds of prey, with that marvelous instinct which always leads them to a dead body, quickly filled the air, and, with discordant cries, swooped down upon the buffalo. An amusing contest ensued; the dogs again and again drove off the intruders, and they, as often, returned reinforced by others who swarmed to the spot. Jack, with his usual impetuosity, wished to send a shot in among the robber band, but I prevented him, for I knew that the bird or two he might kill would be of no use to us, while his shot would not drive away the rest, even had we wished it. Both he and the dogs were at length satisfied, and as it was getting late, I determined to give up for the present the search for the ass, and to return to our camp. We again made our way through the bamboos, but before we left the thicket I cut down one of the smallest of the reeds, the largest of whose joints would form capital little barrels, while those near the tapering top would serve as molds for our next batch of candles.

The buffalo, with a dog on either side and the rope through his nose, was following us passively, and we presently induced him to submit to a package of our goods laid upon his back. We pushed rapidly forward, Jack eager to display our latest acquisition. As we repassed the rocky bed of a stream we had crossed in the morning, Juno dashed ahead, and was about to rush into a cleft between the rocks, when the appearance of a large jackal suddenly checked her further progress. Both dogs instantly flew at the animal, and though she fought desperately, quickly overpowered and throttled her. From the way the beast had shown fight, I concluded that her young must be close by, probably within the very cleft Juno was about to enter.

Directly Jack heard this, he wished to creep in and bring out the young jackals. I hesitated to allow him to do so, for I thought it possible that the male jackal might be still lying in wait within the cave. We peered into the darkness, and, after a while, Jack declared he could discern the little yellow jackals, and that he was quite sure the old one was not there. He then crept in, followed closely by the dogs, and presently emerged, bearing in his arms a handsome cub of a beautiful golden yellow and about the size of a small cat. He was the only one of the brood he had managed to save, for Turk and Juno, without pity for their youth or beauty, had worried all the rest. I did not much regret this, however, for I firmly believe that, had he saved them, Jack would have insisted upon bringing up the whole litter. As it was, I considered that one jackal was, with our young bull, quite sufficient an addition to our livestock.

During the halt we had made I had fastened the buffalo to a small tree, and as I was now again about to move on, I recognized it as the dwarf-palm, whose long, sharp leaves form an excellent barrier if it is planted as a hedge. I determined to return and get some young plants to strengthen our hedge at Tentholm. It was late before we reached our camp, where we found our family anxiously awaiting our return.

The sight of the new animals delighted the children immensely, and in their opinion amply compensated for the loss of our poor donkey. Jack had to answer a host of questions concerning their capture, and to give a minute account of the affray with the buffaloes. This he did, with graphic power certainly, but with so much boasting and self-glorification that I was obliged to check him, and give a plain and unvarnished account of the affair.

Suppertime arrived, and as we sat at that meal, for which Jack and I were heartily thankful, my wife and her party proceeded to give an account of their day's work.

Ernest had discovered a sago-palm, and had, after much labor, contrived to fell it. Franz and his mother had collected dry wood, of which a huge heap now stood before the tent, sufficient to keep up a fire all the rest of the time we should stay on the spot. Fritz had gone off shooting and had secured a good bag. While they had been thus variously employed, a troop of apes had visited the tent, and when they returned, they found the place ransacked and turned upside down. The provisions were eaten and gnawed, the potatoes thrown about, the milk drunk and spilt; every box had been peeped into, every pot and pan had been divested of its lid; the palisade round the hut had been partly destroyed, nothing had been left untouched. Industriously had the boys worked to repair the damage, and when we returned not a sign was to be seen of the disorder. No one would have guessed what had occurred from the delicious supper we were eating.

After matters had been again arranged, Fritz had gone down to the shore, and, among the rocks at Cape Disappointment, had discovered a young eaglet which Ernest declared to be a Malabar or Indian eagle; he was much pleased with his discovery, and I recommended him to bring the bird up and try to train it to hunt as a falcon.

"Look here, though, boys," said I, "you are now collecting a good many pets, and I am not going to have your mother troubled with the care of them all; each must look after his own, and if I find one neglected, whether beast or bird, I set it at liberty. Mark that and remember it!"

My wife looked greatly relieved at this announcement, and the boys promised to obey my directions. Before we retired for the night I prepared the buffalo meat I had brought. I lit a large fire of green wood, and in the smoke of this thoroughly dried both the tongue and steaks. We then properly secured all the animals, Jack took his little pet in his arms, and we lay down and were soon fast asleep.

At daybreak we were on foot, and began to prepare for a return to Falconhurst.

"You are not going to despise my sago, I hope," said Ernest; "you have no idea what a trouble it was to cut it down, and I have been thinking too, that, if we could but split the tree, we might make a couple of long useful troughs, which might, I think, be made to carry water from Jackal River to Tentholm. Is my plan worth consideration?"

"Indeed it is," I replied; "and at all events we must not abandon such a valuable prize as a sago palm. I would put off our departure for a day rather than leave it behind."

We went to the palm, and with the tools we had with us attempted to split the trunk. We first sawed off the upper end, and then with an ax and saw managed to insert a wedge. This accomplished, our task was less difficult, for with a heavy mallet we forced the wedge in further and further, until at length the trunk was split in twain. From one half of the trunk we then removed the pith, disengaging it, with difficulty, from the tough wood fibers; at each end, however, I left a portion of the pith untouched, thus forming a trough in which to work the sago.

"Now, boys," said I, when we had removed the pith from the other half of the trunk, "off with your coats and turn up your shirt-sleeves; I am going to teach you to knead."

They were all delighted, and even little Franz begged to be allowed to help. Ernest brought a couple of pitchers of water, and throwing it in amongst the pith, we set to work quite heartily. As the dough was formed and properly kneaded, I handed it to the mother, who spread it out on a cloth in the sun to dry. This new occupation kept us busy until the evening, and when it was at length completed we loaded the cart with the sago, a store of coconuts, and our other possessions, that we might be ready to start early on the following morning. As the sun rose above the horizon, we packed up our tent and set forth, a goodly caravan. I thought it unfair to the cow to make her drag such a load as we now had alone, and determined if possible to make the young buffalo take the place of our lost donkey: after some persuasion he consented, and soon put his strength to the work and brought the cart along famously. As we had the trough slung under the cart we had to choose the clearest possible route, avoiding anything like a thicket; we, therefore, could not pass directly by the candleberry and caoutchouc trees, and I sent Ernest and Jack aside to visit the store we had made on our outward journey.

They had not long been gone when I was alarmed by a most terrible noise, accompanied by the furious barking of the dogs and shouts from Jack and Ernest. Thinking that the boys had been attacked by some wild beasts, I ran to their assistance. A most ludicrous scene awaited me when I reached the spot. They were dancing and shouting round and round a grassy glade, and I as nearly as possible followed their example, for in the center, surrounded by a promising litter, lay our old sow, whose squeals, previously so alarming, were now subsiding into comfortable grunts of recognition. I did not join my boys in their triumphal dance, but I was nevertheless very much pleased at the sight of the flourishing family, and immediately returned to the cart to obtain biscuits and potatoes for the benefit of the happy mother. Jack and Ernest meanwhile pushed further on and brought back the sack of candleberries and the caoutchouc, and as we could not then take the sow with us, we left her alone with her family and proceeded to Falconhurst.

The animals were delighted to see us back again, and received us with manifestations of joy, but looked askance at the new pets. The eagle especially came in for shy glances, and promised to be no favorite. Fritz, however, determined that his pet should at present do no harm, secured him by the leg to a root of a fig tree and uncovered his eyes. In a moment the aspect of the bird was changed; with his sight returned all his savage instincts, he flapped his wings, raised his head, darted to the full length of his chain, and before any one could prevent him seized the unfortunate parrot, which stood near, and tore it to pieces. Fritz's anger rose at the sight, and he was about to put an end to the savage bird.

"Stop," said Ernest, "don't kill the poor creature, he is but following his natural instincts; give him to me, and I will tame him."

Fritz hesitated. "No, no," he said, "I don't want really to kill the bird, but I can't give him up; tell me how to tame him, and you shall have Master Knips."

"Very well," replied Ernest, "I will tell you my plan, and if it succeeds, I will accept Knips as a mark of your gratitude. Take a pipe and tobacco, and send the smoke all around his head, so that he must inhale it; by degrees he will become stupefied, and his savage nature from that moment subdued."

Fritz was rather inclined to ridicule the plan, but, knowing that Ernest generally had a good reason for anything of the sort that he proposed, he consented to make the attempt. He soon seated himself beneath the bird, who still struggled furiously, and puffed cloud after cloud upward, and as each cloud circled round the eagle's head he became quieter and quieter, until he sat quite still, gazing stupidly at the young smoker.

"Capital!" cried Fritz, as he hooded the bird, "capital, Ernest; Knips is yours."

CHAPTER VIII

Prop our young trees—A lecture on grafting—A new idea broached—Why should we not build stairs within the trunk of our tree?—Jack finds one objection—I make a beehive, and we drive the bees from the tree—Stair-making—Additions to our family of domestic animals—The education of the "pets"—Shoemaking—We lead water from the stream to Falconhurst—A strange animal approaches—Our old ass and his companion—The onager captured—Provisioning our winter quarters—Capture of ruffed grouse—We discover flax—The rainy season.

Next morning the boys and I started with the cart, laden with our bundles of bamboos, to attend to the avenue of fruit trees. The buffalo we left behind, for his services were not needed, and I wished the wound in his nostrils to become completely cicatrized before I again put him to work. We were not a moment too soon; many of the young trees, which before threatened to fall, had now fulfilled their promise, and were lying prostrate on the ground, others were bent, some few only remained erect. We raised the trees, and digging deeply at their roots, drove in stout bamboo props, to which we lashed them firmly with strong broad fibers.

"Papa," said Franz, as we were thus engaged, and he handed me the fibers as I required them, "are these wild or tame trees?"

"Oh, these are wild trees, most ferocious trees," laughed Jack, "and we are tying them up lest they should run away, and in a little while we will untie them and they will trot about after us and give us fruit wherever we go. Oh, we will tame them; they shall have a ring through their noses like the buffalo!"

"That's not true," replied Franz gravely, "but there *are* wild and tame trees, the wild ones grow out in the woods like the crab-apples, and the tame ones in the garden like the pears and peaches at home. Which are these, papa?"

"They are not wild," I replied, "but grafted or cultivated, or, as you call them, tame trees. No European tree bears good fruit until it is grafted!" I saw a puzzled look come over the little boy's face as he heard this new word, and I hastened to explain it. "Grafting," I continued, "is the process of inserting a slip or twig of a tree into what is called an eye; that is, a knot or hole in the branch of another. This twig or slip then grows and produces, not such fruit as the original stock would have borne, but such as the tree from which it was taken would have produced. Thus, if we have a sour crab tree, and an apple tree bearing fine ribston pippins, we would take a slip of the latter, insert it in an eye of the former, and in a year or two the branch which would then grow would be laden with good apples."

"But," asked Ernest, "where did the slips of good fruit trees come from, if none grow without grafting?"

"From foreign countries," I replied. "It is only in the cold climate of our part of the world that they require this grafting; in many parts of the world, in more southern latitudes than ours, the most luscious fruit trees are indigenous to the soil, and flourish and bear sweet, wholesome fruit, without the slightest care or attention being bestowed upon them; while in England and Germany, and even in France, these same trees require the utmost exertion of horticultural skill to make them bring forth any fruit whatever. Thus, when the Romans invaded England they found there nothing in the way of fruit trees but the crab-apple, nut bushes, and bramble bushes, but by grafting on these, fine apples, filberts, and raspberries were produced, and it was the same in our own dear Switzerland—all our fruit trees were imported."

"Were cherries, father? May we not even call cherries Swiss? I always thought they grew nowhere else."

"I am afraid we cannot even claim cherries as our own, not even the name of them; they are called cherries from Cerasus, a state of Pontus, in Asia, whence they were brought to Europe by Lucullus, a Roman general, about seventy years before Christ. Hazelnuts also came from Pontus; walnuts, again, came originally from Persia. As for grapes, they are of the greatest antiquity. We hear, if you remember, of Noah cultivating vines, and they have been brought from one place to another until they now are to be found in most parts of the civilized world."

"Do you think all these trees will grow?" asked Fritz, as we crossed Jackal River and entered our plantation at Tentholm: "here are lemons, pomegranates, pistachio nuts, and mulberries."

"I have little doubt of it," I replied, "we are evidently within the tropics, where such trees as these are sure to flourish. These pines, now, come from France, Spain, and Italy; the olives from Armenia and Palestine; the figs originally from the island of Chios; the peaches and apricots from Persia; plums from Damascus in Syria, and the pears of all sorts from Greece. However, if our countries have not been blessed in the same way with fruit, we have been given wisdom and skill, which has enabled us to import and cultivate the trees of other lands."

We thus talked and worked until every tree that required treatment was provided with a stout bamboo prop, and then, with appetites which a gourmand might well have envied, we returned to Falconhurst. I think the good mother was almost alarmed at the way we fell upon the corned beef and palm-cabbage she set before us, but at length these good things produced the desired effect, and one after another declared himself satisfied. As we sat reclining after our labor and digesting our dinner, we discussed the various projects we had in contemplation. "I wish," said my wife, "that you would invent some other plan for climbing to the nest above us; I think that the nest itself is perfect—I really wish for nothing better, but I should like to be able to get to it without scaling that dreadful ladder every time; could you not make a flight of steps to reach it?"

I carefully thought over the project, and turned over every plan for its accomplishment.

"It would be impossible, I am afraid," said I, "to make stairs outside, but within the trunk it might be done. More than once have I thought that this trunk might be hollow, or partly so, and if such be the case our task would be comparatively easy. Did you not tell me the other day that you noticed bees coming from a hole in the tree?"

"Oh, yes," said little Franz, "and I went to look at them and one flew right against my face and stung me, and I almost cried, but I didn't."

"Brave little boy," said I. "Well, now, if the trunk be sufficiently hollow to contain a swarm of bees, it may be, for all we can tell, hollow the greater part of its length, for like the willow in our own country it might draw all its nourishment through the bark, and in spite of its real unsoundness retain a flourishing appearance."

Master Jack, practical as usual, instantly sprang to his feet to put my conjecture to the proof. The rest followed his example, and they were all soon climbing about like squirrels, peeping into the hole, and tapping the wood to discover by sound how far down the cavity extended.

They forgot, in their eagerness, who were the tenants of this interesting trunk. They were soon reminded of it, however, for the bees, disturbed by this unusual noise, with an angry buzz burst out, and in an instant attacked the causers of the annoyance; they swarmed round them, stung them on the hands, face, and neck, settled in their hair, and pursued them as they ran to me for assistance. It was with difficulty that we got rid of the angry insects and were able to attend to the boys. Jack, who had been the first to reach the hole, had fared the worst, and was soon a most pitiable sight, his face swelled to an extraordinary degree, and it was only by the constant application of cold earth that the pain was alleviated. They were all eager to commence an organized attack upon the bees at once, but for an hour or more, by reason of their pain, they were unable to render me much assistance. In the meanwhile I made my arrangements. I first took a large calabash gourd, for I intended to make a beehive, that, when we had driven the insects from their present abode, we might not lose them entirely. The lower half of the gourd I flattened, I then cut an arched opening in the front for a doorway, made a straw roof as a protection from the rain and heat, and the little house was complete.

Nothing more, however, could then be done, for the irritated bees were still angrily buzzing round the tree. I waited till dark, and then, when all the bees had again returned to their trunk, with Fritz's assistance I carefully stopped up every hole in the tree with wet clay, that the bees might not issue forth next morning before we could begin operations. Very early were we up and at work. I first took a hollow cane, and inserted one end through the clay into the tree; down this tube with pipe and tobacco I smoked most furiously.

The humming and buzzing that went on within was tremendous; the bees evidently could not understand what was going to happen. I finished my first pipeful, and putting my thumb over the end of the cane, I gave the pipe to Fritz to refill. He did so and I again smoked. The buzzing was now becoming less noisy, and was subsiding into a mere murmur. By the time I had finished this second pipe all was still; the bees were stupefied.

"Now then, Fritz," said I, "quick, with a hammer and chisel, and stand here beside me."

He was up in a moment, and, together, we cut a small door by the side of the hole; this door, however, we did not take out, but we left it attached by one corner that it might be removed at a moment's notice; then giving the bees a final dose of tobacco smoke, we opened it.

Carefully but rapidly we removed the insects, as they clung

in clusters to the sides of the tree, and placed them in the hive prepared for their reception. As rapidly I then took every atom of wax and honey from their storehouse, and put it in a cask I had made ready for the purpose.

The bees were now safely removed from the trunk, but I could not tell whether, when they revived from their temporary stupor, they might not refuse to occupy the house with which I had presented them, and insist on returning to their old quarters. To prevent the possibility of this occurrence, I took a quantity of tobacco, and placing it upon a board nailed horizontally within the trunk, I lighted it and allowed it to burn slowly, that the fumes might fill the cavity. It was well I did so, for, as the bees returned to consciousness, they left their pretty hive and buzzed away to the trunk of the tree. They seemed astonished at finding this uninhabitable, and an immense deal of noisy humming ensued. Round and round they flew, backward and forward between the gourd and tree, now settling here and now there, until, at length, after due consideration, they took possession of the hive and abandoned their former habitation to us, the invaders of their territory. By the evening they were quite quiet, and we ventured to open the cask in which we had stored our plunder. We first separated the honey from the honeycomb and poured it off into jars and pots; the rest we then took and threw into a vessel of water placed over a slow fire. It soon boiled and the entire mass became fluid. This we placed in a clean canvas bag, and subjected to a heavy pressure. The honey was thus soon forced out, and we stored it in a cask, and, though not perhaps quite equal to the former batch in quality, it was yet capital. The wax that remained in the bag I also carefully stored, for I knew it would be of great use to me in the manufacture of candles. Then after a hard day's work we turned in.

The internal architecture of the tree had now to be attended to, and early the following morning we prepared for the laborious task. A door had first to be made, so at the base of the trunk we cut away the bark and formed an opening just the size of the door we had brought from the captain's cabin, and which, hinges and all, was ready to be hung. The clearing of the rotten wood from the center of the trunk occupied us some time, but at length we had the satisfaction of seeing it entirely accomplished, and, as we stood below, we could look up the trunk, which was like a great smooth funnel, and see the sky above. It was now ready for the staircase, and first we erected in the center a stout sapling to form an axis round which to build the spiral stairs; in this we cut notches to receive the steps, and corresponding notches in the tree itself to support the outer ends. The steps themselves we formed carefully and neatly of planks from the wreck, and clenched them firmly in their places with stout nails. Upward and upward we built, cutting windows in the trunk as we required, to admit light and air, until we were flush with the top of the center pole. On this pole we erected another to reach the top of the tree, and securing it firmly, built in the same way round it until we at length reached the level of the floor of the nest above. To make the ascent of the stairs perfectly easy we ran a handrail on either side, one round the center pillar, and the other following the curve of the trunk.

This task occupied us a whole month, and by the end of that period, so accustomed had we become to having a definite piece of work before us that we began to consider what other great alteration we should undertake. We were, however, of course not neglecting the details of our colonial establishment. There were all the animals to be attended to; the goats and sheep had both presented us with additions to our flock, and these frisky youngsters had to be seen after; to prevent them straying to any great distance—for we had no wish to lose them—we tied round their necks little bells, which we had found on board the wreck, and which would assist us to track them. Juno, too, had a fine litter of puppies, but, in spite of the entreaties of the children, I could not consent to keep more than two, and the rest disappeared in that mysterious way in which puppies and kittens are wont to leave the earth. To console the mother, as he said, but also, I suspect, to save himself considerable trouble, Jack placed his little jackal beside the remaining puppies, and, to his joy, found it readily adopted. The other pets were also flourishing, and were being usefully trained. The buffalo, after giving us much trouble, had now become perfectly domesticated, and was a very useful beast of burden, besides being a capital steed for the boys. They guided him by a bar thrust through the hole in his nose, which was now perfectly healed, and this served the purpose just as a bit in the mouth of a horse. I began his education by securing round him a broad girth of buffalo hide and fastening to it various articles, to accustom him to carrying a burden. By degrees he permitted this to be done without making the slightest resistance, and soon carried the paniers, before borne by the ass, readily and willingly.

I then made Master Knips sit upon his back and hold the reins I had prepared for him, that the animal might become accustomed to the feeling of a rider, and finally allowed Fritz himself to mount. The education of the eagle was not neglected. Fritz every day shot small birds for his food, and these he placed, sometimes between the wide-spreading horns of the buffalo or goat, and, sometimes upon the back of the great bustard, that he might become accustomed to pounce upon living prey. These lessons had their due effect, and the bird, having been taught to obey the voice and whistle of his master, he was soon allowed to bring down small birds upon the wing, when he stooped and struck his quarry in most sportsmanlike manner. We kept him well away from the poultry yard, lest his natural instincts should show themselves and he should put an untimely end to some of our feathered pets.

Neither was Master Knips allowed to remain idle, for Ernest, now that he was in his possession, wished to train him to be of some use. With Jack's help he made a little basket of rushes, which he so arranged with straps that it might be easily fitted on to the monkey's back. Thus equipped, he was taught to mount coconut palms and other lofty trees, and to bring down their fruit in the hamper.

Jack was not so successful in his educational attempts. Fangs, as he had christened his jackal, used his fangs, indeed, but only on his own account; nothing could persuade him that the animals he caught were not at once to be devoured, consequently poor Jack was never able to save from his jaws anything but the tattered skin of his prey. Not disheartened, however, he determined that Fangs could be trained, and that he would train him.

These, and such like employment, afforded us the rest and recreation we required while engaged in the laborious task of staircase building.

Among minor occupations, I applied myself to the improvement of our candles. Though the former batch had greatly delighted us at first, yet we were soon obliged to acknowledge that the light they gave was imperfect, and their appearance was unsightly; my wife, too, begged me to find some substitute for the threads of our cotton neckties, which I had previously used as wicks. To give the proper shape and smoothness to the candles, I determined to use the bamboo molds I had prepared. My first idea was to pour the wax in at the end of the mold, and then when the candles were cooled to slip them out; but I was soon convinced that this plan would not succeed. I therefore determined to divide the molds length-ways, and then having greased them well, we might pour the melted wax into the two halves bound tightly together, and so be able to take out the candles when cool without injuring them. The wicks were my next difficulty, and as the mother positively refused to allow us to devote our ties and handkerchiefs for the purpose, I took a piece of inflammable wood from a tree, a native of the Antilles, which I thought would serve our purpose; this I cut into long slips, and fixed in the centers of the molds. My wife, too, prepared some wicks from the fibers of the karata tree, which she declared would beat mine completely out of the field. We put them to the proof.

On a large fire we placed a pot, in which we prepared our wax mixture—half beeswax and half wax from the candleberries. The molds, carefully prepared—half with karata fiber, and half with wooden splint wicks—stood on their ends in a tub of cold water, ready to receive the wax. They were filled; the wax cooled;

the candles taken out and subjected to the criticism of all hands. When night drew on, they were formally tested. The decision was unanimous: neither gave such a good light as those with the cotton wicks; but even my wife declared that the light from mine was far preferable to that emitted by hers, for the former, though rather flaring, burned brilliantly, while the latter gave out such a feeble and flickering flame that it was almost useless.

I then turned shoemaker, for I had promised myself a pair of waterproof boots, and now I determined to make them.

Taking a pair of socks, I filled them with sand and then coated them over with a thin layer of clay to form a convenient mold; this was soon hardened in the sun, and was ready for use. Layer after layer of caoutchouc I brushed over it, allowing each layer to dry before the next was put on, until at length I considered that the shoes were of sufficient thickness. I dried them, broke out the clay, secured with nails a strip of buffalo hide to the soles, brushed that over with caoutchouc, and I had a pair of comfortable, durable, respectable-looking waterproof boots.

I was delighted; orders poured in from all sides, and soon every one in the family was likewise provided for.

One objection to Falconhurst was the absence of any spring close by, so that the boys were obliged to bring water daily from the stream; and this involving no little trouble, it was proposed that we should carry the water by pipes from the stream to our present residence. A dam had to be thrown across the river some way up stream, that the water might be raised to a sufficient height to run to Falconhurst. From the reservoir thus made we led the water down by pipes into the turtle's shell, which we placed near our dwelling, and from which the superfluous water flowed off through the hole made in it by Fritz's harpoon. This was an immense convenience, and we formally inaugurated the trough by washing therein a whole sack of potatoes. Thus day after day brought its own work, and day after day saw that work completed. We had no time to be idle, or to lament our separation from our fellow creatures.

One morning, as we were completing our spiral staircase, and giving it such finish as we were capable of, we were suddenly alarmed by hearing a most terrific noise, the roaring or bellowing of a wild beast; so strange a sound was it, that I could not imagine by what animal it was uttered.

Jack thought it perhaps a lion, Fritz hazarded a gorilla, while Ernest gave it as his opinion, and I thought it possible that he was right, that it was a hyena.

"Whatever it is," said I, "we must prepare to receive it; up with you all to the nest while I secure the door."

Then arming the dogs with their collars, I sent them out to protect the animals below, closed the door, and joined my family. Every gun was loaded, every eye was upon the watch. The sound drew nearer, and then all was still; nothing was to be seen. I determined to descend and reconnoiter, and Fritz and I carefully crept down; with our guns at full cock we glided among the trees; noiselessly and quickly we pushed on further and further; suddenly, close by, we heard the terrific sound again. Fritz raised his gun, but almost as quickly again dropped it, and burst into a hearty fit of laughter. There was no mistaking those dulcet tones—he-haw, he-haw, he-haw—resounded through the forest, and our ass, braying his approach right merrily, appeared in sight. To our surprise, however, our friend was not alone: behind him trotted another animal, an ass no doubt, but slim and graceful as a horse. We watched their movements anxiously.

"Fritz," I whispered, "that is an onager. Creep back to Falconhurst and bring me a piece of cord—quietly now!"

While he was gone, I cut a bamboo and split it half-way down to form a pair of pincers, which I knew would be of use to me should I get near the animal. Fritz soon returned with the cord, and I was glad to observe also brought some oats and salt. We made one end of the cord fast to a tree, and at the other end made a running noose. Silently we watched the animals as they approached, quietly browsing; Fritz then arose, holding in one hand the noose and in the other some oats and salt. The ass, seeing his favorite food thus held out, advanced to take it; Fritz allowed him to do so, and he was soon munching contentedly. The stranger, on seeing Fritz, started back; but finding her companion show no signs of alarm, was reassured, and soon approached sniffing, and was about to take some of the tempting food. In a moment the noose left Fritz's adroit hand and fell round her neck; with a single bound she sprang backward the full length of the cord, the noose drew tight, and she fell to the earth half strangled. I at once ran up, loosened the rope, and replaced it by a halter; and placing the pincers upon her nose, secured her by two cords fastened between two trees, and then left her to recover herself.

Every one hastened up to examine the beautiful animal as she rose to the ground and cast fiery glances around. She lashed out with her heels on every side; and, giving vent to angry snorts, struggled violently to get free. All her endeavors were vain: the cords were stout, and after a while she quieted down and stood exhausted and quivering. I then approached: she suffered me to lead her to the roots of our tree, which for the present formed our stables, and there I tied her up close to the donkey, who was likewise prevented from playing truant.

Next morning I found the onager after her night's rest as wild as ever, and as I looked at the handsome creature I almost despaired of ever taming her proud spirit. Every expedient was tried, and at length, when the animal was subdued by hunger, I thought I might venture to mount her; and having given her the strongest curb and shackled her feet I attempted to do so. She was as unruly as ever, and as a last expedient I resolved to adopt a plan which, though cruel, was I knew attended with wonderful success by the American Indians, by whom it is practiced. Watching a favorable opportunity, I sprang upon the onager's back, and seizing her long ear in my teeth, in spite of her kicking and plunging, bit it through. The result was marvelous, the animal ceased plunging, and, quivering violently, stood stock still. From that moment we were her masters, the children mounted her one after the other, and she carried them obediently and quietly. Proud, indeed, did I feel as I watched this animal, which naturalists and travelers have declared to be beyond the power of man to tame, guided hither and thither by my youngest son.

Additions to our poultry yard reminded me of the necessity of providing some substantial shelter for our animals before the rainy season came on; three broods of chickens had been successfully hatched, and the little creatures, forty in all, were my wife's pride and delight. We began by making a roof over the vaulted roots of our tree, forming the framework of bamboo canes, which we laid close together and bound tightly down; others we fixed below as supports. The interstices were filled up with clay and moss; and coating the whole over with a mixture of tar and lime-water, we obtained a firm balcony, and a capital roof impervious to the severest fall of rain. I ran a light rail round the balcony to give it a more ornamental appearance, and below divided the building into several compartments. Stables, poultry yard, hay and provision lofts, dairy, kitchen, larder, and dining-hall were united under one roof.

Our winter quarters were now completed, and we had but to store them with food. Day after day we worked, bringing in provisions of every description.

As we were one evening returning from gathering potatoes, it struck me that we should take in a store of acorns; and sending the two younger boys home with their mother and the cart, I took a large canvas bag, and with Fritz and Ernest, the former mounted on his onager, and the latter carrying his little favorite, Knips, made a detour toward the Acorn Wood.

We reached the spot, tied Lightfoot to a neighboring tree, and began rapidly to fill the sack. As we were thus engaged, Knips sprang suddenly into a bush close by, from which, a moment afterward, issued such strange cries that Ernest followed to see what could be the matter.

"Come!" he shouted; "come and help me! I've got a couple of birds and their eggs. Quick! Ruffed grouse!"

We hurried to the spot. There was Ernest with a fluttering, screaming bird in either hand; while, with his foot, he was endeavoring to prevent his greedy little monkey from seizing the eggs. We quickly tied the legs of the birds, and removing the eggs from the nest, placed them in Ernest's hat; while he gathered some of the long, broad grass, with which the nest was woven, and which grew luxuriantly around, for Franz to play at sword-drill with. We then loaded the onager with the acorns, and moved homeward. The eggs I covered carefully with dry moss, that they might be kept warm, and as soon as possible I handed them over to my wife, who managed the mother so cleverly that she induced her to return to the eggs, and in a few days, to our great delight, we had fifteen beautiful little Canadian chicks.

Franz was greatly pleased with the "swords" his brother brought him; but having no small companion on whom to exercise his valor, he amused himself for a short time in hewing down imaginary foes, and then cut the reeds in slips, and plaited them to form a whip for Lightfoot. The leaves seemed so pliable and strong that I examined them to see to what further use they might be put. Their tissue was composed of long silky fibers. A sudden thought struck me—this must be New Zealand flax. I could not rest till I had announced this invaluable discovery to my wife. She was no less delighted than I was.

"Bring me the leaves!" she exclaimed. "Oh, what a delightful discovery! No one shall now be clothed in rags; just make me a spindle, and you shall soon have shirts and stockings and trousers, all good homespun! Quick, Fritz, and bring your mother more leaves!"

We could not help smiling at her eager zeal; but Fritz and Ernest sprang on their steeds, and soon the onager and buffalo were galloping home again, each laden with a great bundle of flax. The boys dismounted and deposited their offering at their mother's feet.

"Capital!" she exclaimed. "I shall now show you that I am not at all behindhand in ingenuity. This must be retted, carded, spun, and woven, and then with scissors, needle, and thread I will make you any article of clothing you choose."

We decided that Flamingo Marsh would be the best spot for the operation of steeping or "retting" the flax, and next morning we set out thither with the cart drawn by the ass, and laden with the bundles, between which sat Franz and Knips, while the rest of us followed with spades and hatchets. I described to my boys as we went along the process of retting, and explained to them how steeping the flax leaves destroys the useless membrane, while the strong fibers remain.

As we were employed in making beds for the flax and placing it in them, we observed several nests of the flamingo. These are most curiously and skillfully made of glutinous clay, so strong that they can neither be overturned nor washed away. They are formed in the shape of blunted cones, and placed point downward; at the upper and broader end is built a little platform to contain the eggs, on which the female bird sits, with her long legs in the water on either side, until the little birds are hatched and can take to the water. For a fortnight we left the flax to steep, and then taking it out and drying it thoroughly in the sun, stored it for future use at Falconhurst.

Daily did we load our cart with provisions to be brought to our winter quarters: manioc, potatoes, coconuts, sweet acorns, sugarcanes, were all collected and stored in abundance—for grumbling thunder, lowering skies, and sharp showers warned us that we had no time to lose. Our corn was sowed, our animals housed, our provisions stored, when down came the rain.

To continue in our nest we found impossible, and we were obliged to retreat to the trunk, where we carried such of our domestic furniture as might have been injured by the damp. Our dwelling was indeed crowded: the animals and provisions were below, and our beds and household goods around us, hemmed us in on every side; by dint of patience and better packing, we obtained sufficient room to work and lie down in; by degrees, too, we became accustomed to the continual noise of the animals and the smell of the stables. The smoke from the fire, which we were occasionally obliged to light, was not agreeable; but in time even that seemed to become more bearable.

To make more space, we turned such animals as we had captured, and who therefore might be imagined to know how to shift for themselves, outside during the daytime, bringing them under the arched roofs only at night. To perform this duty Fritz and I used to sally forth every evening, and as regularly every evening did we return soaked to the skin. To obviate this, the mother, who feared these continual wettings might injure our health, contrived waterproofs: she brushed on several layers of caoutchouc over stout shirts, to which she attached hoods; she then fixed to these duck trousers, and thus prepared for each of us a complete waterproof suit, clad in which we might brave the severest rain.

In spite of our endeavors to keep ourselves busy, the time dragged heavily. Our mornings were occupied in tending the animals; the boys amused themselves with their pets, and assisted me in the manufacture of carding-combs and a spindle for the mother. The combs I made with nails, which I placed head downward on a sheet of tin about an inch wide; holding the nails in their proper position I poured solder round their heads to fix them to the tin, which I then folded down on either side of them to keep them perfectly firm. In the evening, when our room was illuminated with wax candles, I wrote a journal of all the events which had occurred since our arrival in this foreign land; and, while the mother was busy with her needle and Ernest making sketches of birds, beasts, and flowers with which he had met during the past months, Fritz and Jack taught little Franz to read.

Week after week rolled by. Week after week saw us still close prisoners. Incessant rain battered down above us; constant gloom hung over the desolate scene.

CHAPTER IX

Spring again—We begin to hew a cave—Jack makes a discovery—We drive the foul air from the cavern—The mother and her boys join us—We explore the cave—Fit it up as our winter quarters—The herring-bank—We catch seals—Fishing on a grand scale—Isinglass and caviare—We visit our plantations—An expedition to establish a colony—The building of "Woodlands"—Jack and Fritz return to Falconhurst for provisions—Ernest and I explore—A "beast with a bill"—We build a canoe—Franz undertakes the education of Grumble—We continue our work at the cave—Carpet making—Thanksgiving-day—A startling salute—Athletics and shooting—Prize giving—Manufacture of birdlime—Fritz and Jack ride off for caoutchouc—Shoot a crane and badger—Find "Woodlands" turned upside down by monkeys—Discover ginseng.

The winds at length were lulled, the sun shot his brilliant rays through the riven clouds, the rain ceased to fall—spring had come. No prisoners set at liberty could have felt more joy than we did as we stepped forth from our winter abode, refreshed our eyes with the pleasant verdure around us, and our ears with the merry songs of a thousand happy birds, and drank in the pure, balmy air of spring.

Our plantations were thriving vigorously. The seed we had sown was shooting through the moist earth. All nature was refreshed.

Our nest was our first care; filled with leaves and broken and torn by the wind, it looked indeed dilapidated. We worked hard, and in a few days it was again inhabitable. My wife begged that I would now start her with the flax, and as early as possible I built a drying-oven, and then prepared it for her use; I also, after some trouble, manufactured a beetle-reel and spinning-wheel, and she and Franz were soon hard at work, the little boy reeling off the thread his mother spun.

I was anxious to visit Tentholm, for I feared that much of our precious stores might have suffered. Fritz and I made an excursion thither. The damage done to Falconhurst was as nothing compared to the scene that awaited us. The tent was blown to the ground, the canvas torn to rags, the provisions soaked, and two casks of powder utterly destroyed. We immediately spread such things as we hoped yet to preserve in the sun to dry. The pinnace was safe, but our faithful tub-boat was dashed in pieces, and the irreparable damage we had sustained made me resolve to contrive some safer and more stable winter-quarters before the arrival of the next rainy season. Fritz proposed that we should hollow out a cave in the rock, and though the difficulties such an undertaking would present appeared almost insurmountable, I yet determined to make the attempt; we might not, I thought, hew out a cavern of sufficient size to serve as a room, but we might at least make a cellar for the more valuable and perishable of our stores.

Some days afterward we left Falconhurst with the cart laden with a cargo of spades, hammers, chisels, pickaxes, and crowbars, and began our undertaking. On the smooth face of the perpendicular rock I drew out in chalk the size of the proposed entrance, and then, with minds bent on success, we battered away. Six days of hard and incessant toil made but little impression; I do not think that the hole would have been a satisfactory shelter for even Master Knips; but we still did not despair, and were presently rewarded by coming to softer and more yielding substance; our work progressed, and our minds were relieved.

On the tenth day, as our persevering blows were falling heavily, Jack, who was working diligently with a hammer and crowbar, shouted:

"Gone, father! Fritz, my bar has gone through the mountain!"

"Run around and get it," laughed Fritz; "perhaps it has dropped into Europe—you must not lose a good crowbar."

"But, really, it is through; it went right through the rock; I heard it crash down inside. Oh, do come and see!" he shouted excitedly.

We sprang to his side, and I thrust the handle of my hammer into the hole he spoke of; it met with no opposition, I could turn it in any direction I chose. Fritz handed me a long pole; I tried the depth with that. Nothing could I feel. A thin wall, then, was all that intervened between us and a great cavern.

With a shout of joy, the boys battered vigorously at the rock; piece by piece fell, and soon the hole was large enough for us to enter. I stepped near the aperture, and was about to make a further examination, when a sudden rush of poisonous air turned me giddy, and shouting to my sons to stand off, I leaned against the rock.

When I came to myself I explained to them the danger of approaching any cavern or other place where the air has for a long time been stagnant. "Unless air is incessantly renewed it becomes vitiated," I said, "and fatal to those who breathe it. The safest way of restoring it to its original state is to subject it to the action of fire, a few handfuls of blazing hay thrown into this hole may, if the place is small, sufficiently purify the air within to allow us to enter without danger." We tried the experiment. The flame was extinguished the instant it entered. Though bundles of blazing grass were thrown in, no difference was made.

I saw that we must apply some more efficacious remedy, and sent the boys for a chest of signal rockets we had brought from the wreck. We let fly some dozens of these fiery serpents, which went whizzing in, and disappeared at apparently a vast distance from us. Some flew like radiant meteors round, lighted up the mighty circumference and displayed, as by a magician's wand, a sparkling, glittering roof. They looked like avenging dragons driving a foul, malignant fiend out of a beauteous palace.

We waited for a little while after these experiments, and I then again threw in lighted hay. It burned clearly; the air was purified.

Fritz and I enlarged the opening, while Jack, springing on his buffalo, thundered away to Falconhurst to bear the great and astonishing news to his mother.

Great must have been the effect of Jack's eloquence on those at home, for the timbers of the bridge were soon again resounding under the swift but heavy tramp of his steed; and he was quickly followed by the rest of our party in the cart.

All were in the highest state of excitement. Jack had stowed in the cart all the candles he could find, and we now, lighting these, shouldered our arms and entered. I led the way, sounding the ground as I advanced with a long pole, that we might not fall unexpectedly into any great hole or chasm. Silently we marched—the mother, the boys, and even the dogs seeming overawed with the grandeur and beauty of the scene. We were in a grotto of diamonds—a vast cave of glittering crystal: the candles reflected on the walls a golden light, bright as the stars of heaven, while great crystal pillars rose from the floor like mighty trees, mingling their branches high above us and drooping in hundreds of stalactites, which sparkled and glittered with all the colors of the rainbow.

The floor of this magnificent palace was formed of hard, dry sand, so dry that I saw at once that we might safely take up our abode therein, without the slightest fear of danger from damp.

From the appearance of the brilliant crystals round about us I suspected their nature.

I tasted a piece. This was a cavern of rock salt. There was no doubt about it—here was an unlimited supply of the best and purest salt! But one thing detracted from my entire satisfaction and delight—large crystals lay scattered here and there, which, detached from the roof, had fallen to the ground; this, if apt to recur, would keep us in constant peril. I examined some of the masses and discovered that they had been all recently separated, and therefore concluded that the concussion of the air occasioned by the rockets had caused their fall. To satisfy ourselves, however, that there were no more pieces tottering above us, we discharged our guns from the entrance, and watched the effect. Nothing more fell—our magnificent abode was safe.

We returned to Falconhurst with minds full of wonder at our new discovery, and plans for turning it to the best possible advantage.

Nothing was now talked of but the new house, how it should be arranged, how it should be fitted up. The safety and comfort of Falconhurst, which had at first seemed so great, now dwindled away in our opinion to nothing; it should be kept up, we decided, merely as a summer residence, while our cave should be formed into a winter house and impregnable castle. Our attention was now fully occupied with this new house. Light and air were to be admitted, so we hewed a row of windows in the rock, where we fitted the window cases we had brought from the officers' cabins. We brought the door, too, from Falconhurst, and fitted it in the aperture we had made. The opening in the trunk of the tree I determined to conceal with bark, as less likely to attract the notice of wild beasts or savages should they approach during our absence. The cave itself we divided into four parts: in front, a large compartment into which the door opened, subdivided into our sitting, eating, and sleeping apartments; the right-hand division containing our kitchen and workshop, and the left our stables; behind all this, in the dark recesses of the cave, was our storehouse and powder-magazine. Having already undergone one rainy season, we knew well its discomforts, and thought of many useful arrangements in the laying out of our dwelling. We did not intend to be again smoke-dried; we therefore contrived a properly built fire place and chimney; our stable arrangements, too, were better, and plenty of space was left in our workshop that we should not be hampered in even the most extensive operations.

Our frequent residence at Tentholm revealed to us several important advantages which we had not foreseen. Numbers of splendid turtles often came ashore to deposit their eggs in the sand, and their delicious flesh afforded us many a sumptuous meal. When more than one of these creatures appeared at a time, we used to cut off their retreat to the sea, and, turning them on their backs, fasten them to a stake driven in close by the water's edge, by a cord passed through a hole in their shell. We thus had fresh turtle continually within our reach; for the animals throve well thus secured, and appeared in as good condition, after having been kept thus for several weeks, as others when freshly caught. Lobsters, crabs, and mussels also abounded on the shore. But this was not all; an additional surprise awaited us.

As we were one morning approaching Tentholm, we were attracted by a most curious phenomenon. The waters out at sea appeared agitated by some unseen movement, and as they heaved and boiled, their surface, struck by the beams of the morning sun, seemed illuminated by flashes of fire. Over the water where this disturbance was taking place hovered hundreds of birds, screaming loudly, which ever and anon would dart downward, some plunging beneath the water, some skimming the surface. Then again they would rise and resume their harsh cries. The shining, sparkling mass then rolled onward, and approached in a direct line our bay, followed by the feathered flock above. We hurried down to the shore to further examine this strange sight.

I was convinced as we approached that it was a shoal or bank of herrings.

No sooner did I give utterance to my conjecture than I was assailed by a host of questions concerning this herring-bank, what it was, and what occasioned it.

"A herring-bank," I said, "is composed of an immense number of herrings swimming together. I can scarcely express to you the huge size of this living bank, which extends over a great area many fathoms deep. It is followed by numbers of great ravenous fish, who devour quantities of the herrings, while above hover birds, as you have just seen, ready to pounce down on stragglers near the top. To escape these enemies, the shoal makes for the nearest shore, and seeks safety in those shallows where the large fish cannot follow. But here it meets with a third great enemy. It may escape from the fish, and elude the vigilance of sharp-sighted birds, but from the ingenuity of man it can find no escape. In one year millions of these fish are caught, and yet the roes of only a small number would be sufficient to supply as many fish again."

Soon our fishery was in operation. Jack and Fritz stood in the water with baskets, and baled out the fish, as one bales water with a bucket, throwing them to us on the shore. As quickly as possible we cleaned them, and placed them in casks with salt, first a layer of salt, and then a layer of herrings, and so on, until we had ready many casks of pickled fish.

As the barrels were filled, we closed them carefully, and rolled them away to the cool vaults at the back of our cave.

Our good fortune, however, was not to end here. A day after the herring fishery was over, and the shoal had left our bay, a great number of seals appeared, attracted by the refuse of the herrings which we had thrown into the sea. Though I feared they would not be suitable for our table, we yet secured a score or two for the sake of their skins and fat. The skins we drew carefully off for harness and clothing, and the fat we boiled down for oil, which we put aside in casks for tanning, soap-making, and burning in lamps.

These occupations interfered for some time with our work at Rock House; but as soon as possible we again returned to our labor with renewed vigor.

I had noticed that the salt crystals had for their base a species of gypsum, which I knew might be made of great service to us in our building operations as plaster.

As an experiment, I broke off some pieces, and, after subjecting them to great heat, reduced them to powder. The plaster this formed with water was smooth and white, and as I had then no particular use to which I might put it, I plastered over some of the herring casks, that I might be perfectly certain that all air was excluded. The remainder of the casks I left as they were, for I presently intended to preserve their contents by smoking. To do this, the boys and I built a small hut of reeds and branches, and then we strung our herrings on lines across the roof. On the floor we lit a great fire of brushwood and moss, which threw out a dense smoke, curling in volumes round the fish, and they in a few days seemed perfectly cured.

About a month after the appearance of the herrings, we were favored by a visit from other shoals of fish. Jack espied them first, and called to us that a lot of young whales were off the coast. We ran down and discovered the bay apparently swarming with great sturgeons, salmon, and trout, all making for the mouth of Jackal River, that they might ascend it and deposit their spawn among the stones.

Jack was delighted at his discovery.

"Here are proper fish!" he exclaimed; "none of your paltry fry. How do you preserve these sorts of fish? Potted, salted, or smoked?"

"Not so fast," said I, "not so fast; tell me how they are to be caught, and I will tell you how they are to be cooked."

"Oh! I'll catch them fast enough," he replied, and darted off to Rock House.

While I was still puzzling my brains as to how I should set to work, he returned with his fishing apparatus in hand; a bow and arrow, and a ball of twine.

At the arrow-head he had fastened a barbed spike, and had secured the arrow to the end of the string. Armed with this weapon, he advanced to the river's edge.

His arrow flew from the bow, and, to my surprise, struck one of the largest fish in the side.

"Help, father, help!" he cried, as the great fish darted off, carrying arrow and all with it; "help! Or he will pull me into the water."

I ran to his assistance, and together we struggled with the finny monster. He pulled tremendously, and lashed the water around him; but we held the cord fast, and he had no chance of escape. Weaker and weaker grew his struggles, and, at length, exhausted by his exertions and loss of blood, he allowed us to draw him ashore.

He was a noble prize, and Fritz and Ernest, who came up just as we completed his capture, were quite envious of Jack's success. Not to be behindhand, they eagerly rushed off for weapons themselves.

We were soon all in the water, Fritz with a harpoon, Ernest with a rod and line, and I myself, armed, like Neptune, with an iron trident, or more properly speaking, perhaps, a pitchfork. Soon the shore was strewn with a goodly number of the finest fish—monster after monster we drew to land. At length Fritz, after harpooning a great sturgeon full eight feet long, could not get the fish ashore; we all went to his assistance, but our united efforts were unavailing.

"The buffalo!" proposed my wife, and off went Jack for Storm. Storm was harnessed to the harpoon rope, and soon the monstrous fish lay panting on the sand.

We at length, when we had captured as many fish as we could possibly utilize, set about cleaning and preparing their flesh. Some we salted, some we dried like the herrings, some we treated like the tunny of the Mediterranean—we prepared them in oil. Of the roe of the sturgeon I decided to form caviare, the great Russian dish. I removed from it all the membranes by which it is surrounded, washed it in vinegar, salted it, pressed out all the moisture caused by the wet-absorbing properties of the salt, packed it in small barrels, and stowed it away in our storehouse.

I knew that of the sturgeon's bladder the best isinglass is made, so carefully collecting the air-bladders from all those we had killed, I washed them and hung them up to stiffen. The outer coat or membrane I then peeled off, cutting the remainder into strips, technically called staples. These staples I placed in an iron pot over the fire, and when they had been reduced to a proper consistency I strained off the glue through a clean cloth, and spread it out on a slab of stone in thin layers, letting them remain until they were dry. The substance I thus obtained was beautifully transparent, and promised to serve as an excellent substitute for glass in our window-frames.

Fortunately, in this beautiful climate little or no attention was necessary to the kitchen garden, the seeds sprang up and nourished without apparently the slightest regard for the time or season of the year. Peas, beans, wheat, barley, rye, and Indian corn seemed constantly ripe, while cucumbers, melons, and all sorts of other vegetables grew luxuriantly. The success of our garden at Tentholm encouraged me to hope that my experiment at Falconhurst had not failed, and one morning we started to visit the spot.

As we passed by the field from which the potatoes had been dug, we found it covered with barley, wheat, rye, and peas in profusion.

I turned to the mother in amazement.

"Where has this fine crop sprung from?" said I.

"From the earth," she replied laughing, "where Franz and I sowed the seed I brought from the wreck. The ground was ready tilled by you and the boys; all we had to do was to scatter the seed."

I was delighted at the sight, and it augured well, I thought, for the success of my maize plantation. We hurried to the field. The crop had indeed grown well, and, what was more, appeared to be duly appreciated. A tremendous flock of feathered thieves rose as we approached. Among them Fritz espied a few ruffed grouse, and, quick as thought, unhooding his eagle, he started him off in chase, then sprung on his onager and followed at full gallop. His noble bird marked out the finest grouse, and, soaring high above it, stooped and bore his prey to the ground. Fritz was close at hand, and springing through the bushes he saved the bird from death, hooded the eagle's eyes, and returned triumphantly. Jack had not stood idle, for slipping his pet, Fangs, he had started him among some quails who remained upon the field, and to my surprise the jackal secured some dozen of the birds, bringing them faithfully to his master's feet.

We then turned our steps toward Falconhurst, where we were refreshed by a most delicious drink the mother prepared for us: the stems of the young Indian corn, crushed, strained, and mixed with water and the juice of the sugarcane.

We then made preparations for an excursion the following day, for I wished to establish a sort of semi-civilized farm at some distance from Falconhurst, where we might place some of our animals, which had become too numerous with our limited means to supply them with food. In the large cart, to which we harnessed the buffalo, cow, and ass, we placed a dozen fowls, four young pigs, two couple of sheep, and as many goats, and a pair of hens and one cock grouse. Fritz led the way on his onager, and by a new track we forced a passage through the woods and tall grasses toward Cape Disappointment.

The difficult march was at length over, and we emerged from the forest upon a large plain covered with curious little bushes; the branches of these little shrubs and the ground about them were covered with pure white flakes.

"Snow! Snow!" exclaimed Franz. "Oh, mother, come down from the cart and play snowballs. This is jolly; much better than the ugly rain."

I was not surprised at the boy's mistake, for indeed the flakes did look like snow; but before I could express my opinion, Fritz declared that the plant must be a kind of dwarf cotton tree. We approached nearer and found he was right—soft fine wool enclosed in pods, and still hanging on the bushes or lying on the ground, abounded in every direction. We had indeed discovered this valuable plant. The mother was charmed; and gathering a great quantity in three capacious bags, we resumed our journey.

Crossing the cotton field we ascended a pretty wooded hill. The view from the summit was glorious: luxuriant grass at our feet stretching down the hillside, dotted here and there with shady trees, among which gushed down a sparkling brook, while below lay the rich green forest, with the sea beyond.

What better situation could we hope to find for our new farm? Pasture, water, shade, and shelter, all were here.

We pitched our tent, built our fireplace, and leaving the mother to prepare our repast, Fritz and I selected a spot for the erection of our shed. We soon found a group of trees so situated that the trunks would serve as posts for our intended building. Thither we carried all our tools, and then, as the day was far advanced, enjoyed our supper, and lay down upon most comfortable beds, which the mother had prepared for us with the cotton.

The group of trees we had selected was exactly suited to our purpose, for it formed a regular rectilinear figure, the greatest side of which faced the sea. I cut deep mortices in the trunks about ten feet from the ground, and again ten feet higher up to form a second story. In these mortices I inserted beams, thus forming a framework for my building, and then, making a roof of laths, I overlaid it with bark, which I stripped from a neighboring tree, and fixed with acacia thorns, and which would effectually shoot off any amount of rain.

While clearing up the scraps of bark and other rubbish for fuel for our fire, I noticed a peculiar smell, and stooping down I picked up pieces of the bark, some of which, to my great surprise, I found was that of the terebinth tree, and the rest that of the American fir. The goats, too, made an important discovery among the same heap, for we found them busily rooting out pieces of cinnamon, a most delicious and aromatic spice.

"From the fir," said I to the boys, "we get turpentine and tar, and thus it is that the fir tree becomes such a valuable article of commerce. So we may look forward to preparing pitch for our yacht, with tar and oil, you know, and cart-grease, too, with tar and fat. I do not know that you will equally appreciate the terebinth tree. A gum issues from incisions in the bark which hardens in the sun, and becomes as transparent as amber; when burned it gives forth a most delicious perfume, and when dissolved in spirits of wine, forms a beautiful transparent varnish."

The completion of our new farmhouse occupied us several days; we wove strong lianas and other creepers together to form the walls to the height of about six feet; the rest, up to the roof, we formed merely of a latticework of laths to admit both air and light. Within we divided the house into three parts; one subdivided into stalls for the animals; a second fitted with perches for the birds, and a third, simply furnished with a rough table and benches, to serve as a sleeping apartment for ourselves, when we should find it necessary to pay the place a visit. In a short time the dwelling was most comfortably arranged, and as we daily filled the feeding troughs with the food the animals best liked, they showed no inclination to desert the spot we had chosen for them.

Yet, hard as we had worked, we found that the provisions we had brought with us would be exhausted before we could hope to be able to leave the farm. I therefore dispatched Jack and Fritz for fresh supplies.

During their absence, Ernest and I made a short excursion in the neighborhood, that we might know more exactly the character of the country near our farm.

Passing over a brook which flowed toward the wall of rocks, we reached a large marsh, and as we walked round it, I noticed with delight that it was covered with the rice plant growing wild in the greatest profusion. Here and there only were there any ripe plants, and from these rose a number of ruffed grouse, at which both Ernest and I let fly. Two fell, and Fangs, who was with us, brought them to our feet. As we advanced, Knips skipped from the back of his steed Juno and began to regale himself on some fruit, at a short distance off; we followed the little animal and found him devouring delicious strawberries. Having enjoyed the fruit ourselves, we filled the hamper Knips always carried, and secured the fruit from his pilfering paws with leaves fixed firmly down.

I then took a sample of the rice seeds to show the mother, and we continued our journey.

Presently we reached the borders of the pretty lake which we had seen beyond the swamp. The nearer aspect of its calm blue waters greatly charmed us, and still more so the sight of numbers of black swans, disporting themselves on the glassy surface, in which their stately forms and graceful movements were reflected as in a mirror. It was delightful to watch these splendid birds, old and young, swimming together in the peaceful enjoyment of life, seeking their food, and pursuing one another playfully in the water.

I could not think of breaking in upon their happy, beautiful existence by firing among them, but our dog Juno was by no means so considerate; for all at once I heard a plunge, and saw her drag out of the water a most peculiar-looking creature, something like a small otter, but not above twenty-two inches in length, which she would have torn to pieces had we not hurried up and taken it from her.

This curious little animal was of a soft, dark brown color, the fur being of a lighter shade under the body; its feet were furnished with large claws, and also completely webbed, the head small, with deeply set eyes and ears, and terminating in a broad flat bill like that of a duck.

This singularity seemed to us so droll that we both laughed heartily, feeling at the same time much puzzled to know what sort of animal it could possibly be. For want of a better, we gave it the name of the "Beast with a Bill," and Ernest willingly undertook to carry it, that it might be stuffed and kept as a curiosity.

After this we returned to the farm, thinking our messengers might soon arrive, and sure enough, in about a quarter of an hour Fritz and Jack made their appearance at a brisk trot, and gave a circumstantial account of their mission.

I was pleased to see that they had fulfilled their orders intelligently, carrying out my intentions in the spirit and not blindly to the letter.

Next morning we quitted the farm (which we named Woodlands), after providing amply for the wants of the animals, sheep, goats, and poultry which we left there.

Shortly afterward, on entering a wood, we found it tenanted by an enormous number of apes, who instantly assailed us, with showers of fir-cones, uttering hideous and angry cries, and effectually checking our progress, until we put them to flight by a couple of shots, which not a little astonished their weak minds.

Fritz picked up some of their missiles, and, showing them to me, I recognized the cone of the stone-pine.

"By all means gather some of these cones, boys," said I; "you will find the kernel has a pleasant taste, like almonds, and from it we can, by pressing, obtain an excellent oil. Therefore I should like to carry some home with us."

A hill, which seemed to promise a good view from its summit, next attracted my notice, and, on climbing it, we were more than repaid for the exertion by the extensive and beautiful prospect which lay spread before our eyes. The situation altogether was so agreeable, that here also I resolved to make a settlement, to be visited occasionally, and, after resting awhile and talking the matter over, we set to work to build a cottage such as we had lately finished at Woodlands. Our experience there enabled us to proceed quickly with the work, and in a few days the rustic abode was completed, and received, by Ernest's choice, the grand name of Prospect Hill.

My chief object in undertaking this expedition had been to discover some tree from whose bark I could hope to make a useful light boat or canoe. Hitherto I had met with none at all fit for my purpose, but, not despairing of success, I began, when the cottage was built, to examine carefully the surrounding woods, and, after considerable trouble, came upon two magnificent, tall, straight trees, the bark of which seemed something like that of the birch. Selecting one whose trunk was, to a great height, free from branches, we attached to one of the lower of the boughs the rope ladder we had with us, and Fritz, ascending it, cut the bark through in a circle; I did the same at the foot of the tree, and then, from between the circle we took a narrow perpendicular slip of bark entirely out, so that we could introduce the proper tools by which gradually to loosen and raise the main part, so as finally to separate it from the tree uninjured and entire. This we found possible, because the bark was moist and flexible. Great care and exertion was necessary, as the bark became detached, to support it, until the whole was ready to be let gently down upon the grass. This seemed a great achievement; but our work was by no means ended, nor could we venture to desist from it until, while the material was soft and pliable, we had formed it into the shape we desired for the canoe.

In order to do this, I cut a long triangular piece out of each end of the roll, and, placing the sloping parts one over the other, I drew the ends into a pointed form and secured them with pegs and glue.

This successful proceeding had, however, widened the boat, and made it too flat in the middle, so that it was necessary to put ropes round it, and tighten them until the proper shape was restored before we could allow it to dry in the sun.

This being all I could do without a greater variety of tools, I determined to complete my work in a more convenient situation, and forthwith dispatched Fritz and Jack with orders to bring the sledge (which now ran on wheels taken from gun-carriages) that the canoe might be transported direct to the vicinity of the harbor at Tentholm.

During their absence I fortunately found some wood naturally curved, just suited for ribs to support and strengthen the sides of the boat.

When the two lads returned with the sledge, it was time to rest for the night; but with early dawn we were again busily at work.

The sledge was loaded with the new boat, and everything else we could pack into it, and we turned our steps homeward, finding the greatest difficulty, however, in getting our vehicle through the woods. We crossed the bamboo swamp, where I cut a fine mast for my boat, and came at length to a small opening or defile in the ridge of rocks, where a little torrent rushed from its source down into the larger stream beyond; here we determined to make a halt, in order to erect a great earth wall across the narrow gorge, which, being thickly planted with prickly pear, Indian fig, and every thorny bush we could find, would in time form an effectual barrier against the intrusion of wild beasts, the cliffs being, to the best of our belief, in every other part inaccessible. For our own convenience we retained a small winding-path through this barrier, concealing and defending it with piles of branches and thorns, and also we contrived a light drawbridge over the stream, so that we rendered the pass altogether a very strong position, should we ever have to act on the defensive.

This work occupied two days, and continuing on our way, we were glad to rest at Falconhurst before arriving (quite tired and worn out) at Tentholm.

It took some time to recruit our strength after this long and fatiguing expedition, and then we vigorously resumed the task of finishing the canoe. The arrangements, I flattered myself, were carried out in a manner quite worthy of a ship builder; a mast, sails, and paddles were fitted, but my final touch, although I prized it highly and considered it a grand and original idea, would no doubt have excited only ridicule and contempt had it been seen by a naval man. My contrivance was this: I had a couple of large air-tight bags made of the skins of the dog-fish, well tarred and pitched, inflated, and made fast on each side of the boat, just above the level of the water. These floats, however much she might be loaded, would effectually prevent either the sinking or capsizing of my craft.

I may as well relate in this place what I omitted at the time of its occurrence. During the rainy season our cow presented us with a bull-calf, and that there might never be any difficulty in managing him, I at a very early age pierced his nose and placed a short stick in it, to be exchanged for a ring when he was old enough. The question now came to be, who should be his master, and to what should we train him?

"Why not teach him," said Fritz, "to fight the wild animals, and defend us, like the fighting bulls of the Hottentots? That would be really useful!"

"I am sure I should much prefer a gentle bull to a fighting one!" exclaimed his mother; "but do you mean to say tame oxen can be taught to act rationally on the defensive?"

"I can but repeat what I have heard or read," replied I, as regards the race of Hottentots who inhabit the south of Africa, among all sorts of wild and ferocious animals.

"The wealth of these people consists solely in their flocks and herds, and, for their protection, they train their bulls to act as guards.

"These courageous animals keep the rest from straying away, and when danger threatens, they give instant notice of it, drive the herd together in a mass, the calves and young cows being placed in the center; around them the bulls and strong oxen make a formidable circle with their horned heads turned to the front, offering determined resistance to the fiercest foe.

"These fighting bulls will even sometimes rush with dreadful bellowing to meet the enemy; and should it be a mighty lion or other strong and daring monster, sacrifice their own lives in defense of the herd.

"It is said that formerly, when Hottentot tribes made war on one another, it was not unusual to place a troop of these stout-hearted warriors in the van of the little army, when their heroism led to decisive victory on one side or the other.

"But," continued I, "although I can see you are all delighted with my description of these fine, warlike animals, I think we had better train this youngster to be a peaceable bull. Who is to have charge of him?"

Ernest thought it would be more amusing to train his monkey than a calf. Jack, with the buffalo and his hunting jackal, had quite enough on his hands. Fritz was content with the onager. Their mother was voted mistress of the old gray donkey. And I myself being superintendent-in-chief of the whole establishment of animals, there remained only little Franz to whose special care the calf could be committed.

"What say you, my boy—will you undertake to look after this little fellow?"

"Oh, yes, father!" he replied. "Once you told me about a strong man, I think his name was Milo, and he had a tiny calf, and he used to carry it about everywhere. It grew bigger and bigger, but still he carried it often, till at last he grew so strong that when it was quite a great big ox, he could lift it as easily as ever. And so, you see, if I take care of our wee calf and teach it to do what I like, perhaps when it grows big I shall still be able to manage it, and then—oh, papa—do you think I might ride upon it?"

I smiled at the child's simplicity, and his funny application of the story of Milo of Cortona.

"The calf shall be yours, my boy. Make him as tame as you can, and we will see about letting you mount him some day; but remember, he will be a great bull long before you are nearly a man. Now, what will you call him?"

"Shall I call him Grumble, father? Hear what a low muttering noise he makes!"

"Grumble will do famously."

"Grumble, Grumble. Oh, it beats your buffalo's name hollow, Jack!"

"Not a bit," said he; "why, you can't compare the two names. Fancy mother saying, 'Here comes Franz on Grumble, but Jack *riding on the Storm*.' Oh, it sounds sublime!"

We named the two puppies Bruno and Fawn, and so ended this important domestic business.

For two months we worked steadily at our salt-cave, in order to complete the necessary arrangement of partition walls, so as to put the rooms and stalls for the animals in comfortable order for the next long rainy season, during which time, when other work would be at a standstill, we could carry on many minor details for the improvement of the abode.

We leveled the floors first with clay; then spread gravel mixed with melted gypsum over that, producing a smooth, hard surface, which did very well for most of the apartments; but I was ambitious of having one or two carpets, and set about making a kind of felt in the following way:

I spread out a large piece of sailcloth, and covered it equally all over with a strong liquid, made of glue and isinglass, which saturated it thoroughly. On it we then laid wool and hair from the sheep and goats, which had been carefully cleaned and prepared, and rolled and beat it until it adhered tolerably smoothly to the cloth. Finally it became, when perfectly dry, a covering for the floor of our sitting room by no means to be despised.

One morning, just after these labors at the salt-cave were

completed, happening to awake unusually early, I turned my thoughts, as I lay waiting for sunrise, to considering what length of time we had now passed on this coast, and discovered, to my surprise, that the very next day would be the anniversary of our escape from the wreck. My heart swelled with gratitude to the gracious God, who had then granted us deliverance, and ever since had loaded us with benefits; and I resolved to set tomorrow apart as a day of thanksgiving, in joyful celebration of the occasion.

My mind was full of indefinite plans when I rose, and the day's work began as usual. I took care that everything should be cleaned, cleared, and set in order both outside and inside our dwelling; none, however, suspecting that there was any particular object in view. Other more private preparations I also made for the next day. At supper I made the coming event known to the assembled family.

"Good people, do you know that tomorrow is a very great and important day? We shall have to keep it in honor of our merciful escape to this land, and call it Thanksgiving Day."

Every one was surprised to hear that we had already been twelve months in the country—indeed, my wife believed I might be mistaken, until I showed her how I had calculated regularly ever since the 31st of January, on which day we were wrecked, by marking off in my almanac the Sundays as they arrived for the remaining eleven months of that year.

"Since then," I added, "I have counted thirty-one days. This is the 1st of February. We landed on the 2d, therefore tomorrow is the anniversary of the day of our escape. As my bookseller has not sent me an almanac for the present year, we must henceforth reckon for ourselves."

"Oh, that will be good fun for us," said Ernest. "We must have a long stick, like Robinson Crusoe, and cut a notch in it every day, and count them up every now and then, to see how the weeks and months and years go by."

"That is all very well, if you know for certain the number of days in each month, and in the year. What do you say, Ernest?"

"The year contains 365 days, 5 hours, 48 minutes, and 45 seconds," returned he promptly.

"Perfectly correct!" said I, smiling; "but you would get in a mess with those spare hours, minutes, and seconds in a year or two, wouldn't you?"

"Not at all! Every four years I would add them all together, make a day, stick it into February, and call that year leap year."

"Well done, Professor Ernest! We must elect you astronomer royal in this our kingdom, and let you superintend and regulate everything connected with the lapse of time, clocks and watches included."

Before they went to sleep, I could hear my boys whispering among themselves, about "father's mysterious allusions" to next day's festival and rejoicings; but I offered no explanations, and went to sleep, little guessing that the rogues had laid a counter-plot, far more surprising than my simple plan for their diversion.

Nothing less than roar of artillery startled me from sleep at daybreak next morning. I sprang up and found my wife as much alarmed as I was by the noise, otherwise I should have been inclined to believe it fancy.

"Fritz! Dress quickly and come with me!" cried I, turning to his hammock. Lo, it was empty! Neither he nor Jack were to be seen.

Altogether bewildered, I was hastily dressing, when their voices were heard, and they rushed in shouting:

"Hurrah! Didn't we rouse you with a right good thundering salute?"

But perceiving at a glance that we had been seriously alarmed, Fritz hastened to apologize for the thoughtless way in which they had sought to do honor to the Day of Thanksgiving, without considering that an unexpected cannon-shot would startle us unpleasantly from our slumbers.

We readily forgave the authors of our alarm, in consideration of the good intention which had prompted the deed, and, satisfied that the day had at least been duly inaugurated, we all went quietly to breakfast.

Afterward we sat together for a long time, enjoying the calm beauty of the morning, and talking of all that had taken place on the memorable days of the storm a year ago; for I desired that the awful events of that time should live in the remembrance of my children with a deepening sense of gratitude for our deliverance. Therefore I read aloud passages from my journal, as well as many beautiful verses from the Psalms, expressive of joyful praise and thanksgiving, so that even the youngest among us was impressed and solemnized at the recollections of escape from a terrible death, and also led to bless and praise the name of the Lord our Deliverer.

Dinner followed shortly after this happy service, and I then announced for the afternoon a "Grand Display of Athletic Sports," in which I and my wife were to be spectators and judges.

"Father, what a grand idea!"

"Oh, how jolly! Are we to run races?"

"And prizes! Will there be prizes, father?"

"The judges offer prizes for competition in every sort of manly exercise," replied I. "Shooting, running, riding, leaping, climbing, swimming; we will have an exhibition of your skill in all. Now for it!"

"Trumpeters! Sound for the opening of the lists."

Uttering these last words in a stentorian voice and wildly waving my arms toward a shady spot, where the ducks and geese were quietly resting, had the absurd effect I intended.

Up they all started in a fright, gabbling and quacking loudly, to the infinite amusement of the children, who began to bustle about in eager preparations for the contest, and begging to know with what they were to begin.

"Let us have shooting first, and the rest when the heat of the day declines. Here is a mark I have got ready for you," said I, producing a board roughly shaped like a kangaroo, and of about the size of one. This target was admired, but Jack could not rest satisfied till he had added ears, and a long leather strap for a tail.

It was then fixed in the attitude most characteristic of the creature, and the distance for firing measured off. Each of the three competitors was to fire twice.

Fritz hit the kangaroo's head each time; Ernest hit the body once; and Jack, by a lucky chance, shot the ears clean away from the head, which feat raised a shout of laughter.

A second trial with pistols ensued, in which Fritz again came off victor.

Then desiring the competitors to load with small shot, I threw a little board as high as I possibly could up in the air, each in turn aiming at and endeavoring to hit it before it touched the ground.

In this I found to my surprise that the sedate Ernest succeeded quite as well as his more impetuous brother Fritz.

As for Jack, his flying board escaped wholly uninjured.

After this followed archery, which I liked to encourage, foreseeing that a time might come when ammunition would fail; and in this practice I saw with pleasure that my elder sons were really skillful, while even little Franz acquitted himself well.

A pause ensued, and then I started a running match.

Fritz, Ernest, and Jack were to run to Falconhurst, by the most direct path. The first to reach the tree was to bring me, in proof of his success, a penknife I had accidentally left on the table in my sleeping room.

At a given signal, away went the racers in fine style. Fritz and Jack, putting forth all their powers, took the lead at once, running in advance of Ernest, who started at a good, steady pace, which I predicted he would be better able to maintain than such a furious rate as his brothers.

But long before we expected to see them back, a tremendous noise of galloping caused us to look with surprise toward the bridge, and Jack made his appearance, thundering along on his buffalo, with the onager and the donkey tearing after him riderless, and the whole party in the wildest spirits.

"Hullo!" cried I, "what sort of footrace do you call this, Master Jack?"

He shouted merrily as he dashed up to us; then flinging himself off and saluting us in a playful way:

"I very soon saw," said he, "that I hadn't a chance; so renouncing all idea of the prize, I caught Storm, and made him gallop home with me, to be in time to see the others come puffing in. Lightfoot and old Grizzle chose to join me—I never invited them!"

By and by the other boys arrived, Ernest holding up the knife in token of being the winner; and after hearing all particulars about the running, and that he had reached Falconhurst two minutes before Fritz, we proceeded to test the climbing powers of the youthful athletes.

In this exercise Jack performed wonders. He ascended with remarkable agility the highest palms whose stems he could clasp. And when he put on his shark-skin buskins, which enabled him to take firm hold of larger trees, he played antics like a squirrel or a monkey, peeping and grinning at us, at first on one side of the stem, and then on the other, in a most diverting way.

Fritz and Ernest climbed well, but could not come near the grace and skill of their active and lively young brother.

Riding followed, and marvelous feats were performed, Fritz and Jack proving themselves very equal in their management of their different steeds.

I thought the riding was over, when little Franz appeared from the stable in the cave, leading young Grumble, the bull-calf, with a neat saddle of kangaroo hide, and a bridle passed through his nose ring.

The child saluted us with a pretty little air of confidence, exclaiming:

"Now, most learned judges, prepare to see something quite new and wonderful! The great bull-tamer, Milo of Cortona, desires the honor of exhibiting before you."

Then taking a whip and holding the end of a long cord, he made the animal, at the word of command, walk, trot, and gallop in a circle round him.

He afterward mounted, and showed off Grumble's somewhat awkward paces.

The sports were concluded by swimming matches, and the competitors found a plunge in salt water very refreshing after their varied exertions.

Fritz showed himself a master in the art. At home in the element, no moment betokened either exertion or weariness.

Ernest exhibited too much anxiety and effort, while Jack was far too violent and hasty, and soon became exhausted.

Franz gave token of future skill.

By this time, as it was getting late, we returned to our dwelling, the mother having preceded us in order to make arrangements for the ceremony of prize-giving.

We found her seated in great state, with the prizes set out by her side.

The boys marched in pretending to play various instruments in imitation of a band, and then all four, bowing respectfully, stood before her, like the victors in a tournament of old, awaiting the reward of valor from the Queen of Beauty, which she bestowed with a few words of praise and encouragement.

Fritz, to his immense delight, received, as the prize for shooting and swimming, a splendid double-barreled rifle, and a beautiful hunting-knife.

To Ernest, as winner of the running match, was given a handsome gold watch.

For climbing and riding, Jack had a pair of silver plated spurs, and a riding whip, both of which gave him extraordinary pleasure.

Franz received a pair of stirrups, and a driving whip made of rhinoceros hide, which we thought would be of use to him in the character of bull-trainer.

When the ceremony was supposed to be over, I advanced, and solemnly presented to my wife a lovely work-box, filled with every imaginable requirement for a lady's work-table, which she accepted with equal surprise and delight.

The whole entertainment afforded the boys such intense pleasure, and their spirits rose to such a pitch, that nothing would serve them but another salvo of artillery, in order to close with befitting dignity and honor so great a day. They gave me no peace till they had leave to squander some gunpowder, and then at last their excited feelings seeming relieved, we were able to sit down to supper; shortly afterward we joined in family worship and retired to rest.

Soon after the great festival of our grand Thanksgiving-Day I recollected that it was now the time when, the figs at Falconhurst being ripe, immense flocks of ortolans and wild pigeons were attracted thither, and as we had found those preserved last year of the greatest use among our stores of winter provisions, I would not miss the opportunity of renewing our stock; and therefore, laying aside the building work, we removed with all speed to our home in the tree, where sure enough we found the first detachment of the birds already busy with the fruit.

In order to spare ammunition, I resolved to concoct a strong sort of birdlime, of which I had read in some account of the Palm Islanders, who make it of fresh caoutchouc mixed with oil, and of so good a quality that it has been known to catch even peacocks and turkeys.

Fritz and Jack were therefore dispatched to collect some fresh caoutchouc from the trees, and as this involved a good gallop on Storm and Lightfoot, they, nothing loth, set off.

They took a supply of calabashes, in which to bring the gum, and we found it high time to manufacture a fresh stock of these useful vessels. I was beginning to propose an expedition to the Gourd-tree Wood, regretting the time it would take to go such a distance, when my wife reminded me of her plantation near the potato field.

There to our joy we found that all the plants were flourishing, and crops of gourds and pumpkins, in all stages of ripeness, covered the ground.

Selecting a great number suited to our purpose, we hastened home, and began the manufacture of basins, dishes, plates, flasks, and spoons of all sorts and sizes, with even greater success than before.

When the riders returned with the caoutchouc, they brought several novelties besides.

A crane, for example, shot by Fritz, and an animal which they called a marmot, but which to me seemed much more like a badger.

Aniseed, turpentine, and wax berries for candles, they had also collected, and a curious root which they introduced by the name of the monkey plant.

"And pray wherefore 'monkey plant,' may I ask?"

"Well, for this reason, father," answered Fritz: "we came upon an open space in the forest near Woodlands, and perceived a troop of monkeys, apparently engaged, as Jack said, in cultivating the soil! Being curious to make out what they were at, we tied up the dogs, as well as Storm and Lightfoot, and crept near enough to see that the apes were most industriously grubbing up and eating roots. This they did in a way that nearly choked us with laughter, for when the root was rather hard to pull up, and the leaves were torn off, they seized it firmly in their teeth, and flung themselves fairly heels-over-head in the most ludicrous fashion you ever saw, and up came the root, unable to resist the leverage! Of course we wanted to see what this dainty morsel was like, so we loosed the dogs, and the apes cleared out double quick, leaving plenty of the roots about. We tasted them, and thought them very nice. Will you try one?"

The plant was quite new to me, but I imagined it might be what is called in China 'ginseng,' and there prized and valued beyond everything. The children being curious to hear more about this ginseng, I continued:

"In China it is considered so strengthening and wholesome that it is used as a sort of universal medicine, being supposed to prolong human life.

"The emperor alone has the right to permit it to be gathered, and guards are placed round land where it grows.

"Ginseng is to be found in Tartary, and has lately been discovered in Canada; it is cultivated in Pennsylvania, because the Americans introduce it secretly into China as smuggled merchandise."

Fritz then continued:

"After this we went on to Woodlands; but mercy on us! What a confusion the place was in! Everything smashed or torn, and covered with mud and dirt; the fowls terrified, the sheep and goats scattered, the contents of the rooms dashed about as if a whirlwind had swept through the house."

"What!" I exclaimed, while my wife looked horrified at the news, conjuring up in her imagination hordes of savages who would soon come and lay waste Falconhurst and Tentholm as well as Woodlands. "How can that have happened? Did you discover the authors of all this mischief?"

"Oh," said Jack, "it was easy to see that those dreadful monkeys had done it all. First they must have got into the yards and sheds, and hunted the fowls and creatures about; and then I dare say the cunning rascals put a little monkey in at some small opening, and bid him unfasten the shutters—you know what nimble fingers they have. Then of course the whole *posse* of them swarmed into our nice tidy cottage and skylarked with every single thing they could lay paws on, till perhaps they got hungry all at once, and bethought them of the 'ginseng,' as you call it, out in the woods yonder, where we found them so busy refreshing themselves, the mischievous villains!"

"While we were gazing at all this ruin in a sort of bewilderment," pursued Fritz, "we heard a sound of rushing wings and strange ringing cries, as of multitudes of birds passing high above us, and looking up we perceived them flying quickly in a wedge-shaped flock at a great height in the air. They began gradually to descend, taking the direction of the lake, and separated into a number of small detachments, which followed in a long, straight line, and at a slower rate, the movements of the leaders, who appeared to be examining the neighborhood. We could now see what large birds they must be, but dared not show ourselves or follow them, lest they should take alarm.

"Presently, and with one accord, they quickened their motion, just as if the band had begun to play a quick march after a slow one, and rapidly descended to earth in a variety of lively ways, and near enough for us to see that they must be cranes.

"Some alighted at once, while others hovered sportively over them. Many darted to the ground, and, just touching it, would soar again upward with a strong but somewhat heavy flight.

"After gamboling in this way for a time, the whole multitude, as though at the word of command, alighted on the rice fields, and began to feast on the fresh grain.

"We thought now was our time to get a shot at the cranes, and cautiously approached; but they were too cunning to let themselves be surprised, and we came unexpectedly upon their out-posts or sentinels, who instantly sprang into the air, uttering loud, trumpet-like cries, upon which the whole flock arose and followed them with a rush like a sudden squall of wind. We were quite startled, and it was useless to attempt a shot; but unwilling to miss the chance of securing at least one of the birds, I hastily unhooded my eagle, and threw him into the air.

"With a piercing cry he soared away high above them, then shot downward like an arrow, causing wild confusion among the cranes. The one which the eagle attacked sought to defend itself; a struggle followed, and they came together to the ground not far from where we stood.

"Hastening forward, to my grief I found the beautiful crane already dead. The eagle, luckily unhurt, was rewarded with a small pigeon from my game-bag.

"After this we went back to Woodlands, got some turpentine and a bag of rice—and set off for home."

Fritz's interesting story being ended, and supper ready, we made trial of the new roots, and found them very palatable, either boiled or stewed; the monkey plant, however, if it really proved to be the ginseng of the Chinese, would require to be used with caution, being of an aromatic and heating nature.

We resolved to transplant a supply of both roots to our kitchen garden.

CHAPTER X

Birdlime—A midnight raid—The massacre at Woodlands—Capture of Molucca pigeons—A pigeon-house—Fritz and I prepare a conjuring trick—Great success of our experiment—Lichen and nutmegs discovered—Jack's adventure—The loom manufactured—Winter stores prepared—The rainy season sets in—Interior of our house arranged—We study languages—The return of spring—A stranded whale—An account of coral—We go to work on the whale's carcass—Remarks on the habits of the whale.

On the following morning we were early astir; and as soon as breakfast was over, we went regularly to work with the birdlime. The tough, adhesive mixture of caoutchouc, oil, and turpentine turned out well.

The boys brought rods, which I smeared over, and made them place among the upper branches, where the fruit was plentiful, and the birds most congregated.

The prodigious number of the pigeons, far beyond those of last year, reminded me that we had not then, as now, witnessed their arrival at their feeding-places, but had seen only the last body of the season, a mere party of stragglers, compared to the masses which now weighed down the branches of all the trees in the neighborhood.

The sweet acorns of the evergreen oaks were also patronized; large flocks were then congregated; and from the state of the ground under the trees it was evident that at night they roosted on the branches. Seeing this, I determined to make a raid upon them by torchlight, after the manner of the colonists in Virginia.

Meantime, the birdlime acted well: the pigeons alighting, stuck fast. The more they fluttered and struggled, the more completely were they bedaubed with the tenacious mixture, and at length, with piteous cries, fell to the ground, bearing the sticks with them. The birds were then removed, fresh lime spread, and the snare set again.

The boys quickly became able to carry on the work without my assistance; so, leaving it to them, I went to prepare torches, with pine wood and turpentine, for the night attack.

Jack presently brought a very pretty pigeon, unlike the rest, to show me, as he felt unwilling to kill it; and seeing that it must be one of our own European breed, which we wished to preserve until their numbers greatly increased, I took the trembling captive, and gently cleansed its feet and wings with oil and ashes from the stiff, sticky mess with which it was bedaubed, placing it then in a wicker cage, and telling Jack to bring me any others like it which were caught. This he did; and we secured several pairs, greatly to my satisfaction, as having necessarily let them go free when we landed, they had become quite wild and we derived no advantage from them: whereas now we would have a cot, and pigeon-pie whenever we liked.

When evening drew on, we set out for the wood of sweet acorns, provided merely with long bamboo canes, torches, and canvas sacks.

These weapons appeared very curious and insufficient to the children; but their use was speedily apparent; for darkness having come upon us almost before we reached the wood, I lighted the torches, and perceived, as I expected, that every branch was thickly laden with ortolans and wild pigeons, who were roosting there in amazing numbers.

Suddenly aroused by the glare of light, confusion prevailed among the terrified birds, who fluttered helplessly through the branches, dazzled and bewildered, and many falling, even before we began to use the sticks, were picked up, and put in the bags. When we beat and struck the branches, it was as much as my wife and Franz could do to gather up the quantities of pigeons that soon lay on the ground. The sacks were speedily quite full. We turned homeward, and on reaching Falconhurst, put our booty in safety, and gladly withdrew to rest.

The following day was wholly occupied in plucking, boiling, roasting, and stewing, so that we could find time for nothing else; but next morning a great expedition to Woodlands was arranged, that measures might there be taken to prevent a repetition of the monkey invasion.

I hoped, could I but catch the mischievous rascals at their work of destruction, to inflict upon them such a chastisement as would effectually make them shun the neighborhood of our farm for the future.

My wife provided us with a good store of provisions, as we were likely to be absent several days, while she, with Franz and Turk, remained at home.

I took with me abundance of specially prepared birdlime, far stronger than that which we used for the pigeons; a number of short posts, plenty of string, and a supply of coconut shells and gourds.

The buffalo carried all these things, and one or two of the boys beside. I myself bestrode the ass, and in due time we arrived at a convenient spot in the forest, near Woodlands, well concealed by thick bushes and underwood, where we made a little encampment, pitching the small tent, and tethering the animals. The dogs, too, were tied up, lest they should roam about and betray our presence.

We found the cottage quiet and deserted; and I lost no time in preparing for the reception of visitors, hoping to be all ready for them and out of sight before they arrived.

We drove the stakes lightly into the ground, so as to form an irregular paling round the house, winding string in and out in all directions between them thus making a kind of labyrinth, through which it would be impossible to pass without touching either the stakes or the cords.

Everything was plentifully besmeared with birdlime, and basins of the mixture were set in all directions, strewn with rice, maize, and other dainties for bait.

Night came without any interruption to our proceedings; and all being then accomplished, we retired to rest beneath the shelter of our little tent.

Very early in the morning we heard a confused noise, such as we knew betokened the approach of a large number of apes. We armed ourselves with strong clubs and cudgels, and holding the dogs in leash, made our way silently behind the thickets, till, ourselves unseen, we could command a view of all that went on; and strange indeed was the scene which ensued!

The noise of rustling, cracking, and creaking among the branches, with horrid cries, and shrieks, and chattering, increased to a degree sufficient to make us perfectly giddy; and then out from the forest poured the whole disorderly rabble of monkeys, scrambling, springing, leaping from the trees, racing and tumbling across the grassy space toward the house; when, at once attracted by the novelties they saw, they made for the jars and bowls.

They seemed innumerable; but the confused, rapid way in which they swarmed hither and thither, made it difficult to judge accurately of their numbers. They dashed fearlessly through and over the palings in all directions, some rushing at the eatables, some scrambling on to the roof, where they commenced tugging at the wooden pegs, with a view to forcing an entrance.

Gradually, however, as they rambled over the place, all in turn became besmeared with our birdlime on head, paws, or back or breast. The wretched predicament of the apes increased every instant.

Some sat down, and with the most ludicrous gestures, tried to clean themselves. Others were hopelessly entangled in stakes and cordage, which they trailed about after them, looking the picture of bewildered despair.

Others, again, endeavored to help one another, and stuck fast together; the more they pulled, and tugged, and kicked the worse became their plight.

Many had the gourds and coconut shells lumbering and clattering about with them, their paws having been caught when they sought to obtain the rice or fruit we had put for bait.

Most ridiculous of all was the condition of one old fellow, who had found a calabash containing palm wine, and, eagerly drinking it, was immediately fitted with a mask, for the shell stuck to his forehead and whiskers, of course covering his eyes; and he blundered about, cutting the wildest capers in his efforts to get rid of the encumbrance.

Numbers took to flight; but, as we had spread birdlime on several of the trees around, many apes found themselves fixed to, or hanging from the branches, where they remained in woeful durance, struggling and shrieking horribly.

The panic being now general, I loosed the three dogs, whose impatience had been almost uncontrollable, and who now rushed to the attack of the unfortunate monkeys, as though burning with zeal to execute justice upon desperate criminals.

The place soon had the appearance of a ghastly battlefield; for we were obliged to do our part with the clubs and sticks, till the din of howling, yelling, barking, in every conceivable tone of rage and pain, gave place to an awful silence, and we looked with a shudder on the shocking spectacle around us.

At least forty apes lay mangled and dead, and the boys began to be quite sad and down-hearted, till I, fully sharing their feelings, hastened to turn their thoughts to active employment in removing and burying the slain, burning the stakes, cordage, bowls, everything concerned in the execution of our deadly stratagem.

After that we betook ourselves to the task of restoring order to our dismantled cottage; and seeking for the scattered flock of sheep, goats, and poultry, we gradually collected them, hoping to settle them once more peacefully, in their yards and sheds.

While thus engaged, we repeatedly heard a sound as of something heavy falling from a tree. On going to look, we found three splendid birds, caught on some of the limed sticks we had placed loose in the branches.

Two of these proved to be a variety of the blue Molucca pigeon; the third I assumed to be the Nicobar pigeon, having met with descriptions of its resplendent green, bronze, and steely blue plumage; and I was pleased to think of domesticating them, and establishing them as first tenants of a suitable dwelling near the cave.

"First tenants, father!" said Fritz; "do you expect to catch more like these?"

"Not exactly catch them; I mean to practise a secret art. Much can be done by magic, Fritz!"

Further explanation I declined to give.

In a few days Woodlands was once more set in order, and everything settled and comfortable, so that we returned without further adventure to Falconhurst, where we were joyfully welcomed.

Every one agreed that we must go at once to Tentholm, to make the proposed pigeon-house in the rock. Several other things there also requiring our attention, we made arrangements for a prolonged stay.

My plan for the pigeon-house was to hollow out an ample space in the cliff, facing toward Jackal River, and close to our rocky home, fitting that up with partitions, perches, and nesting places; while a large wooden front was fitted on to the opening, with entrance-holes, slides or shutters, and a broad platform in front, where the birds could rest and walk about.

When, after the work of a few weeks, we thought it was fit for habitation, I set the other children to work at some distance from our cavern, and summoning Fritz:

"Now, my faithful assistant," said I, "it is time to conjure the new colonists to their settlement here. Yes," I continued, laughing at his puzzled look, "I mean to play a regular pigeon-dealer's trick. You must know such gentry are very ingenious, not only in keeping their own pigeons safe, but in adding to their numbers by attracting those of other people. All I want is some soft clay, aniseed, and salt, of which I will compound a mixture which our birds will like very much, and the smell of which will bring others to share it with them."

"I can easily get you those things, father."

"I shall want some oil of aniseed besides," said I, "to put on the pigeon-holes, so that the birds' feathers may touch it as they may pass in and out, and become scented with what will attract the wild pigeons. This I can obtain by pounding aniseed; therefore, bring me the mortar and some oil."

When this was strongly impregnated with the aromatic oil from the seeds (for I did not propose to distill it in regular style), I strained it through a cloth, pressing it strongly; the result answered my purpose, and the scent would certainly remain for some days.

All my preparations being completed, the pigeons were installed in their new residence, and the slides closed. The European birds were by this time quite friendly with the three beautiful strangers; and when the other boys came home, and scrambled up the ladder to peep in at a little pane of glass I had fixed in front, they saw them all contentedly picking up grain, and pecking at the "magic food," as Fritz called it, although he did not betray my secret arts to his brothers.

Early on the third morning I aroused Fritz, and directed him to ascend the rope ladder, and arrange a cord on the sliding door of the dovecot, by which it could be opened or closed from below. Also he poured fresh aniseed oil all about the entrance, after which we returned, and awoke the rest of the family, telling them that if they liked to make haste, they might see me let the pigeons fly.

Everybody came to the dovecot, understanding that some ceremony was to attend the event, and I waved a wand with mock solemnity, while I muttered a seeming incantation, and then gave Fritz a sign to draw up the sliding panel.

Presently out popped the pretty heads of the captives, the soft eyes glanced about in all directions; they withdrew, they ventured forth again, they came timidly out on "the veranda," as little Franz expressed it; then, as though suddenly startled, the whole party took wing, with the shrill whizzing sound peculiar to the flight of pigeons, and circling above us as they rose higher and higher, finally darting quite out of sight.

While we were yet gazing after them, they reappeared, and settled quietly on the dovecot; but as we congratulated ourselves on a return which showed that they accepted this as a home, up sprang the three blue pigeons, the noble foreigners, for whom chiefly I had planned the house, and rising in circles high in air, winged their rapid way direct toward Falconhurst.

Their departure had such an air of determination and resolve about it, that I feared them lost to us forever.

Endeavoring to console ourselves by petting our four remaining birds, we could not forget this disappointment, and all day long the dovecot remained the center of attraction.

Nothing, however, was seen of the fugitive until about the middle of the next day; when most of us were hard at work inside the cavern, Jack sprang in full of excitement, exclaiming:

"He is there! He is come! He really is!"

"Who? Who is there? What do you mean?"

"The blue pigeon, to be sure! Hurrah! Hurrah!"

"Oh, nonsense!" said Ernest. "You want to play us a trick."

"Why should it be 'nonsense'?" cried I. "I fully believe we shall see them all soon!"

Out ran everybody to the dovecot, and there, sure enough stood the pretty fellow, but not alone, for he was billing and cooing to a mate, a stranger of his own breed, apparently inviting her to enter his dwelling; for he popped in and out of the door, bowing, sidling, and cooing, in a most irresistible manner, until the shy little lady yielded to his blandishments, and tripped daintily in. "Now, let's shut the door."

"Pull the cord and close the panel!" shouted the boys, making a rush at the string.

"Stop!" cried I, "let the string alone! I won't have you frighten the little darlings. Besides, the others will be coming—would you shut the door in their faces?"

"Here they come! Here they come!" exclaimed Fritz, whose keen eye marked the birds afar, and to our delight the second blue pigeon arrived, likewise with a mate, whom, after a pretty little flirtation scene of real and assumed modesty on her part, he succeeded in leading home.

The third and handsomest of the new pigeons was the last in making his appearance. Perhaps he had greater difficulty than the others in finding a mate as distinguished in rank and beauty as himself.

However, we fully expected them, and the boys talked of the arrival of "Mr. and Mrs. Nicobar" as a matter of course.

Late in the day Franz and his mother went out to provide for supper, but the child returned directly, exclaiming that we must hasten to the dovecot to see something beautiful.

Accordingly a general rush was made out of the cave, and we saw with delight that the third stranger also had returned with a lovely bride, and encouraged by the presence of the first arrivals, they soon made themselves at home.

In a short time nest-building commenced, and among the materials collected by the birds, I observed a long gray moss or lichen, and thought it might very possibly be the same which, in the West Indies, is gathered from the bark of old trees, where it grows, and hangs in great tuft-like beards, to be used instead of horse-hair for stuffing mattresses.

My wife no sooner heard of it than her active brain devised fifty plans for making it of use. Would we but collect enough, she would clean and sort it, and there would be no end to the bolsters, pillows, saddles, and cushions she would stuff with it.

For the discovery of nutmegs we had also to thank the pigeons, and they were carefully planted in our orchard.

For some time no event of particular note occurred, until at length Jack, as usual, got into a scrape, causing thereby no little excitement at home.

He went off early on one of his own particular private expeditions.

He was in the habit of doing this that he might surprise us with some new acquisition on his return.

This time, however, he came back in most wretched plight, covered with mud and green slime; a great bundle of Spanish canes was on his back, muddy and green like himself; he had lost a shoe, and altogether presented a ludicrous picture of misery, at which we could have laughed had he not seemed more ready to cry!

"My dear boy! What has happened to you? Where have you been?"

"Only in the swamp behind the powder magazine, father," replied he. "I went to get reeds for my wicker-work, because I wanted to weave some baskets and hencoops, and I saw such beauties a little way off in the marsh, much finer than those close by the edge, that I tried to get at them.

"I jumped from one firm spot to another, till at last I slipped and sank over my ankles; I tried to get on toward the reeds, which were close by, but in I went deeper and deeper, till I was above the knees in thick soft mud, and there I stuck!

"I screamed and shouted, but nobody came, and I can tell you I was in a regular fright.

"At last who should appear but my faithful Fangs! He knew my voice and came close up to me, right over the swamp, but all the poor beast could do was to help me to make a row; I wonder you did not hear us! The very rocks rang, but nothing came of it, so despair drove me to think of an expedient. I cut down all the reeds I could reach round and round me, and bound them together into this bundle, which made a firm place on which to lean, while I worked and kicked about to free my feet and legs, and after much struggling, I managed to get astride on the reeds.

"There I sat, supported above the mud and slime, while Fangs ran yelping backward and forward between me and the bank, seeming surprised I did not follow. Suddenly I thought of catching hold of his tail. He dragged and pulled, and I sprawled, and crawled, and waded, sometimes on my reeds like a raft, sometimes lugging them along with me, till we luckily got back to *terra firma*. But I had a near squeak for it, I can tell you."

"A fortunate escape indeed, my boy!" cried I, "and I thank God for it. Fangs has really acted a heroic part as your deliverer, and you have shown great presence of mind. Now go with your mother, and get rid of the slimy traces of your disaster! You have brought me splendid canes, exactly what I want for a new scheme of mine."

The fact was, I meant to try to construct a loom for my wife, for I knew she understood weaving, so I chose two fine strong reeds, and splitting them carefully, bound them together again, that when dry they might be quite straight and equal, and fit for a frame. Smaller reeds were cut into pieces and sharpened, for the teeth of the comb. The boys did this for me without in the least knowing their use, and great fun they made of "father's monster toothpicks."

In time all the various parts of the loom were made ready, and put together, my wife knowing nothing of it, while to the incessant questions of the children, I replied mysteriously.

"Oh, it is an outlandish sort of musical instrument; mother will know how to play upon it."

And when the time came for presenting it, her joy was only equaled by the amusement and interest with which the children watched her movements while "playing the loom," as they always said.

About this time, a beautiful little foal, a son of the onager, was added to our stud, and as he promised to grow up strong and tractable, we soon saw how useful he would be. The name of Swift was given to him, and he was to be trained for my own riding.

The interior arrangements of the cavern being now well forward, I applied myself to contriving an aqueduct, that fresh water might be led close up to our cave, for it was a long way to go to fetch it from Jackal River, and especially inconvenient on washing days. As I wanted to do this before the rainy season began, I set about it at once.

Pipes of hollow bamboo answered the purpose well, and a large cask formed the reservoir. The supply was good, and the comfort of having it close at hand so great, that the mother declared she was as well pleased with our engineering as if we had made her a fountain and marble basin adorned with mermaids and dolphins.

Anticipating the setting in of the rains, I pressed forward all work connected with stores for the winter, and great was the in-gathering of roots, fruits, and grains, potatoes, rice, guavas, sweet acorns, pine-cones; load after load arrived at the cavern, and the mother's active needle was in constant requisition, as the demand for more sacks and bags was incessant.

Casks and barrels of all sorts and sizes were pressed into the service, until at last the raft was knocked to pieces, and its tubs made to do duty in the storerooms.

The weather became very unsettled and stormy.

Heavy clouds gathered in the horizon, and passing storms of wind, with thunder, lightning, and torrents of rain swept over the face of nature from time to time.

The sea was in frequent commotion; heavy ground swells drove masses of water hissing and foaming against the cliffs. Everything heralded the approaching rains. All nature joined in sounding forth the solemn overture to the grandest work of the year.

It was now near the beginning of the month of June, and we had twelve weeks of bad weather before us.

We established some of the animals with ourselves at the salt cave. The cow, the ass, Lightfoot, Storm, and the dogs, were all necessary to us, while Knips, Fangs, and the eagle were sure to be a great amusement in the long evenings.

The boys would ride over to Falconhurst very often to see that all was in order there, and fetch anything required.

Much remained to be done in order to give the cave a comfortable appearance, which became more desirable now that we had to live indoors.

The darkness of the inner regions annoyed me, and I set myself to invent a remedy.

After some thought, I called in Jack's assistance, and we got a very tall, strong bamboo, which would reach right up to the vaulted roof. This we planted in the earthen floor, securing well by driving wedges in round it. Jack ascended this pole very cleverly, taking with him a hammer and chisel to enlarge a crevice in the roof so as to fix a pulley, by means of which, when he descended, I drew up a large ship's lantern, well supplied with oil, and as there were four wicks, it afforded a very fair amount of light.

Several days were spent in arranging the different rooms.

Ernest and Franz undertook the library, fixing shelves, and setting books in order.

Jack and his mother took in hand the sitting room and kitchen, while Fritz and I, as better able for heavy work, arranged the workshops. The carpenter's bench, the turning lathe, and a large chest of tools were set in convenient places, and many tools and instruments hung on the walls.

An adjoining chamber was fitted up as a forge, with fireplace, bellows, and anvil, complete, all which we had found in the ship, packed, together, and ready to set up.

When these great affairs were settled, we still found in all directions work to be done. Shelves, tables, benches, movable steps, cupboards, pegs, door handles, and bolts—there seemed no end to our requirements, and we often thought of the enormous amount of work necessary to maintain the comforts and conveniences of life which at home we had received as matters of course.

But in reality, the more there was to do the better; and I never ceased contriving fresh improvements, being fully aware of the importance of constant employment as a means of strengthening and maintaining the health of mind and body. This, indeed, with a consciousness of continual progress toward a desirable end, is found to constitute the main element of happiness.

Our rocky home was greatly improved by a wide porch which I made along the whole front of our rooms and entrances, by leveling the ground to form a terrace, and sheltering it with a veranda of bamboo, supported by pillars of the same.

Ernest and Franz were highly successful as librarians.

The books, when unpacked and arranged, proved to be a most valuable collection, capable of affording every sort of educational advantage.

Besides a variety of books of voyages, travels, divinity, and natural history (several containing fine colored illustrations), there were histories and scientific works, as well as standard fictions in several languages; also a good assortment of maps, charts, mathematical and astronomical instruments, and an excellent pair of globes.

I foresaw much interesting study on discovering that we possessed the grammars and dictionaries of a great many languages, a subject for which we all had a taste. With French we were well acquainted. Fritz and Ernest had begun to learn English at school, and made further progress during a visit to England. The mother, who had once been intimate with a Dutch family, could speak that language pretty well.

After a great deal of discussion, we agreed to study different languages, so that in the event of meeting with people of other nations, there should be at least one of the family able to communicate with them.

All determined to improve our knowledge of German and French.

The two elder boys were to study English and Dutch with their mother.

Ernest, already possessing considerable knowledge of Latin, wished to continue to study it, so as to be able to make use of the many works on natural history and medicine written in that language.

Jack announced that he meant to learn Spanish, "because it sounded so grand and imposing."

I myself was interested in the Malay language, knowing it to be so widely spoken in the islands of the Eastern Seas, and thinking it as likely as any other to be useful to us.

Our family circle by and by represented Babel in miniature, for scraps and fragments of all these tongues kept buzzing about our ears from morning to night, each sporting his newly acquired word or sentence on every possible occasion, propounding idioms and peculiar expressions like riddles, to puzzle the rest.

In this way, the labor of learning was very considerably lightened, and every one came to know a few words of each language.

Occasionally we amused ourselves by opening chests and packages hitherto untouched, and brought unexpected treasures to light—mirrors, wardrobes, a pair of console tables with polished marble tops, elegant writing tables and handsome chairs, clocks of various descriptions, a musical box, and a chronometer were found; and by degrees our abode was fitted up like a palace, so that sometimes we wondered at ourselves, and felt as though we were strutting about in borrowed plumes.

The children begged me to decide on a name for our salt-cave dwelling, and that of Rockburg was chosen unanimously.

The weeks of imprisonment passed so rapidly, that no one found time hang heavy on his hands.

Books occupied me so much that but little carpentering was done, yet I made a yoke for the oxen, a pair of cotton wool carders, and a spinning wheel for my wife.

As the rainy season drew to a close, the weather for a while became wilder, and the storms fiercer than ever. Thunder roared, lightning blazed, torrents rushed toward the sea, which came in raging billows to meet them, lashed to fury by the tempests of wind which swept the surface of the deep.

The uproar of the elements came to an end at last.

Nature resumed her attitude of repose, her smiling aspect of peaceful beauty; and soon all traces of the ravages of floods and storms would disappear beneath the luxuriant vegetation of the tropics.

Gladly quitting the sheltering walls of Rockburg to roam once more in the open air, we crossed Jackal River, for a walk along the coast, and presently Fritz with sharp eyes observed something on the small island near Flamingo Marsh, which was, he said, long and rounded, resembling a boat bottom upward.

Examining it with the telescope, I could form no other conjecture, and we resolved to make it the object of an excursion next day, being delighted to resume our old habit of starting in pursuit of adventure.

The boat was accordingly got in readiness; it required some repairs, and fresh pitching, and then we made for the point of interest, indulging in a variety of surmises as to what we should find.

It proved to be a huge, stranded whale.

The island being steep and rocky, it was necessary to be careful; but we found a landing-place on the further side. The boys hurried by the nearest way to the beach where lay the monster of the deep, while I clambered to the highest point of the islet, which commanded a view of the mainland, from Rockburg to Falconhurst.

On rejoining my sons, I found them only half-way to the great fish, and as I drew near they shouted in high glee:

"Oh! Father, just look at the glorious shells and coral branches we are finding. How does it happen that there are such quantities?"

"Only consider how the recent storms have stirred the ocean to its depths! No doubt thousands of shellfish have been detached from their rocks and dashed in all directions by the waves, which have thrown ashore even so huge a creature as the whale yonder."

"Yes; isn't he a frightful great brute!" cried Fritz. "Ever so much larger than he seemed from a distance. The worst of it is, one does not well see what use to make of the huge carcass."

"Why, make train oil, to be sure," said Ernest. "I can't say he's a beauty, though, and it is much pleasanter to gather these lovely shells, than to cut up blubber."

"Well, let us amuse ourselves with them for the present," said I, "but in the afternoon, when the sea is calmer, we will return with the necessary implements, and see if we can turn the stranded whale to good account."

We were soon ready to return to the boat, but Ernest had a fancy for remaining alone on the island till we came back, and asked my permission to do so, that he might experience, for an hour or two, the sensations of Robinson Crusoe.

To this, however, I would not consent, assuring him that our fate, as a solitary family, gave him quite sufficient idea of shipwreck on an uninhabited island, and that his lively imagination must supply the rest.

The boys found it hard work to row back, and began to beg of me to exert my wonderful inventive powers in contriving some kind of rowing machine.

"You lazy fellows!" returned I; "give me the great clockwork out of a church tower, perhaps I might be able to relieve your labors."

"Oh, father!" cried Fritz, "don't you know there are iron wheels in the clockwork of the large kitchen-jacks? I'm sure mother would give them up, and you could make something out of them, could you not?"

"By the time I have manufactured a rowing-machine out of a roasting-jack, I think your arms will be pretty well inured to the use of your oars! However, I am far from despising the hint, my dear Fritz."

"Is coral of any use?" demanded Jack suddenly.

"In former times it was pounded and used by chemists; but it is now chiefly used for various ornaments, and made into beads for necklaces, etc. As such, it is greatly prized by savages, and were we to fall in with natives, we might very possibly find a store of coral useful in bartering with them.

"For the present, we will arrange these treasures of the deep in our library, and make them the beginning of a Museum of Natural History, which will afford us equal pleasure and instruction."

"One might almost say that coral belongs at once to the animal, vegetable, and mineral kingdoms," remarked Fritz; "it is hard like stone, it has stems and branches like a shrub, and I believe tiny insects inhabit the cells, do they not, father?"

"You are right, Fritz; coral consists of the calcareous cells of minute animals, so built up as to form a tree-like structure.

"The coral fishery gives employment to many men in the Persian Gulf, the Mediterranean Sea, and other places. The instrument commonly used consists of two heavy beams of wood, secured together at right angles, and loaded with stones. Hemp and netting are attached to the under side of the beams, to the middle of which is fastened one end of a strong rope, by which the apparatus is let down from a boat, and guided to the spots where the coral is most abundant.

"The branches of the coral become entangled in the hemp and network; they are broken off from the rock, and are drawn to the surface of the water.

"Left undisturbed, these coral insects, laboring incessantly, raise foundations, on which, in course of time, fertile islands appear, clothed with verdure, and inhabited by man."

"Why, father, here we are at the landing place!" exclaimed Jack. "It has seemed quite easy to pull since you began to tell us such interesting things."

"Very interesting, indeed; but did you notice that the wind had changed, Jack?" remarked Ernest as he shipped his oar.

The animated recital of our adventures, the sight of the lovely shells and corals, and the proposed work for the afternoon, inspired the mother and Franz with a great wish to accompany us.

To this I gladly consented, only stipulating that we should go provided with food, water, and a compass. "For," said I, "the sea has only just ceased from its raging, and being at the best of times of uncertain and capricious nature, we may chance to be detained on the island, or forced to land at a considerable distance from home."

Dinner was quickly dispatched, and preparations set on foot.

The more oil we could obtain the better, for a great deal was used in the large lantern which burnt day and night in the recesses of the cave; therefore all available casks and barrels were pressed into the service; many, of course, once full of pickled herrings, potted pigeons, and other winter stores, were now empty, and we took a goodly fleet of these in tow.

Knives, hatchets, and the boys' climbing buskins, were put on board, and we set forth, the labor of the oar being greater than ever, now that our freight was so much increased.

The sea being calm, and the tide suiting better, we found it easy to land close to the whale; my first care was to place the boat, as well as the casks, in perfect security, after which we proceeded to a close inspection of our prize.

Its enormous size quite startled my wife and her little boy; the length being from sixty to sixty-five feet, and the girth between thirty and forty, while the weight could not have been less than 50,000 pounds.

The color was a uniform velvety black, and the enormous head about one-third of the length of the entire bulk, the eyes quite small, not much larger than those of an ox, and the ears almost undiscernible.

The jaw opened very far back, and was nearly sixteen feet in length, the most curious part of its structure being the remarkable substance known as whalebone, masses of which appeared all along the jaws, solid at the base, and splitting into a sort of fringe at the extremity. This arrangement is for the purpose of aiding the whale in procuring its food, and separating it from the water.

The tongue was remarkably large, soft, and full of oil; the opening of the throat wonderfully small, scarcely two inches in diameter.

"Why, what can the monster eat?" exclaimed Fritz; "he never can swallow a proper mouthful down this little gullet!"

"The mode of feeding adopted by the whale is so curious," I replied, "that I must explain it to you before we begin work.

"This animal (for I should tell you that a whale is not a fish; he possesses no gills, he breathes atmospheric air, and would be drowned if too long detained below the surface of the water); this animal, then, frequents those parts of the ocean best supplied with the various creatures on which he feeds. Shrimps, small fish, lobsters, various molluscs, and medusæ form his diet. Driving with open mouth through the congregated shoals of these little creatures, the whale engulfs them by millions in his enormous jaws, and continues his destructive course until he has sufficiently charged his mouth with prey.

"Closing his jaws and forcing out, through the interstices of the whalebone, the water which he has taken together with his prey, he retains the captured animals, and swallows them at his leisure.

"The nostrils, or blow-holes, are placed, you see, on the upper part of the head, in order that the whale may rise to breathe, and repose on the surface of the sea, showing very little of his huge carcass.

"The breathings are called 'spoutings,' because a column of mixed vapor and water is thrown from the blow-holes, sometimes to a height of twenty feet.

"And now, boys, fasten on your buskins, and let me see if you can face the work of climbing this slippery mountain of flesh, and cutting it up."

Fritz and Jack stripped, and went to work directly, scrambling over the back to the head, where they assisted me to cut away the lips, so as to reach the whalebone, a large quantity of which was detached and carried to the boat.

Ernest labored manfully at the creature's side, cutting out slabs of blubber, while his mother and Franz helped as well as they could to put it in casks.

Presently we had a multitude of unbidden guests.

The air was filled by the shrill screams and hoarse croaks

and cries of numbers of birds of prey, they flew around us in ever narrowing circles, and becoming bolder as their voracity was excited by the near view of the tempting prey, they alighted close to us, snatching morsels greedily from under the very strokes of our knives and hatchets.

Our work was seriously interrupted by these feathered marauders, who, after all, were no greater robbers than we ourselves. We kept them off as well as we could by blows from our tools, and several were killed, my wife taking possession of them immediately for the sake of the feathers.

It was nearly time to leave the island, but first I stripped off a long piece of the skin, to be used for traces, harness, and other leather-work. It was about three-quarters of an inch thick, and very soft and oily—but I knew it would shrink and be tough and durable.

I also took a part of the gums in which the roots of the baleen or whalebone was still embedded, having read that this is considered quite a delicacy, as well as the skin, which, when properly dressed and cut in little cubes, like black dice, has been compared, by enthusiastic and probably very hungry travelers, to coconut and cream-cheese.

The boys thought the tongue might prove equally palatable, but I valued it only on account of the large quantity of oil it contained.

With a heavy freight we put to sea, and made what haste we could to reach home, and cleanse our persons from the unpleasant traces of the disgusting work in which we had spent the day.

Next morning we started at dawn.

My wife and Franz were left behind, for our proposed work was even more horrible than that of the preceding day; they could not assist, and had no inclination to witness it.

It was my intention to open the carcass completely, and, penetrating the interior, to obtain various portions of the intestines, thinking that it would be possible to convert the larger ones into vessels fit for holding the oil. This time we laid aside our clothes and wore only strong canvas trousers when we commenced operations, which were vigorously carried on during the whole of the day; then, satisfied that we could do so with a clear conscience, we abandoned the remains to the birds of prey, and, with a full cargo, set sail for land.

On the way, it appeared to strike the boys (who had made not the slightest objection to the singularly unpleasant task I had set them), as very strange that I should wish to possess what they had been working so hard to procure for me.

"What can have made you wish to bring away that brute's entrails, father? Are they of any use?"

"There are countries," I replied, "where no wood grows of which to make barrels, and no hemp for thread, string, and cordage. Necessity, the mother of all the more valuable inventions, has taught the inhabitants of these countries, Greenlanders, Esquimaux, and others, to think of substitutes, and they use the intestines of the whale for one purpose, the sinews and nerves for the other."

We were right glad to land, and get rid, for the present, of our unpleasant materials, the further preparation of which was work in store for the following day.

A refreshing bath, clean clothes, and supper, cheered us all up, and we slept in peace.

CHAPTER XI

The blubber of the whale boiled and stored—A unique machine—Expedition to Prospect Hill—Whale's tongue is voted no delicacy—We land on Whale Island—Jack discovers a strange skeleton—Turtle turning—Towed ashore—The loom completed—Return of the herring shoals—Basket making—We manufacture a sedan chair—Ernest's wild ride therein—A boa constrictor appears—He retreats to the marsh—Suspense—Poor Grizzle's fate—An awful scene—Death of the monster—An account of snakes—Remedies for poisoned bites—Ernest writes Grizzle's epitaph—The serpent stuffed and placed in the museum.

"Now for the finishing up of this dirty job," cried I, merrily, as we all woke up next morning at daybreak. And after the regular work was done, we commenced operations by raising a stand or rough scaffold on which the tubs full of blubber were placed and heavily pressed, so that the purest and finest oil overflowed into vessels underneath.

The blubber was afterward boiled in a cauldron over a fire kindled at some distance from our abode, and by skimming and straining through a coarse cloth, we succeeded in obtaining a large supply of excellent train-oil, which in casks, and bags made of the intestines, was safely stowed away in the "cellar," as the children called our roughest storeroom. This day's work was far from agreeable, and the dreadful smell oppressed us all, more especially my poor wife, who, nevertheless, endured it with her accustomed good temper. Although she very urgently recommended that the new island should be the headquarters for another colony, where, said she, "any animals we leave would be safe from apes and other plunderers, and where you would find it so very convenient to boil whale-blubber, strain train-oil, and the like."

This proposal met with hearty approval, especially from the boys, who were always charmed with any new plan; and they were eager to act upon it at once, but when I reminded them of the putrefying carcass which lay there, they confessed it would be better to allow wind and storms, birds and insects to do their work in purging the atmosphere, and reducing the whale to a skeleton before we revisited the island.

The idea of a rowing-machine kept recurring to my brain. I determined to attempt to make one.

I took an iron bar, which when laid across the middle of the boat projected about a foot each way. I provided this bar in the middle with ribbed machinery, and at each end with a sort of nave, in which, as in a cart wheel, four flat spokes, or paddles, were fixed obliquely. These were intended to do the rowers' part.

Then the jack was arranged to act upon the machinery in the middle of the iron cross-bar, in such a way that one of its strong cogwheels bit firmly into the ribs, so that, when it was wound up, it caused the bar to revolve rapidly, of course turning with the paddles fixed at either end, which consequently struck the water so as to propel the boat.

Although this contrivance left much to be desired in the way of improvement, still when Fritz and I wound up the machinery, and went off on a trial trip across the bay, we splashed along at such a famous rate, that the shores rang with the cheers and clapping of the whole family, delighted to behold what they considered my brilliant success.

Every one wanted to go on board, and take a cruise, but as

it was getting late, I could not consent. A trip next day, however, was promised to Cape Disappointment and the little settlement of Prospect Hill.

This proposal satisfied everybody. The evening was spent in preparing the dresses, arms, and food which would be required, and we retired early to rest.

Intending to be out all day, the house was left in good order, and we departed on our expedition, provided, among other things, with spades and mattocks, for I wished to get young coconut trees and shrubs of different kinds, that, on our way back, we might land on Whale Island, and begin our plantation there.

We directed our course toward the opposite side of the bay. The sea was smooth, my rowing machine performed its work easily, and, leaving Safety Bay and Shark Island behind us, we enjoyed at our ease the panorama of all the coast scenery.

Landing near Prospect Hill, we moored the boat, and walked through the woods to our little farm, obtaining some fresh coconuts, as well as young plants, on the way.

Before coming in sight of the cottage at the farm, we heard the cocks crow, and I experienced a sudden rush of emotion as the sound recalled, in a degree painfully vivid, the recollection of many a ride and walk at home, when we would be greeted by just such familiar sounds as we approached some kind friend's house. Here, but for the unconscious animals, utter solitude and silence prevailed, and I with my dear family, whose visit would have been hailed with delight in so many homes, advanced unnoticed to this lonely cottage. So long had been our absence that our arrival created a perfect panic. The original animals had forgotten us, and to their progeny, lambs, kids, and chickens, who had never seen the face of man, we seemed an army of fierce foes.

The boys found it impossible to milk the goats, until, by the use of the lasso, they captured them one after the other, bound their legs, then giving them salt to lick, they soon obtained a supply of excellent milk, which was poured from the coconut shells they used into calabash flasks, so that we could take with us what was not required at dinner.

The fowls were enticed by handfuls of grain and rice, and my wife caught as many as she wished for.

We were by this time very ready for dinner, and the cold provisions we had with us were set forth, the chief dish consisting of the piece of whale's tongue, which, by the boys' desire, had been cooked with a special view to this entertainment.

But woeful was the disappointment when the tongue was tasted! One after another, with dismal face, pronounced it "horrid stuff," begged for some pickled herring to take away the taste of train-oil, and willingly bestowed on Fangs the cherished dainty.

Fortunately there was a sufficient supply of other eatables, and the fresh, delicious coconuts and goat's milk put every one in good humor again.

While the mother packed everything up, Fritz and I got some sugarcane shoots which I wished to plant, and then we returned to the shore and again embarked.

Before returning to Whale Island, I felt a strong wish to round Cape Disappointment and survey the coast immediately beyond, but the promontory maintained the character of its name, and we found that a long sandbank, as well as hidden reefs and rocks, ran out a great way into the sea.

Fritz espying breakers ahead, we put about at once, and aided by a light breeze, directed our course toward Whale Island.

On landing, I began at once to plant the saplings we had brought. The boys assisted me for a while, but wearied somewhat of the occupation, and one after another went off in search of shells and coral, leaving their mother and me to finish the work.

Presently Jack came back, shouting loudly:

"Father! Mother! Do come and look. There is an enormous skeleton lying here; the skeleton of some fearful great beast—a mammoth, I should think."

"Why, Jack!" returned I, laughing, "have you forgot our old acquaintance, the whale? What else could it be?"

"Oh, no, father, it is not the whale. This thing has not fish bones, but real, good, honest, huge beast bones. I don't know what can have become of the whale—floated out to sea, most likely. This mammoth is ever so much bigger. Come and see!"

As I was about to follow the boy, a voice from another direction suddenly cried:

"Father! Father! A great enormous turtle! Please make haste. It is waddling back to the sea as hard as it can go, and we can't stop it."

This appeal being more pressing, as well as more important than Jack's, I snatched up an oar and hastened to their assistance.

Sure enough a large turtle was scrambling quickly toward the water, and was within a few paces of it, although Ernest was valiantly holding on by one of its hind legs.

I sprang down the bank, and making use of the oar as a lever, we succeeded with some difficulty in turning the creature on its back.

It was a huge specimen, fully eight feet long, and being now quite helpless, we left it sprawling, and went to inspect Jack's mammoth skeleton, which, of course, proved to be neither more nor less than that of the whale. I convinced him of the fact by pointing out the marks of our feet on the ground, and the broken jaws where we had hacked out the whalebone.

"What can have made you take up that fancy about a mammoth, my boy?"

"Ernest put it into my head, father. He said there seemed to be the skeleton of an antediluvian monster there, so I ran to look closer, and I never thought of the whale, when I saw no fish bones. I suppose Ernest was joking."

"Whales are generally considered as fishes by those little acquainted with the animal kingdom, but they belong to the class of mammals, which comprises man, the monkey tribes, the bats, the dogs and cats, all hoofed animals, whales and their allies, with other animals, the last on the list being the sloth.

"The name by which they are distinguished is derived from the Latin word 'mamma,' a breast, and is given to them because all the species belonging to this class are furnished with a set of organs called the mammary glands, secreting the liquid known as milk, by which the young are nourished.

"The bones of the whale differ from those of animals, simply in being of a hollow construction, and filled with air so as to render the carcass more buoyant. The bones of birds are also hollow, for the same reason, and in all this we see conspicuously the wisdom and goodness of the great Creator."

"What a marvelous structure it is, father!" said Fritz. "What a ponderous mass of bones! Can we not make use of any of them?"

"Nothing strikes me at this moment; we will leave them to bleach here yet awhile, and perhaps, by sawing them up afterward, make a few chairs, or a reading desk for the museum. But now it is time to return home. Bring the boat round to where the turtle awaits his fate; we must settle how to deal with him."

It was soon decided that he must swim. I fastened the empty water-cask to a long line, one end of which was made fast to the bow of the boat, the other carefully passed round the neck and fore paws of the creature, who was then lifted, so as to let him regain his feet, when he instantly made for the water, plunged in, the cask floated after him, and prevented his sinking. We were all on board in a moment; and the worthy fellow, after vainly attempting to dive, set himself diligently to swim right forward, towing us comfortably after him. I was ready to cut the line on the least appearance of danger, and kept him on the course for Safety Bay by striking the water with a boat-hook, right or left, according as the turtle was disposed to turn too much one way or the other.

The boys were delighted with the fun, and compared me to Neptune in his car, drawn by dolphins, and accompanied by Amphitrite and attendant Tritons.

We landed safely at the usual place, near Rockburg, and the turtle was condemned and executed soon afterward; the shell, which was quite eight feet long, and three broad, was, when cleaned and prepared, to form a trough for the water supply at the cave, and the meat was carefully salted, and stored up for many a good and savory meal.

It had been my intention to bring a piece of land under cultivation before the next rainy season, to be sown with different sorts of grain; but many unforeseen circumstances had intervened to hinder this, and our animals, unaccustomed to the yoke, were not available for the plough.

I therefore gave up the idea for the present, and applied myself, with Ernest's assistance, to completing the loom, which, although the workmanship was clumsy, I succeeded in making quite fit for use. I had fortunately in my younger days spent many hours in the workshops of weavers and other artisans, and therefore I understood more than might have been expected of their various crafts.

Paste or size was required to smear over the threads; but we could not spare floor for such a purpose, and I used isinglass, which kept the warp moist perfectly well, and spared us the necessity of setting up the loom in a damp uncomfortable place, which has often to be done to prevent the over-drying of the web.

Of this isinglass I also made thin plates, to be used as window-panes; they were at least as transparent as horn, and when fixed deep in the rock, and beyond the reach of rain, did good service in admitting light.

Success encouraging me to persevere, I next began harness-making; the spoils of the chase having furnished us with plenty of leather, with which I covered light frames of wood, using a hairy moss or lichen for stuffing, and ere long the animals were equipped with saddles, stirrups, bridles, yokes, and collars, to the very great satisfaction of their youthful riders and drivers.

This occupation was followed by a great deal of work connected with the annual return of the herring shoals, which now took place; to them succeeding, as on former occasions, shoals of other fish, and many seals. More than ever aware of the value of all these, we did not fail to make good use of our opportunities, and captured large numbers.

The boys were getting anxious for another shooting expedition; but before undertaking that, I wished to do some basket-making, as sacks were beginning to fail us, and there was constant demand for baskets in which to carry and keep our roots and fruits. Our first attempts were clumsy enough; but, as usual, perseverance was rewarded, and we produced a good supply of all sorts and sizes. One very large basket I furnished with openings through which to pass a strong stick, so that it might, when heavily laden, be carried by two persons.

No sooner did the children see the force of this idea, than they got a bamboo, and popping little Franz into the basket, carried him about in triumph.

This amusement suggested a fresh notion to Fritz. "Oh, father," cried he, "don't you think we might make something like this for mother, and carry her much more comfortably than jolting along in the cart?"

The boys shouted with glee at the proposal, and though their mother thought the plan feasible enough, she confessed that she did not much like the thoughts of sitting in the middle of a basket, and just looking out now and then over the rim.

However, I assured her it should be a well-shaped, comfortable sedan-chair, or litter; and the next question was how it should be carried, since the boys could not play the part of Indian palanquin-bearers, either with safety to their mother, or with any pleasure to themselves.

"The bull and the buffalo!" cried Jack. "Why not use them for it? Let's go and try them now!"

Off ran the boys, and in a short time the basket was securely hung between Storm and Grumble. Fritz and Jack sprang into their saddles, and Ernest very gingerly deposited himself in the "cradle," as Franz called it; they set forth at a most sober pace, the animals, who were perfectly docile, appearing only a little surprised at the new arrangement.

"Oh, it is so pleasant, mother, it is a delightful motion," cried Ernest, as they passed us; "it swings and rocks really soothingly. Quicker, Fritz! Go quicker!" and the trot pleasing him equally well, the pace gradually quickened, till the animals were going along at a rate which shook and jolted the basket about most fearfully. Ernest called and screamed in vain for a halt. His brothers thought it capital fun to "shake up" the "professor," and made the circuit of the level ground near Rockburg, finally pulling up in front of us, like performers stopping to receive the applause of spectators.

It was impossible to help laughing, the scene was so ridiculous, but Ernest was very angry with his brothers, his reproaches provoked high words in reply, and a quarrel was imminent, but I interfered, and showed them how easily a joke, carried too far, would lead to disputes and bad feeling, urging them to avoid on all occasions any breach of the good-fellowship and brotherly love which was the mainstay of our strength and happiness.

Good humor was soon restored, Ernest himself helped to unharness the beasts, and got some handfuls of salt and barley to reward their exertions, saying that they must have some more palanquin-practice another day.

I was seated with my wife and Fritz beneath the shade of the veranda, engaged in wicker-work, and chatting pleasantly, when suddenly Fritz got up, advanced a step or two, gazing fixedly along the avenue which led from Jackal River, then he exclaimed:

"I see something so strange in the distance, father! What in the world can it be? First it seems to be drawn in coils on the ground like a cable, then uprises as if it were a little mast, then that sinks, and the coils move along again. It is coming toward the bridge."

My wife took alarm at this description, and calling the other boys, retreated into the cave, where I desired them to close up the entrances, and keep watch with firearms at the upper windows. These were openings we had made in the rock at some elevation, reached within by steps, and a kind of gallery which passed along the front of the rooms.

Fritz remained by me while I examined the object through my spyglass.

"It is, as I feared, an enormous serpent!" cried I; "it advances directly this way, and we shall be placed in the greatest possible danger, for it will cross the bridge to a certainty."

"May we not attack it, father?" exclaimed the brave boy.

"Only with the greatest caution," returned I; "it is far too formidable, and too tenacious of life, for us rashly to attempt its destruction. Thank God, we are at Rockburg, where we can keep in safe retreat, while we watch for an opportunity to destroy this frightful enemy. Go up to your mother now, and assist in preparing the firearms; I will join you directly, but I must further observe the monster's movements."

Fritz left me unwilling, while I continued to watch the serpent, which was of gigantic size, and already much too near the bridge to admit of the possibility of removing that means of access to our dwelling. I recollected, too, how easily it would pass through the walls. The reptile advanced with writhing and undulatory movements, from time to time rearing its head to the height of fifteen or twenty feet, and slowly turning it about, as though on the lookout for prey.

As it crossed the bridge, with a slow, suspicious motion, I withdrew, and hastily rejoined my little party, which was preparing to garrison our fortress in warlike array, but with considerable trepidation, which my presence served in a measure to allay.

We placed ourselves at the upper openings, after strongly barricading everything below, and, ourselves unseen, awaited with beating hearts the further advance of the foe, which speedily became visible to us.

Its movements appeared to become uncertain, as though puzzled by the trace of human habitation; it turned in different directions, coiling and uncoiling, and frequently rearing its head, but keeping about the middle of the space in front of the cave, when suddenly, as though unable to resist doing so, one after another the boys fired, and even their mother discharged her gun. The shots took not the slightest effect beyond startling the monster, whose movements were accelerated. Fritz and I also fired with steadier aim, but with the same want of success, for the monster, passing on with a gliding motion, entered the reedy marsh to the left, and entirely disappeared.

A wonderful weight seemed lifted from our hearts, while all eagerly discussed the vast length and awful though magnificent appearance of the serpent. I had recognized it as the boa constrictor. It was a vast specimen, upward of thirty feet in length.

I explained to the children that its name in South America is Boaguacu; the first syllable of that word, with the Latin addition, which indicates that it kills its prey by pressure, or "constriction," gives the name by which it is commonly known.

The near neighborhood of this terrific reptile occasioned me the utmost anxiety; and I desired that no one should leave the house on any pretense whatever, without my express permission.

During three whole days we were kept in suspense and fear, not daring to stir above a few hundred steps from the door, although during all that time the enemy showed no sign of his presence.

In fact, we might have been induced to think the boa had passed across the swamp, and found his way by some cleft or chasm through the wall of cliffs beyond, had not the restless behavior of our geese and ducks given proof that he still lurked in the thicket of reeds which they were accustomed to make their nightly resting place.

They swam anxiously about, and with much clapping of wings and disturbed cackling showed their uneasiness; finally taking wing they crossed the harbor, and took up their quarters on Shark Island.

My embarrassment increased, as time passed on. I could not venture to attack with insufficient force a monstrous and formidable serpent concealed in dense thickets amidst dangerous swamps; yet it was dreadful to live in a state of blockade, cut off from all the important duties in which we were engaged, and shut up with our animals in the unnatural light of the cave, enduring constant anxiety and perturbation.

Out of this painful state we were at last delivered by none other than our good old simple-hearted donkey; not, however, by the exercise of a praiseworthy quality, such as the vigilance of the time-honored geese of the Capitol, but by sheer stupidity.

Our situation was rendered the more critical from having no great stock of provisions, or fodder for the animals; and the hay failing us on the evening of the third day, I determined to set them at liberty by sending them, under guidance of Fritz, across the river at the ford.

He was to ride Lightfoot, and they were to be fastened together until safely over.

Next morning we began to prepare for this by tying them in a line, and while so engaged my wife opened the door, when old Grizzle, who was fresh and frolicsome after the long rest and regular feeding, suddenly broke away from the halter, cut some awkward capers, then bolting out, careened at full gallop straight for the marsh.

In vain we called him by name. Fritz would even have rushed after him, had not I held him back. In another moment the ass was close to the thicket, and with the cold shudder of horror, we beheld the snake rear itself from its lair, the fiery eyes glanced around, the dark, deadly jaws opened widely, the forked tongue darted greedily forth—poor Grizzle's fate was sealed.

Becoming aware on a sudden of his danger, he stopped short, spread out all four legs, and set up the most piteous and discordant bray that ever wrung echo from the rocks.

Swift and straight as a fencer's thrust, the destroyer was upon him, wound round him, entangled, enfolded, compressed him, all the while cunningly avoiding the convulsive kicks of the agonized animal.

A cry of horror arose from the spectators of this miserable tragedy.

"Shoot him, father! Oh, shoot him—do save poor Grizzle!"

"My children, it is impossible!" cried I. "Our old friend is lost to us for ever! I have hopes, however, that when gorged with his prey we may be able to attack the snake with some chance of success."

"But the horrible wretch is never going to swallow him all at once, father?" cried Jack. "That will be too shocking!"

"Snakes have no grinders, but only fangs, therefore they cannot chew their food, and must swallow it whole. But although the idea is startling, it is not really more shocking than the rending, tearing, and shedding of blood which occurs when the lions and tigers seize their prey."

"But," said Franz, "how can the snake separate the flesh from the bones without teeth? And is this kind of snake poisonous?"

"No, dear child," said I, "only fearfully strong and ferocious. And it has no need to tear the flesh from the bones. It swallows them, skin, hair, and all, and digests everything in its stomach."

"It seems utterly impossible that the broad ribs, the strong legs, hoofs, and all, should go down that throat," exclaimed Fritz.

"Only see," I replied, "how the monster deals with his victim; closer and more tightly he curls his crushing folds, the bones give way, he is kneading him into a shapeless mass. He will soon begin to gorge his prey, and slowly but surely it will disappear down that distended maw!"

The mother, with little Franz, found the scene all too horrible, and hastened into the cave, trembling and distressed.

To the rest of us there seemed a fearful fascination in the dreadful sight, and we could not move from the spot. I expected that the boa, before swallowing his prey, would cover it with saliva, to aid in the operation, although it struck me that its very slender forked tongue was about the worst possible implement for such a purpose.

It was evident to us, however, that this popular idea was erroneous.

The act of lubricating the mass must have taken place during the process of swallowing; certainly nothing was applied beforehand.

This wonderful performance lasted from seven in the morning until noon. When the awkward morsel was entirely swallowed, the serpent lay stiff, distorted, and apparently insensible along the edge of the marsh.

I felt that now or never was the moment for attack!

Calling on my sons to maintain their courage and presence of mind, I left our retreat with a feeling of joyous emotion quite new to me, and approached with rapid steps and leveled gun the outstretched form of the serpent. Fritz followed me closely.

Jack, somewhat timidly, came several paces behind; while Ernest, after a little hesitation, remained where he was.

The monster's body was stiff and motionless, which made its rolling and fiery eyes and the slow, spasmodic undulations of it tail more fearful by contrast.

We fired together, and both balls entered the skull; the light of the eye was extinguished, and the only movement was in the further extremity of the body, which rolled, writhed, coiled, and lashed from side to side.

Advancing closer, we fired our pistols directly into its head, a convulsive quiver ran through the mighty frame, and the boa constrictor lay dead.

As we raised a cry of victory, Jack, desirous of a share in the glory of conquest, ran close to the creature, firing his pistol into its side, when he was sent sprawling over and over by a movement of its tail, excited to a last galvanic effort by the shot.

Being in no way hurt, he speedily recovered his feet, and declared he had given it its quietus.

"I hope the terrible noise you made just now was the signal of victory," said my wife, drawing near, with the utmost circumspection, and holding Franz tightly by the hand. "I was half afraid to come, I assure you."

"See this dreadful creature dead at our feet; and let us thank God that we have been able to destroy such an enemy."

"What's to be done with him now?" asked Jack.

"Let us get him stuffed," said Fritz, "and set him up in the museum among our shells and corals."

"Did anybody ever think of eating serpents?" inquired Franz.

"Of course not!" said his mother. "Why, child, serpents are poisonous—it would be very dangerous."

"Excuse me, my dear wife," said I. "First of all, the boa is not poisonous; and then, besides that, the flesh of even poisonous snakes can be eaten without danger; as, for instance, the rattlesnake, from which can be made a strong and nourishing soup, tasting very like good chicken broth—of course, the cook must be told to throw away the head, containing the deadly fangs.

"It is remarkable that pigs do not fear poisonous snakes, but can kill and eat them without injury. An instance of this occurs to my memory. A vessel on LakeSuperior, in North America, was wrecked on a small island abounding in rattlesnakes, and for that reason uninhabited.

"The vessel had a cargo of live pigs. The crew escaped to the mainland in a boat, but the pigs had to be left for some time, till the owner could return to fetch them, but with the small hope of finding many left alive.

"To his surprise, the animals were not only alive, but remarkably fat and flourishing, while not a single rattlesnake remained on the island. The pigs had clearly eaten the serpents."

"But might not some other cause have been assigned for their disappearance?" asked Ernest. "Suppose, for example, that a great flight of secretary birds had arrived, they might have cleared the island of rattlesnakes."

"Oh, what is a secretary bird?" interrupted Franz. "I thought a secretary meant a man who wrote letters."

"So it does, Franz, and the bird Ernest spoke of has curious long feathers projecting from either side of its head, something like pens stuck behind a man's ear; hence its name.

"It is perfectly true that it lives on snakes, lizards, toads, and frogs, but, Ernest, I cannot give up my pigs; for, in the first place, the secretary bird is an inhabitant of Southern Africa, and is never seen in North America, neither does it ever fly in a flock; still, so ravenous is its appetite, that, no doubt, even one or two, had they by some miracle found themselves on Lake Superior, would have been able to give a very good account of the deadly reptiles, and at least shared in the glory of their extermination."

My wife having gone to prepare dinner, we continued talking as we rested in the shade of some rocks, near the serpent, for a considerable time. The open air was welcome to us after our long imprisonment: and we were, besides, desirous to drive off any birds of prey who might be attracted to the carcass, which we wished to preserve entire.

My boys questioned me closely on the subject of serpents in general; and I described to them the action of the poison fangs; how they folded back on the sides of the upper jaw; and how the poison-secreting glands and reservoir are found at the back and sides of the head, giving to the venomous serpents that peculiar width of head which is so unfailing a characteristic.

"The fangs are hollow," said I, "and when the creature bites, the pressure forces down a tiny drop of the liquid poison which enters the wound, and, through the veins, quickly spreads over the entire system. Sometimes, if taken in time, cures are effected, but in most cases the bite of a serpent is followed by speedy death."

The children were much interested in my account of the snake-charmers of India, how they fearlessly handle the most deadly of the serpent tribe, the Cobra di Capello—or hooded cobra—cause them to move in time to musical sounds from a small pipe, twine the reptile about their arms and bare necks, and then, to prove that the poison fangs have not been removed, make them bite a fowl, which soon dies from the effects.

"How is it possible to extract the fangs, father!" asked Ernest.

"No instrument is required," replied I; "I have read the account written by a gentleman in India, who saw a snake-charmer catch a large cobra in the jungle, and for the purpose of removing the fangs, hold up a cloth at which the irritated snake flew, and the fangs being caught in it, the man seized the reptile by the throat, extracted them, and then squeezed out the poison, a clear oily substance, upon a leaf."

"What does the rattle of the rattlesnake look like? And how does it sound?"

"At the tip of the tail are a number of curious, loose, horny structures formed of the same substance as the scales. A very good idea of the structure of the rattle may be formed by slipping a number of thimbles loosely into each other.

"The rattlesnake lies coiled with its head flat, and the tip of its tail elevated; when alarmed or irritated it gives a quivering movement to the tail which causes the joints of the rattle to shake against each other with a peculiar sound not easily described; all animals, even horses newly brought from Europe, tremble at this noise, and try to escape."

"What is the best thing to be done for the bite of a serpent?" inquired Fritz.

"Remedies are very various, very uncertain, and differ with the species inflicting the bite.

"Suction, ammonia, oil, the use of the knife, application of fresh mold, lunar caustic, leaves of certain plants, all these and more are mentioned. There is a creeping plant, called *Aristolochia indica*, the leaves of which have in repeated instances done wonders for fearful bites. It is found in many parts of the world, but most plentifully in the hotter regions.

"A mode of cure adopted by natives of India, Ceylon, and parts of Africa, is by the application of a remarkable object called snake-stone. These are described as flattish, something like half an almond with squared ends, rather light, bearing a very high polish, and of an intense jetty black.

"On being bitten by a cobra, the sufferer applies one of these 'stones' to each puncture, where they adhere strongly for a time, five or six minutes being about the average. They seem to absorb the blood as it flows from the wound, and at last fall off, when the danger is considered to be over.

"But now we must leave this fertile subject of discussion, and I can only say I sincerely trust we may never have cause to resume it from the appearance of another serpent here of any sort, size, or description.

"Come, Ernest, can you not give us an epitaph for our unfortunate friend the donkey?

"We must afford him more honorable sepulture than he enjoys at present, when we proceed, as we speedily must, to disembowel his murderer."

Ernest took the matter quite seriously, and planting his elbows on his knees, he bent his thoughtful brow in his hands, and remained wrapt in poetic meditation for about two minutes.

"I have it!" cried he; "but perhaps you will all laugh at me?"

"No, no, don't be shy, old fellow; spit it out!" and thus encouraged by his brother, Ernest, with the blush of a modest author, began:

"Beneath this stone poor Grizzle's bones are laid,
A faithful ass he was, and loved by all.
At length, his master's voice he disobeyed,
And thereby came his melancholy fall.
A monstrous serpent, springing from the grass,
Seized, crushed, and swallowed him before our eyes
But we, though yet we mourn our honest ass,
Are grateful; for he thereby saved the lives
Of all the human beings on this shore—
A father, mother, and their children four."

"Hurrah for the epitaph! Well done, Ernest!" resounded on all sides, and taking out a large red pencil I used for marking wood, the lines were forthwith inscribed on a great flat stone, being, as I told the boy, the very best poetry that had ever been written on our coast.

We then had dinner, and afterward went to work with the serpent.

The first operation was to recover the mangled remains of the ass, which being effected, he was buried in the soft marshy ground close by, and the hole filled up with fragments of rock.

Then we yoked Storm and Grumble to the serpent, and dragged it to a convenient distance from Rockburg, where the process of skinning, stuffing, and sewing up again afforded occupation of the deepest interest to the boys for several days.

We took great pains to coil it round a pole in the museum, arranging the head with the jaws wide open, so as to look as alarming as possible, and contriving to make eyes and tongue sufficiently well to represent nature; in fact, our dogs never passed the monster without growling, and must have wondered at our taste in keeping such a pet.

Over the entrance leading to the museum and library were inscribed these words:

NO ADMITTANCE FOR ASSES

The double meaning of this sentence pleased us all immensely.

CHAPTER XII

We examine the marsh—A cave discovered—We find the floor covered with fuller's earth—Discharge our pistols—Jack's fright—Ernest captures an eel—An expedition toward the Gap—Visit Falconhurst and Woodlands and examine the country round—Franz shoots a capybara—Ernest and Knips fight the rats—A lecture on musk—Cinnamon apples—A peccary hunt—We prepare the peccary meat—Disasters at Prospect Hill—An exploring expedition through the Gap—We find our barrier broken down across the desert—Strange objects in the distance—An account of ostriches—An ostrich slain—We discover the nest—A mud tortoise—We encounter bears—A desperate fight—Back again to camp—We skin the bears and smoke their flesh—Pepper found—Three of the boys start on an expedition—I discover talc.

The greatest danger to which we had yet been exposed was now over, but there remained much anxiety in my mind lest another serpent might, unseen by us, have entered the swamp, or might appear, as this had done, from the country beyond Falconhurst.

I projected then two excursions, the first to make a thorough examination of the thicket and morass; the next right away to the Gap, through which alone the archenemy could have entered our territory.

On summoning my sons to accompany me to the marsh, I found neither Ernest nor Jack very eager to do so, the latter vowing he had the cold shivers each time he thought how his ribs might have been smashed by the last flap of the snake's tail; but I did not yield to their reluctance, and we finally set about crossing the marsh by placing planks and wicker hurdles on the ground, and changing their places as we advanced.

Nothing was discovered beyond tracks in the reeds and the creature's lair; where the rushes, grass, and bog-plants were beaten down.

Emerging beyond the thicket we found ourselves on firm ground, near the precipitous wall of rock, and perceived a clear sparkling brook flowing from an opening, which proved to be a cave or grotto of considerable size.

The vaulted roof was covered with stalactites, while many formed stately pillars, which seemed as though supporting the roof. The floor was strewn with fine snow-white earth, with a smooth soapy feeling, which I felt convinced was fuller's earth.

"Well, this is a pleasant discovery!" said I. "This is as good as soap for washing, and will save me the trouble of turning soap-boiler."

Perceiving that the streamlet flowed from an opening of some width in the inner rock, Fritz passed through, in order to trace it to its source, presently shouting to me that the opening widened very much, and begging me to follow him.

I did so, leaving the other boys in the outer cave, and fired a pistol-shot—the reverberating echoes of which testified to the great extent of the place; and lighting the bit of candle I always carried with me, we advanced, the light burning clear and steadily, though shedding a very feeble light in so vast a space.

Suddenly Fritz exclaimed:

"I verily believe this is a second cave of salt! See how the walls glance! And how the light is reflected from the roof!"

"These cannot be salt crystals," said I; "the water which flows over them leaves no track, and tastes quite sweet. I am rather inclined to believe that we have penetrated into a cave of rock crystal!"

"Oh, how splendid! Then we have discovered a great treasure!"

"Certainly, if we could make any use of it; otherwise, in our situation, it is about as valuable as the lump of gold found by good old Robinson Crusoe."

"Anyhow, I will break off a piece for a specimen. See, here is a fine bit, only rather dull, and not transparent; what a pity! I must knock off another."

"You must go more carefully to work, or it will look as dull as the first. You destroyed its true form, which is that of a pyramid, with six sides or faces."

We remained some time in this interesting grotto, but our light burnt low after we had examined it in different directions; and Fritz having secured a large lump, which exhibited several crystals in perfection, we quitted the place, Fritz discharging a farewell shot for the sake of hearing the grand echoes.

On reaching the open air we saw poor Jack sobbing bitterly, but as soon as we appeared he ran joyfully toward us, and threw himself into my arms.

"My child, what is the matter?" I cried anxiously.

"Oh, I thought you were lost! I heard a noise twice, as if the rocks had shattered down; and I thought you and Fritz were crushed in the ruins! It was horrible! How glad I am to see you!"

I comforted the child, and explained the noises he had heard, inquiring why he was alone?

"Ernest is over there among the reeds: I daresay he did not hear the shots."

I found Ernest busily engaged in weaving a basket in which to catch fish; he had devised it ingeniously, with a funnel-shaped entrance; through which the fish passing would not easily find their way out, but would remain swimming about in the wide part of the apparatus.

"I shot a young serpent while you were away, father," said he. "It lies there covered with rushes; it is nearly four feet long, and as thick as my arm."

"A serpent!" cried I, hurrying toward it in alarm, and fearing there must be a brood of them in the swamp after all.

"A fine large eel, you mean, my boy. This will provide an excellent supper for us tonight. I am glad you had the courage to kill it, instead of taking to your heels and fleeing from the supposed serpent."

"Well, I thought it would be so horrid to be pursued and caught that I preferred facing it; my shot took effect, but it was very difficult to kill the creature outright, it moved about although its head was smashed."

"The tenacity of life possessed by eels is very remarkable," I said. "I have heard that the best mode of killing them is to grasp them by the neck and slap their tails smartly against a stone or post."

We made our way back more easily by keeping close to the cliffs, where the ground was firmer, and found the mother washing clothes at the fountain. She rejoiced greatly at our safe return, and was much pleased with the supply of fuller's earth, as she said there was now very little soap left. The eel was cooked for supper, and during the evening a full account was given of our passage through the swamp, and discovery of the rock-crystal cavern.

It was most important to ascertain whether any serpent lurked among the woods of our little territory between the cliffs and the sea. Preparations were set on foot for the second and greater undertaking of a search throughout the country beyond the river, as far as the Gap. I wished all the family to go on the expedition, a decision which gave universal satisfaction.

Intending to be engaged in this search for several weeks, we took the small tent and a store of all sorts of necessary provisions, as well as firearms, tools, cooking utensils, and torches.

All these things were packed on the cart, which was drawn by Storm and Grumble. Jack and Franz mounted them, and acted at once the part of riders and drivers. My wife sat comfortably in the cart, Fritz rode in advance, while Ernest and I walked; we were protected in flank by the dogs and Fangs, the tame jackal.

Directing our course toward Woodlands, we saw many traces of the serpent's approach to Rockburg. In some places, where the soil was loose, the trail, like a broad furrow, was very evident indeed.

At Falconhurst we made a halt, and were, as usual, welcomed by the poultry, as well as by the sheep and goats.

We then passed on to Woodlands, where we arrived at nightfall. All was peaceful and in good order; no track of the boa in that direction; no signs of visits from mischievous apes; the little farm and its inhabitants looked most flourishing.

Next day was passed in making a survey of the immediate neighborhood, at the same time collecting a quantity of cotton, which was wanted for new pillows and cushions. In the afternoon Franz was my companion, carrying a small gun entrusted to him for the first time.

We took Fan and Bruno with us, and went slowly along the left bank of the lake, winding our way among reedy thickets, which frequently turned us aside a considerable distance from the water. The dogs hunted about in all directions, and raised duck, snipe, and heron. These usually flew directly across the lake so that Franz got no chance of a shot. He began to get rather impatient, and proposed firing at the black swans we saw sailing gracefully on the glassy surface of the lake.

Just then a harsh booming sound struck our ears. I paused in wonder as to whence the noise proceeded, while Franz exclaimed, "Oh, father, can that be Swift, our young onager?"

"It cannot possibly be Swift," said I; adding, after listening attentively a minute or two, "I am inclined to think it must be the cry of a bittern, a fine handsome bird of the nature of a heron."

"Oh! May I shoot it, father? But I wonder how a bird can make that roaring noise! One would think it was an ox, it is more like lowing than braying."

"The noise creatures make depends more on the construction of the windpipe, its relation to the lungs and the strength of the muscles which force out the breath, than on their size. As, for example, how loud is the song of the nightingale and the little canary bird. Some people say the bittern booms with his long bill partly thrust into the boggy ground, which increases the hollow muffled sound of its very peculiar cry."

Franz was very anxious that the first trophy of his gun should be so rare a bird as the bittern; the dogs were sent into the wood, and we waited some distance apart, in readiness to fire.

All at once there was a great rustling in the thicket, Franz fired, and I heard his happy voice calling out:

"I've hit him! I've hit him!"

"What have you hit?" shouted I in return.

"A wild pig," said he; "but bigger than Fritz's."

"Aha! I see you remember the agouti! Perhaps it is not a hog at all but one of our little pigs from the farm. What will the old sow say to you, Franz?"

I soon joined my boy, and found him in transports of joy over an animal certainly very much like a pig, although its snout was broad and blunt. It was covered with bristles, had no tail, and in color was a yellowish gray.

Examining it carefully, and noticing its webbed feet and its curious teeth, I decided that it must be a capybara, a water-loving animal of South America, and Franz was overjoyed to find that he had shot "a new creature," as he said. It was difficult to carry it home, but he very sensibly proposed that we should open and clean the carcass, which would make it lighter—and then putting it in a game bag, he carried it till quite tired out; he then asked if I thought Bruno would let him strap it on his back. We found the dog willing to bear the burden, and reached Woodlands soon afterward.

There we were surprised to see Ernest surrounded by a number of large rats which lay dead on the ground.

"Where can all these have come from?" exclaimed I. "Have you and your mother been rat-hunting instead of gathering rice as you intended?"

"We came upon these creatures quite unexpectedly," he replied, "while in the rice swamp. Knips, who was with us, sprang away to a kind of long-shaped mound among the reeds, and pounced upon something, which tried to escape into a hole. He chattered and gnashed his teeth, and the creature hissed and squeaked, and running up I found he had got a big rat by the tail; he would not let go, and the rat could not turn in the narrow entrance to bite him, but I soon pulled it out and killed it with my stick.

"The mound was a curious looking erection, so I broke it open with some difficulty, and in doing this dislodged quite a dozen of the creatures. Some I killed, but many plunged into the water and escaped.

"On examining their dwelling I found it a vaulted tunnel made of clay and mud, and thickly lined with sedges, rushes, and water-lily leaves.

"There were other mounds or lodges close by, and seeking an entrance to one I stretched my game bag across it, and then hammered on the roof till a whole lot of rats sprang out, several right into the bag. I hit away right and left, but began to repent of my audacity when I found the whole community swarming about in the wildest excitement, some escaping, but many stopping in bewilderment, while others actually attacked me.

"It was anything but pleasant, I assure you, and I began to think of Bishop Hatto in the Mouse Tower on the Rhine. Knips liked it as little as I did, and skipped about desperately to get out of their way, though he now and then seized a rat by the neck in his teeth.

"Just as I began to shout for help, Juno came dashing through the reeds and water, and made quick work with the enemy, all flying from her attack.

"My mother had great difficulty in forcing her way through the marsh to the scene of action, but reached me at last; and we collected all the slain to show you, and for the sake of their skins."

This account excited my curiosity, and I went to examine the place Ernest described: where I found, to my surprise, an arrangement much like a beaver dam, though on a small scale, and less complete.

"You have discovered a colony of beaver rats," said I to Ernest, "so called from their resemblance in skill and manner of life to that wonderful creature.

"Muskrat, musquash, and ondatra are other names given to them. They have, you see, webbed feet and flattened tails, and we shall find that they carry two small glands containing the scented substance called musk. The sooner we strip off the skins the better; they will be useful for making caps."

We went back to the house, and met Fritz and Jack just returned from their excursion, reporting that no trace of serpents, great or small, had been met with.

Jack carried in his hat about a dozen eggs; and Fritz had shot a couple of heath fowls, a cock and hen.

We sat down to supper, Franz eager to partake of his capybara. Even he himself made a face at the peculiar flavor of the meat.

"It is the musk which you taste," said I; and I described to them the various animals in which this strange liquid is found; the musk deer, musk ox, crocodile, muskrat of India (also called coudeli, which taints a corked bottle of wine, if it only runs across it), concluding with an account of the civet, called also civet-cat.

"The civet," said I, "is a handsome black and white animal, and the perfume obtained from it was formerly considered a valuable medicine; in the present day it is used chiefly as a scent. This odoriferous substance is secreted, *i.e.*, formed, in a double glandular pouch near the tail, and the Dutch keep the creature in captivity, so that it shall afford them a continual supply.

"The method of removing the civet perfume is ingenious. The animal is very quick and elastic in its movements, and having sharp teeth it is not pleasant to handle. So it is put into a long, narrow cage in which it cannot turn round, a horn spoon is then introduced, and the perfume, a thick, oily stuff something like butter, is coolly scraped from the pouch, the plundered civet being then released from strait durance, until the supply is reformed."

Presently Jack ran for his game bag, producing some fruit which he had forgotten. Several pale green apples, quite new to us, excited general attention.

"Why, what are those? Are they good?" I asked.

"I hope so, for we sadly want something to take away the taste of Franz's beast," said Jack: "but Fritz and I were afraid of eating some awful poison or other, like the manchineel, so we brought them for the inspection of the learned master Knips."

I took one and cut it in two, remarking that it contained a circle of seeds or pips, instead of the stone of the manchineel. At that moment Knips slyly came behind me, and snatching up one half, began to munch it with the liveliest satisfaction, an example which the boys were so eager to follow that a general scramble ensued, and I had some trouble in securing a couple of apples for myself and their mother.

I imagined this to be the cinnamon apple of the Antilles.

Every one seeming wearied by the fatigues of the day, our mattresses and pillows were arranged, and the inmates of Woodlands betook themselves to repose.

With early light we commenced the next day's journey, directing our course to a point between the sugar-brake and the Gap, where we had once made a sort of arbor of the branches of trees; as this remained in pretty good condition, we spread a sailcloth over the top of it, instead of pitching the tent, and made it very comfortable quarters for the short time I proposed to stay there.

Our object being to search the neighborhood for traces of the boa constrictor, or any of his kindred, Fritz, Jack, and Franz went with me to the sugarcane brake, and satisfied ourselves that our enemy had not been there. It was long since we had enjoyed the fresh juice of these canes, and we were refreshing ourselves therewith, when a loud barking of dogs, and loud rustling and rattling through the thicket of canes, disturbed our pleasant occupation, and, as we could see nothing a yard off where we stood, I hurried to the open ground, and with guns in readiness we awaited what was coming.

In a few minutes a herd of creatures like little pigs issued from the thicket, and made off in single file at a brisk trot; they were of a uniform gray color, and showed short sharp tusks.

My trusty double-barrel speedily laid low two of the fugitives;

the others continued to follow the leader in line, scarcely turning aside to pass the dead bodies of their comrades, and maintaining the same steady pace, although Fritz and Jack also fired and killed several.

I felt certain that these were peccaries, and recollected that an odoriferous gland in the back must be removed immediately, otherwise the meat will become tainted, and quite unfit to eat. This operation, with the help of my boys, I accordingly performed at once.

Presently, hearing shots in the direction of the hut where we had left Ernest and his mother, I sent Jack to their assistance, desiring him to fetch the cart, that the booty might be conveyed to our encampment, employing the time of his absence in opening and cleaning the animals, thus reducing their weight.

Ernest came back with Jack and the cart, and told us that the procession of peccaries had passed near the hut, and that he, with Juno's help, had secured three of them.

I was glad to hear this, as I had determined to cure a good supply of hams, and we made haste to load the cart; the boys adorned it with flowers and green boughs, and with songs of triumph which made the woods ring they conveyed the valuable supply of game to the hut, where their mother anxiously waited for us.

After dinner we set to work upon our pigs, singeing and scalding off the bristles; I cut out the hams, divided the flitches, bestowed considerable portions of the carcass on the dogs, and diligently cleansed and salted the meat, while the boys prepared a shed, where it was to be hung to be cured in the smoke of fires of green wood.

This unexpected business of course detained us in the place for some time. On the second day, when the smoking shed was ready, the boys were anxious to cook the smallest porker in the Otaheitian fashion. For this purpose they dug a hole, in which they burned a quantity of dry grass, sticks, and weeds, heating stones, which were placed round the sides of the pit.

While the younger boys made ready the oven, Fritz singed and washed his peccary, stuffing it with potatoes, onions, and herbs, and a good sprinkling of salt and pepper.

He then sewed up the opening, and enveloped the pig in large leaves to guard it from the ashes and dust of its cooking place.

The fire no longer blazed, but the embers and stones were glowing hot; the pig was carefully placed in the hole, covered over with hot ashes, and the hole with earth, so that it looked like a big mole heap.

Dinner was looked forward to with curiosity, as well as appetite; my wife, as usual, distrusting our experiments, was not sanguine of success, and made ready some plain food as a *pis aller.*

She was well pleased with the curing-hut, which was roomy enough to hang all our hams and bacon. On a wide hearth in the middle we kindled a large fire, which was kept constantly smouldering by heaping it with damp grass and green wood. The hut being closed in above, the smoke filled it, and penetrated the meat thoroughly; this process it had to undergo for several days.

In a few hours Fritz gave notice that he was going to open his oven.

Great excitement prevailed as he removed the earth, turf, and stones, and a delicious appetizing odor arose from the opening. It was the smell of roast pork, certainly, but with a flavor of spices which surprised me, until I thought of the leaves in which the food had been wrapped up.

The peccary was carefully raised, and when a few cinders were picked off, it looked a remarkably well-cooked dish. Fritz was highly complimented on his success, even by his mother.

The scented leaves were, I thought, those of a tree which I knew to be found in Madagascar, called by the natives ravensara, or "good leaf." It is said to combine the scent of the nutmeg, clove, and cinnamon. The fruit is a species of nut, possessing the scent of the leaves in a more delicate degree, and from it an oil or essence is distilled, which is highly valued in native cookery.

During the process of curing our large supply of hams

and bacon, which occupied several days, we roamed about the neighborhood in all directions, finding no trace of the serpent, but making many valuable acquisitions, among which were some gigantic bamboos, from fifty to sixty feet in length and of proportionate thickness. These, when cut across near the joints, formed capital casks, tubs and pots; while the long sharp thorns, which begirt the stem at intervals, were as strong and useful as iron nails.

One day we made an excursion to the farm at Prospect Hill, and were grievously provoked to find that the vagabond apes had been there, and wrought terrible mischief, as before at Woodlands.

The animals and poultry were scattered, and everything in the cottage so torn and dirtied, that it was vain to think of setting things right that day. We therefore very unwillingly left the disorder as we found it, purposing to devote time to the work afterward.

When all was in readiness for the prosecution of our journey, we closed and barricaded the hut, in which, for the present, we left the store of bacon; and arranging our march in the usual patriarchal style, we took our way to the Gap, the thorough defense of which defile was the main object we had in view.

Our last halting-place being much enclosed by shrubs, bamboos, and brushwood, we had during our stay opened a path through the cane thicket in the direction we were about to travel; this we now found of the greatest assistance, and the loaded cart passed on without impediment.

The ground was open and tolerably level beyond, so that in a few hours we arrived at the extreme limit of our coast territory.

We halted on the outskirts of a little wood, behind which, to the right, rose the precipitous and frowning cliffs of the mountain gorge, while to the left flowed the torrent, leaving between it and the rocks the narrow pass we called the Gap, and passing outward to mingle its water with the sea.

The wood afforded us pleasant shelter, and standing high and within gunshot of the mouth of the rocky pass, I resolved to make it our camping place. We therefore unpacked the cart, and made our usual arrangements for safety and comfort, not forgetting to examine the wood itself, so as to ascertain whether it harbored any dangerous animals.

Nothing worse than wild cats was discovered. We disturbed several of these creatures in their pursuit of birds and small game, but they fled at our approach.

By the time dinner was ready we felt much fatigued, and some hours of unusually sultry and oppressive heat compelled us to rest until toward evening, when returning coolness revived our strength. We pitched the tent, and then occupied ourselves with preparations for the next day, when it was my intention to penetrate the country beyond the defile, and make a longer excursion across the Savannah than had yet been undertaken.

All was ready for a start at an early hour; my brave wife consented to remain in camp with Franz as her companion, while the three elder boys, and all the dogs, except Juno, went with me.

We expected to find it somewhat difficult to make our way through the narrowest part of the pass, which had been so strongly barricaded and planted with thorny shrubs, but found on the contrary that the fences and walls were broken down and disarranged. It was thus very evident that the great snake, as well as the herd of peccaries, had made an entrance here.

This barricade was the first check that had been placed by hand of man upon the wild free will of nature in this lonely place.

With one consent storms, floods, torrents, and the wild beasts of the forest, had set themselves to destroy it.

We resolved to make the defenses doubly strong, being convinced that the position was capable of being barricaded and fortified so as to resist the invaders we dreaded.

The prospect which opened before us on emerging from the rocky pass was wide and varied. Swelling hills and verdant wooded vales were seen on one hand, while a great plain stretched before us, extending from the banks of the river toward a chain of lofty mountains, whose summits were rendered indistinct in the haze of the distance.

We crossed the stream, which we named East River, filling our flasks with water, and it was well we did so, for in continuing our journey, we found the soil become more arid and parched than we had expected; in fact we soon appeared surrounded by a desert.

The boys were astonished at the altered appearance of the country, part of which had been explored when we met with the buffaloes. I reminded them of the difference of the season; that the expedition had been made directly after the rains, when vegetation had clothed with transient beauty this region, which, possessing no source of moisture itself, had become scathed and bare during the blazing heat of summer.

Our march proceeded slowly, and many were the uncomplimentary remarks made on the "new country."

It was "Arabia Petrea," groaned one. "Desert of Sahara," sighed another. "Fit abode for demons," muttered a third. "Subterranean volcanic fires are raging beneath our feet."

"Patience, my dear fellows!" cried I; "you are too easily discouraged. Look beyond the toilsome way to those grand mountains, whose spurs are already stretching forward to meet us. Who knows what pleasant surprises await us amid their steep declivities? I, for my part, expect to find water, fresh grass, trees, and a lovely resting-place."

We were all glad to repose beneath the shade of the first overhanging rock we came to, although, by pressing further upward, we might have attained to a pleasanter spot.

Looking back toward the Gap, we marked the strange contrast of the smiling country bordering the river, and the dreary, monotonous plain we had traversed.

After gazing on the distant scene, we produced our store of provisions, and were busily engaged, when Knips (our constant companion) suddenly began to snuff and smell about in a very ridiculous way; finally, with a shriek which we knew was expressive of pleasure, he set off at a full speed, followed by all the dogs, up a sort of glen behind us.

We left them to their own devices, being far too pleasantly engaged with our refreshments to care much what fancy the little rogue had got in his head.

When hunger was somewhat appeased, Fritz once more cast his eyes over the expanse of plain before us, and after looking fixedly for a moment, exclaimed:

"Is it possible that I see a party of horsemen riding at full gallop toward us! Can they be wild Arabs of the desert?"

"Arabs my boy! Certainly not; but take the spyglass and make them out exactly. We shall have to be on our guard, whatever they are!"

"I cannot see distinctly enough to be sure," said he presently, "and imagination supplies the deficiency of sight in most strange fashion. I could fancy them wild cattle, loaded carts, wandering haycocks, in fact most anything I like."

The spyglass passed from hand to hand; Jack and Ernest agreed in thinking the moving objects were men on horseback; but when it came to my turn to look, I at once pronounced them to be very large ostriches.

"This is fortunate, indeed!" I exclaimed; "we must try to secure one of these magnificent birds; the feathers alone are worth having."

"A live ostrich, father! That would be splendid. Why, we might ride upon him!"

As the ostriches approached, we began to consider in what way we should attempt a capture. I sent Fritz and Jack to recall the dogs, and placed myself with Ernest behind some shrubs which would conceal us from the birds as they came onward.

The boys did not rejoin us for some little time; they found Knips and the dogs at a pool of water formed by a small mountain stream, which the monkey's instinct had detected; his sudden departure was thus accounted for, and they availed themselves right gladly of his discovery, filling their flasks, and hastily bathing before their return.

The ostriches continued to come in our direction, varying

their pace as though in sport, springing, trotting, galloping, and chasing each other round and round, so that their approach was by no means rapid.

I could now perceive that of the five birds one only was a male, the white plumes of the wings and tail contrasting finely with the deep glossy black of the neck and body.

The color of the females being ashen brown, the effect of their white plumes was not so handsome.

"I do not believe we shall have a chance with these birds," said I, "except by sending Fritz's eagle in pursuit; and for that we must bide our time, and let them come as near as possible."

"In what way, then, are ostriches caught by the natives of the African deserts?" inquired Fritz.

"Sometimes by chase on horseback; but their speed is so very great, that even that must be conducted by stratagem.

"When these birds are pursued, they will run for hours in a wide circle; the hunter gallops after them, but describes a much smaller circle, and can therefore maintain the pace for a longer time, waiting to make the attack until the bird is fatigued.

"Among the Bushmen, the hunter sometimes envelopes himself in the skin of an ostrich, his legs doing duty for those of the bird, and his arm managing the head and neck so as to imitate the movements of the bird when feeding. The enterprising hunter is thus enabled to get among a flock of ostriches, and to shoot them with arrows one after another.

"When aware of an enemy they defend themselves desperately, using their powerful legs as weapons, always kicking forward, and inflicting dreadful injuries on dogs, and even on men, if attacked without due precaution. But let us take up our positions, and keep perfectly still, for the ostriches are at hand!"

We held the dogs concealed as much as possible; the stately birds suddenly perceiving us, paused, hesitated, and appeared uneasy. Yet as no movement was made, they drew a few steps nearer, with outstretched necks, examining curiously the unwonted spectacle before them.

The dogs became impatient, struggled from our grasp, and furiously rushed toward our astonished visitors. In an instant they turned and fled with the speed of the wind; their feet seemed not to touch the ground, their wings aiding the marvelously rapid progress.

In a few moments they would have been beyond our reach, but as they turned to fly the eagle was unhooded. Singling out the male bird the falcon made his fatal swoop, and piercing the skull, the magnificent creature was laid low. Before we could reach the spot the dogs had joined the bird of prey, and were fiercely tearing the flesh and bedabbling the splendid plumes with gore.

The sight grieved us.

"What a pity we could not capture this glorious bird alive!" exclaimed Fritz, as we took its beautiful feathers; "it must, I am sure, have stood more than six feet high, and two of us might have mounted him at once!"

"In the vast sandy deserts where nothing grows, what can flocks of these birds find to live upon?" inquired Ernest.

"That would indeed be hard to say, if the deserts were utterly barren and unfruitful," returned I; "but over these sandy wastes a beneficent Providence scatters plants of wild melons, which absorb and retain every drop of moisture, and which quench the thirst as well as satisfy the hunger of the ostriches and other inhabitants of the wilds. These melons, however, do not constitute his entire diet; he feeds freely on grasses, dates, and hard grain, when he can obtain them."

"Does the ostrich utter any cry?"

"The voice of the ostrich is a deep, hollow, rumbling sound, so much resembling the roar of a lion as to be occasionally mistaken for it. But what does Jack mean by waving his cap and beckoning in that excited fashion? What has the boy found, I wonder!"

He ran a little toward us, shouting:

"Eggs, father! Ostriches' eggs! A huge nest full—do come quick!"

We all hastened to the spot, and in a slight hollow of the ground beheld more than twenty eggs, as large as an infant's head.

The idea of carrying more than two away with us was

preposterous, although the boys, forgetting what the weight would be, seriously contemplated clearing the nest.

They were satisfied when a kind of landmark had been set up, so that if we returned we might easily find the nest.

As each egg weighed about three pounds, the boys soon found the burden considerable, even when tied into a handkerchief and carried like a basket. To relieve them, I cut a strong elastic heath stick, and suspending an egg in its sling at each end, laid the bent stick over Jack's shoulder, and like a Dutch dairy-maid with her milk pails, he stepped merrily along without inconvenience.

We presently reached a marshy place, surrounding a little pool evidently fed by the stream which Knips had discovered. The soft ground was trodden and marked by the footsteps of many different sorts of animals; we saw tracks of buffaloes, antelopes, onagas or quaggas, but no trace whatever of any kind of serpent; hitherto our journey in search of monster reptiles had been signalized by very satisfactory failure.

By this brook we sat down to rest and take some food; Fangs presently disappeared, and Jack calling to his pet discovered him gnawing at something which he had dug from the marsh. Taking it for a root of some sort, Jack brought it for my inspection. I dipped it in water to clear off the mud, and to my surprise found a queer little living creature, no bigger than half an apple, in my hand. It was a small tortoise.

"A tortoise, I declare!" cried Fritz. "What a long way from the sea. How came it here, I wonder?"

"Perhaps there has been a tortoise-shower," remarked Ernest. "One reads of frog-showers in the time of the ancient Romans."

"Hullo, Professor! You're out for once," said I. "This is nothing but a mud-tortoise, which lives in wet, marshy ground and fresh water. They are useful in gardens; for although they like a few lettuce leaves now and then, they will destroy numbers of snails, grubs, and worms."

Resuming our journey, we arrived at a charming valley, verdant, fruitful, and shaded by clumps of graceful trees. It afforded us the greatest delight and refreshment to pass along this cool and lovely vale, which we agreed to call Glen Verdant.

In the distance we could see herds of antelopes or buffaloes feeding; but as our dogs continually ranged a long way ahead of us, they were quickly startled, and vanished up one or other of the narrow gorges which opened out of the valley.

Following the imperceptible windings of the vale, we were surprised, on quitting it for the more open ground, to find ourselves in a country we were already acquainted with, and not far from the Jackal Cave, as we called the place where Fangs had been captured in cubhood.

On recognizing the spot, Ernest, who was in advance with one of the dogs, hastened toward it. We lost sight of him for a few minutes, and then arose a cry of terror, violent barking, and deep, surly growls.

As we rushed forward, Ernest met us, looking white as ashes, and calling out:

"A bear, a bear, father! He is coming after me!"

The boy clung to me in mortal fear. I felt his whole frame quivering.

"Courage, my son!" cried I, disengaging myself from his grasp; "we must prepare for instant defense!"

The dogs dashed forward to join the fray, whatever it was; and not long were we in doubt. To my no small consternation, an enormous bear made his appearance, quickly followed by another.

With leveled guns, my brave Fritz and I advanced slowly to meet them. Jack was also ready to fire, but the shock had so unnerved Ernest that he fairly took to his heels. We fired together, one at each bear; but though hit, the monsters were unfortunately only wounded. We found it most difficult to take aim, as the dogs beset them on all sides. However, they were much disabled, one having the lower jaw broken, and the other, with a bullet in his shoulder, was effectually lamed. The dogs, perceiving their advantage, pressed more closely round their foes, who yet defended themselves furiously, with frightful yells of pain and rage. Such was the confusion and perpetual movement of the struggle, that I dared not fire again, seeing that even slightly wounding one of our gallant hounds would instantly place him in the power of the raging bears.

Watching our opportunity, we suddenly advanced with loaded pistols to within a very few paces of the animals, and firing, both fell dead, one shot through the head, the other, in the act of rearing to spring on Fritz, received his charge in its heart.

"Thank Heaven!" cried I, as with dull groans the brutes sank to the ground. "We have escaped the greatest peril we have yet encountered!"

The dogs continued to tear and worry the fallen foe, as though unwilling to trust the appearance of death. With feelings somewhat akin, I drew my hunting-knife, and made assurance doubly sure.

Seeing all safe, Jack raised a shout of victory, that poor Ernest might gain courage to approach the scene of conflict, which at last he did, and joined us in examining the dangerous animals, as they lay motionless before us.

Every point was full of interest, their wounds, their sharp teeth, their mighty claws, the extraordinary strength of neck and shoulder, all were remarked and commented on, and observing that the shaded brown hair was tipped with glossy white, I thought that these might be the silver bears mentioned in Captain Clarke's journey to the northwest coasts of America.

"Well, my lads," said I, "if we have failed to catch sight of serpents, we have at least made good riddance of some other bad rubbish! These fellows would one day have worked us woe, or I am much mistaken. What's to be done next?"

"Why, skin them, to be sure," said Fritz. "We shall have a couple of splendid bearskin rugs."

As this process would take time and evening drew on, we dragged the huge carcasses into their den, to await our return, concealing them with boughs of trees and fencing the entrance as well as we could. The ostrich eggs we also left behind us, hidden in a sandy hole.

By sunset we reached the tent, and joyfully rejoined the mother and Franz, right glad to find a hearty meal prepared for us, as well as a large heap of brushwood for the watch-fire.

When a full account of our adventures had been given, with a minute and special description of the bear fight, the mother related what she had done during our absence. She and Franz had made their way through the wood up to the rocks behind it, and discovered a bed of pure white clay, which it seemed to her might be used for making porcelain. Then she had contrived a drinking trough for the cattle out of a split bamboo.

She had arranged a hearth in a sheltered place by building up large stones, cemented with the white clay; and, finally, she had cut a quantity of canes and brought them, on the cart, to be in readiness for the building we had in hand.

I praised the thoughtful diligence which had effected so much that was of real and definite use. In order to try the clay, I put some balls of it in the fire now kindled, to burn during the night, and we then betook ourselves to rest under shelter of our tent.

I awoke at dawn and aroused my little party. My first idea was to examine the clay balls, which I found baked hard and finely glazed, but too much melted down by the heat—a fault which, seeing the excellent quality of the clay, I knew it would be well worth while to remedy.

After breakfast, and our accustomed devotions, we harnessed the cart, and took the way to the bears' den. Fritz headed the party, and, coming in sight of the entrance to the cave, called out softly:

"Make haste and you will see a whole crowd of wild turkeys, who seem to have come to attend the funeral obsequies of their respected friend and neighbor, Bruin, here. But there appears to be a jealous watcher who is unwilling to admit the visitors to the bed of state!"

The Watcher, as Fritz called him, was an immensely large bird, with a sort of comb on his head, and a loose, fleshy skin hanging from beneath the beak. Part of the neck was bare, wrinkled, and purplish-red, while around it, resting on the shoulders, was a downy collar of soft, white feathers. The plumage was grayish-brown, marked here and there with white patches; the feet appeared to be armed with strong claws. This great bird guarded the entrance to the cave, occasionally retiring into it himself for a few minutes; but as soon as the other birds came pressing in after him, he hurried out again, and they were forced to retire.

We stopped to observe this curious scene, and were startled suddenly by a mighty rush of wings in the air above us. We looked up; at the same moment Fritz fired, and an enormous bird fell heavily head foremost on the rocks, by which its neck was broken, while blood flowed from a wound in the breast.

We had been holding back the dogs, but they, with Fritz, now rushed toward the cave, the birds rising around them and departing with heavy, ungainly flight, leaving only Fritz's prize, and one of the other birds killed by the large one in its fall.

With the utmost caution I entered the cave, and rejoiced to find that the tongue and eyes only of the bears had been devoured; a little later and we should have had the handsome skins pecked and torn to rags, and all chance of steaks and bears' paws gone.

On measuring the wings of the large bird from tip to tip, I found the length exceeded eleven feet, and concluded it to be a condor; it was evidently the mate of the "Watcher," as Fritz called the first we saw.

To work we now went on the bears, and no slight affair we found it to skin and cut them up, but by dint of perseverance, we at last succeeded in our object.

Determining to smoke the meat on the spot, we cut magnificent hams, and took off the rest of the meat in slices after the manner of the buccaneers in the West Indies, preserving the paws entire to be cooked as a delicacy, and obtaining from the two bears together a prodigious supply of lard, which my wife gladly undertook to melt and prepare for keeping.

The bones and offal we drew to some distance with the help of our cattle, and made the birds of the air most welcome to feast upon it. This, with the assistance of all sorts of insects, they did so effectually that before we left the place the skulls were picked perfectly clean, the sun had dried them, and they were ready for us to carry off to our museum.

The skins had to be very carefully scraped, washed, salted, cleansed with ashes, and dried; which occupied fully two days.

I was lamenting our distance from the rascusara tree, the leaves of which had flavored our roast peccary so nicely, when I observed among the brushwood which the boys had brought from the thickets around us, a climbing plant, whose leaves had a very strong smell; the stem resembled a vine, and the fruit grew in clusters like currants. Some were red, and some of a green color, which I supposed to denote various degrees of ripeness. They were hard, and the outer skin was quite thin.

I recognized in this the pepper plant, a discovery particularly agreeable at this moment.

The boys soon gathered a large supply; the red berries were soaked in salt and water for several days, then washed and rubbed, and finally, becoming perfectly white, were dried in the sun. The treatment of the green berries was simple; they were merely exposed to the sun's heat for a day or two, and then stored: in this way we obtained enough, both of black and white pepper, to last us a very long time.

I took also a number of young plants, that we might have pepper growing at Rockburg and our various settlements. Some roots of another plant were also taken, which, from the pods, appeared to be a kind of bean.

We were glad of this occupation during the tedious business of smoking the bears' meat, and availed ourselves of the leisure time by also preparing for stuffing the condor and the turkey buzzard, urubu or black vulture—for I could not determine to which species the smaller bird belonged.

The four boys at length became so weary of inaction, that I determined to let them make an excursion alone on the Savannah. Three of them received this permission with eager delight, but Ernest said he would prefer to remain with us; to which, as the expedition was to be entirely one of pleasure, I could make no objection.

Little Franz, on the other hand, whom I would willingly have kept with us, was wild to go with his brothers, and I was obliged to consent, as I had made the proposal open to all, and could not draw back.

In the highest spirits they ran to bring their steeds (as we were fain to call the cattle they rode) from their pasturage at a short distance. Speedily were they saddled, bridled, and mounted—the three lads were ready to be off.

It was my wish that our sons should cultivate a habit of bold independence, for well I knew that it might be the will of God to deprive them easily of their parents; when, without an enterprising spirit of self-reliance, their position would be truly miserable.

My gallant Fritz possessed this desirable quality in no small degree, and to him I committed the care of his young brothers, charging them to look up to and obey him as their leader.

They were well armed, well mounted, had a couple of good dogs; and, with a hearty "God speed and bless you, my boys!" I let them depart.

We, who remained behind, passed the day in a variety of useful occupations.

The bears' meat, which was being cured in a smoking shed such as that we set up for the peccary hams, required a good deal of attention from my wife. Ernest had a fancy for making ornamental cups from the ostrich eggs, while I investigated the interior of the cave.

I found the inner wall to consist of a kind of talc, mingled with threads of asbestos, and also indications of mica. Examining further, I detached a large block, and found to my joy that I could split it into clear transparent sheets, which would serve admirably for window panes.

My wife saw this substitute for glass with unfeigned satisfaction, declaring, that although she would not complain, yet the want of glass for windows had been a downright trouble to her.

CHAPTER XIII

The boys return and give an account of their adventures—How they captured the antelopes—How Fritz caught the rabbits and Jack rode down the gazelles—How they followed the honey bird and Jack tried to rob the bees' bike—We sup on the bears' paws—Across the desert again—Sight three ostriches—The male bird captured—We secure him between Storm and Grumble—The mother's astonishment at our new pet—Return to Woodlands—Home again—We establish colonies on Shark and Whale Islands—Turn our attention to agriculture—The difficulties of ostrich training—My patent saddle and bridle—I exercise my ingenuity in various trades.

As evening approached, the bears' paws, which were stewing for supper, sent forth savory odors; and we sat talking round the fire, while listening anxiously for sounds heralding the return of our young explorers.

At last the tramp and beat of hoofs struck our ears; the little troop appeared, crossing the open ground before us at a sharp trot, and a shrill ringing cheer greeted us as we rose and went to meet them.

They sprang from their saddles, the animals were set at liberty to refresh themselves, and the riders eagerly came to exhibit their acquisitions and give an account of themselves.

Funny figures they cut! Franz and Jack had each a young kid slung on his back, so that the four legs, tied together, stuck out under their chins.

Fritz's game bag looked remarkably queer—round lumps, sharp points, and an occasional movement seemed to indicate a living creature or creatures within.

"Hurrah! For the chase, father!" cried Jack. "Nothing like real hunting after all. And just to see how Storm and Grumble go along over a grassy plain! It is perfectly splendid! We soon tired out the little antelopes, and were able to catch them."

"Yes, father," said Franz; "and Fritz has two Angora rabbits in his bag, and we wanted to bring you some honey. Only think! such a clever bird—a cuckoo, showed us where it was!"

"My brothers forget the chief thing," said Fritz. "We have driven a little herd of antelopes right through the Gap into our territory; and there they are, all ready for us to hunt when we like—or to catch and tame!"

"Well done!" cried I; "here is indeed a list of achievements. But to your mother and me, the chief thing of all, is God's goodness in bringing you safe back to us. Now, let us hear the whole story, that we may have a definite idea of your performances."

"We had a splendid ride," said Fritz, "down Glen Verdant, and away to the defile through our Rocky Barrier, and the morning was so cool and fresh that our steeds galloped along, nearly the whole way, at the top of their speed. When we had passed through the Gap we moderated our furious pace and kept our eyes open on the lookout for game; we then trotted slowly to the top of a grassy hill, from whose summit we saw two herds of animals, whether antelopes, goats, or gazelles, we did not know, grazing by the side of the stream below us. We were about to gallop down and try to get a shot at them, when it struck me that it would be wiser to try and drive the whole herd through the Gap into our own domain, where they would be shut up, as it were, in a park, free and yet within reach. Down the hill we rode as hard as we could go, formed in a semi-circle behind the larger herd—magnificent antelopes—and, aided by the dogs, with shouts and cries drove them along the stream toward the Gap; as we came near the opening they appeared inclined to halt and turn, like sheep about to be driven into the butcher's yard; and it was all we could do to prevent them from bolting past us; but, at length, one made a rush at the opening and, the rest following, they were soon all on the other side of the frontier, and inhabitants of New Switzerland."

"Capital," I said, "capital, my boy! But I don't see what is to make them remain inhabitants of our domain, or to prevent them from returning through the Gap whenever they feel inclined."

"Stop, father," he replied, "you interrupt me too soon; we thought of that possibility too, and provided against it. We stretched a long line right across the defile and strung on it feathers and rags and all sorts of other things, which danced and fluttered in the wind, and looked so strange that I am perfectly certain that the herd will never attempt to pass it; in fact, Levaillant, from whom I learned the trick, says, in his *Voyage au Cap de Bonne Espérance*, that the Hottentots make use of the method for penning in the antelopes they have caught in the chase."

"Well done," said I, "I am glad to see that you remember what you have read. The antelopes are welcome to New Switzerland, but, my boy," I added, "I cannot say the same for the rabbits you have there; they increase so rapidly that if you establish a colony of the little wretches your next difficulty will be to get rid of them."

"True," he replied, "but my idea was to place them upon Whale Island, where they would find abundant food, and at the same time in no way trouble us. May I not establish a warren there? It would be so useful. Do you know, my eagle caught these pretty little fellows for me? I saw a number of them running about and so unhooded him, and in a few minutes he brought me three—one dead, with whose body I rewarded him, and these two here, unhurt."

"Now, father," said Jack, interrupting him, "do listen to me and hear my story, or else Fritz will begin upon my adventures and tire you out with his rigmarole descriptions."

"Certainly, Jack," I said, "I am quite ready to listen to you. First and foremostly, how did you bring down those beautiful little animals you have there?"

"Oh, we galloped them down. The dogs sniffed about in the grass while Fritz was away after the rabbits, out popped those little fawns, and away they went bounding and skipping at the rate of thirty miles an hour, with Storm, Grumble, and the dogs at their heels. In about a quarter of an hour we had left the dogs behind and were close upon our prey. Down went the little creatures in the grass, and, overcome with terror and fatigue, were at our mercy. So we shouted to Fritz, and——"

"My dear boy," said I, "according to your statement, Fritz must have been seven miles and a half off."

"Oh, well, father, perhaps we did not ride for quite a quarter of an hour, and, of course, I can't say exactly how fast we were going; and then, you see, the fawns did not run in a straight line; at any rate Fritz heard us, and he and Franz and I leashed the legs of the pretty creatures, and then we mounted again, and presently saw a wretch of a cuckoo, who led us ever so far out of our course by cuckooing and making faces at us, and then hopping away. Franz declared it must be an enchanted princess, and so I thought I would rid it of its spell; but Fritz stopped me shooting it, and said it was a 'Honey Indicator,' and that it was leading us probably to a bees' bike, so we spared its life, and presently, sure enough, it stopped close by a bees' nest in a hollow tree. This was capital, we thought, and, as we were in a great hurry to taste the honey, I threw in a lot of lighted lucifer matches, but somehow it did not kill the bees at all, but only made them awfully angry, and they flew out in a body and stung me all over. I rushed to Storm and sprang on his back, but, though I galloped away for bare life, it was an age before I got rid of the little wretches, and now my face is in a perfect fever. I think I will get mother to bathe it for me;" and off rushed the noisy boy, leaving Fritz and me to see to the fawns and examine the rabbits. With these latter I determined to do as Fritz proposed, namely, to colonize Whale Island with them. I was all the more willing to do this because I had been considering the advisability of establishing on that island a fortress to which we might retreat in any extreme danger, and where we should be very thankful, in case of such a retreat, to possess means of obtaining a constant supply of animal food.

Having ministered to the wants of the antelopes, I tried to interest the boys in my discovery of the block of talc, but just then their mother summoned us to dinner.

The principal dish in this meal consisted of the bears' paws—most savory smelling delicacies, so tempting that their close resemblance to human hands, and even the roguish "Fee-fo-fum" from Jack, did not prevent a single member of the family from enjoying them most heartily.

Supper over, we lit our watch-fire, retired to our tent, and slept soundly.

We had been working very diligently; the bears' meat was smoked, the fat melted down and stored, and a large supply of bamboos collected. But I wished to make yet another excursion, and at early dawn I aroused the boys.

Fritz mounted the mule, I rode Lightfoot, Jack and Franz took their usual steeds, and, with the two dogs, we galloped off—first to visit the euphorbia to collect the gum, and then to discover whether the ostrich had deserted her eggs in the sand.

Ernest watched us depart without the slightest look or sigh of regret, and returned to the tent to assist his mother and study his books.

Our steeds carried us down the Green Valley at a rapid rate, and we followed the direction we had pursued on our former expedition. We soon reached Turtle Marsh, and then, filling our water-flasks, we arrived at the rising ground where Fritz discovered the mounted Arabs.

As Jack and Franz wanted a gallop, I allowed them to press forward, while Fritz and I visited the euphorbia trees. A quantity of the red gum had exuded from the incisions I had made, and as this had coagulated in the sun, I rolled it into little balls and stored it in a bamboo jar I had brought with me for the purpose.

As we rode after the boys, who were some way ahead, Fritz remarked:

"Did you not tell me that the juice of that tree was poisonous, father; why have you collected such a quantity?"

"I did indeed say so," I replied; "it is a most deadly poison. The inhabitants of the Cape of Good Hope use it to poison the springs where wild animals assemble to quench their thirst; and they thus slaughter an immense number of the creatures for the sake of their hides. I intend, however, to use it to destroy the apes should they again commit depredations, and also in preparing the skins of animals to protect them from the attacks of insects."

The two boys were still at some distance from us, when suddenly four magnificent ostriches rose from the sand where they had been sitting.

Jack and Franz perceived them, and, with a great shout, drove them toward us. In front ran a splendid male bird, his feathers of shining black, and his great tail plume waving behind. Three females of an ashen gray color followed him. They approached us with incredible swiftness, and were within gunshot before they perceived us. Fritz had had the forethought to bind up the beak of his eagle so that, should he bring down an ostrich, he might be unable to injure it.

He now threw up the falcon which, towering upward, swooped down upon the head of the foremost bird, and so confused and alarmed him, that he could not defend himself nor continue his flight. So greatly was his speed checked that Jack overtook him, and hurling his lasso, enfolded his wings and legs in its deadly coils and brought him to the ground. The other ostriches were almost out of sight, so leaving them to their own devices, we leaped from our steeds and attempted to approach the captured bird. He struggled fearfully, and kicked with such violence, right and left, that I almost despaired of getting him home alive.

It occurred to me, however, that if we could cover his eyes, his fury might be subdued. I instantly acted upon this idea, and flung over his head my coat and hunting-bag, which effectually shut out the light.

No sooner had I done this than his struggles ceased, and we were able to approach. We first secured round his body a broad strip of sealskin, on each side of which I fastened a stout piece of cord, that I might be able to lead him easily. Then, fastening another cord in a loop round his legs that he might be prevented from breaking into a gallop, we released him from the coils of the lasso.

"Do you know," said I to the boys, "how the natives of India secure a newly captured elephant?"

"Oh, yes!" said Fritz; "they fasten him between two tame elephants. We'll do that to this fine fellow, and tame him double quick."

"The only difficulty will be," remarked Jack, "that we have no tame ostriches. However, I daresay Storm and Grumble will have no objection to perform their part, and it will puzzle even this great monster to run away with them."

So we at once began operations. Storm and Grumble were led up on either side of the recumbent ostrich, and the cords secured to their girths. Jack and Franz, each armed with a stout whip, mounted their respective steeds, the wrappers were removed from the bird's eyes, and we stood by to watch what would next occur.

For some moments after the return of his sight he lay perfectly still, then he arose with a bound and, not aware of the cords which hampered him, attempted to dash forward. The thongs were stout, and he was brought to his knees. A fruitless struggle ensued, and then at length, seeming to accommodate himself to circumstances, he set off at a sharp trot, his guards making the air re-echo with their merry shouts. These cries stimulated the ostrich to yet further exertions, but he was at length brought to a stand by the determined refusal of his four-footed companions to continue such a race across loose sand.

The boys having enjoyed the long run, I told them to walk with the prisoner slowly home, while Fritz and I returned to examine the ostrich's nest. The eggs were quite warm, and I was certain that the mother had quite recently left the nest; leaving about half, I packed the rest of the eggs in a large bag I had brought for the purpose, and slung it carefully on the saddle before. We soon caught up our advance guard, and without other notable incident reached our tent.

Astonishment and dismay were depicted on the face of the mother as we approached.

"My dear husband," she exclaimed, "do you think our provisions so abundant that you must scour the deserts to find some great beast to assist us to devour them. You must discover an iron mine next, for iron is what ostriches chiefly live on, is it not? Oh! I do wish you would be content with the menagerie you have already collected, instead of bringing in a specimen of every beast you come across. And this is such a useless monster!"

"Useless! Mother," exclaimed Jack; "you would not say so had you seen him run; why, he will be the fleetest courser in our stables. I am going to make a saddle and bridle for him, and in future he shall be my only steed. Then as for his appetite, father declares it is most delicate, he only wants a little fruit and grass, and a few stones and tenpenny nails to help his digestion."

The way in which Jack assumed the proprietorship of our new prize seemed to strike his brothers as rather cool, and there was instantly a cry raised on the subject.

"Very well," said Jack, "let us each take possession of the part of the ostrich we captured. Your bird, Fritz, seized the head, keep that; father shall have the body, I'll have the legs, and Franz a couple of feathers from the tail."

"Come, come," said I, "I think that Jack has a very good right to the ostrich, seeing that he brought it to the ground, and if he succeeds in taming it and converting it into a saddle horse it shall be his. From this time, therefore, he is responsible for its training."

The day was now too far advanced to allow us to think of setting out for Rockburg, so we fastened up the ostrich between two trees, and devoted the remainder of the evening to making preparations for our departure.

At early dawn our picturesque caravan was moving homeward. The ostrich continued so refractory that we were obliged to make him again march between Storm and Grumble, and as these gallant steeds were thus employed, the cow was harnessed to the cart, laden with our treasures. Room was left in the cart for the mother. Jack and Franz mounted Storm and Grumble, I rode Lightfoot, and Fritz brought up the rear on Swift.

At the mouth of the Gap we called a halt, and replaced the cord the boys had strung with ostrich feathers by a stout palisade of bamboos. I also took the opportunity of collecting a store of pipeclay, as I intended during the winter months, which were close at hand, to try my hand at china making.

When we reached the sugarcane grove, we again stopped to collect the peccary hams we had left to be smoked; and my wife begged me to gather some seeds of an aromatic plant which grew in the neighborhood, and which had the scent of vanilla. I obtained a good supply, and we moved forward toward Woodlands, where we intended to rest for the night, after our long and fatiguing march.

Our tent was pitched, and on our beds of cotton we slept soundly.

Next morning early we examined our farmyard, which appeared in a most prosperous and flourishing condition. The sight of all these domestic animals made us long even more than ever for our home at Rockburg, and we determined to hasten thither with all possible speed.

The number of our pigs, goats, and poultry had greatly increased since we had last visited our colony; and some of these, two fine breeds of chickens especially, my wife wished to take back with her.

We found that the herd of antelopes, which Fritz and Jack had driven through the Gap, had taken up their abode in the neighborhood, and several times we saw the beautiful animals browsing among the trees.

While at the farm, we repaired both the animals' stalls and our dwelling room, that the former might be more secure against the attacks of wild beasts, and the latter fitted for our accommodation when we should visit the spot.

Everything at length being satisfactorily arranged, we again retired to rest, and early next morning completed our journey to Rockburg.

By midday we were once more settled at home. Windows and doors were thrown open to admit fresh air; the animals established in their stalls; and the cart's miscellaneous cargo discharged and arranged.

As much time as I could spare, I devoted to the ostrich, whom we fastened, for the present, between two bamboo posts in front of our dwelling.

I then turned my attention to the eggs we had brought, and which I determined to hatch, if possible, by artificial heat. For this purpose I arranged a stove, which I maintained at a uniform temperature, and on it I placed the eggs, carefully wrapped in cotton wool.

Next morning Fritz and I went off in the boat, first to Whale Island, there to establish our colonists, the Angora rabbits, and then to Shark Island, where we placed the dainty little antelopes. Having made them happy with their liberty and abundance of food, we returned as quickly as possible to cure the bearskins, and add the provisions we had brought to the stores lying in our cellar.

As we returned, we caught up Jack, making his way in great glee toward Rockburg. He was carrying, in a basket, an immense eel, which he and Ernest had secured.

Ernest had set, on the previous night, a couple of lines; one had been dragged away, but on the other they found this splendid fellow.

It proved delicious. Half was prepared for dinner, and the other half salted and stowed away.

We now, for a short time, again turned our attention to our duties about the house.

Thinking that the veranda would be greatly improved by some creepers, I sowed, round the foot of each bamboo pillar, vanilla and pepper-seeds, as well as that of other creeping plants, which would not only give the house a pleasanter aspect, but also afford us shade during the summer months.

I constructed a couple of hencoops too, for the hens and their little chicks which we had brought from Woodlands, for I knew that if I left them unprotected, the inquisitive dispositions of Knips and Fangs might induce them to make anatomical experiments which would be detrimental to the welfare of the youngsters.

Ernest's rat skins were voted a nuisance within doors, and were tied together and hung up outside; so powerful was the odor they emitted, that even then Jack would pretend to faint every time he passed near them.

The museum received its addition: the condor and vulture were placed there, to be stuffed when we should find time during the rainy season. The mica and asbestos, too, were brought in for the present, not to lie there idle, but to wait until I could use them as I intended, for china and lampwicks.

Having occupied two days in this way, we turned our attention to other duties: the cultivation of a wheat, barley, and maize field, the management of the ostrich's eggs, and the taming of the captives.

As agriculture was, though the least to our taste, the most important of these several duties, we set about it first. The animals drew the plough, but the digging and hoeing taxed our powers of endurance to the utmost.

We worked two hours in the morning and two in the evening. Fully did we realize the words of Scripture: "In the sweat of thy face shalt thou eat bread."

In the interval we devoted our attention to the ostrich. But our efforts on behalf of his education seemed all in vain. He appeared as untameable as ever. I determined, therefore, to adopt the plan which had subdued the refractory eagle.

The effect of the tobacco fumes almost alarmed me. The

ostrich sank to the ground and lay motionless. Slowly, at length, he arose, and paced up and down between the bamboo posts.

He was subdued, but to my dismay resolutely refused all food. I feared he would die; for three days he pined, growing weaker and weaker each day.

"Food he must have!" said I to my wife; "food he must have!" The mother determined to attempt an experiment. She prepared balls of maize flour, mixed with butter. One of these she placed within the bird's beak. He swallowed it, and stretched out his long neck, looking inquiringly for a second mouthful. A second, third, and fourth ball followed the first. His appetite returned, and his strength came again.

All the wild nature of the bird had gone, and I saw with delight that we might begin his education as soon as we chose. Rice, guavas, maize, and corn he ate readily—*washing it down*, as Jack expressed it, with small pebbles, to the great surprise of Franz, to whom I explained that the ostrich was merely following the instinct common to all birds; that he required these pebbles to digest his food, just as smaller birds require gravel.

After a month of careful training, our captive would trot, gallop, obey the sound of our voice, feed from our hand; and, in fact, showed himself perfectly docile. Now our ingenuity was taxed to the utmost. How were we to saddle and bridle a bird? First, for a bit for his beak. Vague ideas passed through my mind, but every one I was obliged to reject. A plan at length occurred to me. I recollected the effect of light and its absence upon the ostrich, how his movements were checked by sudden darkness, and how, with the light, power returned to his limbs.

I immediately constructed a leathern hood, to reach from the neck to the beak, cutting holes in it for the eyes and ears.

Over the eyeholes I contrived square flaps or blinkers, which were so arranged with whalebone springs that they closed tightly of themselves. The reins were connected with these blinkers, so that the flaps might be raised or allowed to close at the rider's pleasure.

When both blinkers were open, the ostrich would gallop straight ahead; close his right eye and he turned to the left, close his left and he turned to the right, shut both and he stood stock still.

I was justly proud of my contrivance, but, before I could really test its utility, I was obliged to make a saddle. After several failures, I succeeded in manufacturing one to my liking, and in properly securing it; it was something like an old-fashioned trooper's saddle, peaked before and behind—for my great fear was lest the boys should fall. This curious-looking contrivance I placed upon the shoulders as near the neck as possible, and secured it with strong girths round the wings and across the breast, to avoid all possibility of the saddle slipping down the bird's sloping back.

I soon saw that my plan would succeed, though skill and considerable practice was necessary in the use of my patent bridle. It was difficult to remember that to check the courser's speed it was necessary to slacken rein, and that the tighter the reins were drawn, the faster he would fly. We at length, however, all learned to manage Master Hurricane, and the distance between Rockburg and Falconhurst was traversed in an almost incredibly short space of time. The marvelous speed of the bird again revived the dispute as to the ownership, and I was obliged to interfere.

"Jack shall retain the ostrich," said I, "for it is most suited to him; he is a lighter weight than either of you his elder brothers, and Franz is not yet strong enough to manage such a fleet courser. But he is so far to be considered common property, that all may practice on him occasionally; and, in a case of necessity, any one may mount him."

Our field work was by this time over. The land had been ploughed and sown with wheat, barley, and maize. On the other side of Jackal River we had planted potatoes and cassava roots, and all sorts of other seeds had been carefully sown.

We had not neglected the ostrich's eggs, and one day Fritz introduced me with great glee to three little ostriches. But alas, the little creatures were not destined to enjoy life long. One died almost as soon as it was hatched, and the others, after tottering about on their stilt-like legs for a few days, followed its example.

I now found time to turn my attention to the bears' skins, which required preparation before they would be fit for use as leather. They had been salted and dried, and now required tanning. I had no tan, however. This was unfortunate; but not to be deterred from my purpose, I determined to use a mixture of honey and water in its place.

The experiment proved successful. When the skins were dried they remained flexible and free from smell, while the fur was soft and glossy.

This was not the only result of the experiment, for the honey-water which I boiled appeared so clear and tempting, that it struck me that I might prepare from it an excellent drink. I put by some of the liquid before making use of it as tan, and reboiled it with nutmeg and cinnamon. The preparation, which much resembled English mead, was pronounced delicious, and the mother begged me to brew a large supply. As our cellar was now well stocked with provisions for the winter, and our other preparations were completed, I was able to turn my attention to details of lesser importance. The boys had been clamoring for hats, and as my success in so many trades had surprised me, I agreed to turn hatter for the nonse. With the rat skins and a solution of India rubber, I produced a kind of felt, which I dyed a brilliant red with cochineal, and stretching this on a wooden block I had prepared, I passed over it a hot iron, to smooth the nap, and by next morning had the satisfaction of presenting to my wife a neat little red Swiss cap, to be lined and finished by her for one of the boys. The mother admired the production immensely, and lining it with silk, added yet more to its gay appearance by adorning it with ribbons and ostrich feathers, and finally placed it upon the head of little Franz.

So delighted was every one with the hat, that all were eager to be similarly provided, and begged me to manufacture more. I readily agreed to do so, as soon as they should furnish me with the necessary materials, and advised them to make half a dozen rat traps, that they might secure the water rats with which the stream abounded, and whose rich glossy fur would serve admirably for felt.

Every fifth animal that they brought me I told them should be mine, that I might obtain material for a hat for myself and their mother.

The boys at once agreed to this arrangement, and began the manufacture of the traps, which were all so made that they should kill the rats at once, for I could not bear the idea of animals being tortured or imprisoned.

While they were thus engaged I applied myself to the manufacture of porcelain. I first cleaned the pipeclay and talc from all foreign substances, and made them ready to be beaten down with water into a soft mass, and then prepared my molds of gypsum plaster. These preparations were at length made, and the molds received a thin layer of the porcelain material. When this was partly baked, I sprinkled over it a powder of colored glass beads which I had crushed, and which looked very pretty in patterns upon the transparent porcelain.

Some of my china vessels cracked with the heat of the stove, some were very ill-shaped; but, after many failures, I succeeded in producing a set of white cups and saucers, a cream-jug, a sugar-basin, and half a dozen small plates.

I must allow that my china was far from perfect; the shape of some of the vessels was faulty, and none were really transparent; nevertheless, the general appearance gave great satisfaction, and when the plates were filled with rosy and golden fruit resting on green leaves, and fragrant tea filled the cups, it greatly added to the appearance of the table.

CHAPTER XIV

The rainy season again—The building of the kayak—The mother invents a swimming dress—A visit to our colonies—Mysterious seaweed—The mother's surprise—A visit to Whale Island—Mischievous pigs—The three boys return from a day's hunting—They display their treasures—A new skinning apparatus—We make a crushing machine—An early harvest—We prepare a threshing floor—Reaping in Italian fashion—Threshing also in Italian fashion—Return of the herring shoals.

Scarcely had I completed my pottery, when great black clouds and terrific storms heralded the approach of another winter. The rainy season having set in, we were compelled to give up our daily excursions.

Even in the spacious house which we now occupied, and with our varied and interesting employments, we yet found the time dragging heavily. The spirits of all were depressed, and even occasional rapid rides, during a partial cessation of the rain, failed permanently to arouse them. Fritz, as well as I, had perceived this, and he said to me:

"Why, father, should we not make a canoe, something swifter and more manageable than those vessels we as yet possess? I often long for a light skiff, in which I might skim over the surface of the water."

The idea delighted all hands, but the mother, who was never happy when we were on the sea, declared that our chances of drowning were, with the pinnace and canoe, already sufficiently great, and that there was not the slightest necessity for our adding to these chances by constructing another craft which would tempt us out upon the perfidious element. My wife's fears were, however, speedily allayed, for I assured her that the boat I intended to construct should be no flimsy cockle-shell, but as safe and stout a craft as ever floated upon the sea. The Greenlander's kayak I intended to be my model, and I resolved not only to occupy the children, but also to produce a strong and serviceable canoe—a masterpiece of art.

The boys were interested, and the boat-building was soon in operation. We constructed the skeleton of whalebone, using split bamboo canes to strengthen the sides and also to form the deck, which extended the whole length of the boat, leaving merely a square hole in which the occupant of the canoe might sit.

The work engrossed our attention most entirely, and by the time it was complete the rain had passed away and the glorious sun again shone brightly forth.

Our front door was just wide enough to admit of the egress of our boat, and we completed her construction in the open air. We quickly cased the sides and deck with sealskin, making all the seams thoroughly watertight with caoutchouc.

The kayak was indeed a curious looking craft, yet so light that she might be lifted easily with one hand, and when at length we launched her she bounded upon the water like an India rubber ball. Fritz was unanimously voted her rightful owner, but before his mother would hear of his entering the frail-looking skiff she declared that she must contrive a swimming dress, that "should his boat receive a puncture from a sharp rock or the dorsal of a fish and collapse, he might yet have a chance of saving his life."

Though I did not consider the kayak quite the soap bubble the mother imagined it, I yet willingly agreed to assist her in the construction of the dress.

The garment we produced was most curious in appearance, and I must own that I doubted its efficiency. It was like a double waistcoat, made of linen prepared with a solution of India rubber, the seams being likewise coated with caoutchouc, and the whole rendered perfectly air-tight. We so arranged it that one little hole was left, by means of which air could be forced into the space between the outer covering and the lining, and the dress inflated.

Meanwhile I perceived with pleasure the rapid vegetation the climate was producing. The seeds we had scattered had germinated, and were now promising magnificent crops. The veranda, too, was looking pleasant with its gay and sweet-scented creepers, which were already aspiring to the summit of the pillars. The air was full of birds, the earth seemed teeming with life.

The dress was at length completed, and Fritz one fine afternoon offered publicly to prove it. We all assembled on the beach, the boy gravely donned and inflated the garment, and, amid roars of laughter from his brothers, entered the water. Quickly and easily he paddled himself across the bay toward Shark Island, whither we followed in one of our boats.

The experiment was most successful, and Ernest, Jack, and Franz, in spite of their laughter at their brother's garment, begged their mother to make for each of them a similar dress.

While on the island we paid a visit to the colonists whom we had established there the previous autumn. All was well; we could perceive by the footprints that the antelopes had discovered and made use of the shelter we had erected for them, and feeling that we could do nothing more we scattered handfuls of maize and salt, and strolled across to the other side of the island. The shore was covered with lovely shells, many of which, with beautiful pieces of delicate coral, the boys collected for their museum; strewn by the edge of the water too lay a great quantity of seaweed of various colors, and as the mother declared that much of it was of use, the boys assisted her to collect it and store it in the boat. As we pulled back to the land I was surprised to see that my wife chose from among the seaweed a number of curious leaves with edges notched like a saw. When we reached home she carefully washed these and dried them in the oven. There was evidently something mysterious about this preparation, and my curiosity at length prompted me to make an attempt to discover the secret.

"Are these leaves to form a substitute for tobacco?" said I; "do you so long for its refreshing smell?"

My wife smiled, for her dislike to tobacco was well known, and she answered in the same jocular tone:

"Do you not think that a mattress stuffed with these leaves would be very cool in summer?"

The twinkle in her eyes showed me that my curiosity must still remain unsatisfied, but it nevertheless became greater than ever.

The boys and I had one day made a long and fatiguing expedition, and, tired out, we flung ourselves down in the veranda. As we lay there resting, we heard the mother's voice.

"Could any of you enjoy a little jelly?"

She presently appeared, bearing a porcelain dish laden with most lovely transparent jelly. Cut with a spoon and laid before us it quivered and glittered in the light.

"Ambrosia!" exclaimed Fritz, tasting it. It was indeed delicious, and, still marveling from whence the mother could have obtained a dish so rare, we disposed of all that she had set before us.

"Aha," laughed the mother, "is not this an excellent substitute for tobacco, far more refreshing than the nasty weed itself. Behold the product of my mysterious seaweed."

"My dear wife," exclaimed I, "this dish is indeed a masterpiece of culinary art, but where had you met with it? What put it into your head?"

"While staying with my Dutch friends at the Cape," replied she, "I often saw it, and at once recognized the leaves on Shark Island. Once knowing the secret, the preparation of the dish is extremely simple; the leaves are soaked in water, fresh every day, for a week, and then boiled for a few hours with orange juice, citron, and sugar."

We were all delighted with the delicacy, and thanked the mother for it most heartily, the boys declaring that they must at once go off again to the island to collect as many of the leaves as they could find. I agreed to accompany them, for I wished to examine the plantations we had made there.

All were flourishing, the palms and mangroves had shot up in a most marvelous manner, and many of the seeds which I had cast at random among the cliffs in the rocks had germinated, and promised to clothe the nakedness of the frowning boulders.

Away up among the rocks, too, we discovered a bright sparkling spring of delicious water, at which, from the footprints around, we saw that the antelopes must have refreshed themselves.

Finding everything so satisfactory, we were naturally anxious to discover how our colony and plantations on Whale Island had fared. It was evident at a glance that the rabbits had increased; the young and tender shoots of the trees bore the marks of many greedy, mischievous little teeth. The coconut palms alone had they spared.

Such depredations as these could not be allowed, and with the help of the boys I erected round each stem a hedge of prickly thorn, and then prepared again to embark; before we did so, however, I noticed that some of the seaweed had also been gnawed by the rabbits, and wondering what it could have been to tempt them, I collected some of it to examine more fully at home.

The skeleton of the whale, too, attracted our attention, for, picked clean by the birds and bleached by the sun and rain, the bones had been purified to a most perfect whiteness. Thinking that the joints of the vertebræ might be made of use, I separated some ten or twelve, and rolled them down to the boat, and then returned to the shore, towing them after us.

A scheme now occupied my mind for the construction of a crushing machine, which would prove of the greatest service to us. I knew that to make such a machine of stone was far beyond my power, but it had struck me that the vertebræ of the whale might serve my purpose.

I determined next morning to look out a tree from which I might cut the blocks of wood that I should require to raise my crushers.

My expedition was destined to be a solitary one, for when I went to the stables for a horse, I discovered that the boys had gone off by themselves with their guns and traps, and had left to me a choice between the bull and buffalo.

With Storm, therefore, I was fain to be content. I crossed the bridge, but as I reached the cassava field I noticed to my great annoyance that it had been overrun and laid waste by some mischievous animals. I examined the footprints, and seeing that they greatly resembled those of pigs, determined to follow the trail, and see who these invaders of our territory would prove to be. The track led me on for some way until I almost lost sight of it near our old potato field. For some time I hunted backward and forward without seeing a sign of the animals; at length a loud barking from Floss and Bruno, who were with me, announced that they had been discovered.

The whole family of our old sow, and she herself, were standing at bay, showing their teeth and grunting so savagely, that the dogs feared to approach them.

I raised my gun and fired twice among the herd; two of the pigs fell, and the rest fled, followed by the dogs. I picked up the pigs, and calling back the pursuers, continued my way through the forest.

A tree suited to my purpose was soon found; I marked it and returned home.

Ernest, who had remained at home, assisted me to flay the young porkers, and I handed them over to the mother to prepare for supper; by which time I hoped the other lads would have returned.

Late in the evening we heard the sounds of trampling hoofs, and presently Jack appeared, thundering along upon his two-legged steed, followed in the distance by Fritz and Franz. These latter carried upon their cruppers game bags, the contents of which were speedily displayed; four birds, a kangaroo, twenty muskrats, a monkey, two hares, and half a dozen beaver rats, were laid before me. Besides these, Fritz threw down, without a word of explanation, a bundle of thistles.

The boys seemed almost wild with excitement at the success of their expedition, and presently Jack exclaimed:

"Oh, father, you can't think what grand fun hunting on an ostrich is; we flew along like the wind; sometimes I could scarcely breathe, we were going at such a rate, and was obliged to shut my eyes because of the terrific rush of air; really, father, you must make me a mask with glass eyes to ride with, or I shall be blinded one of these fine days."

"Indeed!" replied I, "I must do no such thing."

"Why not?" asked he, with a look of amazement upon his face.

"For two reasons; firstly, because I do not consider that I *must* do anything that you demand; and, secondly, because I think that you are very capable of doing it yourself. However, I must congratulate you upon your abundant supply of game; you must have indeed worked hard. Yet I wish that you would let me know when you intend starting on such a long expedition as this; you forget that though you yourselves know that you are quite safe, and that all is going on well, yet that we at home are kept in a constant state of anxiety. Now, off with you, and look to your animals, and then you may find supper ready."

Presently the boys returned, and we prepared for a most appetizing meal which the mother set before us.

While we were discussing the roast pig, and washing it down with fragrant mead, Fritz described the day's expedition.

They had set their traps near Woodlands, and had there captured the muskrats, attracting them with small carrots, while with other traps, baited with fish and earth-worms, they had caught several beaver rats, and a duck-billed platypus. Hunting and fishing had occupied the rest of the day, and it was with immense pride that Jack displayed the kangaroo which he had run down with his swift courser. Contributions to the garden had not been forgotten, and Fritz handed over to his mother several cuttings from cinnamon and sweet-apple trees. Finally, when all the other treasures had been displayed, Fritz begged me to examine his thistles which he had gathered, thinking, he said, that it was a plant used in the manufacture of wool. He was perfectly right, for I recognized it at once as the "fuller's teazle," a plant whose sharp little thorns, which cover the stem and leaves, are used to raise the nap of cloth.

We resolved to be up betimes the following morning, that we might attend to the preparation of the booty, and as I now noticed that the boys were all becoming extremely drowsy, I closed the day with evening devotions.

The number of the creatures we killed rendered the removal of their skins a matter of no little time and trouble. It was not an agreeable task at any time, and when I saw the array of animals the boys had brought me to flay, I determined to construct a machine which would considerably lessen the labor. Among the ship's stores, in the surgeon's chest, I discovered a large syringe. This, with a few alterations, would serve my purpose admirably. Within the tube I first fitted a couple of valves, and then, perforating the stopper, I had in my possession a powerful air pump.

The boys stared at me in blank amazement when, armed with this instrument, I took up the kangaroo, and declared myself ready to commence operations.

"Skin a kangaroo with a squirt?" said they, and a roar of laughter followed the remark.

I made no reply to the jests which followed, but silently hung the kangaroo by its hind legs to the branch of a tree. I then made a small incision in the skin, and inserting the mouth of the syringe forced air with all my might between the skin and the body of the animal. By degrees the hide of the kangaroo distended, altering the shape of the creature entirely.

Still I worked on, forcing in yet more air until it had become a mere shapeless mass, and I soon found that the skin was almost entirely separated from the carcass. A bold cut down the belly, and a few touches here and there where the ligatures still bound the hide to the body, and the animal was flayed.

"What a splendid plan!" cried the boys; "but why should it do it?"

"For a most simple and natural reason," I replied; "do you not know that the skin of an animal is attached to its flesh merely by slender and delicate fibers, and that between these exist thousands of little bladders or air chambers; by forcing air into these bladders the fibers are stretched, and at length, elastic as they are, cracked. The skin has now nothing to unite it to the body, and, consequently, may be drawn off with perfect ease. This scientific fact has been known for many years; the Greenlanders make constant use of it; when they have killed a seal or walrus, they distend the skin that they may tow the animal more easily ashore, and then remove its hide at a moment's notice."

The remaining animals were subjected to the same treatment, and, to my great joy, in a couple of days the skins were all off, and being prepared for use.

I now summoned the boys to assist me in procuring blocks of wood for my crushing machine, and the following day we set forth with saws, ropes, axes, and other tools. We soon reached the tree I had selected for my purpose, and I began by sending Fritz and Jack up into the tree with axes to cut off the larger of the high branches that, when the tree fell, it might not injure its neighbors. They then descended, and Fritz and I attacked the stem. As the easiest and most speedy method we used a saw, such a one as is employed by sawyers in a saw-pit, and Fritz taking one end and I the other, the tree was soon cut half through. We then adjusted ropes that we might guide its fall, and again began to cut. It was laborious work, but when I considered that the cut was sufficiently deep we took the ropes and pulled with our united strength. The trunk cracked, swayed, tottered, and fell with a crash.

The boughs were speedily lopped off, and the trunk sawed into blocks four feet long.

To cut down and divide this tree had taken us a couple of days, and on the third we carted home four large and two small blocks, and with the vertebræ joints of the whale I, in a very short time, completed my machine.

While engaged on this undertaking I had paid little attention to our fields of grain, and, accordingly, great was my surprise when one evening the fowls returned, showing most evident indifference to their evening meal, and with their crops perfectly full. It suddenly struck me that these birds had come from the direction of our cornfield. I hurried off to see what damage they had done, and then found to my great joy that the grain was perfectly ripe.

The amount of work before us startled my wife. This unexpected harvest, which added reaping and threshing to the fishing, salting, and pickling already on hand, quite troubled her.

"Only think," said she, "of my beloved potatoes and manioc roots! What is to become of them, I should like to know? It is time to take them up, and how to manage it, with all this press of work, I can't see."

"Don't be down-hearted, wife," said I; "there is no immediate hurry about the manioc, and digging potatoes in this fine, light soil is easy work compared to what it is in Switzerland, while as to planting more, that will not be necessary if we leave the younger plants in the ground. The harvest we must conduct after the Italian fashion, which, although anything but economical, will save time and trouble, and as we are to have two crops in the year, we need not be too particular."

Without further delay, I commenced leveling a large space of firm, clayey ground to act as a threshing floor; it was well sprinkled with water, rolled, beaten, and stamped; as the sun dried the moisture it was watered anew, and the treatment continued until it became as flat, hard, and smooth as threshing floor need be.

Our largest wicker basket was then slung between Storm and Grumble; we armed ourselves with reaping hooks, and went forth to gather in the corn in the simplest and most expeditious manner imaginable.

I told my reapers not to concern themselves about the length of the straw, but to grasp the corn where it was convenient to them, without stooping; each was to wind a stalk around his own handful, and throw it into the basket; in this way great labor was saved. The plan pleased the boys immensely, and in a short time the basket had been filled many times, and the field displayed a quantity of tall, headless stubble, which perfectly horrified the mother, so extravagant and untidy did she consider our work.

"This is dreadful!" cried she; "you have left numbers of ears growing on short stalks, and look at that splendid straw completely wasted! I don't approve of your Italian fashion at all."

"It is not a bad plan, I can assure you, wife, and the Italians do not waste the straw by not cutting it with the grain; having more arable than pasture land, they use this high stubble for their cattle, letting them feed in it, and eat what grain is left; afterward, allowing the grass to grow up among it, they mow all together for winter fodder. And now for threshing, also in Italian fashion. We shall find it spare our arms and backs as much in that as in reaping."

The little sheaves were laid in a large circle on the floor, the boys mounted Storm, Grumble, Lightfoot, and Hurry, starting off at a brisk trot, with many a merry jest, and round they went, trampling and stamping out the grain, while dust and chaff flew in clouds about them.

My wife and I were incessantly occupied with hay-forks, by means of which we shook up and moved the sheaves over which the threshers rode, so as to throw them in the track.

From time to time the animals took mouthfuls of the tempting food they were beating out; we thought they well deserved it, and called to mind the command given to the Jews, "Thou shalt not muzzle the ox that treadeth out the corn."

After threshing, we proceeded to winnowing; by simply throwing the threshed corn with shovels high in the air when the land or sea-breeze blew strong, the chaff and refuse was carried away by the wind and the grain fell to the ground.

During these operations our poultry paid the threshing-floor many visits, testifying a lively interest in the success of our labors, and gobbling up the grain at such a rate that my wife was obliged to keep them at a reasonable distance; but I would not have them altogether stinted in the midst of our plenty. I said, "Let them enjoy themselves; what we lose in grain, we gain in flesh. I anticipate delicious chicken-pie, roast goose, and boiled turkey!"

When our harvest stores were housed, we found that we had reaped sixty, eighty, even a hundred fold what had been sown. Our garner was truly filled with all manner of store.

Expecting a second harvest, we were constrained to prepare the field for sowing again, and immediately therefore commenced mowing down the stubble. While engaged in this, flocks of quails and partridges came to glean among the scattered ears. We did not secure any great number, but resolved to be prepared for them next season, and by spreading nets, to catch them in large quantities.

My wife was satisfied when she saw the straw carried home and stacked; our crop of maize, which of course had not been threshed like the other corn, afforded soft leaves which were used for stuffing mattresses, while the stalks, when burnt, left ashes so rich in alkali as to be especially useful.

I changed the crops sown on the ground to rye, barley, and oats, and hoped they would ripen before the rainy season.

The shoals of herring made their appearance just as we finished our agricultural operations. This year we pickled only two barrels of them; but we were not so merciful toward the seals, which arrived on the coast directly afterward. We hunted them vigorously, requiring their skins for many purposes, more especially for the completion of the kayak. On the little deck of that tiny vessel I had made a kind of magazine, in which to store pistols, ammunition, water, and provisions, and this I meant to cover with sealskin, so as to be quite watertight. A couple of harpoons furnished with seal bladders were to be suspended alongside.

CHAPTER XV

Trial of the kayak—Fritz kills a walrus—We carry home its head—The storm—Where is Fritz?—Safe at last—The fishing season—An expedition proposed—Three of the boys start for Woodlands—Pigeon post—Encounter with a hyena—Wood Lake explored—A tapir—Prospect Hill pillaged—A tragedy—The boys in danger—We join them—We build a summer house—Discover the cacao plant—Fritz ascends the stream—He sees elephants and hippopotami—Jack's "moist secret"—We return to Rockburg—Grace and beauty—Shark Island is fortified.

At last came the day when Fritz was to make his trial trip with the kayak. Completely equipped in swimming costume—trousers, jacket, and cap—it was most ludicrous to see him cower down in the canoe and puff and blow till he began to swell like the frog in the fable.

All trace of his original figure was speedily lost, and shouts of laughter greeted his comical appearance. Even his mother could not resist a smile, although the dress was her invention.

I got the other boat out, that my wife might see we were ready to go to his assistance the moment it became necessary.

The kayak was launched from a convenient shelving point, and floated lightly on the sea-green ocean mirror. Fritz with his paddles then began to practice all manner of evolutions: darting along with arrowy swiftness, wheeling to the right, then to the left; and at last, flinging himself quite on his side, while his mother uttered a shriek of terror, he showed that the tiny craft would neither capsize nor sink. Then, recovering his balance, he sped securely on his further way.

Encouraged by our shouts of approbation, he now boldly ventured into the strong current of Jackal River, and was rapidly carried out to sea.

This being more than I had bargained for, I lost no time in giving chase in the boat, with Ernest and Jack; my wife urging us to greater speed, and declaring that some accident could not fail to happen to "that horrid soap-bubble."

We soon arrived outside the bay, at the rocks where formerly lay the wreck, and gazed in all directions for signs of the runaway.

After a time we saw, at a considerable distance, a faint puff of smoke, followed by the crack of a pistol. Upon this we fired a signal shot, which was presently answered by another, and, steering in the direction of the sound, we soon heard the boy's cheery halloo; the kayak darted from behind a point of land, and we quickly joined company.

"Come to this rocky beach," cried Fritz, "I have something to show you."

With blank amazement we beheld a fine, well-grown young walrus, harpooned and quite dead.

"Did you kill this creature, my dear Fritz?" I exclaimed, looking round in some anxiety, and half expecting to see a naked savage come to claim the prize.

"To be sure, father! Don't you see my harpoon? Why do you doubt it?"

"Well, I scarcely know," replied I, laughing; "but success so speedy, so unexpected, and so appropriate, to an amateur Greenlander, took me by surprise. I congratulate you, my boy! But I must tell you that you have alarmed us by making this long trip. You should not have gone out of the bay. I left your mother in grievous trouble."

"Indeed, father, I had no idea of passing out of sight, but once in the current, I was carried along, and could not help myself. Then I came on a herd of walruses, and I did so long to make a prize of one that I forgot everything else, and made chase after them when beyond the influence of the current, until I got near enough to harpoon this fine fellow. He swam more slowly, and I struck him a second time; then he sought refuge among these rocks, and expired. I landed, and scrambled to where he lay, but I took care to give him the contents of my pistol before going close up, having a salutary recollection of the big serpent's parting fling at you, Jack."

"You ran a very great risk," said I. "The walrus is an inoffensive creature; but when attacked and wounded, it often becomes furious, and, turning upon its pursuer, can destroy, with its long tusks, a strongly built whale boat. However, thank God for your safety! I value that above a thousand such creatures. Now, what's to be done with him? He must be quite fourteen feet long, although not full grown."

"I am very glad you followed me, father," said Fritz; "but our united strength will not remove this prodigious weight from among these rocks; only do let me carry away the head, with these grand, snow-white tusks! I should so like to fasten it on the prow of the kayak, and name it the *Sea-horse*."

"We must certainly carry away the beautiful ivory tusks," said I; "but make haste; the air feels so excessively close and sultry, I think a storm is brewing."

"But the head! The head! We must have the whole head," cried Jack; "just think how splendid it will look on the kayak!"

"And how splendid it will smell too, when it begins to putrefy," added Ernest; "what a treat for the steersman?"

"Oh, we will prepare for that," said Fritz; "it shall be soaked and cleaned, and dried until it is as hard as a wooden model; it shall not offend your delicate nose in the least, Ernest!"

"I supposed the walrus to be an animal peculiar to the Arctic regions," remarked Ernest.

“And so it is,” I replied; “though they may occasionally be seen elsewhere; these may have wandered from the Antarctic seas. I know that on the eastern coast of Africa is found a smaller species of walrus called the dugong; it has long incisor teeth, but not tusks; and certainly resembles a seal, rather than a walrus.”

While thus speaking, we were actively engaged in the decapitation of the walrus, and in cutting off long strips of its skin. This took some time, as we had not the proper implements, and Fritz remarked that in future the kayak must be provided with a hunting-knife and a hatchet; adding that he should like to have a small compass in a box, with a glass top, fixed in front of the hole where the steersman sits. I saw the necessity of this, and I promised it should be done.

Our work being accomplished, we were ready to go, and I proposed to take Fritz and the canoe on board our boat, so that we might all arrive together; but I yielded to his earnest wish to return alone as he came; he longed to act as our avant-courier, and announce our approach to his mother; so he was soon skimming away over the surface of the water, while we followed at a slower rate.

Black clouds meanwhile gathered thick and fast around us, and a tremendous storm came on. Fritz was out of sight, and beyond our reach.

We buckled on the swimming belts and firmly lashed ourselves to the boat, so that we might not be washed overboard by the towering seas which broke over it.

The horizon was shrouded in darkness, fearful gusts of wind lashed the ocean into foam, rain descended in torrents, while livid lightning glared athwart the gloom. Both my boys faced the danger nobly; and my feelings of alarm were mingled with hope on finding how well the boat behaved.

The tempest swept on its way, and the sky began to clear as suddenly as it had been overcast; yet the stormy waves continued for a long time to threaten our frail bark with destruction, in spite of its buoyancy and steadiness.

Yet I never lost hope for ourselves—all my fears were for Fritz; in fact I gave him up for lost, and my whole agonized heart arose in prayer for strength to say, "Thy will be done!"

At last we rounded the point, and once more entering Safety Bay, quickly drew near the little harbor.

What was our surprise—our overwhelming delight—when there we saw the mother with Fritz, as well as her little boy, on their knees in prayer so earnest for our deliverance, that our approach was unperceived, until with cries of joy we attracted their notice. Then indeed ensued a happy meeting, and we gave thanks together for the mercy which had spared our lives.

Returning joyfully to Rockburg, we changed our drenched garments for warm, dry clothes; and, seated at a comfortable meal, considered and described at our ease the perils of the storm.

Afterward, the head of the walrus was conveyed to our workshop; where it underwent such a skillful and thorough process of cleaning, embalming, and drying, that ere long it was actually fixed on the prow of the kayak, and a most imposing appearance it presented!

The strips of hide, when well tanned and prepared, made valuable leather.

Much damage had been done by the late storm. The heavy rain had flooded all the streams, and injured crops which should have been housed before the regular rainy season.

The bridge over Jackal River was partly broken down, and the water tanks and pipes all needed repair. So our time was much occupied in restoring things to order.

On going to work one day, near the cascade, we found a great number of dark red berries scattered on the ground; they were about the size of ordinary hazelnuts, with small leafy coronets at the tip.

The boys thought them so inviting, that they tasted them at once, but angry exclamations and much spitting and spluttering followed the experiment; even Knips rejected them, and they would have been cast aside with contempt, had not the smell induced me to examine them. I decided that this was the fruit of the clove.

Some plants were immediately set in the nursery garden, and my wife was pleased to have this excellent spice wherewith to flavor her boiled rice and other dishes, in lieu of pepper—a very welcome variety to everyone.

Having a good supply of clay, brought from the bed near Falconhurst, I proposed to use it for making aqueducts; and, observing how much the recent rain had promoted the growth of our young corn, I determined to irrigate the fields with the drainage from our crushing mill.

The fishing season was again successful. Large takes of salmon, sturgeon, and herring rewarded our annual exertions, and our storeroom again assumed a well-stocked appearance. Much as I wished that we could obtain a constant supply of these fish fresh, I was obliged to reject the naïve proposal from Jack, that we should tether a shoal of salmon by the gills to the bottom of the bay as we had secured the turtles.

Many quiet uneventful days passed by, and I perceived that the boys, wearied by the routine of farm work at Rockburg, were longing for a cruise in the yacht or an expedition into the woods, which would refresh both mind and body.

"Father," said Fritz at length, "we want a quantity of hurdles, and have scarcely any more bamboos of which to make them. Had we not better get a supply from Woodlands? And you said, too, the other day, that you wished you had some more of the fine clay: we might visit the Gap at the same time."

I had really no objection to propose; and it was shortly afterward settled that Fritz, Jack, and Franz should start together; and that Ernest, who had no great desire to accompany his brothers, should remain with his mother and me, and assist in the construction of a sugar mill, the erection of which I had long contemplated.

Before they started, Fritz begged some bear's meat from the mother, to make pemmican.

"And what may pemmican be?" she asked.

"It is food carried by the fur-traders of North America on their long journeys through the wild country they traverse; and consists of bear or deer's flesh, first cooked and then pounded or ground to powder. It is very portable, and nourishing."

His mother consented "to humor him," as she said, although without much faith in the value of the preparation; and in the course of two days a stock of pemmican, sufficient for a Polar expedition, was fabricated by our enthusiastic son.

They were ready to start, when I observed Jack quietly slip a basket, containing several pigeons, under the packages in the cart.

"Oh, oh!" thought I, "the little fellow has his doubts about that pemmican, and thinks a tough old pigeon would be preferable."

The weather was exquisite; and, with exhortations to prudence and caution from both me and their mother, the three lads started in the very highest spirits. Storm and Grumble, as usual, drew the cart, and were ridden by Fritz and Franz; while Hurry carried Jack swiftly across the bridge in advance of them; followed by Floss and Bruno, barking at his heels.

The sugar mill occupied us for several days, and was made so much like our other mills that I need not now describe it.

On the evening of the first day, as we sat resting in the porch at Rockburg, we naturally talked of the absentees, wondering and guessing what they might be about.

Ernest looked rather mysterious, and hinted that he might have news of them next morning.

Just then a bird alighted on the dovecot, and entered. I could not see, in the failing light, whether it was one of our own pigeons or an intruder. Ernest started up, and said he would see that all was right.

In a few minutes he returned with a scrap of paper in his hand.

"News, father! The very latest news by pigeon post, mother!"

"Well done, boys! What a capital idea!" said I, and taking the note I read:

"Dearest Parents and Ernest:

"A brute of a hyena has killed a ram and two lambs. The dogs seized it. Franz shot it. It is dead and skinned. The pemmican isn't worth much, but we are all right. Love to all.

"Fritz

"Woodlands, 15th instant."

"A true hunter's letter!" laughed I; "but what exciting news. When does the next post come in, Ernest?"

"Tonight, I hope," said he, while his mother sighed, and doubted the value of such glimpses into the scenes of danger through which her sons were passing, declaring she would much rather wait and hear all about it when she had them safe home again.

Thus the winged letter-carriers kept us informed from day to day of the outline of adventures which were afterward more fully described.

On approaching the farm at Woodlands, the boys were startled by hearing, as they thought, human laughter, repeated again and again; while, to their astonishment, the oxen testified the great uneasiness, the dogs growled and drew close to their masters, and the ostrich fairly bolted with Jack into the rice swamp.

The laughter continued, and the beasts became unmanageable.

"Something is very far wrong!" cried Fritz. "I cannot leave the animals; but while I unharness them, do you, Franz, take the dogs, and advance cautiously to see what is the matter."

Without a moment's hesitation, Franz made his way among the bushes with his gun, closely followed by the dogs; until, through an opening in the thicket, he could see, at a distance of about forty paces, an enormous hyena, in the most wonderful state of excitement; dancing round a lamb just killed, and uttering, from time to time, the ghastly hysterical laughter which had pealed through the forest.

The beast kept running backward and forward, rising on its hind legs, and then rapidly whirling round and round, nodding its head, and going through most frantic and ludicrous antics.

Franz kept his presence of mind very well; for he watched till, calming down, the hyena began with horrid growls to tear its prey; and then, firing steadily both barrels, he broke its foreleg, and wounded it in the breast.

Meanwhile Fritz, having unyoked the oxen and secured them to trees, hurried to his brother's assistance. The dogs and the dying hyena were by this time engaged in mortal strife; but the latter, although it severely wounded both Floss and Bruno, speedily succumbed, and was dead when the boys reached the spot. They raised a shout of triumph, which guided Jack to the scene of action; and their first care was for the dogs, whose wounds they dressed before minutely examining the hyena. It was as large as a wild boar; long stiff bristles formed a mane on its neck, its color was gray marked with black, the teeth and jaws were of extraordinary strength, the thighs muscular and sinewy, the claws remarkably strong and sharp altogether. But for his wounds he would certainly have been more than a match for the dogs.

After unloading the cart at the farm, the boys returned for the carcass of the tiger-wolf, as it is sometimes called, and occupied themselves in skinning it during the remainder of the day, when, after dispatching the carrier-pigeon to Rockburg, they retired to rest on their bearskin rugs, to dream of adventures past and future.

The following day they devised no less a scheme than to survey the shores of Wood Lake, and place marks wherever the surrounding marsh was practicable, and might be crossed either to reach the water or leave it.

Fritz in the kayak, and the boys on shore, carefully examined the ground together; and when they found firm footing to the water's edge, the spot was indicated by planting a tall bamboo, bearing on high a bundle of reeds and branches.

They succeeded in capturing three young black swans, after considerable resistance from the old ones. They were afterward brought to Rockburg, and detained as ornaments to Safety Bay.

Presently a beautiful heron thrust his long neck from among the reeds, to ascertain what all the noise on the lake was about. Before he could satisfy his curiosity, Fritz unhooded his eagle, and though vainly he flapped and struggled, his legs and wings were gently but firmly bound, and he had to own himself vanquished, and submit to the inspection of his delighted captors.

It was their turn to be alarmed next, for a large powerful animal came puffing, with a curious whistling sound, through the dense thicket of reeds, passing close by and sorely discomposing them by its sudden appearance. It was out of sight immediately, before they could summon the dogs, and from their description it must have been a tapir, the color dark brown, and in form resembling a young rhinoceros, but with no horn on the nose, and the upper lip prolonged into a trunk something like that of an elephant on a smaller scale. It is a gentle creature, but when attacked becomes a fierce opponent, and can wound dogs dangerously with its powerful teeth.

The tapir can swim and dive with perfect ease, and abounds in the densely wooded swamps and rivers of tropical America.

Fritz in his kayak followed for a time the direction in which the tapir proceeded, but saw no more of it.

Meanwhile the other two boys returned to the farm by the rice fields, and there fell in with a flock of cranes, five or six of which they caught alive, among them two demoiselles or Numidian cranes. These birds they shot at with arrows arranged in a skillful and original way, with loops of cord dipped in birdlime attached to them, so that it often happened that the bird aimed at was entangled and brought down uninjured.

The young hunters seemed to have lived very comfortably on peccary ham, cassava bread and fruit, and plenty of baked potatoes and milk.

One trial of the pemmican was sufficient, and it was handed over to the dogs. Fritz, however, determined again to attempt the manufacture, knowing its value when properly prepared.

After collecting a supply of rice and cotton, they took their way to Prospect Hill; "and," said Fritz, as he afterward vividly described the dreadful scene there enacted, "when we entered the pine wood, we found it in possession of troops of monkeys, who resolved to make our passage through it as disagreeable as possible, for they howled and chattered at us like demons, pelting us as hard as they could with pine cones.

"They became so unbearable, that at last we fired a few shot right and left among them; several bit the dust, the rest fled, and we continued our way in peace to Prospect Hill, but only to discover the havoc the wretches had made there.

"Would you believe it, father? The pleasant cottage had been overrun and ruined by apes just as Woodland last summer! The most dreadful dirt and disorder met our eyes wherever we turned, and we had hard work to make the place fit for human habitation; and even then we preferred the tent. I felt quite at loss how to guard the farm for the future; but seeing a bottle of the poisonous gum of the euphorbia in the tool chest, I devised a plan for the destruction of the apes which succeeded beyond my expectations.

"I mixed poison with milk, bruised millet, and anything I thought the monkeys would eat, and put it in coconut shells, which I hung about in the trees, high enough to be out of reach of our own animals. The evening was calm and lovely; the sea murmured in the distance, and the rising moon shed a beauty over the landscape which we seemed never before to have so admired and enjoyed. The summer night closed around us in all its solemn stillness, and our deepest feelings were touched; when suddenly the spell was broken by an outburst of the most hideous and discordant noises. As by one consent, every beast of the forest seemed to arise from its den, and utter its wild nocturnal cry. Snorting, snarling, and shrieking filled the wood beneath us.

"From the hills echoed the mournful howl of the jackals, answered by Fangs in the yard, who was backed up by the barking and yelping of his friends Floss and Bruno. Far away beyond the rocky fastnesses of the Gap, sounded unearthly, hollow snortings and neighings, reminding one of the strange cry of the hippopotamus; above these, occasional deep majestic roaring made our hearts quail with the conviction that we heard the voices of lions and elephants.

"Overawed and silent, we retired to rest, hoping to forget in sleep the terrors of the midnight forest, but ere long the most fearful cries in the adjoining woods gave notice that the apes were beginning to suffer from the poisoned repast prepared for them.

"As our dogs could not remain silent amid the uproar and din, we had not a wink of sleep until the morning. It was late, therefore, when we rose, and looked on the awful spectacle presented by the multitude of dead monkeys and baboons thickly strewn under the trees round the farm. I shall not tell you how many there were. I can only say, I wished I had not found the poison, and we made all haste to clear away the dead bodies, and the dangerous food, burying some deep in the earth, and, carrying the rest to the shore, we pitched them over the rocks into the sea. That day we traveled on to the Gap."

The same evening that the boys reached the rocky pass, a messenger pigeon arrived at Rockburg, bearing a note which concluded in the following words:

"The barricade at the Gap broken down. Everything laid waste as far as the sugar-brake, where the hut is knocked to pieces, and the fields trampled over by huge footmarks. Come to us, father—we are safe, but feel we are no match for this unknown danger."

I lost not an instant, but saddled Swift, late as it was, in order to ride to the assistance of our boys, desiring Ernest to prepare the small cart, and follow me with his mother at daybreak, bringing everything we should require for camping out for some days.

The bright moonlight favored my journey, and my arrival at the Gap surprised and delighted the boys, who did not expect me till the next day. Early on the following morning I inspected the footprints and ravages of the great unknown. The cane brake had, without doubt, been visited by an elephant. That great animal alone could have left such traces and committed such fearful ravages. Thick posts in the barricade were snapped across like reeds; the trees in the vicinity, where we planned to build a cool summer-house, were stripped of leaves and branches to a great height, but the worst mischief was done among the young sugarcane plants, which were all either devoured or trampled down and destroyed.

It seemed to me that not one elephant, but a troop must have invaded our grounds. The tracks were very numerous, and the footprints of various sizes; but, to my satisfaction, I saw that they could be traced not only from the Gap, but back to it in evidently equal numbers.

We did not, therefore, suppose that the mighty animals remained hidden in the woods of our territory; but concluded that, after this freebooting incursion, they had withdrawn to their native wilds, where, by greatly increasing the strength of our ramparts, we hoped henceforth to oblige them to remain.

In what manner to effect this we laid many plans, during the night of my arrival, when, sitting by an enormous watch-fire, I chatted with my boys, and heard details of their numerous adventures, so interesting for them to relate, and for me to hear, that every one was more disposed to act sentinel than retire to sleep.

The mother and Ernest arrived next day, and she rejoiced to find all well, making light of trodden fields and trampled sugarcanes, since her sons were sound in life and limb.

A systematic scheme of defense was now elaborated, and the erection of the barricade occupied us for at least a month, as it was to be a firm and durable building, proof against all invasion. As our little tent was unsuited to a long residence of this sort, I adopted Fritz's idea of a Kamchatkan dwelling, and, to his great delight, forthwith carried it out.

Instead of planting four posts, on which to place a platform, we chose four trees of equal size, which, in a very suitable place, grew exactly in a square, twelve or fourteen feet apart. Between these, at about twenty feet from the ground, we laid a flooring of beams and bamboo, smoothly and strongly planked. From this rose, on all four sides, walls of cane; the frame of the roof was covered so effectually by large pieces of bark that no rain could penetrate.

The staircase to this tree-cottage was simply a board plank with bars nailed across it for steps. The flooring projected like a balcony in front of the entrance door, and underneath, on the ground, we fitted up sheds for cattle and fowls.

Various ornaments in Chinese or Japanese style were added to the roof and eaves, and a most convenient, cool, and picturesque cottage, overhung and adorned by the graceful foliage of the trees, was the result of our ingenuity.

I was pleased to find that the various birds taken by the boys during this excursion seemed likely to thrive; they were the first inmates of the new sheds, and even the black swans and cranes soon became tame and sociable.

Constantly roaming through the woods, the children often made new discoveries.

Fritz brought one day, after an excursion to the opposite side of the stream beyond the Gap, a cluster of bananas, and also of cacao beans, from which chocolate is made.

The banana, although valuable and nourishing food for the natives of the tropical countries where it grows, is not generally liked by Europeans, and probably this variety was even inferior to many others, for we found the fruit much like rotten pears, and almost uneatable.

The cacao seeds tasted exceedingly bitter, and it seemed wonderful that by preparation they should produce anything so delicious as chocolate.

My wife, who now fancied no manufacture beyond my skill, begged for plants, seeds, or cuttings to propagate in her nursery garden, already fancying herself in the enjoyment of chocolate for breakfast, and I promised to make a cacao plantation near home.

"Let me have bananas also," said she, "for we may acquire a

taste for that celebrated fruit, and, at all events, I am sure I can make it into an excellent preserve."

The day before our return to Rockburg, Fritz went again to the inland region beyond the river to obtain a large supply of young banana plants, and the cacao fruit. He took the kayak, and a bundle of reeds to float behind him as a raft to carry the fruit, plants, and anything else he might wish to bring back.

In the evening he made his appearance, coming swiftly down stream. His brothers rushed to meet him, each eager to see and help to land his cargo.

Ernest and Fritz were quickly running up the bank, with arms full of plants, branches, and fruits, when Fritz handed to Jack a dripping wet bag which he had brought along partly under water. A curious pattering noise proceeded from this bag, but they kept the contents a secret for the present, Jack running with it behind a bush before peeping in, and I could just hear him exclaim:

"Hullo! I say, what monsters they are. It's enough to make a fellow's flesh creep to look at them!"

With that he hastily shut up the bag, and put it away safely out of sight in water.

Securing the kayak, Fritz sprang toward us, his handsome face radiant with pleasure, as he exhibited a beautiful waterfowl.

Its plumage was rich purple, changing on the back to dark green; the legs, feet, and a mark above the bill, bright red. This lovely bird I concluded to be the sultan cock described by Buffon, and as it was gentle, we gladly received it among our domestic pets.

Fritz gave a stirring account of his exploring trip, having made his way far up the river, between fertile plains and majestic forests of lofty trees, where the cries of vast numbers of birds, parrots, peacocks, guinea fowls, and hundreds unknown to him, quite bewildered, and made him feel giddy.

"It was in the Buffalo Swamp," continued he, "that I saw the splendid birds you call sultan cocks, and I set my heart on catching one alive, which, as they seemed to have little fear of my approach, I managed by means of a wire snare. Farther on I saw a grove of mimosa trees, among which huge dark masses were moving in a deliberate way. Guess what they were!"

"Savages?" asked Franz timidly.

"Black bears, I bet!" cried Jack.

"Your words suggest to my mind the manner and appearance of elephants," said Ernest.

"Right you are, Professor!" exclaimed Fritz gaily, the words producing quite a sensation on the whole attentive family. "From fifteen to twenty elephants were feeding peacefully on the leafy boughs, tearing down branches with their trunks and shoving them into their mouths with one jerk, or bathing in the deep waters of the marsh for refreshment in the great heat. You cannot imagine the wild grandeur of the scene! The river being very broad, I felt safe from wild animals, and more than once saw splendid jaguars crouched on the banks, their glossy skin glancing in the sunlight.

"While considering if it would be simply foolhardy to try a shot at one of these creatures, I was suddenly convinced that discretion is the better part of valor, and urging my canoe into the center current, made a rapid retreat down the river. For just before me, in the calm deep water of a sheltered bay where I was quietly floating, there arose a violent boiling, bubbling commotion, and for an instant I thought a hot spring was going to burst forth—instead of that, up rose the hideous head and gaping jaws of a hippopotamus, who, with a hoarse, terrific snort, seemed about to attack me. I can tell you I did not wait to see the rest of him! A glimpse of his enormous mouth and its array of white gleaming tusks was quite enough. 'Right about face!' said I to myself, and shot down the stream like an arrow, never pausing till a bend in the river brought me within sight of the Gap, where I once more felt safe, and joyfully made my way back to you all."

This narrative was of thrilling interest to us, proving the existence of tribes of the most formidable animals beyond the rocky barrier which defended, in so providential a manner, the small and fertile territory on which our lot was cast.

During the absence of the adventurer we had been busily

engaged in making preparations for our departure—and everything was packed up and ready by the morning after his return.

After some hesitation I yielded to his great wish, which was to return by sea in his kayak round Cape Disappointment, and so meet us at Rockburg.

He was much interested in examining the outlines of the coast and the rugged precipices of the Cape. These were tenanted by vast flocks of sea fowl and birds of prey; while many varieties of shrubs and plants, hitherto unknown to us, grew in the clefts and crevices of the rocks, some of them diffusing a strong aromatic odor. Among the specimens he brought I recognized the caper plant, and, with still greater pleasure, a shrub which was, I felt sure, the tea-plant of China—it bore very pretty white flowers, and the leaves resembled myrtle.

Our land journey was effected without accident or adventure of any kind.

Jack, mounted as usual on Hurry, the ostrich, carried the mysterious wet bag very carefully slung at his side, and when near home started off at a prodigious rate in advance of us.

He let fall the drawbridge, and we saw no more of him until, on reaching Rockburg, he appeared leisurely returning from the swamp, where apparently he had gone to deposit his "moist secret," as Franz called it.

We were all glad to take up our quarters once more in our large and convenient dwelling, and my first business was to provide for the great number of birds we now had on our hands, by establishing them in suitable localities, it being impossible to maintain them all in the poultry yard. Some were, therefore, taken to the islands; and the black swans, the heron, the graceful demoiselle cranes, and our latest acquisition, the splendid sultan cock, soon became perfectly at home in the swamp, greatly adding to the interest of the neighborhood of Safety Bay.

The old bustards were the tamest of all our feathered pets, and never more so than at meal times. They were unfailing in their attendance when we dined or supped in the open air.

Toward evening, as we sat in the veranda listening to Fritz's account of his trip round the Cape, an extraordinary hollow, roaring noise sounded from the swamp not unlike the angry bellowing of a bull.

The dogs barked, and the family rose in excitement; but I remarked a look of quiet humor in Fritz's eye, as he stood leaning against one of the veranda pillars, watching Jack, who, in some confusion, started off toward the marsh.

"Come back, you silly boy!" cried his mother; "the child has not so much as a pistol, and is rushing off alone to face he knows not what!"

"Perhaps," said I, looking at Fritz, "this is not a case requiring the use of firearms. It may be only the booming of a bittern which we hear."

"You need not be uneasy, mother," said Fritz; "Jack knows what he is about; only this charming serenade took him by surprise, and I fancy he will have to exhibit his treasures before they reach perfection. Yes, here he comes!"

Lugging his "moist secret" along with him, Jack, flushed and breathless, came up to us, exclaiming:

"They were to grow as big as rabbits before you saw them! Such a shame! I never thought they would kick up a row like that. Now for it!"—and he turned out the bag. "This is 'Grace,' and this is 'Beauty.'"

Two immense frogs rolled clumsily on the ground, and recovering their feet, sat squat before us, swelling and puffing with a ludicrous air of insulted dignity, while peals of laughter greeted them on all sides.

"Ladies and Gentleman, these are two very handsome young specimens of the famous African bullfrog," said Jack, pretending to be offended at the mingled disgust and amusement occasioned by their appearance; "they are but half-grown, and I hoped to maintain them in seclusion until they reached full size, when I would have introduced them with proper *éclat*. But since their talent for music has brought them precociously into public notice,

I must beg for your kind and indulgent patronage, and—leave to take them back to the swamp!"

Great clapping of hands followed Jack's speech.

"Grace" and "Beauty" were examined, and commented on with much interest, and voted decidedly handsome "in their way."

Their general color was greenish brown, mottled and spotted with reddish brown and yellow; the sides green and black; the under part yellow, mottled with orange. The eyes were positively beautiful, of a rich chestnut hue, covered with golden white dots, which shone with a metallic luster. The skin of the body was puckered into longitudinal folds.

By general consent they were remanded to the swamp.

Shortly after our return to Rockburg, my wife drew my attention to the somewhat neglected state of our dear old summer residence at Falconhurst, begging me to devote some time to its restoration and embellishment.

This I most willingly undertook, and we removed thither, as soon as the boys had completed the arrangement of the artificial salt-lick to their satisfaction.

At Falconhurst things were quickly in good order, and we made a great improvement by completing the broad terrace supported on the arching roots of the trees—it was better floored—and rustic pillars and trellis-work sustained a bark roof which afforded a pleasant shade.

After this was done, I was compelled to consent to a plan long cherished by Fritz, who wished to construct a watch-tower and mount a gun on Shark Island. After great exertion, both mental and bodily, this piece of military engineering was completed; and a flagstaff erected, on which the guard at this outpost could run up a white flag to signal the approach of anything harmless from the sea, while a red flag would be shown on the least appearance of danger.

To celebrate the completion of this great work, which occupied us during two months, we hoisted the white flag, and fired a salute of six guns.

CHAPTER XVI

Ten years afterward—Our farms and farmyards—Fritz makes a voyage of discovery—Cape Minster and the swallows' nests—Pearl oysters—A magnificent bay—The strange message—An excursion to Pearl Bay—Fritz proposes to search for the stranger, and prepares his canoe for her reception—The pearl fishery—An encounter with a wild boar—Jack's accident—Truffles—A midnight alarm—The lion and his mate—Our enemies overcome—Juno's death—We set sail for Rockburg—Fritz leaves us.

"We spend our years as a tale that is told," said King David.

These words recurred to me again and again as I reviewed ten years, of which the story lay chronicled in the pages of my journal.

Year followed year; chapter succeeded chapter; steadily, imperceptibly, time was passing away.

The shade of sadness cast on my mind by retrospect of this kind was dispelled by thoughts full of gratitude to God, for the welfare and happiness of my beloved family during so long a period. I had cause especially to rejoice in seeing our sons advance to manhood, strengthened by early training for lives of usefulness and activity wherever their lot might fall.

And my great wish is, that young people who read this record of our lives and adventures should learn from it how admirably suited is the peaceful, industrious, and pious life of a cheerful, united family, to the formation of strong, pure, and manly character.

None take a better place in the great national family, none are happier or more beloved than those who go forth from such homes to fulfill new duties, and to gather fresh interests around them.

Having given a detailed account of several years' residence in New Switzerland, as we liked to call our dominion, it is needless for me to continue what would exhaust the patience of the most long-suffering, by repeating monotonous narratives of exploring parties and hunting expeditions, wearisome descriptions of awkward inventions and clumsy machines, with an endless record of discoveries, more fit for the pages of an encyclopedia than a book of family history.

Yet before winding up with the concluding events, I may mention some interesting facts illustrative of our exact position at the time these took place.

Rockburg and Falconhurst continued to be our winter and summer headquarters, and improvements were added which made them more and more convenient, as well as attractive in appearance.

The fountains, trellised verandas, and plantations round Rockburg, completely changed the character of the residence which, on account of the heat and want of vegetation, had in former days been so distasteful to my wife. Flowering creepers overhung the balconies and pillars; while shrubs and trees, both native and European, grew luxuriantly in groves of our planting.

In the distance, Shark Island, now clothed with graceful palms, guarded the entrance to Safety Bay, the battery and flagstaff prominently visible on its crested rock.

The swamp, cleared and drained, was now a considerable lake, with just marsh and reeds enough beyond it to form good cover for the waterfowl whose favorite retreat it was.

On its blue waters sailed stately black swans, snow-white geese, and richly colored ducks; while out and in among the water plants and rushes would appear at intervals glimpses of the brilliant sultan, marsh-fowl, crimson flamingos, soft, blue-gray, demoiselle cranes, and crested heron, all associating in harmony, and with no fear of us, their masters.

The giant frogs, Grace and Beauty, delighted Jack by actually attaining in time to the size of small rabbits; and, perfectly knowing their very appropriate names, would waddle out of the marsh at his call, to eat a grasshopper or dainty fly.

Beneath the spreading trees, and through the aromatic shrubberies, old Hurry, the ostrich, was usually to be seen marching about, with grave and dignified pace, as though monarch of all he surveyed. Every variety of beautiful pigeon nested in the rocks and dovecots, their soft cooing and glossy plumage making them favorite household pets.

By the bridge alone could Rockburg be approached; for higher up the river, where, near the cascade, it was fordable a dense and impenetrable thicket of orange and lemon trees, Indian figs, prickly pears, and all manner of thorn-bearing shrubs, planted by us, now formed a complete barrier.

The rabbit warren on Shark Island kept us well supplied with food, as well as soft and useful fur; and, as the antelopes did not thrive on Whale Isle, they also were placed among the shady groves with the rabbits, and their own island devoted to such work as candle-making, tanning, wool-cleaning, and any other needful but offensive operations.

The farm at Woodlands flourished, and our flocks and herds supplied us with mutton, beef, and veal, while my wife's dairy was almost more than she could manage.

My boys retained their old love for giving names to the animals. They had a beautiful creamy-white cow called Blanche, and a bull with such a tremendous voice, that he received the name of Stentor. Two fleet young onagers were named Arrow and Dart; and Jack had a descendant of his old favorite Fangs, the jackal, which he chose to call Coco, asserting that no word could be distinguished at a distance without the letter "o" in it, giving illustrations of his theory, till our ears were almost deafened.

Excellent health had been enjoyed by us all during these ten years, though my wife occasionally suffered from slight attacks of fever, and the boys sometimes met with little accidents.

They were all fine, handsome fellows; Fritz, now twenty-four, was of moderate height, uncommonly strong, active, muscular, and high-spirited.

Ernest, two years younger, was tall and slight; in disposition, mild, calm, and studious; his early faults of indolence and selfishness were almost entirely overcome. He possessed refined tastes and great intellectual power.

Jack, at twenty, strongly resembled Fritz, being about his height, though more lightly built, and remarkable rather for active grace and agility than for muscular strength.

Franz, a lively youth of seventeen, had some of the qualities of each of his brothers; he possessed wit and shrewdness, but not the arch drollery of Jack.

All were honorable, God-fearing young men, dutiful and affectionate to their mother and myself, and warmly attached to each other.

Although so many years had elapsed in total seclusion, it continued to be my strong impression that we should one day be restored to the society of our fellow-men.

But time, which was bringing our sons to manhood, was also carrying their parents onward to old age; and anxious, gloomy thoughts relating to their future, should they be left indeed alone, sometimes oppressed my heart.

On such occasions, I would not communicate the sense of depression to my family, but, turning in prayer to the Almighty Father, laid my trouble before Him, with never-failing renewal of strength and hope.

My elder sons often made expeditions of which we knew nothing until their return after many hours; when any uneasiness

I might have felt was dissipated by their joyous appearance, and reproof always died away on my lips.

Fritz had been absent one whole day from Rockburg, and not until evening did we remark that his kayak was gone, and that he must be out at sea.

Anxious to see him return before nightfall, I went off to Shark Island with Ernest and Jack, in order to look out for him from the watch tower there, at the same time hoisting our signal flag, and loading the gun.

Long we gazed across the expanse of ocean glittering in the level beams of the setting sun, and finally discerned a small black speck in the distance which, by the telescope, was proved to be the returning wanderer.

I remarked that his skiff sailed at a slower rate than usual toward the shore. The cannon was fired to let him know that his approach was observed, and then we joyfully hurried back to receive him at the harbor.

It was easy to see, as he drew near, what had delayed his progress. The kayak towed a large sack, besides being heavily laden.

"Welcome, Fritz!" I cried. "Welcome back, wherever you come from, and whatever you bring. You seem to have quite a cargo there!"

"Yes, and my trip has led to discoveries as well as booty," answered he; "interesting discoveries which will tempt us again in the same direction. Come, boys, let's carry up the things, and while I rest I will relate my adventures."

As soon as possible all assembled round him.

"I think my absence without leave deserves reproach instead of this warm reception, father, and I must apologize for it," he began. "But ever since I possessed the kayak it has been my ambition to make a voyage of discovery along the coast, which we have never explored beyond the point at which I killed the walrus.

"In order to be ready to start without delay when a convenient opportunity offered, I made preparations beforehand, such as provisioning my skiff, fixing the compass in front of my seat, arranging conveniently rifle, harpoon, ax, boat-hook, and fishing net. I also resolved to take with me Pounce, my eagle, and this I always will do in future.

"This morning dawned magnificently; the calm sea, the gentle breeze, all drew me irresistibly to the fulfillment of my purpose.

"I left the harbor unperceived, the current quickly bore me out to sea, and I rounded the point to the left, passing just over the spot where, beneath the waves, lie the guns, cannon balls, ironwork, and all that was indestructible about our good old wreck. And would you believe it? Through the glassy clear water, undisturbed by a ripple, I actually saw many such things strewn on the flat rocky bottom.

"Pursuing my way, I passed among rugged cliffs and rocks which jutted out from the shore, or rose in rugged masses from the water. Myriads of sea fowl inhabited the most inaccessible of these, while on the lower ridges, seals, sea bears, and walruses were to be seen, some basking lazily in the sun, some plunging into the water, or emerging awkwardly from it, hoisting their unwieldy bodies up the rocks by means of their tusks.

"I must confess to feeling anything but comfortable while going through the places held in possession by these monsters of the deep, and used every effort to pass quickly and unnoticed. Yet it was more than an hour and a half before I got clear of the rocks, cliffs, and shoals to which they resorted, and neared a high and precipitous cape, running far out to sea. Right opposite me, in the side of this rocky wall, was a magnificent archway, forming, as it first appeared to me, a lofty entrance to an immense vaulted cavern. I passed beneath this noble portal and examined the interior. It was tenanted by numbers of a small species of swallow, scarcely larger than a wren, and the walls were covered by thousands of their nests. They were rudely built, and their peculiarity was that each rested on a kind of platform, something like a spoon without the handle. I detached a number, and found that they had a curious appearance, seemingly made of something fibrous and gelatinous, and more like a set of sponges, corals, or fungi, than nests of birds. I have brought them home in my fishing net."

"If we had commercial dealings with the Chinese," said I, "your discovery would be of value; these are doubtless edible birds' nests. The bird is called the esculent swallow, and the trade in this strange article of diet is a very large one. The nests are of different value, but those which are quite new, and nearly white, are held in such esteem that they are worth their weight in silver.

"There are tremendous caverns in Java and other places where, at great risk, these nests are procured; the annual weight obtained being upward of fifty thousand pounds, and the value more than £200,000.

"When placed in water and well soaked, they soften and swell, and are made into soup of very strengthening and restorative quality.

"I think you might try your hand on these, mother, just for curiosity's sake."

"I can't say I fancy the look of the queer things," said she, "but I don't mind trying if they will turn to jelly; though boiling birds' nests is cookery quite out of my line."

"Oh, do, mother; let us taste birds' nests as soon as you can, though the idea makes me fancy a mouth full of feathers!" laughed Jack.

"It is really a most curious formation," said Fritz. "From whence are the swallows supposed to get this kind of gelatine?"

"It has never been exactly ascertained," I replied, "whether the birds discover or produce this curious substance. But whatever may be its basis, it is clear that a very large portion of it is furnished by certain glands, which pour out a viscid secretion."

"After laying in my store of nests," continued Fritz, "I pursued my way through this vaulted cave or corridor; which, presently turning, opened into a very lonely bay, so calm and lake-like, that, although of considerable size, I concluded at once it must be nearly land locked. Its shores, beyond the rocky boundary through which I penetrated, extended in a fertile plain toward what seemed the mouth of a river, beyond which lay rough, and probably marshy, ground, and a dense forest of cedars, which closed the view.

"The water beneath me was clear as crystal; and, gazing into its depths and shallows, I perceived beds of shellfish, like large oysters, attached to the rocks and to each other by tufts of hairy filaments.

"'If these are oysters,' thought I, 'they must be better worth eating, as far as size goes, than our little friends in Safety Bay,' and thereupon I hooked up several clusters with my boat-hook, and landing soon after on the beach, I flung them on the sand, resolving to fetch another load, and then tow them after me in the fishing-net.

"The hot sun disagreed with their constitution, I suppose; for when I came back the shells were all gaping wide open; so I began to examine them, thinking that after all they were probably much less delicate than the small oysters we have learnt to like so much.

"Somehow, when a thing is to be 'examined,' one generally needs a knife. The blade met with resistance here and there in the creature's body; and still closer 'examination' produced from it several pearly balls like peas, of different sizes. Do you think they can be pearls? I have a number here in a box."

"Oh, show them to us, Fritz!" cried the boys. "What pretty shining things! And how delicately rounded, and how softly they gleam!"

"You have discovered treasure, indeed!" I exclaimed; "why these are most beautiful pearls! Valueless, certainly, under present circumstances; but they may prove a source of wealth, should we ever again come into contact with the civilized world. We must visit your pearl-oyster beds at the earliest opportunity."

"After resting for some time, and refreshing myself with food," pursued Fritz, "I resumed my survey of the coast, my progress somewhat impeded by the bag of shellfish, which I drew after me; but I proceeded without accident past the mouth of the stream to the further side of the bay, which was there enclosed by a point corresponding to that through which I had entered; and between these headlands I found a line of reefs and sandbanks, with but a single channel leading out to the open sea; from which, therefore, Pearl Bay, as I named it, lies completely sheltered.

"The tide was setting strongly in shore, so that I could not then attempt a passage through it, but examined the crags of the headland, thinking I might perchance discover a second vaulted archway. I saw nothing remarkable, however, but thousands of sea fowl of every sort and kind, from the gull and sea swallow to the mighty albatross.

"My approach was evidently regarded as an invasion and trespass; for they regularly beset me, screaming and wheeling over my head, till, out of all patience, I stood up, and hit furiously about me with the boat-hook; when, rather to my surprise, one blow struck an albatross with such force, that he fell stunned into the water.

"I now once more attempted to cross the reef by the narrow channel, and happily succeeding, found myself in the open sea, and speeding homeward, joyfully saw our flag flying, and heard the welcome salute you fired."

Here ended the narrative; but next morning Fritz drew me aside, and confided to me a most remarkable sequel, in these words:

"There was something very extraordinary about that albatross, father. I allowed you to suppose that I left it as it fell, but in reality I raised it to the deck of the canoe, and then perceived a piece of rag wound round one of its legs. This I removed, and, to my utter astonishment, saw English words written on it, which I plainly made out to be: 'Save an unfortunate Englishwoman from the smoking rock!'

"This little sentence sent a thrill through every nerve: my brain seemed to whirl. I doubted the evidence of my senses.

"'Is this reality, or delusion?' thought I. 'Can it be true, that a fellow-creature breathes with us the air of this lonely region?'

"I felt stupefied for some minutes: the bird began to show

signs of life, which recalled me to myself; and, quickly deciding what must be done, I tore a strip from my handkerchief, on which I traced the words—'Do not despair! Help is near!'

"This I carefully bound round one leg, replacing the rag on the other, and then applied myself to the complete restoration of the bird. It gradually revived; and after drinking a little, surprised me by suddenly rising on the wing, faltering a moment in its flight, and then rapidly disappearing from my view in a westerly direction.

"Now, father, one thought occupies me continually: will my note ever reach this Englishwoman? Shall I be able to find, and to save her?"

I listened to this account with feelings of the liveliest interest and astonishment.

"My dear son," said I, "you have done wisely in confiding to me alone your most exciting discovery. Unless we know more, we must not unsettle the others by speaking of it; for it appears to me quite possible that these words were penned long ago on some distant shore, where, by this time, the unhappy stranger may have perished miserably. By the 'smoking rock' must be meant a volcano. There are none here."

Fritz was not disposed to look at the case from this gloomy point of view; did not think the rag so very old; believed smoke might rise from a rock which was not volcanic; and evidently cherished the hope that he might be able to respond effectually to this touching appeal.

I was in reality as anxious as himself on the subject, but judged it prudent to abate rather than excite hopes of success which might be doomed to bitter disappointment.

After earnest consultation on the subject, we decided that Fritz should go in search of the writer of the message, but not until he had so altered the canoe as to fit it for carrying two persons, as well as provisions sufficient to admit of his absence for a considerable time. Impatient as he was, he could not but see the wisdom of this delay.

We returned to the house, and saw the boys busily opening the oysters, which they had had no time to do the previous night, and greatly excited as ever and anon a pearl was found.

"May we not establish a pearl fishery at once, father?" shouted they. "We might build a hut on the shore of the bay, and set about it regularly."

An excursion to Pearl Bay was now the event to which all thoughts turned, and for which preparations on a grand scale were made. It was to form, as it were the basis of the more important voyage Fritz had in view, and to which, unsuspected by the rest, he could devote all his attention.

I took an opportunity, one day, when all were present, to remark in a serious tone:

"I have been considering, dear wife, that our eldest son is now of an age to be dependent on himself. I shall, therefore, henceforth leave him at liberty to act in all respects according to his own judgment; and, especially in the matter of voyages or excursions, he must not be hampered by the fear of alarming us should he choose to remain absent longer than we expect. I have such entire confidence in his prudence, and at the same time in his affection for us, that I am certain he will never needlessly cause us anxiety."

Fritz looked gratefully toward me as I spoke; and his mother ratified my words, embracing him affectionately, and saying, with emotion, "God bless and preserve thee, my boy!"

It took some time to make several raking or scraping machines, which I invented for the purpose of detaching and lifting the oysters from their native rocks; but that gave Fritz leisure to change the fittings of his canoe, so as to have a spare seat in it.

His brothers naturally concluded he meant to take one of them as shipmate on board, and he allowed the mistake to continue. They occupied themselves in making various articles they expected to be of use, and bore the delay with tolerable patience.

At last came the day, when, taking leave of the mother and Franz, we went on board the yacht, accompanied by some of the dogs; while Jack, proudly occupying the new seat beside Fritz in the canoe, shared with him the honor of leading the way in the character of pilots.

We passed safely through the rocks and shoals near Walrus Island into an expanse of calm water, sheltered by jutting cliffs, where the sea glanced like a mirror, and for the first time we observed the fairy-like shells of the paper-nautilus sailing lightly over the dazzling surface.

It was impossible to see these lovely seafarers without wishing to obtain specimens; and the canoe accordingly gave chase, presently securing half a dozen, which were handed to us in the yacht to be carefully preserved for the museum, and the place was ever after called Nautilus Creek.

Further on we rounded a short promontory, flat, with an abrupt rock at the extremity, to which we gave the name of Cape Pug-Nose; and then, at some distance, appeared the grand cliffs of a headland running far out to sea.

This I suppose we should have to weather, but my pilots made no change in our course, and, following the canoe, we soon came in sight of the majestic archway which offered us a short passage to Pearl Bay.

The wonderfully architectural appearance of the pillars, arches, and pinnacles, surrounding and surmounting this noble entrance, struck me with admiration, resembling parts of a fine gothic cathedral, and inducing me to propose for it the name, Cape Minster.

A perfect cloud of little swallows darted from the cavernous entrance on our approach, divided into flocks, soared, wheeled, flew right and left, and finally returned in a body as swiftly as they came, to the sides of the long dark tunnel, which were festooned with their nests.

We detached a number of these as we passed, taking care to leave those containing eggs of young. The best were at a considerable height, but the broken shelving rocks afforded, in some places, footing for such daring and active climbers as Fritz and Jack, and they quickly obtained as many as we could possibly require.

Our progress was much assisted by the tide, which, like a current, bore us onward along the nave of this natural cathedral; aisles, transepts, screens, and side-chapels appearing between the columns and arches which in the "dim religious light" were revealed to our wondering eyes.

On emerging into the dazzling sunshine, we found ourselves floating in the calm expanse of Pearl Bay; but it was some minutes before we could look around on the bright and lovely scene.

Fritz had not over-rated its beauty, and the romantic islets which studded its waters seemed to give the effect of a pleasant smile to features already perfect.

We cruised about for some time, surveying the coast with its fertile meadows, shady groves, gently swelling hills, and murmuring brooks, seeking a convenient landing place in the vicinity of the shallows where lay the oyster-beds.

This we found, close to a sparkling streamlet; and, as the day was fast declining, we made speedy arrangements for burning a watch-fire; after which we partook of a hasty supper, and leaving the dogs, with Coco, the jackal, to sleep on shore, we returned on board the yacht for the night, anchoring within gunshot of the land.

The coast being quite strange to us, I knew not what wild beasts might frequent it; but, though I did not fear that any would approach us by swimming, yet I was glad to have with us our lively little ape, Mercury (the successor of our old favorite, Knips, long since gathered to his fathers), for he occupied at night a cosy berth on deck, and was certain to give vociferous notice should anything alarming occur.

Fritz moored the kayak alongside, and came on board. The night passed in peace, although for a time we were disturbed by the yelping of jackals, with whom Coco persisted in keeping up a noisy conversation.

We awoke it daybreak, and after breakfast *à la fourchette*, we repaired in haste with nets, scrapers, and all other requisites, to the oyster-beds, where we worked with such diligence and success that in the course of two days we had an immense pile of shells built up like a stack on the beach, and left to decay.

I collected a quantity of seaweed to spread over them, which was afterward burnt to make alkali, when we returned to secure our harvest of pearls.

Every evening we went out shooting in the neighborhood, and kept ourselves supplied with game of one sort or another. The last day of our fishery we started earlier, intending to make a longer excursion into the woods.

Ernest set off first with Floss; Jack and Coco strolling after them. Fritz and I were still employed in taking on board the last load of our tools, when we suddenly heard a shot, a loud cry of pain or fear, and then another shot.

At the first alarm, the other two dogs rushed away from us toward the spot, and Fritz, who had just called Pounce from his perch, to accompany us in the ramble, let him fly, and seizing his rifle darted off in the same direction.

Before I could reach the scene of action, more shots were heard, and then a shout of victory; after which appeared through the stems of the trees the disconsolate figure of Jack, hobbling along like a cripple, supported on each side by his brothers.

When they came near me they stopped; and poor Jack moaning and groaning, began to feel himself all over, as if to search for broken bones, crying out:

"I'm pounded like a half-crushed pepper-corn!"

On examination I found some severe bruises.

"Who or what has been pommeling the boy?" I exclaimed; "one would think he had been beaten."

"It was a huge wild boar," said Ernest, "with fierce eyes, monstrous tusks, and a snout as broad as my hand."

We took Jack down to the yacht, bathed his bruises, gave him a cooling drink, and he soon fell fast asleep in his berth, where I left him and returned to the shore.

"Now, Ernest," said I, "enlighten me on the subject of this adventure! What you and the boar did, is quite a mystery to me."

"Floss and I were going quietly along," replied he, "when suddenly there was a rustling and snorting close by, and a great boar broke through the brushes, making for the outskirts of the wood. Floss gave chase directly, and the boar turned to bay. Then up came Jack with Coco, and the gallant little jackal attacked the monster in the rear. In another moment, however, he was sent sprawling upon his back, and this so provoked his master that he fired a hasty ill-directed shot. The brute's notice and fury at once turned upon Jack, who prudently took to his heels, when I attempted to check the career of the boar by a shot, which, however, only slightly wounded it. Jack stumbled and fell over the root of a tree, just as the animal came up with him. 'Help! Murder,' shouted he; and if the other dogs had not then arrived, and all together tackled the boar, I fear it would have been a case of murder indeed! As it was, the poor fellow got mauled and trampled upon dreadfully.

"As I was waiting for an opportunity to fire without any risk of hitting Jack, Pounce rushed through the air and darted upon the beast, and Fritz came up quickly and shot it dead with a pistol.

"While we were helping Jack along, and passing a place where the boar had been grubbing, I noticed some such curious knotty roots or tubercles, that I brought away specimens. Are they worth anything, do you think? They have a strong smell."

"If I may trust my nose," said I, "you have brought something by no means to be despised. Yes!" I continued, putting them to my lips, "these are very fine truffles! Taste them, Fritz."

"Indeed, they are excellent," said he; "very different from the tough, leathery things I remember in Europe; these are tender and well flavored."

"Because they are fresh," said I. "You have before tasted those only which have been brought from a distance. They are found in different parts of Europe, buried at a depth of ten or twelve inches in the soil of oak or beech woods. A small dog is employed to hunt for them, who perceives their musky odor in a singularly acute way, and at once scratches at the spot where they lie."

"Have the truffles no leaves or stalks," inquired Fritz, "by which they might be found without the help of the dog?"

"They have nothing of the sort," I replied; "they are discovered simply by scent, and are considered to belong to the tribe of Fungi."

By this time it was late; we took supper, made up the watch-fire, and withdrew to our yacht, where we slept peacefully.

Early next morning we proceeded to visit the field of battle. The wild boar, which I had not before seen, proved to be much larger and more formidable in appearance than I had imagined, and Jack's escape seemed to be perfectly marvelous.

The boys took it as a matter of course that we were to cut out hams and flitches; and we therefore did so, though I warned them that they need not expect much pleasure in eating bacon from a tough old African boar like this. We conveyed the mighty hams to the beach, each on a sledge of plaited boughs and twigs, and drawn by one of the dogs. The monstrous head traveled in the same way, and we collected a large number of truffles before quitting the forest.

As soon as the dogs were released, they rushed back to the scene of operations in the wood, comprehending that they were now free to feast on what remained there.

There was so much to be done in consequence of this affair that Fritz, who had hoped to set out on his solitary expedition that day, deferred it until the next; and was, therefore, fortunately with us, when late in the evening we desisted from our labors, and, having supped, were preparing to retire to rest.

All at once a deep, fearful sound echoed through the neighboring woods. It made our blood curdle in our veins. We listened with straining ears, hoping it would not be repeated. With a shudder we heard the dread voice roar again, yet nearer to us, and an answer peal from the distance.

"We must find out who are the performers in this concert!" exclaimed Fritz, springing to his feet and snatching up his rifle. "Make the fire blaze; get on board the yacht, and have all the guns in readiness. I am off to reconnoiter in the canoe."

We mechanically obeyed his rapid orders, while the bold youth disappeared in the darkness; and, after heaping fuel on the fire, we went on board and armed ourselves with cutlasses, besides loading all the guns, waiting in readiness either to land again or to quit the coast.

We presently saw the whole pack of our dogs, as well as Coco, the jackal, and the little ape, Mercury (who had been tempted by the truffles to stay with them in the woods), come galloping at full speed up to the fire.

Mercury was evidently excessively discomposed at finding us gone; he gnashed his teeth, and chattered, as though in fear, looking hopelessly at the water, through which he could not venture.

The dogs planted themselves by the fire, gazing fixedly landward, with ears erect, and occasionally uttering a barking challenge, or a suppressed howl.

Meantime, the horrid roarings approached nearer, and I concluded that a couple of leopards or panthers had been attracted by the scent of the boar's carcass.

But not long after I had expressed this opinion, we beheld a large, powerful animal spring from the underwood, and, with a bound, and muttered roar, approach the fire. In a moment I recognized the unmistakable outlines of the form of a lion, though in size he far surpassed any I had ever seen exhibited in Europe.

The dogs slunk behind the fire, and the lion seated himself almost like a cat on his hind legs, glaring alternately at them, and at the great boar hams which hung near, with doubtless a mixed feeling of irritation and appetite, which was testified by the restless movement of his tail.

He then arose, and commenced walking up and down with a slow and measured pace, occasionally uttering short, angry roars, quite unlike the prolonged, full tones we had heard at first.

At times he went to drink at the brook, always returning with such haste, that I fully expected to see him spring.

Gradually his manner became more and more threatening; he turned toward us, crouched, and with his body at full stretch, waved his tail, and glared so furiously, that I was in doubt whether to fire, or retreat, when through the darkness rang the sharp crack of a rifle.

"That is Fritz!" exclaimed every one; while, with a fearful roar, the lion sprang to his feet, stood stock still, tottered, sank on his knees, rolled over, and lay motionless on the sand.

"We are saved!" I cried; "that was a masterly shot. The lion is struck to the heart; he will never stir again. Stay on board, boys. I must join my brave Fritz."

In a few moments I landed; the dogs met me with evident tokens of pleasure, but kept whining uneasily, and looking toward the deep darkness of the woods whence the lion had come.

This behavior made me cautious; and, seeing nothing of Fritz, I lingered by the boat, when suddenly a lioness bounded from the shadow of the trees, into the light diffused by the fire.

At sight of the blazing faggots she paused, as though startled; passed with uncertain step round the outskirts of the illuminated circle; and uttered roarings, which were evidently calls to her mate, whose dead body she presently discovered.

Finding him motionless, her manner betokened the greatest concern; she touched him with her fore-paws, smelt round him, and licked his bleeding wounds. Then, raising her head, she gnashed her teeth, and gave forth the most lamentable and dreadful sound I ever heard; a mingled roar and howl, which was like the expression of grief, rage, and a vow to be revenged, all in one.

Crack! Another shot: the creature's right forepaw was lamed; and the dogs, seeing me raise my gun, suddenly gathered courage, and ran forward just as I fired. My shot also wounded the lioness, but not mortally, and the most terrific combat ensued.

It was impossible to fire again, for fear of wounding the dogs. The scene was fearful beyond description. Black night surrounded us; the fitful blaze of the fire shed a strange, unnatural light on the prostrate body of the huge dead lion, and on the wounded lioness, who fought desperately against the attack of the four gallant dogs; while the cries, roars, and groans of anguish and fury uttered by all the animals were enough to try the stoutest nerves.

Old Juno, staunch to the last, was foremost in the fray. After a time, I saw her change her plan of attack, and spring at the throat of the lioness; who, in an instant, raised her left paw, and at one blow the cruel claws had laid open the body of the dog, and destroyed the life of the true and faithful companion of so many years.

Just then Fritz appeared. The lioness was much weakened, and we ventured to go near enough to fire with safety to ourselves; and finally I dispatched her by plunging a hunting-knife deep in her breast.

Ernest and Jack were summoned from the yacht to witness the completed victory; and I regretted having left them on board, when I saw how greatly the noise and tumult had alarmed them, unable, as they were, to ascertain what was going on.

They hastened toward us in great agitation, and their joy on seeing us safe was only equaled by the grief they felt on learning the death of Juno.

The night was now far advanced; the fire burnt low; but we piled on more wood, and, by the renewed light, drew poor Juno from between the paws of the lioness; and by the brookside, washed and bound up the torn body, wrapped it carefully in canvas, and carrying it with us on board the yacht, that it might be buried at Rockburg, whither on the following day it was our purpose to return.

Wearied and sorrowful, but full of thankfulness for our personal safety, we at length lay down to sleep, having brought all the dogs on board.

Next morning, before quitting Pearl Bay, we once more landed, that we might possess ourselves of the magnificent skins of the lion and lioness, whose visit, fatal to themselves, had caused such a commotion during the night.

In about a couple of hours we returned to the yacht, leaving the flayed carcasses to the tender mercies of the birds of prey sure to be attracted to them.

"Homeward bound," sang out the boys, as they cheerily weighed anchor, and prepared to stand out to sea. I could see, though he did not complain, that poor Jack had not recovered from the boar's rough treatment, and moved very stiffly.

"You must pilot us through the channel in the reef this time, Fritz," said I; adding, in a lower tone, "and then is it to be 'farewell,' my son!"

"Yes, dear father—*Au revoir*!" returned he, brightly, with a glance full of meaning, while he threw into his canoe a cushion and a fur cloak.

"Thanks, Fritz! But I'm going to honor them with the care of my battered bones in the yacht here. You are awfully considerate though, old fellow," remarked Jack, not for a moment doubting that his brother expected him to return, as he came, beside him in the kayak.

Fritz laughed, and commended his decision. Then springing into his skiff, he led the way toward the open sea.

We followed, carefully, and soon passed the reef; after which the boys were very busy with the sails, putting the vessel on the homeward course, when, waving his hand to me, Fritz turned in the opposite direction, and quickly vanished behind the point, which I afterward named Cape Farewell.

When missed by his brothers, I said he had a fancy to explore more of the coast, and if he found it interesting he might, instead of only a few hours, remain absent for two or three days.

Toward evening, we sailed into Safety Bay.

CHAPTER XVII

Juno's epitaph—Fritz does not appear—We start in search of him—A cachalot whale—The unexpected appearance of a savage—Fritz in a dusky disguise—He leads us to Fair Isle, and shows us the wonders therein—The stranger—Fritz narrates his adventures—How he saw Toucans—Encountered a tiger—Lost Pounce—Found the Smoking Rock, and Jenny Montrose—The history of the stranger—Wolves dispute our right to the whale—Coco joins his brethren—Jack and Jenny search for the truant—We leave Pearl Bay—A hearty reception—A visit to Falconhurst—Jack displays our stud—The rainy season again.

The mother and Franz, though somewhat startled by the unexpected absence of Fritz, were delighted to see us return safely, and listened with eager interest to our adventures. My wife shuddered, and scarcely suppressed an involuntary scream as she heard of our desperate encounter with the lion and his mate. Jack's danger and providential escape, too, made her tremble; and so pale did he still look, that she could scarcely believe he was uninjured.

Tears came into Franz's eyes when he heard of the sad death of poor old Juno; and he inquired most tenderly whether her remains had been brought back, that they might be interred near the house which had been her home for so many years.

Next day he saw her buried carefully; and Ernest, at his request, produced an epitaph, which was inscribed upon a slab of stone above her grave.

JUNO,
A servant true lies here;
A faithful friend,
A Dog,
To all most dear;
Who met her end
Fighting right bravely in her master's cause.

The flesh of the wild boar and the truffles were handed over to the mother, who received them with delight, promising us therefrom many a savory dish. She would fain have had the boar's head too; but my word was pledged to Ernest that it should adorn his museum, and, though my lips watered to taste it baked in Hottentot fashion, I would not break my promise.

This splendid head, therefore, together with the lions' skins, we carried to the tannery on Whale Island, where they were cleaned and dressed.

Five days passed, but Fritz still remained absent. I could not conceal my anxiety, and at length determined to follow him. All were delighted at the proposal, and even the mother, when she heard that we were to sail in the pinnace, agreed to accompany us.

The boat was stored, and on a bright morning, with a favorable breeze, we five, with the dogs, stepped aboard, and ran for Cape Minster.

Our beautiful little yacht bounded over the water gaily, and the bright sunshine and delicious sea breeze put us all in the highest spirits. The entrance of the archway was in sight, and thither I was directing the boat's course. Suddenly, right ahead, I saw a dark and shadowy mass just below the surface of the water. "A sunken rock!" I thought to myself, "and yet it is strange that

I never before noticed it." I put down the helm in a moment, but a catastrophe seemed inevitable.

We surged ahead! A slight shock, and all was over! The danger was passed!

I glanced astern, to look again at the dangerous spot; but the rock was gone, and, where but a moment before I had distinctly seen its great green shadow, I could now see nothing. Before we had recovered from our amazement, a shout from Jack surprised me.

"There is another," he exclaimed, "to starboard, father!"

Sure enough, there lay, apparently, another sunken rock.

"The rock is moving!" shouted Franz; and a great black body emerged from the sea, while from the upper extremity rushed a column of water, which, with a mighty noise, rose upward, and then fell like rain all around. The mystery was explained; for, as the great beast emerged yet further from the water, I recognized, from its enormous size and great length of head, the cachalot whale.

The monster was apparently enraged at the way we had scratched his back; for, retreating to a short distance, he evidently meditated a rush upon us.

Fearful stories occurred to me of the savage temper of this whale, how he has been known to destroy boat after boat, and even ships, and with a feeling of desperation I sprang to one of the guns. Jack leaped to the other, and almost simultaneously we fired. Both shots apparently took effect; for the whale, after lashing the water violently for a few seconds, plunged beneath its surface, and disappeared. We kept a sharp lookout for him, for I was unwilling to lose such a valuable prize, and, reloading, stood toward the shore, in which direction he was apparently making. Presently we again sighted him in shallow water, lashing fearfully with his tail, and dyeing the waves around him with blood. Approaching the infuriate animal as nearly as I dared, we again fired.

The struggles of the whale seemed for a few moments to

become even yet more frantic, and then, with a quiver from head to tail, he lay motionless—dead!

The boys were about to raise the cry of victory, but checked the shout upon their very lips; for darting behind a rock they espied a canoe paddled by a tall and muscular savage, who now stood up in his skiff and appeared to be examining us attentively. Seeing that we were standing toward him, the swarthy native seized his paddle and again darted behind a rock. An awful thought now took possession of me. There must be a tribe of blacks lurking on these shores, and Fritz must have fallen into their hands. We, however, I determined should not be easily taken; and our guns were loaded and run out.

Presently a dusky face appeared, peeping at us from a lofty rock; it vanished, and we saw another peeping at us from lower down. Then, again, the skiff put out as though to make a further reconnoiter. All, even Jack, looked anxious, and glanced at me for orders.

"Hoist a white flag," said I, "and hand me the speaking-trumpet."

I seized the instrument and uttered such peaceable words in the Malay language as I could recall; neither the flag nor my words seemed to produce any effect, and the savage was about to return to the shore.

Jack hereupon lost patience, and in his turn took up the trumpet.

"Come here, you black son of a gun," he exclaimed. "Come on board and make friends, or we'll blow you and your——"

"Stop! Stop! You foolish boy," I said; "you will but alarm the man, with your wild words and gestures."

"No! But, see," he cried, "he is paddling toward us!"

And sure enough the canoe was rapidly approaching.

Presently a cry from Franz alarmed me. "Look! Look!" he shrieked, "the villain is in Fritz's kayak. I can see the walrus' head."

Ernest alone remained unmoved. He took the speaking-trumpet:

"Fritz, ahoy!" he shouted; "welcome, old fellow!"

The words were scarcely out of his mouth when I, too, recognized the well-known face beneath its dusky disguise.

In another minute the brave boy was on board, and in spite of his blackened face was kissed and welcomed heartily. He was now assailed with a storm of questions from all sides: "Where had he been?" "What had kept him so long, and why had he turned blackamoor?"

"The last question," replied he, with a smile, "is the only one I will now answer; the others shall be explained when I give a full account of my adventures. Hearing guns fired, my mind was instantly filled with ideas of Malay pirates, for I never dreamed that you could be here in the yacht, so I disguised myself as you now see me, and came forth to reconnoiter. When you addressed me in Malay you only added to my terror, for it left not a doubt in my mind that you were pirates."

Having in our turn described to him our adventure with the cachalot whale, I asked him if he knew of a suitable spot for the anchorage of the yacht.

"Certainly," he replied, casting toward me a glance full of meaning; "I can lead you to an island where there is a splendid anchorage, and which is itself well worth seeing, for it contains all sorts of strange things." And after removing the stains from his skin, and turning himself once more into a civilized being, he again sprang into his canoe and piloted us to a picturesque little island in the bay.

Now that there could be no doubt as to the success of Fritz's expedition, I no longer hesitated to give to my wife an account of his project, and to prepare her mind for the surprise which awaited her. She was greatly startled, as I expected, and seemed almost overcome with emotion at the idea of seeing a human being, and that being one of her own sex.

"But why," she asked, "did you not tell me of this at first? Why wait until the last moment with such joyful news?"

"I was unwilling," I replied, "to raise hopes which might never be realized: but now, thank Heaven, he has succeeded, and there is no need for concealment."

The boys could not at all understand the evident air of mystery and suppressed excitement which neither their mother, Fritz, nor I could entirely conceal. They cast glances of the greatest curiosity toward the island, and as soon as the sails were furled and the anchor dropped, they sprang eagerly ashore. In a body we followed Fritz, maintaining perfect silence. Presently we emerged from the thicket through which we were passing, and saw before us a hut of sheltering boughs, at the entrance of which burned a cheerful fire.

Into this leafy bower Fritz dived, leaving his brothers without, mute with astonishment. In another moment he emerged, leading by the hand a slight, handsome youth, by his dress apparently a young English naval officer. The pair advanced to meet us; and Fritz, with a countenance radiant with joy, briefly introduced his companion as Edward Montrose.

"And," he continued, looking at his mother and me, "will you not welcome him as a friend and a brother to our family circle?"

"That will we, indeed!" I exclaimed, advancing and holding out my hands to the fair young stranger. "Our wild life may have roughened our looks and manners, but it has not hardened our hearts, I trust."

The mother, too, embraced the seeming youth most heartily. The lads, and even the dogs, were not behind hand in testifying their gratification at the appearance of their new friend—the former delighted at the idea of a fresh companion, and the latter won by her sweet voice and appearance.

From the expression made use of by Fritz I perceived that the girl wished her sex to remain unrevealed to the rest of the party until the mother could obtain for her a costume more suited to her real character.

The young men then ran down to the yacht to bring up what was necessary for supper, as well as to make preparations for a camp in which we might spend the night. This done the mother hastened to set before us a substantial meal, while the boys, anxious to make their new acquaintance feel at home among them, were doing their best to amuse her. She herself, after the first feeling of strangeness had worn off, entered fully into all their fun; and by the time they sat down to supper was laughing and chattering as gaily as any one of the rest. She admired the various dishes, tasted our mead, and, without alluding once to her previous life, kept up a lively conversation.

The mere fact of meeting with any human being after so many years of isolation was in itself sufficient to raise the boys to the greatest state of excitement; but that this being should be one so handsome, so gay, so perfectly charming, seemed completely to have turned their heads; and when I gave the sign for breaking up of the feast, and their new friend was about to be led to the night quarters which had been prepared for her on board the yacht, the health of Edward Montrose was proposed, and drank in fragrant mead, amid the cheers and acclamations of all hands.

When she was gone, and silence had been restored, Jack exclaimed:

"Now, then, Fritz, if you please, just tell me where you came across this jolly fellow. Did you take your mysterious voyage in search of him, or did you meet him by chance? Out with your adventures, while we sit comfortably round the fire."

So saying, Jack cast more wood upon the blazing pile, and throwing himself down in his usual, careless fashion, prepared to listen attentively.

Fritz, after a few moments' hesitation, began:

"Perhaps you remember," said he, "how, when I returned from my expedition in the kayak the other day, I struck down an albatross. None but my father at the time knew, however, what became of the wounded bird, or even thought more about it. Yet it was that albatross who brought me notice of the shipwrecked stranger and he, too, I determined should carry back a message, to cheer and encourage the sender.

"I first, as you know, prepared my kayak to carry two persons; and then, with a heart full of hope and trust, left you and the yacht, and, with Pounce seated before me, made for the open sea. For several hours I paddled steadily on, till, the wind freshening, I thought it advisable to keep in nearer shore; that, should a regular storm arise, I might find some sheltered bay in which to weather it.

"It was well I did so; for, scarcely had I reached a quiet cove which promised to afford me the protection I desired than the sea appeared one mass of foam: great surging waves arose; and even in the comparative calm of the bay I felt that I was in some danger.

"I passed the night in my kayak; and next morning, after a frugal meal of pemmican, and a draught of water from my flask, once more ventured forth. The wind had subsided, and the sea was tolerably smooth; and, keeping my eyes busily employed in seeking in every direction to detect, if possible, the slightest trace of smoke, or other sign of human life, I paddled on till noon.

"The aspect of the coast now began to change: the shores were sandy, while further inland lay dense forests, from whose gloomy depths I could ever and anon hear the fierce roar of beasts of prey, the yell of apes, the fiendish laugh of the hyena, or the despairing death cry of a hapless deer. Seldom have I experienced a greater feeling of solitude than while listening to these strange sounds, and knowing that I, in this frail canoe, was the only human being near. Giving myself up to contemplation, I rested my paddle, and allowed my kayak to drift slowly on.

"As I neared the shore, I noticed a large number of stranger looking birds, who would sometimes flutter round me, and then dart back again to the border of the forest, where they were feeding on what appeared to be the pepper plant; they seized the berries in their great, ponderous beaks, threw them up into the air, and then dexterously caught them in their fall. Their beaks were really something extraordinary: they looked as though they must give their owners a perpetual headache, from their immense weight. The only thing that relieved the extreme ugliness of these great appendages was their gorgeous color, which was only rivaled by the gay hue of the plumage. I wished now that I had brought home a specimen; but at the time I was so much amused by watching the grotesque antics of the birds that I did not think of obtaining one. When I left the spot, I settled in my own mind that they were toucans: was I right, Ernest?"

The Professor, unwilling to interrupt the narrative, merely gave an oracular nod, and Fritz continued:

"For some hours after this I paddled quickly on, sometimes passing the mouth of a stream, sometimes that of a broad river. Had I been merely on an exploring expedition, I should have been tempted, doubtless, to cruise a little way up one of these pathways into the forest; but now such an idea did not enter my head. On, on, on, I felt I must go, until I should reach the goal of my voyage.

"The shades of night at length drew on, and, finding a sheltered cove, I moored my kayak, and stepped on shore. You may imagine how pleasant it was to stretch my legs, after sitting for so long in the cramped position which my kayak enforces. It would not do, however, to sleep on shore; so after preparing and enjoying my supper, I returned on board, and there spent the night.

"Next morning Pounce and I again landed for breakfast. I lit my fire, and hung before it a plump young parrot to roast. As I was so doing, I heard a slight rustle among the long grass behind me. I glanced round, and there, with glaring eyes and his great tail swaying to and fro, I saw an immense tiger.

"In another moment his spring would have been made. I should have been no more, and our young guest would have been doomed to, God only knows how many, years of frightful solitude!

"My gun was lying by my side. Before I could have stooped to pick it up, the monster would have seized me.

"Pounce saw and comprehended my danger: the heroic bird darted upon my enemy, and so blinded him with his flapping wings, and the fierce blows of his beak, that his spring was checked, and

I had time to recover my self-possession. I seized my gun, and fired; and the brute, pierced to the heart, gave one spring, and then rolled over at my feet.

"My enemy was dead; but beside him, alas! Lay poor Pounce, crushed and lifeless. One blow of the great beast's paw had struck him down, never to rise again!"

Fritz's voice shook as he came to this point; and, after remaining silent for a moment or two, he continued hurriedly:

"With a sad and desolate feeling at my heart, I buried the faithful bird where he had met his death; and then, unable longer to continue near the spot, I returned to my kayak, and leaving the great tiger lying where he fell, paddled hastily away.

"My thoughts were gloomy. I felt as though, now that my companion was gone, I could no longer continue the voyage. The albatross, I thought, may have flown for hundreds of miles before it reached me. This stranger may be on different shores from these entirely; every stroke of my paddle may be carrying me further from the blazing signal: who knows?

"This feeling of discouragement was not, however, to be of long duration; for in a moment more a sight presented itself, which banished all my doubts and fears, and raised me to the highest pitch of excitement.

"A high point of land lay before me. I rounded it, and beyond found a calm and pleasant bay, from whose curved and thickly wooded shores ran out a reef of rocks. From the point of this reef rose a column of smoke, steadily and clearly curling upward in the calm air. I could scarcely believe my senses, but stopped gazing at it, as though I were in a dream; then, with throbbing pulse and giddy brain, I seized my paddle, and strained every nerve to reach it.

"A few strokes seemed to carry me across the bay, and, securing my canoe, I leaped upon the rock, on which the beacon was blazing, but not a sign of a human being could I see. I was about to shout, for as the fire had evidently been recently piled up, I knew the stranger could not be far off; but, before I could do so, I saw a slight figure passing along the chain of rocks toward the spot on which I stood. You may all imagine my sensations.

"I advanced a few paces; and then mastering my emotion as best I could, I said in English:

"'Welcome, fair stranger! God, in his mercy, has heard your call, and has sent me to your aid!'

"Miss Montrose came quickly forward——"

"Who? What?" shouted the boys, interrupting the narrative; "who came forward?" and amid a general hubbub, Ernest, rising and advancing to his brother, said in his quiet way:

"I did not like to make any remark till you actually let out the secret, Fritz, but we need no longer pretend not to see through the disguise of Edward Montrose."

Fritz, though much disconcerted by the discovery of the secret, recovered his self-possession; and, after bearing with perfect equanimity the jokes with which his brothers assailed him, joined in three cheers for their new sister, and when the confusion and laughter which ensued had subsided, continued his story:

"Miss Montrose grasped my hands warmly, and guessing from my pronunciation, I am afraid, that I was not in the habit of speaking English every day of my life, said in French:

"'Long, long, have I waited since the bird returned with your message. Thank God, you have come at last!'

"Then, with tears of joy and gratitude, she led me to the shore, where she had built a hut and a safe sleeping-place, like Falconhurst on a small scale, among the branches of a tree. I was delighted with all she showed me, for indeed her hut and its fittings evinced no ordinary skill and ingenuity. Round the walls hung bows, arrows, lances, and bird-snares; while on her work-table, in boxes and cases, carved skillfully with a knife, were fish-hooks of mother-of-pearl, needles made from fish-bones, and bodkins from the beaks of birds, fishing-lines of all sorts, and knives and other tools. These latter she told me were, with a chest of wearing apparel, almost the only things washed ashore after the wreck, when three years ago she was cast alone upon this desolate coast.

I marveled more and more at the wonderful way in which this girl had surmounted obstacles, the quarter of which would completely have appalled the generality of her sex. The hut itself was a marvel of skill; stout posts had been driven into the ground, with cross pieces of bamboo, to form a framework; the walls had been woven with reeds, the roof thatched with palm-leaves, and the whole plastered smoothly with clay, an open space being left in the center of the roof for a chimney to carry off the smoke of the fire.

"As we entered, a cormorant, with a cry of anger, flew from under the table toward me, and was about to attack me fiercely. Miss Montrose called it off, and she then told me she had captured and tamed the bird soon after first landing, and since that time had contrived to train it to assist her in every conceivable way; it now not only was a pleasant companion, but brought her food of every description, fish, flesh and fowl, for whether it dived into the waters, according to its natural habit, struck down birds upon the wing, or seized rabbits and other small animals upon the land, it laid all its booty at her feet.

"Before darkness closed in, all the curiosities and ingenious contrivances of the place had been displayed—the kitchen stove, cooking utensils, skin bottles, shell plates and spoons, the fishing raft and numberless other things—and then, sitting down with my fair hostess to a most appetizing meal, she gave me a short account of her life:

"Jenny Montrose was the daughter of a British officer, who had served for many years in India, where she herself was born. At the early age of three years she lost her mother.

"After the death of his wife, all the colonel's love and care was centered upon his only child; under his eye she was instructed in all the accomplishments suited to her sex; and from him she imbibed an ardent love of field sports. By the time she was seventeen, she was as much at home upon her horse in the field as in her father's drawing room. Colonel Montrose now received orders to return home with his regiment, and as for certain reasons he did not wish her to accompany him in the ship with the troops, he obtained a passage for her on board a vessel which was about to sail at the same time.

"The separation was extremely painful to both the old soldier and his daughter, but there was no alternative. They parted, and Miss Montrose sailed in the *Dorcas* for England. A week after she had left Calcutta, a storm arose and drove the vessel far out of her course; more bad weather ensued; and at length, leaks having been sprung in all directions, the crew were obliged to take to the boats. Jenny obtained a place in one of the largest of these. After enduring the perils of the sea for many days, land was sighted; and, the other boats having disappeared, an attempt was made to land. The boat was capsized, and Miss Montrose alone reached the shore. For a long time she lay upon the sand almost inanimate; but, reviving sufficiently to move, she at length obtained some shellfish, and by degrees recovered her strength. From that time forth until I appeared she never set eyes upon a human being. To attract any passing vessel, and obtain assistance, however, she kept a beacon continually blazing at the end of the reef; and, with the same purpose in view, attached missives to the feet of any birds she could take alive in her snares. The albatross, she told me, she had kept for some time, and partially tamed; but, as it was in the habit of making long excursions on its own account, she conceived the idea of sending it also with a message, that should it by chance be seen and taken alive, it might return with an answer.

"Our supper was over, and, at length, both wearied out with the anxieties and excitement of the day, we retired to rest, she to her leafy bower, and I to sleep in the hut below.

"Next morning, having packed her belongings in the kayak, we both went on board; and bidding adieu to her well-known bay she took her seat before me, and I made for home.

"We should have reached Rockburg this evening had not an accident occurred to our skiff and compelled us to put in at this island. The boat was scarcely repaired when I heard your first shots. I instantly disguised myself; and, never doubting that Malay pirates were near, came forth to reconnoiter. Glad, indeed, I was to find my fears ungrounded."

All had listened attentively to Fritz's story, but now a dreadful yawn from Franz, followed by others from Jack, Ernest, and Fritz, and a great desire on my own part to follow their example, warned me that it was time to dismiss the party for the night. Fritz retired to his kayak, the boys and I to the deck of the yacht, and the remainder of the night passed quietly away.

Next morning, as we assembled for breakfast, I took the opportunity of begging Miss Montrose no longer to attempt to continue her disguise, but to allow us to address her in her real character.

Jenny smiled; for she had noticed, as the young men met her when she came from the cabin, a great alteration in their manner, and had at once seen that her secret was guessed.

"After all," she said, "I need not be ashamed of this attire; it has been my only costume for the last three years, and in any other I should have been unable to manage all the work which during that time has been necessary."

Our pleasant meal over, I prepared to start for home, but Fritz reminded me of the cachalot, and although he confessed he should not care to repeat the operation of cutting up a whale, he thought it would be a pity to lose such a chance of obtaining a supply of spermaceti.

I fully agreed with him; and embarking, we quickly reached the sandbank on which the monster lay. No sooner did we come near, than the dogs leaped ashore, and before we could follow, rushed round to the other side of the great beast; snarling, growling, and howling ensued, and when we reached the spot we found a terrific combat going on. A troop of wolves were disputing fiercely with the dogs their right to the prey. Our appearance, however, quickly settled the matter; two of the brutes already lay dead, and those that now escaped our guns galloped off. Among the pack were a few jackals, and no sooner did Coco catch sight of these, his relations, than, suddenly attracted by his instinct, he left his master's side, and in spite of our shouts and cries, joined them, and disappeared into the forest.

As it would have been uscless and dangerous to attempt to follow the deserter into the woods, we left him alone, trusting that he would return before we again embarked. Fritz then climbed up the mountain of flesh, and with his hatchet quickly laid open the huge skull; Jack and Franz joined him—Ernest having remained on the island, where we had left the mother and Jenny—and with buckets assisted him to bail out the spermaceti. The few vessels we possessed were soon full, and having stored them in the yacht, we once more embarked and arrived at the little island shortly before the dinner hour.

A capital meal had been prepared for us, and, when we had made ourselves presentable, we sat down to it, and related our adventures. The account of Coco's desertion was received with exclamations of surprise and sorrow. "Yet," said Jenny, after a time, "I do not think you should despair of his recovery, for animals in their native state seldom care to allow those that have been once domesticated to consort with them. My poor albatross even, though he was never thoroughly tamed, and certainly did finally desert me, yet used to return at intervals; and I am pretty sure that were you, Jack, to search the wood early tomorrow morning, you would find your pet only too willing to come back to civilized life; or, if you like, I will go myself and find him, for I should immensely like to have a paddle in the kayak all by myself."

Jack was delighted at the former suggestion, and though he would not listen for a moment to Jenny's request to be allowed to go alone, he agreed, if she cared for the fun of an early cruise, to accompany her in the canoe next morning, and to return to the yacht in time to start for Rockburg.

At sunrise they were off, armed with "bait" in the shape of meat and biscuit, and a muzzle and chain which Jack had manufactured in the evening to punish the runagate for his offenses, should they catch him. Arrived at the sandbank, they landed; and, after entering the forest and shouting "Coco, Coco!" till the woods rang again, they presently espied the truant, slouching disconsolately toward them, looking very miserable and heartily ashamed of himself.

With torn ears, and coat ruffled and dirty, he sneaked up. There was no need to use the bait to entice him; and when the poor beast thus came, unhappy and begging forgiveness, Jack had not the heart to degrade him further with the muzzle and chain. He had evidently attempted to join his wild brethren, and by them had been scouted, worried, and hustled, as no true jackal; and, as Jenny had foretold, was now only too glad to return to bondage and to comfort.

Poor Coco had recovered his spirits slightly by the time the yacht was reached; and, after a hearty meal, again took his place among the dogs, whom I had little doubt he would never again desert.

All was now bustle and activity; and breakfast over, we went aboard the yacht. Fritz and Jack stepped into the canoe; and we soon left Fair Isle and Pearl Bay far behind.

The morning was delightful. The sea, excepting for the slight ripple raised by the gentle breeze wafting us homeward, was perfectly calm. Slowly and contentedly we glided on through the wonders of the splendid archway, threaded our passage among the rocks and shoals, and passed out to the open sea. So slowly did we make our way, that the occupants of the kayak announced that they could not wait for us when they had once piloted us out from among the shoals and reefs, and plied their paddles to such good purpose that they were soon out of sight. Nautilus Bay and Cape Pug-Nose were in due time passed, however, and Shark Island hove in sight. With great astonishment Jenny gazed at our watch tower, with its guard-house, the fierce-looking guns, and the waving flag upon the heights. We landed, that she might visit the fortification; when we displayed all our arrangements with great pride. When they and the herd of lovely gazelles had been sufficiently admired, we again embarked, and steered toward Deliverance Bay. On reaching the entrance, a grand salute of twelve shots welcomed us and our fair guest to Rockburg. Not pleased with the even number, however, Ernest insisted upon replying with thirteen guns, an odd number being, he declared, absolutely necessary for form's sake.

As we neared the quay, Fritz and Jack stood ready to receive us, and with true politeness handed their mother and Jenny ashore. They turned and led the way to the house through the gardens, orchards, and shrubberies which lay on the rising ground that sloped gently upward to our dwelling.

Jenny's surprise was changed to wonder as she neared the villa itself—its broad, shady balcony, its fountains sparkling in the sun, the dovecots, the pigeons wheeling above, and the bright, fresh creepers twined round the columns, delighted her. She could scarcely believe that she was still far from any civilized nation, and that she was among a family wrecked like herself upon a lonely coast.

My amazement, however, fully equaled that of my little daughter when, beneath the shade of the veranda, I saw a table laid out with a delicious luncheon. All our china, silver, and glass had been called into requisition, and was arranged upon the spotless damask cloth.

Wine sparkled in the decanters, splendid pineapples, oranges, guavas, apples, and pears resting on cool green leaves, lay heaped in pyramids upon the porcelain dishes. A haunch of venison, cold fowl, hams, and tongues occupied the ends and sides of the table, while in the center rose a vase of gay flowers, surrounded by bowls of milk and great jugs of mead. It was, indeed, a perfect feast, and the heartiness of the welcome brought tears of joy into the lovely eyes of the fair girl in whose honor it had been devised.

All were soon ready to sit down; and Jenny, looking prettier than ever in the dress for which she had exchanged her sailor's suit, took the place of honor between the mother and me. Ernest and Franz also seated themselves; but nothing would induce Fritz and Jack to follow their example. They considered themselves our entertainers, and waited upon us most attentively, carving the joints, filling our glasses, and changing the plates; for, as Jack declared to Miss Montrose, the servants had all run away in our absence, and, for the next day or two, perhaps we should be obliged to wait upon ourselves.

When the banquet was over, and the waiters had satisfied their appetites, they joined their brothers, and with them displayed all the wonders of Rockburg to their new sister. To the house, cave, stables, gardens, fields and boathouses, to one after the other did they lead her.

Not a corner would they have left unnoticed, had not the mother, fearing they would tire the poor girl out, come to the rescue, and led her back to the house.

On the following day, after an early breakfast, we started, while it was yet cool, for Falconhurst; and as I knew that repairs and arrangements for the coming winter would be necessary, and would detain us for several days, we took with us a supply of tools, as well as baskets of provisions, and other things essential to our comfort.

The whole of our stud, excepting the ostrich, were in their paddocks near the tree; but Jack, saying that his mother and Jenny really must not walk the whole way, to the great amusement of the latter, leaped on Hurry, and fled away in front of us. Before we had accomplished one quarter of the distance, we heard the thundering tread of many feet galloping down the avenue, and presently espied our motley troop of steeds being driven furiously toward us. Storm, Lightfoot, Swift, Grumble, Stentor, Arrow and Dart were there, with Jack, on his fleet two-legged courser, at their heels. At his saddlebow hung a cluster of saddles and bridles, the bits all jangling and clanking, adding to the din and confusion, and urging on the excited animals, who thoroughly entered into the fun, and with tails in the air, ears back, and heels ever and anon thrown playfully out, seemed about to overwhelm us.

We stepped aside to shelter ourselves behind the trees from the furious onset; but a shout from Fritz brought the whole herd to a sudden halt, and Jack spurred toward us.

"Which of the cattle shall we saddle for you, Jenny?" he shouted; "they're all as gentle as lambs, and as active as cats. Every one has been ridden by mother; and knows what a side-saddle means, so you can't go wrong."

To his great delight, Jenny quickly showed her appreciation of the merits of the steeds by picking out Dart, the fleetest and most spirited in the whole stud.

The ostrich was then relieved of his unusual burden, the animals were speedily equipped, and Lightfoot bearing the baskets and hampers, the whole party mounted and trotted forward. Jenny was delighted with her palfrey, and henceforward he was reserved for her special use.

The work at Falconhurst, as I had expected, occupied us for some time, and it was a week before we could again return to Rockburg. Yet the time passed pleasantly; for though the young men were busy from morning to night, the presence of their new companion, her lively spirits and gay conversation, kept them in constant good humor.

When the repairs were all finished, we remained yet a day or two longer, that we might make excursions in various directions to bring in poultry from Woodlands, stores of acorns for the pigs, and grass, willows, and canes, to be manufactured during the winter into mats, baskets, hurdles, and hencoops.

Many a shower wetted us through during these days, and we had scarcely time to hurry back to Rockburg and house our cattle and possessions before the annual deluge began.

Never before had this dreary season seemed so short and pleasant; with Jenny among us, the usual feeling of weariness and discontent never appeared; the English language was quickly acquired by all hands, Fritz, in particular, speaking it so well that Jenny declared she could scarcely believe he was not an Englishman. She herself already spoke French, and therefore easily learned our native language and spoke it fluently before we were released from our captivity.

CHAPTER XVIII

Spring and its accompanying work—The mysterious guns—Who fired them—A storm—Fritz and I reconnoiter—The English brig—We visit her in the yacht—Captain Littlestone—We are cordially welcomed—Mr. Wolston and his family—An earnest consultation—Our visitors at Rockburg—The supper—Who is for Europe and who for New Switzerland?—The decision—Farewell.

Many wondrous tales were told or read in turn by the boys and Jenny during the long evenings as we sat drawing, weaving, and plaiting in our cozy study. In fact this winter was a truly happy time, and when at length the rain ceased and the bright sun again smiled upon the face of nature, we could scarcely believe, as we stepped forth and once more felt the balmy breath of spring, that, for so many weeks, we had been prisoners within our rocky walls.

All was once more activity and life; the duties in field, garden, and orchard called forth the energy of the lads, while their mother and sister found abundant occupation in the poultry yard and house.

Our various settlements and stations required attention. Falconhurst, Woodlands, Prospect Hill, Shark and Whale Islands were in turn visited and set in order. The duty of attending to the island battery fell to Jack and Franz.

They had been busy all day repairing the flagstaff, rehoisting the flag, and cleaning and putting into working order the two guns.

Evening was drawing on and our day's work over; the rest of us were strolling up and down upon the beach, enjoying the cool sea breeze. They loaded and ran out their guns, and paddling off with an empty tub in the kayak, placed it out at sea as a mark for practice. They returned and fired, and the barrel flew in pieces, and then, with a shout of triumph, they cleaned the guns and ran them in.

Scarcely had they done so when, as though in answer to their shots, came the sound of three guns booming across the water from the westward.

We stopped, speechless. Was it fancy? Had we really heard guns from a strange ship? Or had the boys again fired? No! There were the lads leaping into their canoe and paddling in hot haste toward us. They, too, had heard the sound.

A tumult of feelings rushed over us—anxiety, joy, hope, doubt, each in turn took possession of our minds. Was it a European vessel close upon our shores, and were we about to be linked once more to civilized life? Or did those sounds proceed from a Malay pirate, who would rob and murder us! What was to be the result of meeting with our fellow beings; were they to be friends who would help us, enemies who would attack us, or would they prove unfortunate creatures in need of our assistance? Who could tell?

Before we could express these thoughts in words the kayak had touched the shore, and Jack and Franz were among us.

"Did you hear them? Did you hear them?" they gasped. "What shall we do? Where shall we go?"

"O Fritz," continued my youngest son, "it must be a European ship. We shall find her. We shall see our Fatherland once more," and in an emotion of joy he grasped his brother's hands.

Till then I knew not what a craving for civilized life had been aroused in the two young men by the appearance of their European sister.

All eyes were turned toward me. What would I advise?

"At present," I said, "we can do nothing, for night is drawing on. We must make what preparations we can, and pray for guidance."

In the greatest excitement we returned to the house, all talking eagerly, and till late no one could be persuaded to retire to rest.

Few slept that night. The boys and I took it in turn to keep watch from the veranda, lest more signals might be fired, or a hostile visit might be paid us. But about midnight the wind began to rise, and before we reassembled to discuss our plans a fearful storm was raging; so terrific was the sea that I knew no boat could live, and had a broadside been fired at the entrance of the bay we should not have heard it through the howling of the blast. For two days and two nights the hurricane continued, but on the third day the sun again appeared, and, the wind lulling, the sea went rapidly down. Full of anxiety, I readily complied with the boys' desire to put off to Shark Island and discharge the guns; for who could tell what had been the result of the gale; perhaps the vessel had been driven upon the rocky shore, or, fearing such a fate, she had left the coast and weathered the storm out at sea; if so, she might never return.

With these thoughts I accompanied Jack and Franz to the fort. One—two—we fired the guns and waited.

For some minutes there was no reply, and then an answering report rolled in the distance. There was no longer room for doubt; the strangers were still in the vicinity, and were aware of our presence. We waved the flag as a signal to those on shore that all was well, and quickly returned. We found the whole family in a state of the greatest excitement, and I felt it necessary to calm them down as much as possible, for neither could I answer the questions with which I was besieged, nor could I conceal the fact that the visit of the vessel might not prove so advantageous as they expected.

Fritz and I at once prepared to make a reconnoitre; we armed ourselves with our guns, pistols, and cutlasses, took a spyglass, seated ourselves in the kayak, and with a parting entreaty from the mother to be cautious, paddled out of the bay and round the high cliffs on our left. For nearly an hour we advanced in the direction from which the reports of the guns seemed to proceed. Nothing could we see, however, but the frowning rocks and cliffs, and the waves beating restlessly at their base. Cape Pug-Nose was reached, and we began to round the bluff old point. In a moment all our doubts were dispelled, and joy and gratitude to the Great Giver of all good filled our hearts. There, in the little sheltered cove beyond the cape, her sails furled, and anchor dropped, lay a brig of war with the English colors at her masthead.

With the glass I could discern figures upon the deck, and upon the shore beyond several tents pitched under the shelter of the trees, and the smoke of fires rising among them. As I handed the glass to Fritz, I felt a sudden misgiving. "What," said I to myself, "can this English vessel be doing thus far from the usual track of ships?" and I called to mind tales of mutinous crews who had risen against their officers, have chosen some such sheltered retreat as this; have disguised the vessel, and then sailed forth to rob and plunder upon the high seas.

Fritz then exclaimed: "I can see the captain, father; he is speaking to one of the officers, and I can see his face quite well; he is English, I am certain he is English, and the flag speaks the truth!" and he put the glass again in my hand that I might see for myself.

Still keeping under the shelter of the cliff, I carefully surveyed the vessel. There was no doubt that Fritz was right, and my fears were once more dispelled; all was neatness and regularity on board; the spotless decks, the burnished steel and brass, and the air of perfect order which pervaded both ship and camp, betokened that authority and discipline there reigned. For some minutes longer we continued our examination of the scene, and then, satisfied by the appearance of the camp on shore that there was no chance of the brig quitting the coast for several days, we resolved to return without betraying our presence, for I was unwilling to appear before these strangers until we could do so in better form, and in a manner more in accordance with our actual resources.

We again landed at Rockburg, where our family awaited our arrival in eager expectation, and as fully as possible we told them of all we had seen. They thoroughly approved of our caution, and even Jenny, whose hopes had been excited to the highest pitch by our description of the English vessel, and who longed to meet her countrymen once more, agreed to postpone the visit until the following day, when, having put our yacht into good order, we might pay our respects to the captain, not as poor shipwrecked creatures begging assistance, but as lords and masters of the land, seeking to know for what purpose strangers were visiting the coast.

The rest of the day was occupied in making our preparations. Our dainty little craft was made to look her very best; her decks were scrubbed, her brass guns burnished, all lumber removed and put ashore, and the flag of England hoisted to her peak. The mother overhauled our wardrobes, and the neatest uniforms were put ready for the boys and me, for though neither my wife nor Jenny had ever dreamed of appearing otherwise than they would have done had they been at home among civilized people in Europe, yet we, accustomed daily to rough and often even dirty work, had adopted just that custom which best suited our comfort and inclination. We should indeed have surprised the smart man-o'-war's men, had we appeared in our great, shapeless, wide-brimmed hats, our linen coats and trousers, our broad leathern belts and hairy buskins; so we next day readily donned the more becoming costumes.

At the break of that eventful morn, when we were destined once more to set our eyes upon our fellow-men, and to hear news of the outer world, from which for so many years we had been exiled, we assembled in our little breakfast room. The meal was eaten hurriedly and almost in silence, for our hearts were too full, and our minds too busily occupied, to allow of any outward display of excitement. Fritz and Jack then slipped quietly out, and presently returned from the garden with baskets of the choicest fruits in fresh and fragrant profusion, and with these, as presents for the strangers, we went on board our yacht.

The anchor was weighed, the sails set, and with the canoe in tow the little vessel, as though partaking of our hopes and joyous expectation, bounded merrily over the waters of Safety Bay, gave a wide berth to the Reef, against whose frowning rocks the sea still lashed itself to foam, and kept away from the cove, where the English ship unconsciously awaited us. The Pug-Nosed Cape was reached, and, to the surprise and utter amazement of the strangers, we rounded the point and brought up within hail. Every eye on board and on shore was turned toward us, every glass was produced and fixed upon our motions; for of all the strange sights which the gallant crew may have looked for, such an anomaly as a pleasure yacht, manned by such a party as ours, and cruising upon this strange and inhospitable shore, was the furthest from their thoughts.

Fritz and I stepped into our boat and pulled for the brig. In another minute we were upon her deck. The captain, with the simple frankness of a British seaman, welcomed us cordially, and having led us into his cabin, begged us to explain to what good fortune he owed a visit from residents upon a coast generally deemed uninhabited, or the abode of the fiercest savages.

I gave him an outline of the history of the wreck, and of our sojourn upon these shores, and spoke to him, too, of Miss Montrose, and of the providential way in which we had been the means of rescuing her from her lonely position.

"Then," said the gallant officer, rising and grasping Fritz by the hand, "let me heartily thank you in my own name, and in that of Colonel Montrose; for it was the hope of finding some trace of that brave girl that led me to these shores. The disappearance of the *Dorcas* has been a terrible blow to the colonel, and yet, though for three years no word of her or any of those who sailed in her has reached England, he has never entirely abandoned all hope of again hearing of his daughter. I knew this, and a few weeks ago, when I was about to leave Sydney for the Cape, I found three men who declared themselves survivors of the *Dorcas* and said that their boat, of four which left the wreck, was the only one which, to their knowledge, reached land in safety. From them I learned all particulars, and applying for permission to cruise in these latitudes, I sailed in hopes of finding further traces of the unfortunate crew. My efforts have been rewarded by unlooked-for success."

Fritz replied most modestly to the praises which he received, and then the captain begged to be introduced to my wife and Miss Montrose.

"And," he continued, "if it be not contrary to your rules of discipline for the whole ship's company to be absent at once, I will now send a boat for the remainder of your party."

One of the officers was accordingly dispatched to the yacht with a polite message, and the mother, Jenny, and the boys were presently on board.

Our kind host greeted them most warmly, and he and his officers vied with one another in doing us honor. They proved, indeed, most pleasant entertainers, and the time passed rapidly away. At luncheon the captain told us that there had sailed with him from Sydney an invalid gentleman, Mr. Wolston, his wife, and two daughters; but that, though the sea voyage had been recommended on account of his health, yet it had not done Mr. Wolston so much good as had been anticipated, and he had suffered so greatly from the effects of the storm, which had driven the *Unicorn* into the bay for repairs, that he had been eager to rest for a short time on land.

We were anxious to meet the family, and in the afternoon it was decided that we should pay them a visit. Tents had been pitched for their accommodation under the shady trees, and when we landed we found Mr. Wolston seated by one of them, enjoying the cool sea breeze. He and his family were delighted to see us, and so much did we enjoy their society, that evening found us still upon the shore. It was too late then to return to Rockburg, and the captain kindly offered tents for the accommodation of those who could not find room in the yacht. The boys spent the night on land.

That night I had a long and serious consultation with my wife, as to whether or not we really had any well grounded reason for wishing to return to Europe. It would be childish to undertake a voyage thither simply because an opportunity offered for doing so.

Neither knew to what decision the feelings of the other inclined; each was afraid of expressing what might run counter to those feelings; but gradually it began to appear that neither entertained any strong wish to leave the peaceful island; and finally we discovered that the real wish which lay at the bottom of both our hearts was to adopt New Switzerland as thenceforward our home.

What can be more delightful than to find harmony of opinion in those we love, when a great and momentous decision has to be taken?

My dear wife assured me that she desired nothing more earnestly than to spend the rest of her days in a place to which she had become so much attached, provided I, and at least two of her sons, also wished to remain.

From the other two she would willingly part, if they chose to return to Europe, with the understanding that they must endeavor to send out emigrants of a good class to join us, and form a prosperous colony, adding that she thought the island ought to continue to bear the name of our native country, even if inhabited in future time by colonists from England, as well as from Switzerland.

I heartily approved of this excellent idea, and we agreed to mention it, while consulting with Captain Littlestone on the subject of placing the island under the protection of Great Britain.

Then came the question as to which of our sons were best suited to remain with us, and which to go away.

This point we left undecided, thinking that in the course of a few days they would probably make a choice of their own accord, which they did, even sooner than we anticipated.

After breakfast, it was proposed that Captain Littlestone should bring his ship round to Safety Bay, that we might receive a visit from him and his party, at Rockburg—where we invited the invalid, Mr. Wolston, and his family, in hopes that his health might benefit by a comfortable residence on shore.

No sooner was this plan adopted, than Fritz and Jack hurried off in the canoe to prepare for their reception, being followed in more leisurely style by the brig and our yacht.

But what words can express the amazement of our guests, when, rounding the Rocky Cape at the entrance, Safety Bay, the beautiful domain of Rockburg lay before them.

Still greater was their astonishment, as a salute of eleven guns boomed from the battery on Shark Island, where the royal standard of England was displayed and floated majestically on the morning breeze.

A glow of surprise and pleasure beamed on every countenance, and poor Wolston's spirits appeared to revive with the very idea of peace and happiness to be enjoyed in such a home.

He was carried on shore with the utmost care and tenderness, and comfortably established in my room, a camp-bed for Mrs. Wolston being added to the furniture there, that she might be able conveniently to attend on her husband.

Meantime the scene at the harbor and all round Rockburg was of the liveliest description; merriment and excitement prevailed in all directions, as the beauties and wonders of our residence were explored, so that a summons to dinner scarcely attracted notice.

However, as a visit to Falconhurst was projected, the company was at length induced to be seated, and to partake of our good cheer, but the spirit of restlessness soon returned, and the young people kept roaming about through our hitherto quiet lawns, avenues, and shrubberies, until I was ready to believe their number three times what it actually was.

Toward evening the universal excitement began to abate, and the party assembled for supper with tolerable composure.

Mr. Wolston was able to join us, as the rest he had enjoyed, and the pleasure inspired by the hope of a residence among us, seemed to have given him new life. This wish he now distinctly expressed in his own name, and in that of his wife; inquiring what our intentions were, and proposing, if agreeable to us, that they, with their eldest daughter, whose health, like his own, was delicate, should make a long stay on the island, while the younger daughter went for the present to her brother at the Cape of Good Hope.

In the event of his ultimately deciding to settle altogether among us, Mr. Wolston would propose that his son should leave the Cape, and join our colony.

With sincere satisfaction I welcomed this proposal, saying that it was my wish and that of my wife to remain for the rest of our days in New Switzerland.

"Hurrah for New Switzerland!"

"New Switzerland forever!" shouted the whole company enthusiastically, as they raised their glasses, and made them touch with a musical ring, which so expressively denotes a joyful unanimity of sentiment.

"Prosperity to New Switzerland: long may she flourish;" echoed on all sides.

"Long life and happiness to those who make New Switzerland their home!" added Ernest, to my great surprise, leaning forward as he spoke, to ring his glass with mine, his mother's, and Mr. Wolston's.

"Won't somebody wish long life and prosperity to those who go away?" inquired Jenny, with a pretty, arch look. "Much as I long to return to England and my father, my inclination will waver if all the cheers are for New Switzerland!"

"Three cheers for England and Colonel Montrose," cried Fritz; "success and happiness to us who return to Europe!" and while the vaulted roofs rang with the cheering elicited by this toast, a glance from Jenny showed him how much she thanked him for appreciating her wish, to return to her father, notwithstanding her attachment to our family.

"Well," said I, when silence was restored, "since Fritz resolves to go to England, he must undertake for me the duty of bringing happiness to a mourning father by restoring to him this dear daughter, whom I have been ready to regard as my own, by right of her cast on the shores of my island.

"Ernest chooses to remain with me. His mother and I rejoice heartily in this decision, and promise him all the highest scientific appointments in our power to bestow.

"And now what is Jack's choice? The only talent I can say he possesses is that of a comic actor, and to shine on the stage he must needs go to Europe."

"Jack is not going to Europe, however," was his reply. "He means to stay here, and when Fritz is gone he will be the best rider and the best shot in New Switzerland, which is the summit of his ambition.

"The fact is," he continued, laughing, "I rather stand in awe of their European schools, and should expect to find myself caught and clapped into one if I ventured too near them."

"A good school is exactly what I want," said Franz. "Among a number of students there is some emulation and enthusiasm, and I shall have a chance of rising in the world."

"Fritz will probably return here some day; but it might be well for one member of the family to go home with the intention of remaining there altogether, and as I am the youngest I could more easily than the rest adapt myself to a different life. My father, however, will decide for me."

"You may go, my dear son," I replied; "and God bless all our plans and resolutions. The whole earth is the Lord's, and where, as in his sight, you lead good and useful lives, there is your home.

"And now that I know your wishes, the only question is whether Captain Littlestone will kindly enable you to carry them out?"

All eyes were fixed eagerly upon him, and after a moment's pause the gallant officer spoke as follows:

"I think my way in this matter is perfectly clear, and I consider that I have been providentially guided to be the means of once more placing this family in communication with their friends and with the civilized world.

"My orders were to search for a shipwrecked crew.

"Survivors from two wrecks have been discovered.

"Three passengers express a wish to leave my ship here, instead of at the Cape, while, at the same time, I am requested to give to three persons a passage to England.

"Could anything suit better? I am most willing to undertake the charge of those who may be committed to my care.

"Every circumstance has been wonderfully ordered and linked together by Divine Providence, and if England gains a prosperous and happy colony, it will prove a fitting clasp to this fortunate chain of events. Three cheers for New Switzerland!"

Deep emotion stirred every heart as the party separated for the night. Many felt that they were suddenly standing on the threshold of a new life, while, for myself, a weight was rolled from my heart, and I thanked God that a difficulty was solved which, for years, had oppressed me with anxiety.

After this nothing was thought of but making preparations for the departure of the dear ones bound for England. Captain Littlestone allowed as much time as he could spare; but it was necessarily short, so that incessant movement and industry pervaded the settlement for several days.

Everything was provided and packed up that could in any way add to our children's comfort on the voyage, or benefit them after their arrival in England, and a large share of my possessions in pearls, corals, furs, spices, and other valuables would enable them to take a good position in the world of commerce.

I committed to their care private papers, money, and jewels which I knew to have been the personal property of the captain of our ill-fated ship, desiring them to hand them over, if possible, to his heirs. A short account of the wreck, with the names of the crew, a list of which I had found, was given to Captain Littlestone.

Fritz, having previously made known to me, what indeed was very evident, the attachment between himself and Jenny, I advised him to mention it to Colonel Montrose as soon as possible after being introduced to him, and ask for his sanction to their engagement. I, on my part, gladly bestowing mine, as did his mother, who loved the sweet girl dearly, and heartily grieved to part with her.

On the evening before our separation, I gave to Fritz the journal in which, ever since the shipwreck, I had chronicled the events of our life, desiring that the story might be printed and published.

"It was written, as you well know," said I, "for the instruction and amusement of my children, but it is very possible that it may be useful to other young people, more especially to boys.

"Children are, on the whole, very much alike everywhere, and you four lads fairly represent multitudes, who are growing up in all directions. It will make me happy to think that my simple narrative may lead some of these to observe how blessed are the results of patient continuance in well-doing, what benefits arise from the thoughtful application of knowledge and science, and how good and pleasant a thing it is when brethren dwell together in unity, under the eye of parental love."

Night has closed around me.

For the last time my united family slumbers beneath my care.

Tomorrow this closing chapter of my journey will pass into the hands of my eldest son.

From afar I greet thee, Europe!

I greet thee, dear old Switzerland!

Like thee, may New Switzerland flourish and prosper—good, happy, and free!